G000168153

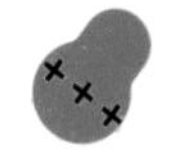

THE BLACK ORCHID

ALSO BY ANNIS BELL

The Girl at Rosewood Hall

THE BLACK ORCHID

A LADY JANE MYSTERY

ANNIS BELL

TRANSLATED BY EDWIN MILES

amazon crossing

This is a work of fiction. Names, characters, organizations, places, events, and incidents are either products of the author's imagination or are used fictitiously.

Text copyright © 2016 Annis Bell
Translation copyright © 2016 Edwin Miles
All rights reserved.

No part of this book may be reproduced, or stored in a retrieval system, or transmitted in any form or by any means, electronic, mechanical, photocopying, recording, or otherwise, without express written permission of the publisher.

Previously published as *Die schwarze Orchidee* by Amazon Publishing in Germany in 2016. Translated from German by Edwin Miles. First published in English by AmazonCrossing in 2016.

Published by AmazonCrossing, Seattle

www.apub.com

Amazon, the Amazon logo, and AmazonCrossing are trademarks of Amazon.com, Inc., or its affiliates.

ISBN-13: 9781503952751
ISBN-10: 1503952754

Cover design by Cyanotype Book Architects

Printed in the United States of America

Child's Song

What is gold worth, say,
Worth for work or play,
Worth to keep or pay,
Hide or throw away,
Hope about or fear?
What is love worth, pray?
Worth a tear?

Golden on the mould
Lie the dead leaves roll'd
Of the wet woods old,
Yellow leaves and cold,
Woods without a dove;
Gold is worth but gold;
Love's worth love.

Algernon Charles Swinburne (1837–1909)

Thirl Moor, Cheviot Hills, Northumberland, November 1860

The moor burbled and seethed like a living thing. *Like an animal that might rise at any moment and swallow me whole,* thought Rachel, and she raised the lantern higher to ensure she did not lose the path in front of her. She knew it was sheer stupidity to go traipsing around there at night, but some things made it worth the risk.

Rachel smiled. Not *things*, no; for this particular man, she would have risked everything, and she was overjoyed that he had finally realized just how devoted to him she was. He was so handsome and could no doubt have almost any woman he wanted wrapped around his little finger. But Rachel was well aware of her body's feminine curves and the way her raven hair shone. Her slightly almond-shaped eyes and the full lips of her doll's mouth added to her mysterious allure. She had not yet given herself to a man, but with this man things would be different. With this man, she would have a future. They could go away together, leave that terrible, gloomy house far behind, build a life of their own.

Winton Park, Rachel sniffed. Before Winton Park, she'd had a post in a house in Devon but had lost it because one of the lord's sons had become altogether too insistent. After that, she had taken the job here. She had not been happy about moving back to the cold, inhospitable north. But her roots were in Crookham, just thirty miles north of Winton Park, and the thought of seeing her family again had been a good enough reason to make the long journey back. Her wages were reasonable, too, and she counted herself lucky to have found a new post again so quickly.

A bitter wind cut between the hills and pierced through the wool of her cape, which was now wet to the touch. Damp and cold . . . that was how she remembered the moor, and so it was on that November night. The place was no better in summer, for then one had to put up with countless mosquitoes, little beasts that brought nothing but the fever to which three of her siblings and her aunt had fallen victim.

Her new mistress also seemed to find the northern climate unbearable. The poor woman was as pale as a shroud and looked to be terribly frail. Rachel felt sorry for Lady Charlotte, because despite her friendly nature, the woman did not have an easy time of it with her husband; Sir Frederick was moody and brusque and quick to lash out. *Let him rot in his hothouse,* thought Rachel, then let out a small squeal of delight when she finally saw the light ahead.

The hut in the moor was used by the gamekeeper and his men, but it was also the ideal place for a secret tryst. Apart from the residents of Winton Park, no one knew about it, except, perhaps, for the gypsies who sometimes camped in the area. Gypsies seemed to know their way around, wherever they were. Rachel liked the itinerant folk; her mother had always told her that she had inherited the gypsy blood of her grandmother. Her father never liked to hear that. He was a shepherd from a long line of English shepherds, and marrying a Romany woman had caused him enough problems, though eventually his family had accepted their match.

So Rachel's wild blood and her love of wandering were her grandmother's legacy. As she approached the hidden hut and saw a dark figure standing before it, she smiled. But the person's silhouette quickly disappeared. She felt like calling out, but the man apparently feared that someone might discover them. Yet apart from them there was no one out on the moor, no one but two people who wanted to share a bed that night.

Rachel began to breathe faster, and she slowed her steps. Sweeping her hair away from the damp skin of her face, she bit her lips to make them red and enticing. She heard an owl screech, and something fluttered past her ear: bats were out on the hunt. She loved the creatures of the dark. They were exceptionally sensitive, she knew, with abilities that other animals lacked. And that night she also wanted to be a creature of the dark, wanted to forget that she was no more than a simple housemaid. She reached into her skirt pocket as if to reassure herself that the letter that had lured her into the darkness was real. The paper felt firm under her fingers, a promise of good things to come.

Slowly, she moved on. She drew her shoulders back, imagining she was a gypsy princess on the way to meet her lover. Winton Park was so terribly oppressive! Sir Frederick's presence created a tense atmosphere, for no one wanted to be taken to task by him. And as kind as Lady Charlotte was, she could not be counted on in a crisis because she always bowed to her husband's will. The kitchen was ruled by Mrs. Elwood, a gruff and sharp-tongued woman, who had no interest in anything but the meals she prepared and who flew into a fury if anyone so much as took an apple without permission. Good God, there were enough apples in the house! Such people had no idea what it was like to be hungry, what the gnawing pain in your stomach felt like when you'd had nothing but water and groats for days.

The other servants in the place were decent enough, but the housekeeper in charge of the female staff, Mrs. Gubbins, was an ill-tempered piece of work. And the governesses always seemed to be a problem, because they spent most of their time with the ladies and gentlemen of the house and therefore felt themselves to be above everyone else.

Melissa Molan was no exception. Though she did not eat with Sir Frederick and Lady Charlotte, neither did she lower herself to eat in the kitchen with the rest of the domestic staff.

When the clouds momentarily parted, the moon bathed the moorscape in a silvery shimmer, and the branches of the birch trees reached into the night sky like arms sprouting a thousand fingers. A gust of wind whipped a willow branch into Rachel's face. Startled, Rachel lost her footing and stepped off the path. In her attempt to keep her balance, the lantern fell from her fingers. Her foot immediately sank into the mire, and to make matters worse, her skirt caught in the creeping roots of a mountain pine. The heavy material began to greedily suck its fill of water. All Rachel's anticipation and confidence gave way to naked fear: every child learned not to mock the spirits of the moor. Should they catch an inattentive wanderer in their clammy fangs, there was little hope of escape.

"Help me!" Rachel cried, just as she was able to catch hold of a strong willow branch and pull her foot out of the morass. But her skirt was still caught in the pine root, and as she struggled she heard the fabric tear.

"The deuce! My lovely new dress!" Rachel grumbled, looking around. He must have seen her, must have heard her! Where the devil was he?

"All this hide-and-seek is wearing very thin," she muttered. She pulled herself free with a jerk but could not prevent a large piece of cloth from being left behind in the roots.

She bent down to pick up the dropped lantern, which had gone out when it fell. "I shall not move from this spot! My light is out, and the last thing I want in this world is to suffer another fall into this rotten swamp!" she called out, her voice angry but also tinged with fear.

When a dark figure finally separated from the shadows of the hut, she initially felt relieved. But something wasn't right. Why didn't he simply come out to meet her? What game was this?

"Please, help me . . . ," she whispered, frightened, and she stood unmoving on the tiny bit of safe earth left to her in the darkness.

The moon disappeared again behind a barricade of clouds, and everything suddenly turned pitch-black. "Holy Mother of God, protect me!" Rachel murmured, reaching instinctively for the silver medallion she wore around her neck.

The soft earth swallowed the sound of rushing feet, but she felt the vibration through the ground. Before she felt the impact, she noticed a particular odor. The smell was not unfamiliar to her, but she had no time to consider it further because her attacker hit her with such force that she pitched backward and landed hard, sending a sharp pain shooting up her spine. Why would—

Before her senses faded completely, she realized that someone was rolling her deeper into the mire. She did not struggle this time as the soft, gurgling ooze wrapped itself almost consolingly around her limbs.

Barranquilla, Colombia, September 25, 1860

Dear Sir Frederick,

Two weeks have now passed since our departure from Barranquilla. I hope that my telegram reached you. I had hoped to get far more from Mexico and hope just as fervently that the four boxes containing your plants arrive in a reasonable condition. I sent them in care of my longtime associate, Howard Murray, as far as Caracas. The pickings were meager, I'm afraid, which was at least partly due to the fact that the Yucatán has taken its toll on my health. I lay an entire week in the "Orient Lounge"—at least, that's what the flea-trap called itself. I can find no better words to describe the hut where I kept myself alive by consuming as much quinine as my body would tolerate. The people here are composed chiefly of thieves, con men, and cutthroats, and I mean that quite literally! I was forced to pay dearly for the quinine and used my last pennies to make it to Barranquilla. It cost me a great deal of strength to restore my health and my appearance to a fair state.

Without Murray's help, I would not be in any condition today to even write this letter and would instead be filling the bellies of caimans. On a mule and with my last remaining bearer at my side, I made it to the delta along a tributary of the Magdalena. The bearer was not a good guide—or perhaps he wanted to lure me to my death—for he pointed out a place where I might access the shallow-seeming water. But the current washed out the sand from underneath me, and I sank almost immediately. It just so happened that Murray was approaching the same spot with a boat and a load of plants from the south at that moment. When he saw me, he immediately tied up at the shore and sent his people out to rescue me. I must say that more money certainly makes for better workers, and I again implore you, as a matter of urgency, to send me a more substantial sum. You know that I am loyal to you and that I supply no other master. My entire fortitude and all my efforts serve a single goal: to find you the best and most beautiful orchids.

I am now in a position to tell you something that will certainly arouse your greatest interest. Unless I am very much mistaken—and you know that I like to be certain before I utter so much as a syllable about something—I am closing in on the legendary sacred orchid! Yes, the same Sobralia mystica *that has so far been seen by just one white man, who was unable to send back so much as a single specimen. Until now, I can only report what I have heard and not yet anything I have experienced or encountered for myself, and you will understand why.*

In the region to which we will be departing tomorrow, there dwells a tribe of Chibcha Indians known as the Motilone. The Motilones are said to worship a holy orchid, unmatched in splendor, size, and beauty. No mention is made of this orchid being black; this Sobralia *is rather said to be an extraordinarily delicate white or yellow, its petals in the form of a cross and sprinkled with red points as if spattered with a light spray of paint. I am certain that this orchid will cause a sensation, and if you are able to cultivate it, you will be able to ask extraordinary prices. We both know the excitement caused merely by Douglas's story and his drawing; a shame that he succumbed to yellow fever in Peru. Douglas was the only one who knew the exact location of the* Sobralia. *My search now leads me into the Sierra de Perijá and the southern parts of the cordillera. My feelings toward this expedition are mixed, for it is one thing to fell trees in order to collect orchids, but quite another to steal the holy flower of an entire tribe. I have managed to put together a new bearer team, more or less trustworthy people, all of whom speak with awe of the Motilone Indians. There seems to be hardly anyone who has ever seen a member of this tribe face-to-face. Apparently, they are intelligent and form friendships with no one, including the half-blood settlers among the Sierra foothills. One of my bearers tells me that the Motilones are a peaceful people, as long as one does not intrude on them or trespass on their territory. But should one disturb their hunting grounds, then they turn to implacable revenge and drive out the interlopers with every treacherous means at their disposal. Again and again, one hears of savage disputes arising between the settlers and the Motilones.*

As for myself, I have seen a lot of the world, and poisoned arrows can't frighten me. Chiggers were more bothersome; they almost cost me the toes of my left foot. The little beasts burrow beneath your nails at night, gorge themselves, and swell into little balls as hard as pearls. If you don't get them out at once, they cause infection and suppurating abscesses. From another traveler, I learned that the trick is to rub the soles of one's feet with petroleum, and now I no longer have any trouble with the chiggers. You once asked me what helps against the mosquitoes. The most effective treatment I have yet found is still mustard oil.

But I have lost my thread; I wanted to tell you more of what I know about the Motilone Indians and their sacred orchid, to inform you of what awaits us. It is a mystery to me as to how Douglas managed to see the orchid for himself, for the flower is kept hidden from the eyes of whites and half bloods. The Motilones are a religious lot, ruled by their priests. If one breaks the laws of the priests, the penalty is death. The priests have even succeeded, it seems, in keeping their own tribesmen away from the holy flower. What I have learned is rather confusing, but from what meager information I've managed to glean, I understand that the Sobralia mystica *is surrounded by swarms of malevolent insects and that their bites or stings lead to blood poisoning. The priests alone know of an ointment that protects them from the insects, and that thus allows them to approach the sacred bloom unmolested. Whether that is truly the case I will—God willing!—find out for myself. We will decamp tomorrow morning and attempt to make contact with the Motilones. I am confident of success, because our informant struck me as trustworthy.*

It goes without saying that I will continue to keep my eyes open for the black orchid. But for now, the wonder-orchid of the Motilones seems more within reach, and I am therefore giving it priority.

An observation I made before my departure from Barranquilla is causing me some concern. While there, I saw Mungo Rudbeck in a public house. Rudbeck, as you know, works for Sir Robert. He saw me, too, I am sure of it, but pretended to ignore me. My association with Mungo is not the best, for I have an aversion to liars and cheats, and he is both. Every second word that falls from his mouth is a lie! He has cheated me out of my dues on several occasions. What's more, he is known for his brutality, and just recently I heard that he had murdered a rival in Venezuela. There was no proof against him, but that means nothing—in the jungle, anyone who is not your friend is your enemy. I have conducted my research with the greatest of discretion, and only those I trust know the true nature of my expedition. Still, I seem unable to shake off the uneasy feeling that Mungo prompts in me. I was unable to find out anything about the reasons for his being in Barranquilla. I would find it extremely disagreeable, were Mungo to be pursuing similar goals to my own. His despicable methods and intrigues revolt me, as does the house he represents.

I remain,
Your obedient servant,
Derek Tomkins

1.

Mulberry Park, Cornwall, November 1860

Jane stretched and blinked in the weak morning sunlight that filtered through the curtains. It was already cold, more so than usual for November. The farmers were talking about a hard winter ahead. Shivering, she pulled the blankets all the way up to the chilly tip of her nose, noting that the fire in the fireplace seemed to have gone out. A low, throaty growl reminded her that she was not alone. Well, if she had to share her bed, then at least she wouldn't freeze. She pushed her feet across to where she knew David's warm body was, because it was also where most of the blanket had gone.

"What the . . . !" came a muffled cry of protest, then the blanket was thrown back. David, quick as a flash, turned to Jane, threw his arms around her, and pulled her body close.

So much had happened since that fateful night at the ball in February, and her life had taken a turn that she had never expected. With the death of her uncle, she had lost the only person—aside from her parents—she truly loved. Back then, a marriage of convenience with the aloof Captain Wescott seemed the only way to save herself from the guardianship of her hated cousin. But that same Captain Wescott—a stranger from whom she expected no more than the fulfillment of a contract, the protection offered by a paper marriage—showed her that friendship and loyalty could turn into something more. *Far more,* thought Jane. She smiled.

The lips that had been nuzzling so gently at her throat and collarbone drew back. "What do you find so amusing, Jane?"

Propping himself up on an elbow, David ran his fingers over the rise of her breasts. Dreamily, she opened her eyes and reached out a hand to him. His dark hair tumbled to his powerful shoulders. She touched his upper arm, where a bullet had left a scar. His back and belly were likewise marked by old wounds—a thrust from a bayonet here, a shot from a duel there, although he had yet to reveal to her the reason for the duel.

Her hand slid up to his neck, and she briefly touched the scar that ran from his chin to his right temple. It was among his more recent injuries, but it was no longer as red as it had been in February. "Sometimes, it amazes me that you are here with me."

His dark eyes, with such mysterious hidden depths, were full of warmth. "Why?"

She flicked at a stray strand of his hair, her eyes teasing him. "Perhaps you could have done better than me. I am well-off but not rich. I am, let's say, challenging. I'm not beautiful, my nose is too large, and you've had all kinds of trouble with me."

"If by 'trouble' you mean that you act impetuously and that I have been seriously worried about your life more than once, then, yes, I agree. But that rubbish about your nose . . ." He kissed the tip of it. "I find it classical. And your chin? It matches your passionate, defiant personality, which I happen to find fascinating, albeit a little unconventional at times . . ."

He kissed her, taking his time, savoring the contours of her body. Finally, he looked up and asked, "Do you need any more reasons?"

Breathlessly, all teasing forgotten, Jane replied, "Not for the moment."

She had learned that she could not badger him with too many questions, although there was so much she wanted to know. He rarely spoke about his father and never about his mother. Whenever he was called to London by mail, he made excuses about leaving for business, but she knew perfectly well that the letters came from the palace. She gathered that he worked for the royal intelligence services; he had once admitted as much, only to then turn around and deny it with his next breath, saying that all he did was offer advice based on his wartime experience. But Jane practiced patience, a virtue she was willing to learn when it came to David. She would never have believed it possible to feel what she did for this man; no one had ever told her what it meant to be in love.

Her vague, girlish notions of heady romantic love had absolutely nothing to do with what she felt for David. During their first night together, he had seduced her with tenderness and passion, showing her that physical intimacy did not have to be shameful. As a result, she had discovered what she called a dark side within herself, a side of her that only David knew and, it seemed, wanted to celebrate abundantly.

"Hettie will be coming in any moment," she offered in weak protest as her nightdress floated to the floor.

"Hettie knows when she is not welcome."

Later, wearing a brown riding outfit and with her hair pinned up, Jane sat with her husband at the breakfast table. David studied the morning paper, frowning.

"A new war?" Jane asked as she buttered her toast and tore off a piece for Rufus. The Great Dane with its trusting eyes lay at her feet.

"Hmm . . . our troops have destroyed the Summer Palace in Peking," David said, looking up. "That does not bode well. All it does is lead to resentment and revenge. They learn nothing from these wars," he murmured, turning back to the article about the aftermath of the Opium War that Britain and France had been waging against the Chinese.

"Good morning, my lady." Floyd, the butler, brought in the post on a silver tray.

He was still favoring one leg a little. Jane had offered her long-serving butler a pension and a small cottage at the coast, but Floyd had remained at Mulberry Park. She was happy that he had, because having Floyd nearby conjured up precious memories of her Uncle Henry.

"Thank you, Floyd." Two letters lay on the tray. She took the one addressed to her. "How is Mrs. Roche?"

The housekeeper had been ill with a troubling cough, but Mrs. Roche's sense of discipline and duty prevented her from admitting that she would be better off in her bed rather than here in the house. Jane had called in Dr. Woodfall, and it was only on his say-so that Mrs. Roche finally accepted the prescribed bed rest.

"Thank you for asking, my lady. She is quite recovered and back to her usual self, if I may say so." A hint of a smile flickered across his face.

"Wonderful. I would like a fruitcake for tea and fish this evening. Would you like that, David?" she said, turning back to her husband.

"Hmm? Yes, of course," he answered, opening the letter Floyd had handed him.

"Will that be all, my lady?" Floyd asked.

"Yes, thank you. And Floyd, make sure there is enough wood to warm the staff quarters as well as the main house." Jane could not understand how in other houses the domestic staff was forced to live in freezing rooms. Not only did a lack of heat mean excessive moisture in the house, but also no one had much use for a sick servant.

"Very good, my lady." The butler bowed and left.

Jane reached for her fruit knife and opened the letter. She immediately recognized the flowing hand of her friend Alison, but a moment later she caught her breath, because what she read did not sound at all like the cheerful, uncomplaining Alison she knew. If her friend wasn't chatting about plays in London or the latest scandals or fashions, then she must have some very serious concerns indeed. And as she read on, Jane's fears turned out to be well-founded:

Dearest Jane,

I miss you very much and wish you could be here! I should have listened to Thomas and not traveled to this wasteland! I'm in my seventh month, as you know, and this pregnancy is causing me more difficulties than the last one. But Charlotte's letter sounded so despairing that I simply could not leave her to her own devices. Have I ever told you about my cousin Charlotte? We were always very close, at least until she married Sir Frederick Halston! I warned her at the time and advised her not to marry that horrible man, who is much older than she is.

But you don't know Charlotte. She is so terribly dutiful that she does everything her parents tell her to. Simply everything! If her dreadful father told her to jump into the Thames, she would. Imagine that! But, oh, that's just the way she is, and there's no changing it; she simply had to move here. She lives in Northumberland, outside a godforsaken town called Allenton. The village lies in the Cheviot Hills, a treacherous expanse of moors and bogs. A moor, of all places! You have no idea what an inhospitable place this is, but that might also have something to do with Sir Frederick, who I have yet to see in a good mood. He prowls through the rooms here at Winton Park with the grouchiest, most unpleasant expression on his face, and that's if he decides to show his face at all.

And another thing I haven't told you: He's one of these fanatical flower collectors that seem to be crawling all over the place these days. But no, he doesn't collect just flowers. He collects orchids! Oh, I don't know what people see in those crippled-looking little plants. The flowers have hardly any scent at all, and they look somehow indecent . . . then again, perhaps that is what makes them so attractive. Dearest Jane, please don't let your husband read this, or he will think me depraved. But I must also say, I think you have had the greatest luck in having Captain Wescott as your husband, and that makes me very happy for you, Jane! You are my very best friend, and I could not bear to see you unhappy.

You have to come and pay me a visit in this cold district. I am not allowed to get out of bed—the doctor has forbidden it! It is torture! But I have to stay here, or I might lose the child, and he fears for my life if my labor comes early or, worse, if I start to bleed. I suffered some bleeding just after I arrived, but the child is still alive, and I am as well as can be so far. But as I said, I cannot leave my bed.

No doubt you are thinking: What does spoiled little Alison have to complain about? She has her cousin there for company, after all. Well, Charlotte has two children of her own. Eleanor has just turned five, and Charlotte's son, Cedric, is seven. Cedric is a little beast, a repulsive creature who maltreats not only his sister but also animals. And you know how I hate when children do that. Charlotte has changed in the two years since I last saw her. She has become terribly pale and is no more than a shadow of her former self. The children run rings around her, and she can't count on Sir Frederick for anything, for he spends all his time in his precious hothouse.

And now I come to the real reason I am writing: I am afraid! Jane, I am worried about Charlotte. Something about this house isn't right at all, and I am convinced that all is not as it appears. I cannot put into words what I find so inexplicable here, but there is something evil at work, and I fear the worst for my cousin! You are the only one who understands me. Thomas is tied up in London, and in any case he would think me hysterical.

Please come and visit as soon as you can! They can't turn you away if you are coming to help me, and then you can find out what is going on here. Please, my dearest friend, don't make me linger here alone!

Your truest friend,

Ally

Jane put the letter down and looked at her husband. "Ally's written, David. She isn't well, and I must go to her."

David, who had finished reading his own missive, folded it and nodded. "Nothing simpler. I also have to travel to London. We can go together."

Jane shook her head. "She isn't there. She's in Northumberland, in Allenton, staying with her cousin Charlotte."

"Northumberland? That's out of the question. Winter is coming. The roads are either quagmires or frozen over, and we'll have our first snow within the week. You can't travel to the north now." His words sounded final.

"But I have to! There's a train from London to York and another on to Durham, if I remember correctly. From Durham with a coach—"

"No! Jane, it is too dangerous this time of year!" said David, louder than intended, then he smoothed out his newspaper and continued more quietly. "Please, Jane, maybe you will indeed reach York and even Allenton. But once winter closes in, you'll be trapped up there till springtime!"

Jane cleared her throat. "David, I have to go to Alison. She's worried about her cousin. More than worried . . . I know Ally, and she would not write what she did if she did not have grounds to do so."

"That may be, but—"

"No buts, David. She is my best and oldest friend, and if she asks for my help, then I will not deny her that. You have to understand! You would never leave a friend in the lurch, would you?"

David Wescott ran his hand through his thick, dark mane. "No, I would not. But you are a woman, Jane. You are my wife, and I cannot allow anything to happen to you."

Jane felt her anger slowly rising. "May I remind you that we have a contract? One in which we are supposedly equal partners."

He raised one eyebrow. "And partners look after each other, don't they? It is my duty to be concerned about your well-being, and what you are planning to do is foolish!"

"Don't exaggerate! I'm going to take a train with my maid and travel to the north. From there, a coach will take us to a village somewhere in the vicinity of Hadrian's Wall, which is extremely interesting in itself, I think. I've always wanted to visit Hadrian's Wall."

"But not in winter!" David stated flatly.

"I don't have a choice. Alison needs me now, not in the spring when the sun is shining and my husband thinks the time is right for a vacation." Her lips hardened into a tight line, and she challenged him with her gaze, rather disappointed that he had so little confidence in her.

"You're questioning my judgment," he said, his tone cool.

"Your judgment?" Jane's voice grew tremulous; she could no longer contain her disappointment about his dominating tone. Rising slowly to her feet, she pressed the letter to her chest and said quietly, "I was questioning nothing, because I always believed that we respected each other fully. But now it looks as if I might have been mistaken. Perhaps our marriage itself was a mistake."

David leaped angrily to his feet. "You make things very easy for yourself, Jane. There has always been someone watching over you, caring for you. You've never had to worry about anything. But if just once you don't get what you want, you become petulant."

"My heart is simply more sympathetic than yours! Where would Mary be today if I hadn't gone looking for her? Dead or in a brothel, that's where!"

David's eyes flashed angrily at the mention of Mary, an orphan girl whom Jane had rescued earlier in the year from the clutches of a depraved nobleman. "If it hadn't been for Blount and me watching over you like hawks, you'd be dead yourself! But you're quite content to forget that particular point, aren't you? Do you seriously believe that a woman and her lady's maid could resist the likes of Devereaux without any help? Good God, Jane, think again!"

"Don't you think I know that? But this is not about orphanages and the secret carousings of perverse aristocrats. I want to visit my friend!" She softened her tone, relenting somewhat because she suspected that more awaited her in Winton Park than the company of her bedridden friend.

David took a deep breath. They were standing facing each another, and Jane could see a vein pulsing in his neck. His furrowed brow relaxed a little, and a smile crept into the corners of his mouth. Relieved, she took a step toward him and smoothed out the tails of his frock coat.

"I won't do anything that could put Hettie or me in harm's way."

Taking her hand, he suddenly smiled and pulled her into his arms. "If only I could believe that, Jane." He kissed her, then pulled back slightly and tapped the letter still in her hand. "May I read it?"

She pushed the letter into her skirt pocket and jokingly said, "Of course not! Alison writes all sorts of confidential gossip, women's matters that would make even you blush."

"I doubt that very much. I know Thomas well enough to know that his wife, unlike you, is as innocent as a lamb. You just don't trust me."

"You two talk about us? I see. And what do you tell him about me?" She flirtingly made as if to turn away, but David put an arm around her waist and looked intently into her eyes.

"What's in the letter?"

Jane held his gaze. "I already told you. What's in your letter?"

He released her. "We'll go to London together. You wanted to see the Royal Academy exhibition, if I remember right. We'll visit Thomas and then decide whether it is really necessary for you to travel to the north."

That's a step in the right direction, thought Jane, who had already made up her mind.

2.

Seymour Street, London, November 1860

Jane climbed the stairs to the second floor and looked around. Little had changed since her departure from London months earlier. Levi was as reserved as ever, and slender little Josiah still shadowed the elderly man.

"Josiah, put the bags in here," Levi ordered the boy, who puffed into Jane's bedroom with two traveling cases.

"Thank you. It's lovely to be back. How are you, Levi?" Jane asked the man, whose eastern European accent was still unmistakable.

"I can't complain, my lady. Josiah, don't just stand around. Run and fetch the rest of the luggage." Levi's expression betrayed no emotion, but his intelligent eyes belied his submissive manner.

One day I'll discover your secret, thought Jane, pulling open the curtains. She heard Hettie laughing in the hall. The young woman had spent the entire trip talking about a play she hoped to see and a certain dashing actor whose name Jane could not bother to remember.

It was raining, and the city seemed gray and desolate, just like the wintry garden the window overlooked. Out in the country, bad weather didn't bother her. It watered the plants and felt cleansing. But in the city, the rain seemed dirtier—though that may have been because all the sidewalks turned into slippery, muddy mires, with women's long skirts absorbing the grime and moisture.

The doors to David's adjoining bedroom opened, and her husband stepped through. "That will be all, Levi."

Tipping his head, the servant left the room. Jane turned to her husband and smiled. "Nothing has changed, except that Josiah is a little taller. How old is he? Ten, or already eleven? He should go to school."

David, wearing a mustard-colored vest beneath a dark suit jacket, unknotted the scarf around his neck. "We can't rescue and send every child to school, you know. He has a job and is satisfied."

"That's something I would like to hear from him," Jane shot back, tossing her shawl onto the bed.

"Please, Jane. I am tired from the long drive. Let's not argue. Just believe me that Josiah is in good hands." He leaned back against one of the solid bedposts. "Would you still like to go out, or would you prefer a warm bath and something to eat?"

She undid the pins holding her hair in place at her neck and sighed. "A bath would be wonderful. Our compartment was terribly drafty, and my bones are aching."

He looked at her sympathetically. "And you want to travel to the Scottish border?"

She bit her lip; that was exactly what she was planning. "Where's Hettie? She's supposed to help me get out of this dress!"

"I could help you . . ." With a look Jane had come to understand well, he reached a hand toward her.

"Oh, no! What will Josiah think of us?" Laughing, she moved out of reach.

"Jane." David's voice was full of warmth and made her pause. "Everything has changed."

She swallowed and watched him go into his room. He left the door open.

When Jane woke the next morning, she found the bed beside her empty. Levi told her that David had left early, but he had left a message to say that he would collect her in time for their dinner with Thomas. *At least he managed to find time amid all his business dealings to think of me.* Jane poured some deliciously aromatic Darjeeling tea into her teacup, then stirred in a little milk. Her irritation was basically jealousy over David's busy life. While he was out meeting interesting people and talking about important political problems, she was supposed to manage the household and spend her time paying boring visits to other bored women. She drank her tea while gazing out the window. It wasn't raining, but gray clouds covered London's November sky, and the branches of the large chestnut tree just outside swayed in the chilly wind.

The grandfather clock struck nine. Maybe she should spend the hours until midday at the library and read up a little about orchids. Alison's cousin's husband was an orchid breeder, after all, and it paid to be prepared.

"Hettie?" she called out in the hallway, and her maid's head appeared over the second-floor balustrade.

"I'll be down in a moment!"

"Not necessary. Get dressed. We're going out!"

Hettie squealed in delight, and Jane smiled. She liked her bubbly young maid very much. Hettie was inquisitive, sometimes a little frivolous, and always in a good mood.

"My lady, these letters have just arrived for you." Levi, in his dark, perfectly fitted suit, had almost silently come to stand beside her.

"Thank you. Please have a cab out front in ten minutes." Jane took the letters from the tray and headed back upstairs.

Hettie was already waiting for her in Jane's dressing room. "I've laid out the warm coat with the fur collar, ma'am. It's very windy and cold today. Winter's coming early, I tell you. I feel so sorry for the children out on the street. Oh, ma'am, all those hungry little mouths to feed. Josiah told me that where he comes from, they lost at least one child from each family in the village every winter."

Even in England, Jane thought, things were far from ideal. "Where exactly does he come from?"

"Well, I wasn't actually clear on that. He and Levi belong to a people who are hounded by the Russians and others because of their culture and religion. Circassians, or something along those lines? Josiah says the mountains they lived in lay in front of the Black Sea, and that they had to leave their homeland in the Crimean War. They both lost their families, and Levi has looked after Josiah ever since. They're not actually related at all." Hettie set out Jane's sturdy boots.

"No?" Jane was glad she had decided against the hoop skirt. Etiquette be hanged, the bulky thing always got in the way. "And how did they wind up in England?"

"Your husband brought them here, ma'am. Josiah says the captain was thought of most highly by everyone who knew him. You've landed yourself a fine man, ma'am, if I may say so."

"Yes, Hettie, you're right about that," Jane murmured. She was now a little ashamed that she hadn't shared the letter with David so that he could understand more fully why she wanted to visit Alison.

"Oh, is that one from Mary?" Hettie pointed to the topmost letter on the small pile; the handwriting on it looked like a child's. "Is she all right?"

While Hettie laced up her boots, Jane opened the letter and scanned the lines, which were indeed written in an immature hand. The girl was getting along well at her boarding school and wrote regularly about her new friends, the teachers—most of whom were nice, and sometimes she even sent along little drawings. Indeed, there was a sketch in the envelope, of the school building. The girl had talent, Jane was pleased to see.

Sadly, Mary's letters almost always ended with a question about Fiona, and this one was no exception. When Jane had rescued Mary, she had been too late to save Fiona—another orphan girl and Mary's best friend—who had already been put aboard an Australia-bound transport ship. Jane handed the letter to Hettie. "We shall find Fiona. I'm not going to give up, but trying to get information from Australia certainly isn't easy."

Hettie nodded and tucked a few strands of hair under her bonnet. "We can't just go off to Australia, can we? My goodness, that would take months!"

"I remember very well the voyage from India to England. It was no pleasure cruise." The still-fresh loss of her parents and homeland had made the stormy passage even worse. Jane had no desire to undertake another long seafaring journey. "Besides, we've got a trip to the cold north coming up."

"We do? Where are we going?" asked Hettie curiously.

Jane had not yet mentioned the trip to her maid, but now the idea was out in the open, and Hettie would have to keep the news to herself. "My dear friend, Lady Alison, needs me. She is visiting her cousin in Northumberland, and she is desperately worried about the woman's well-being."

Jane opened the second letter, which was from Alison, who'd sent it to London after Jane had telegrammed that she'd be here. It unnerved Jane that her friend had written a second letter so quickly.

Seeing Jane's expression, her maid's round eyes grew wide. "Is she in danger?" Hettie whispered.

As she read the letter, all the color drained from Jane's face. "Not Ally, but her cousin! Now her cousin has taken ill, and nobody knows what's wrong with her. Very mysterious. Something strange is going on in that house."

"Is . . . is it haunted?" Hettie asked, her voice trembling.

"I don't believe in ghosts, Hettie. But if Ally is writing about spooky noises in the night, then something isn't right at all."

"And your friend can't do anything?"

"She is seven months pregnant and not allowed to get out of bed." It was clear from Ally's letters that she had kept the strange happenings at Winton Park from her husband to prevent him from traveling north and taking her back to London. Thomas had no time for tomfoolery and his wife's silly imaginings. If Thomas took his wife back to London, Ally's cousin would then be all alone in that terrible house, and no one would be able to help her.

"Now I'm really concerned, Hettie, but the captain doesn't want to let us travel in this weather."

Hettie flashed her mistress a conspiratorial grin. "But we're going anyway, aren't we? How will we get away?"

"We will know that tonight, after dinner at Sir Thomas's," Jane replied thoughtfully.

"A new adventure! I was starting to fear that we were getting a little . . . domesticated." Hettie giggled.

The library was in an imposing building that was part of the British Museum on Montague Place. Hettie stood reverently between the enormous columns at the museum's entrance. At such an early hour, there were not many visitors yet, so they could stroll undisturbed among the ample halls with their treasures from every corner of the world.

"May I stay here in the Egyptian section?" Hettie gazed in fascination at the stone deities and sarcophagi from Egypt.

"All right, but make sure to stay here, and don't go talking to strange men!" Jane warned, casting a doubtful look at a man wearing a top hat who was examining a relief.

"No, ma'am. When I tell my sister about this . . . She's never even been out of Cornwall, ma'am." A small figure made of black stone caught Hettie's eye. "That one has a dog's head!"

"Make sure it doesn't bite you!" Jane continued into the library and discovered that there were few comprehensive works devoted to orchids. Lindley's *The Genera and Species of Orchidaceous Plants* was among the most complete. The botanist had dedicated his life to researching and categorizing plants, and the volume contained numerous illustrations of orchids. Another work by James Bateman focused on the orchids of Mexico, but Jane soon pushed the books aside with disappointment. She simply did not understand the fascination with what to her were rather unsightly plants.

She thanked the librarian who had brought her the books. "I think I prefer roses. What is it that makes people pull these flowers off trees and ship them across the ocean?"

Behind a pair of pince-nez, the librarian's eyes widened in surprise, and his moustache quivered indignantly. "My dear lady, these positively regal flowers have no rivals. If I could afford to, I would grow them myself. Just last week, a new species from Ecuador was displayed at Messrs. Loddiges. It was a delicate violet color with small brown sprinkles on the sepals, and—"

Jane interrupted the man before he could drift any farther into his enraptured discourse. "I guess I will simply have to visit one of these greenhouses and see for myself what all the fuss is about. Maybe I will become a disciple of this new religion after all."

The man beamed. "I'm sure of it, my lady. I would certainly recommend Loddiges. And Kew, of course."

With its large park and two impressive greenhouses, the Royal Botanic Gardens at Kew were the pride of Queen Victoria. As a child,

Jane had been there several times with her uncle but had never spent much time with the garden's orchids, an oversight she now had to correct.

A visit to Kew would take a while, and she still had to change for dinner, so Jane decided instead to pay a quick visit to the Royal Exotic Nursery of Veitch and Sons in Chelsea. It was situated on the King's Road, south of Hyde Park, and surrounded by high boxwood hedges. What looked like a park was in fact a large and carefully laid-out nursery for young bushes and trees.

"Wait for us," Jane instructed the coach driver. Then she and Hettie climbed the steps to the entrance of Veitch and Sons.

Inside, an elegantly dressed young salesman who wore his pomaded hair parted in the center immediately came to greet them. "Good day, my lady. May I be of service?"

Jane looked around the large salesroom, which contained potted plants along with some cut flowers. "I'm interested in an orchid."

The nurseryman's expression brightened. "Of course. May I accompany you to our greenhouse? Nepenthes—that's the name of our hothouse—recently received a very good write-up in *The Gardeners' Chronicle*, you know."

"And that's exactly why I'm here. They say that Veitch and Sons has some highly sought-after plants in its collection." She followed him along a brightly lit corridor into an atrium-like courtyard where the wind swirled cold city air into the corners.

The greenhouse, marked more by its practicality than by any architectural elegance, welcomed them into its refreshingly warm interior. Surprised, Jane exclaimed, "Oh, I had imagined it would be much hotter and more humid!"

The nurseryman ran his fingers affectionately over the leaves of several plants standing in rows on stone benches along the narrow walkway. "Many make that mistaken assumption, but the orchids don't like it if conditions are too warm. We try to acclimatize them gradually. Just imagine what the small plants have been through by the time they reach England, after having been cooped up for months in a crate. Often, they can't be kept away from the seawater, which will kill them, as will the cold when the ships sail the northern route home. Sometimes there are ants in the containers, and those will also destroy the plants."

He stopped beside several showy yellow orchids. "What color did you have in mind?"

"Yellow is pretty. I'd like to take one with me, if I may."

The man lifted the plant from the bench with the utmost care. "*Dendrobium dalhousieanum*, named for Lord Dalhousie, the former governor-general of India."

"I'd like to have a plant named after me," said Hettie, stroking a leaf.

"Don't touch!" said the nurseryman sharply. "They are very sensitive and *very* expensive."

"You must know most of the orchid growers and collectors in England. Sir Frederick Halston, the husband of a close friend of mine, is mad about orchids," Jane remarked as they walked out.

"Sir Frederick? Oh, yes! He was a good customer of ours. This way, please."

"Was? If I were an orchid fancier, this place would be at the top of my list," she said flatteringly.

Protecting the orchid with his jacket, the gardener hurried through the cold courtyard toward the main building. "He has enough money to afford his own orchid hunter. We do the same, of course, although it must be said that we employ two dozen men on two continents."

3.

Going up the stairs to his house the next evening, David Wescott sensed that something was different. It wasn't the north wind, driving winter ahead of it with icy blasts. He paused and glanced up at the second-story windows. He suddenly knew that she was no longer there.

He moved slowly, letting the door knocker fall loudly against its metal plate. Blount opened the door, and when David saw the stony expression on his steadfast companion's face, he took a deep breath.

"When did she leave?"

"This morning, Captain, after you went into the office. She left a letter for you on the desk."

David nodded grimly and entered his study. Typical! It was just like her. Impulsive, without a thought for possible danger! He tugged at his cravat and undid his top button. At Thomas's house the previous evening, she had been remarkably bright and cheerful, and she had looked so seductive in her dark-green dress. He walked over to his desk and found a letter written in her hand, set beside a yellow orchid.

She knew how much he liked to see her in that dress, and she had worn it fully intending to have her way with him later. He'd held her in his thoughts a long time that morning, the scent of her still in his nose, her passion and her supple body still fresh in his memory. He'd never believed that he could become as emotionally bound to a woman as he was to Jane. But then, he had never met another woman like her. Her compassion for others was honest, and her sympathy for the fate of the less fortunate moved him. At the same time, those traits had gotten her into difficulties more than once.

Now, knowing she was gone, he already missed her, though he did not want to. His life was hard enough, and his own family was a catastrophe. What he had been through was not something he wished to inflict on anyone, least of all the woman whom he had sworn to protect from evil. She had no idea who her husband was, and by God she should never find out what abysses lay behind the honorable St. Amand façade.

He tore open the letter and quickly read it, frowning.

My dearest David,

Please don't be concerned about me. I am with Hettie on my way to Winton Park. It is simply impossible to do anything else. Ally needs me, and you know how much she helped with the search for Mary. Please try to understand. It is not in my nature to abandon friends in their hour of need. I will send word by telegram the moment I arrive.

Always yours,

Jane

P.S. The nights in cold Northumberland will be lonely without you.

The postscript brought a smile to his face, but it did not ease his utter frustration. She could not simply leave like that, without discussing it more with him!

"Blount!" he shouted, throwing the letter on the desk.

It took a mere moment for the quiet man in his brown suit to appear at the door. "I'm sorry, Captain. Unfortunately, you were right to suspect that she would steal away, but I followed your instructions and let her go. They took the nine-thirty to York."

"Hmm. I can't leave London right now. Palmerston is dithering and stalling, but it seems we can at least continue to rely on the support of the Russians and French in China. That said, a conflict with Napoleon over the Italian question is looming." David drummed his fingers on the desk. He hated all these political machinations, but his loyalties belonged to the Queen, and when she needed his services, he did his duty.

"I'm going to the club, Blount, and will probably spend the night there." The house felt empty without Jane; it was a new sensation for him.

"Very good, Captain. Then would it be all right with you if Levi took his evening off tonight? If I have understood correctly, there's a house where refugees from his homeland meet. They play music and try to keep up the old customs."

"Certainly, as long as he isn't moving in any conspiratorial circles. Do we know the people there?"

He had a lot of respect for Levi, whom he considered a gifted musician, but the man had a veiled past, like practically every refugee. That had never been a problem before, because Levi kept to himself and rarely left the house. But if that was changing, there had to be a reason for it. David hoped that Levi was sensible enough not to start associating with any radical revolutionaries. God knows, there were enough of those among Russian immigrants.

Blount stroked the short beard he had been sporting for several weeks now. He was an intelligent man and had proven himself both in war and on dangerous missions alike to be completely loyal and reliable. Indeed, they had saved each other's lives on several occasions. It had been Blount who carried a seriously injured David from the battlefield.

And it was Blount who had convinced him, in the weeks he lay convalescing in the field hospital, that there was a life beyond military service. "The house is in Holborn, and I've been asking around. The only politically interesting name that's come up is Sergej Gundorov. Everyone else seems more interested in reminiscing about their homeland."

"Gundorov? I heard that name just recently, at a meeting with Lord John Russell. Because of his dissident activities, Gundorov can expect the death penalty if he ever returns to Russia. I'll sit down and talk to Levi in the next few weeks. Thank you, Blount. And make sure—discreetly, of course—that Josiah doesn't accompany him to this meeting tonight. Boys like him are easy prey for foolish, subversive ideas."

The coach rolled slowly over the bumpy cobblestones of St. James Street. Gas lanterns lit the sidewalks; at this late hour, most of the pedestrians were men. Black top hats, fur-lined overcoats, and gilded knobs atop walking sticks were all signs that two of the most eminent gentlemen's clubs in London were nearby. A slim figure with an exceptionally proud bearing caught David's attention. Something in the way the man moved seemed familiar and caused a knot to form in David's stomach. As the coach rolled closer to the man, who was deep in conversation with his companion, David recognized the angular profile of his father.

The Duke of St. Amand's sideburns were silvery white, while the family's signet rings sparkled on his hand. He used a walking stick, on which he seemed to be leaning more heavily than usual, and he looked tired. When the coach drew level with him, St. Amand turned his head and looked right at his son.

David knocked on the wall behind the driver's box. "Drive faster, man!"

Given the darkness inside the coach, David knew it was not possible for his father to have actually seen him, and yet the fleeting encounter evoked images that David only ever saw in his nightmares. The duke naturally spent his time in the conservative atmosphere of Boodle's, a dignified building that extended a long way behind its façade, and which offered its members every conceivable comfort. David grimaced at the thought of all the fine gentlemen who pretended to be men of honor and upholders of morality. Many a righteous mask needed only to be scratched for its thin material to fall away.

His own club was a little farther up the street, not that the clientele of Brooks's was significantly different from that of Boodle's. But the average age was somewhat younger, and the politics there were more liberal, for which David was prepared to overlook quite a lot. He could not change the world, but when he talked to daring young idealists, he had the feeling, at least for a while, that there was hope. Hope for change to a social system that was unjust and in dire need of reform.

Jane was right when she pointed out the evils of orphanages and the poorer neighborhoods. A hard winter would mean even more victims than usual, but a great deal of water would flow through the Thames before any real change would come. And Jane had to learn that there were people in this world who would stop at nothing to hold on to their privileges.

The damp, wintry London air battered him as he strode the short distance from the coach to the club entrance. The doorman, who knew every Brooks's member by name, greeted him formally and opened the door. All of the servants who worked at the club were men. Indeed, women were expressly not permitted. For many members, the club represented a welcome respite from home, where a shrewish wife ruled the roost.

David handed over his hat and coat and asked the butler, Mr. Bale, about Thomas. Mr. Bale, who knew everything and everyone yet was the epitome of discretion, replied, "Baron Latimer is at one of the gaming tables, Captain."

"Thank you." Walking away, David greeted a young man with soft features and wavy blond hair; as he entered the gambling lounge and searched for Thomas, he wondered where he had seen the young man before.

Thomas was standing at a table where a game of dice was underway. Hazard was a popular game, and a good way to quickly lose a lot of money if you let yourself get carried away. Neither David nor Thomas played for more than they could comfortably afford to lose, but there were a number of club members who had run up sizable debts. Businessmen like Devereaux exploited such weaknesses only too readily. At the thought of the fugitive criminal, David recalled how he knew the pale young man. Everett Ralston was the son of Lord Ralston, chief justice of the Royal Courts.

"David! Wonderful to see you!" Thomas had noticed him enter, and he passed the dice cup along. "Gentlemen, thank you." He gathered a handful of coins and notes, then slipped them into a pocket. "Did you want to play?"

"No, I'd like to talk to you. Let's find somewhere quieter." They left the busy lounge together and went in search of a corner in the large library, where men met to smoke and chat. David had nothing against a cigar now and then, but after his experiences in Crimea and India, he categorically refused anything stronger. Thomas, tall and well-built, was more of a hedonist than David, and it was beginning to show. They found two leather armchairs, and a servant appeared the moment they sat down. They ordered whisky and cigars, and as the first smoke rings drifted into the air, Thomas looked at David inquiringly.

"I passed young Ralston in the hall just now," David began. "He seemed nervous. Is he mixed up in that scandal with Josephine Simpson after all?"

Stretching his long legs, Thomas sipped his whisky. His custom-tailored suit, made of the finest cloth, and his expensive tiepin left no doubt that he was a scion of one of the wealthiest and most influential families in England. It was not only Thomas's prudence in relation to the Devereaux case that had spurred his and David's mutual appreciation.

Indeed, David's government work had led to fruitful collaborations with Thomas and his department on several occasions. Thomas was responsible for matters of domestic security, which included cases of impropriety—when members of the House of Lords got involved with prostitutes, for example, and revealed information that might put the nation at risk.

"Josephine has taken things too far. She likes to play with fire, indeed so much that I worry about her pretty neck." Thomas flicked the ash of his cigar lazily in the general direction of an ashtray, but most of it landed on the floor.

Josephine Simpson was one of a number of beautiful courtesans who plied their trade among society's uppermost circles and who had the temerity to ride horseback through Hyde Park, although doing so was a privilege reserved for true high-society women. Yet Josephine had the money to take riding lessons and could even afford her own horse. She could often be seen riding through the park, head held high, wearing a riding outfit that showed off her physical virtues to great advantage. Whenever she went out, she created a stir, increasing her popularity among her clientele. For several months now, a persistent rumor had been circulating that she was having an affair with someone close to Lord Russell.

"Everett Ralston is known for his dissolute lifestyle, to be sure, but that doesn't include prostitutes . . ." Thomas paused and looked at David.

"I know that he prefers the company of other men. A thorn in the side for the judge, that. He wants to marry the boy off. But what's the connection between Everett and Josephine Simpson? There must be something there, or am I mistaken?"

"No, you're absolutely right on the money. Something is going on, some intrigue that's supposed to catch Russell in its tangled web. We're keeping our eyes and ears open." Thomas drew on his cigar, then laid the glowing stump in the ashtray. "Is that what you wanted to talk to me about?"

David sighed loudly, drained his glass, and, measuring his words, said, "That, too, but . . . has Ally spoken to you about Jane?"

Thomas raised his eyebrows. "You know what those two are like. I'm the last to find out anything. Ally is still up in Northumberland with her cousin Charlotte. The doctor has forbidden her from leaving her bed during her pregnancy, but she is still healthy, and I believe she's overdramatizing things a bit because she is worried about Charlotte." He cleared his throat. "Charlotte's husband, Sir Frederick, is an eccentric old fossil. I dare say Charlotte doesn't have it easy, and with Ally tied to her bed anyway, then why shouldn't she offer her cousin some company?"

"She asked Jane up to Northumberland, too," David said.

"Well, I must say that is certainly going too far. Poor Sir Frederick! I'd turn into an eccentric myself!" Thomas laughed. "You talked her out of it, I hope?"

"I tried . . . ," David replied grimly. "It will soon be snowing, and they could be stuck there for weeks!"

Thomas grinned. "If Jane wants to do something, she does it. Simple as that. In all the years we've known each other, I can't remember one time when she didn't follow whatever bee got into her bonnet."

"That may be true, but she doesn't think things through. She acts irrationally and impulsively and puts herself in danger as a result!"

"But certainly not up there, not in the wilds of the Cheviot Hills. Don't worry, David. What could happen? Sir Frederick breeds orchids, and Charlotte has her two children. The women will sit around and gossip about children and pregnancy. Better get used to it."

"What? But Jane isn't . . . at least, she hasn't said anything." David looked at his friend in surprise.

"No? Well, she will be, sooner or later, and then you'll understand. I'm actually happy when Ally talks about those things with her friends.

We have a good nanny to look after the twins. My mother also stops by sometimes, but not too often, thank God." Thomas waved the footman over. "Two more!"

"There's something she's not telling me. Ally wrote that Charlotte is afraid of something," said David thoughtfully.

"Did she? I wouldn't take it too seriously. Charlotte has a nervous constitution, and she's extremely insecure. And Winton Park is a gloomy old box. I was only there once, briefly, for the daughter's christening. And I'll tell you, I was very happy to leave." Thomas took another cigar out of the humidor on the table and drank in the scent of the tobacco. "Mmm, exquisite."

With Thomas's reassurances, David's concerns now seemed less urgent, and he leaned back in his armchair. "I only hope Jane is back before Christmas."

"You miss her!" Thomas snipped the tip off the cigar.

"I'm worried about her."

"That's something you'd better not get used to."

Far too late for that, thought David as he took a large, consoling mouthful of whisky.

4.

Winton Park, Northumberland, November 1860

Jane and Hettie climbed out of the coach and stretched their chilled and aching limbs. After the long, bumpy drive through the wintry moorscape of the Cheviot Hills, they were looking forward to a blazing fire, a hot bath, and a relaxed supper.

"D'you think this place is haunted, ma'am?" Hettie whispered.

Standing in the courtyard below the main entrance, Jane stared doubtfully at the grim, cold walls perched atop a hill, partially hidden behind strangely trimmed boxwood hedges and an enormous oak tree. The main house, a Jacobean mansion, had two façades, each with a pointed gable. Houses had their own character, she believed, and this one emanated hostility. Perhaps it was the small windows on the third floor, arranged like pairs of eyes, or the chimneys lurking above the rooftops like dagger blades, or the dark stones that probably came from local quarries. Then there were the windows on the second floor, divided into four panes and so narrow that one could easily have mistaken them for arrow slits.

Jane pulled the fur collar of her coat closer and raised her chin. "I wouldn't be at all surprised, Hettie, but I think that humans are fundamentally more dangerous than ghosts."

Hettie didn't seem to be listening, for she was staring at the main door, set back beneath an arch. Small stone sculptures decorated the house's façade, and as they got closer, Jane could make out grotesque, grimacing faces. She pushed Hettie onward.

The door opened, and a butler appeared on the landing beneath the arch and greeted them stiffly. "Good day, my lady. We have been expecting you. May I show you into the drawing room?"

Jane estimated that the man was nearing forty, which was young for a position as important as that of butler in a manorial home. The man had a high forehead and attractive features, which no doubt endeared him to the housemaids. Hettie seemed to have noticed this, too; feeling perhaps a little overawed, she stayed close behind Jane.

Before the butler opened the door to the drawing room, he turned to Hettie. "The domestic quarters are down this way, miss."

After the sparsely lit hall, the drawing room was a refreshing surprise. The leafy pattern on the wallpaper and the paintings of exotic animals and landscapes evoked the impression of a garden. A small collection of armchairs was arranged in front of an open fire, while light refreshments and tea had already been prepared and set on a sideboard. Though her stomach roiled with hunger, Jane suppressed the feeling and waited by the fire for her hostess.

Suddenly, Jane heard loud thumping and banging and the sound of children's voices, and a boy of about seven and a younger girl came charging into the room. The girl was crying and reaching for a stuffed toy bear that the boy was waving triumphantly in the air.

"Come and get it, Elly! Here's Mr. Boggle, and he says he doesn't need his arm anymore!" Making a hateful face, the boy tugged threateningly at the bear's arm.

The girl cried out so wretchedly that Jane could no longer simply stand and watch, and instead she snatched the toy out of the boy's hand. She crouched down and held the bear out to the girl. "Here. Your brother was just having fun."

With the face and hair of a blond angel, the boy crossed his arms across his chest and gave Jane a sour look. "Elly is a crybaby. All she does is cry, cry, cry. Who are you? You don't belong to this house."

"You must be Cedric. Nice to meet you, young man. I'm visiting your mother and my friend, Lady Alison." The girl was still sniffling but had accepted the stuffed bear and was hugging it to her chest.

The boy took a rude tone. "My father says that there are already too many females in this house and—"

"Cedric!" snapped a sharp, female voice that made the boy fall silent. Jane glanced up to see a young woman in a plain gray dress. "Please excuse the boy. High spirits is all it is. He's full of mischief, but that's what boys his age are like," the woman said.

This must be the governess, thought Jane, registering the self-consciously humble posture the woman adopted. Her voice, however, and the look in her eye—sizing up the situation—bespoke a woman who could get her way if she needed to, which would certainly be to great advantage with a boy like Cedric.

"We still have an hour until supper. Please excuse us, my lady." The governess led the children by the hand out of the room.

Jane heard the governess speak briefly outside the door to another woman, who entered a moment later. With outstretched hands, a pretty woman with brown hair approached Jane. Everything about her was petite. Her hands were soft and looked so fragile that Jane was afraid just touching them might cause the woman injury.

"My dear Lady Jane, what a pleasure to meet you! Alison has been talking about nothing else for days, and I could hardly believe that you would undertake the long journey up here . . . but please, do sit down. Hasn't anyone offered you tea or sandwiches yet? Unforgivable. I don't know what you must think of us."

Jane smiled and eased herself into one of the armchairs, hoping that her grumbling stomach wouldn't give her away. "Thank you, that's very kind of you. We've only just arrived. Your children have already stopped by!"

She bit hungrily into a slice of bread topped with butter and cress.

Her hostess looked at her with concern. "That is so typical! Mr. Draycroft, the butler, should have seen to your well-being immediately! No one in this house listens to me. But dinner tonight will definitely not disappoint. The cook, Mrs. Elwood, came to Winton Park with me. She knows I place great store in dishes that have been prepared with care."

After a second sandwich and a cup of strong, sweet tea, Jane was much revived. She felt sorry for the mistress of the house, who struck her as unsure of herself and unhappy. Ally might have been exaggerating, but even so, this poor creature could certainly use a little support.

They chatted for a few minutes, before, without warning, Charlotte Halston sighed and slumped in her armchair. The teacup almost slipped out of her hand, but Jane was alert enough to jump to her feet and take it from her. "Lady Charlotte, whatever is the matter? Where's the bell—"

"No! Don't call anyone, please. It will pass. Smelling salts, or . . ." Her eyelids fluttered, and her skin turned deathly pale and appeared suddenly waxy. Jane was deeply concerned.

Jane took a handkerchief out of her bag, dunked it in the pitcher of drinking water, and laid it across Charlotte's forehead. She discovered a bottle of smelling salts on the fireplace mantel, opened the little vial, and waved it beneath Charlotte's nose. The effect, however, was minimal, and Charlotte only raised her head and coughed before sinking back again. Jane patted her cheeks, which felt cold to the touch. Determined, she pulled Charlotte's armchair as close as possible to the fireplace to let the heat envelop the poor woman, then half-filled a teacup with tea and added three spoonfuls of sugar.

"Drink this, please."

With her heart-shaped lips, Charlotte sipped the tea like a weak little bird. The sweet drink brought some color back to her face, and the warmth of the fire also seemed to have some effect.

"Oh . . . what was that?" Charlotte murmured. She was wearing a magenta silk dress with cream lace trim. She touched the collar of her dress, which closed at her throat.

"Should I fetch help?" Jane asked uncertainly, unable to simply sit and watch Charlotte's obvious distress.

But Charlotte had regained her senses, first sitting up straight then slowly getting to her feet. "Thank you. It is already passing. Please don't say a word to my husband about this. Please!" Her large brown eyes pleaded with Jane, who could only nod her agreement.

"Of course I won't. Has that happened to you often? Have you talked to a doctor? There could be all kinds of reasons for a dizzy spell."

Quietly, as she smoothed her dress, Charlotte said, "It's happened several times in the last few weeks, but it could just be the weather. I've never been much good in this climate. I'm sure it will settle down again, but now I'd like to take you to Alison."

Whereas the drawing room had been pleasantly green and welcoming, the stairway and corridors of the house proved dark and inhospitable. The Halston ancestors stared down from the walls in old oil-painted likenesses, alternately grim and arrogant, accompanying them all the way up to the second floor. Weapons and old maps added to the gloomy décor. "My bedroom is there, the children's room is at the end of the corridor, and the guest rooms are down here."

They turned into the guest wing of the house. A maid scurried by with an armful of washing. Despite the children being there, it was very quiet in the house. Everyone seemed at pains to move as silently as possible. "In here."

Charlotte knocked at a door and waited until Alison's personal maid, Nora, opened it. "We'll be taking dinner at eight," Charlotte said, and left a surprised Jane at Alison's door.

"Hello, Nora!" Jane said, and the young woman beamed. She had not been with Alison long. Ally had found her in a factory where the women sewed in dim light for fourteen hours a day for scant pay. Nora had a warm smile, and although she was still shy, she learned quickly and was a pleasant companion for Ally.

"Jane? Is that you?" Ally called from inside.

The two friends embraced tearfully. Jane patted Ally's cheeks and sat beside her bed. "I am so happy that you're well!" Jane squeezed her friend's hand and looked her over thoroughly. Ally, seven months pregnant, was as round as one might expect. Her blond hair gleamed, and her cheeks were rosier than usual.

"Oh, I'm doing splendidly! You know that pregnancy never did me any harm. I mean, the twins cost me a lot of strength, of course, but this is a stroll by comparison. It will be a boy, I'd say, from the way he's kicking." Smiling, she took Jane's hand and laid it on the swell of her belly.

Jane felt some movement beneath her fingers, and she leaned over and kissed Ally's belly. "Now don't annoy my best friend, little one."

Then she looked around the room. The four-poster bed was covered with light-green velvet, the curtains and wallpaper were mustard yellow, and Jane spotted two magnificent orchids on a table. Gas lamps radiated a muted light, and a fire was crackling in the fireplace.

"At least it looks more or less pleasant in your room. This house has something . . . repellent about it, I don't know how else to say it. It's simply dark and unwelcoming. By the way, Charlotte had a dizzy spell just now, but she didn't want me to mention a word of it to anyone, least of all to her husband."

Alison frowned. "Again? Can you understand why I'm worried? It's been getting worse ever since I arrived. It's like Charlotte is fading away, as if there's less and less of her every day. She never used to be sick at all!"

"Has Nora been able to learn anything from the servants?" asked Jane quietly.

"She's been trying all along to get something out of them, but they're banding together and not telling her much. There's something very strange going on here, Jane, something sinister!" Ally looked at her friend, wide-eyed.

"I assume those orchids are from Sir Frederick? Could all this have anything to do with him?"

"I don't know. We hardly ever get so much as a glimpse of the man. Heaven knows, I've never especially liked him, but I've never had anything bad to say about him, either. He is a grumpy old fellow who likes to spend his time in his greenhouse with his orchids more than anything else. There are a lot of men like him. He only married to preserve his family line. Now that he has an heir, Charlotte has done her duty, and so he looks after his plants." Ally rolled her eyes. "Jane, these orchids are pretty, I admit, but all the money he puts into it . . . do you understand his obsession?"

Jane shook her head thoughtfully. "Frankly, no. Not entirely, anyway. My uncle was mad about plants, but he had other interests, too. He loved life, and he lived it to the fullest. Oh, Ally, I still miss him so much."

"My poor Jane," said Alison with compassion in her voice. "Henry was a special man, and he holds a special place in your heart. Nothing will ever change that."

Jane cleared her throat. "And there's David, now, too. He didn't want to let me come up here. I left in secret."

Alison stared at her, aghast. "You didn't!" Then she let out a ringing laugh. "You are incorrigible! I wager he has cursed the day he signed that marriage certificate!"

"More than once, I'm afraid," Jane said. She laughed herself, then immediately grew serious again. "But we actually get along well together. Very well, in fact. It's just that sometimes he's inclined to forget that we are partners and that I don't need a nursemaid. At least he didn't send Blount after me."

"Jane, don't be unfair. Without him, you would be—"

"Oh, I know. Well, what do we do now? Can you get out of bed for meals?"

"No. I have to stay lying down. The doctor's instructions were very clear, although I will certainly be driving back to London with you before Christmas. But between now and then, we have to find out who in this household is trying to harm my cousin."

Jane swallowed. "You really think that is true?"

"Yes, but I don't know who or why, and no one would believe a hysterical pregnant woman in any case! Jane, you'll be dining with Sir Frederick this evening. Tell me what you think of him. And there's also Melissa Molan, the governess. She doesn't have an easy time of it with the children. The girl is harmless, but watch out for Cedric. He's one of these little boys who likes to carry out pranks on others, and I don't mean harmless little tricks."

"I'll start a list, I think, and keep notes of what everyone in the house does."

Ally nodded and took Jane's hand. "I am so happy you're here."

Sierra Nevada, Colombia, October 3, 1860

Dear Sir Frederick,

The past week has fully depleted us. Some unpleasant events have moved us farther from the Motilones' dominions than planned. Without José, a local mulatto fellow who is exceptionally knowledgeable, we would all be dead! The man knows the Sierra like the palm of his hand, so at least I have one man I can rely on. By God, he has already proved his worth!

I have no desire to go on at length about the confused political situation here. Suffice it to say that the loose alliance of nations presently calls itself the Granadine Confederation. Colombia is part of this alliance, which will certainly not be permanent, not with people on all sides slaughtering each other in a civil war. It is the same thing everywhere, the conservatives fighting the liberals. But I tell you, new ideas will win out in the end. The war has been going on for nine years, since the day that slaves officially became paid laborers.

Some cry for freedom, others for bread, and who can blame them if they reach for weapons? One evening, our small party came to a narrowing of our trail, where it passed between the river on one side and a mountain on the other. Our group consists of me, four bearers—the aforementioned José and three Indians, all taciturn fellows—and a young fellow countryman.

Dennis Brendon, a botanist from Durham, had contracted a disease of some sort and was left behind by his expedition in a mountain village. The poor chap, it seems, spent three months up there in a hut, receiving only the most meager attention and food from the Indians of the cordillera, who have little as it is for themselves. These mountain Indians are small in stature, but certainly strong; I have seen two of them carry a piano between them up a mountain for hours! The young Dennis has become a pleasant traveling companion for me, in part because of the depth of his knowledge about all kinds of plants. Unfortunately, his constitution suffered greatly during the months of his fever, and he can count himself lucky if he comes through this journey with no lasting damage.

One evening, our little group arrived at a narrow point on the trail, as I mentioned, that was supposed to lead us a little farther down the river to a place to spend the night. José told us that we had to hurry and find shelter before dark. We were perhaps a little inattentive, which in turn caused us not to see the four figures beneath a rocky outcrop. It is hard to say whether they had pitched their camp there for the night or had been waiting at exactly that place for us to come along. They were two former slaves and two mulatto men; they blocked our path and demanded money from us. They seemed intoxicated, and two of them spat chewed leaves onto the ground.

José talked to them in Spanish, which they could at least partly understand. Among themselves, they spoke in a foreign dialect that none of us could fathom. I also tried to speak to them in a friendly tone, but the moment I opened my mouth their countenances grew grim, and they began to shout abuse at me. It was clear that the two blacks, in particular, saw me as their despicable enemy, a representative of the race that had forced them into servitude all those years.

During our argument, Dennis had become even paler than usual. He has an Englishman's light skin and blond hair, and he stands out among the dark-skinned members of our little troop. As for me, I cannot say when my skin could last have been called white; I have been out exploring the countries of the world far too long. One of these treacherous fellows was holding a machete and staring at us with bloodthirsty eyes. All he seemed to be waiting for was a signal from his leader to carry out his bloodlust. But José managed to convince them that our only interest was in flowers, and when they examined the baskets containing our collected plants, they sniffed and snorted most unfavorably.

Orchid collectors may well be rich in plants, but we are not wealthy in money, and even these cutthroats seemed to know that. They tore our cargo apart, laughed and joked about our bags and baskets filled with seeds and seedlings, and, to my horror, threw most of what we had gathered into the river. They acted as if they were befuddled and not in control of themselves. Finally, one of the mulattos shouted, "Bolívar." The others took up the shout, and José also cried out, "Bolívar, our great liberator!"

Simón Bolívar, though already thirty years dead, is still a great hero and revered in these parts. He freed the Colombians from the Spanish yoke, after all. So I gave Dennis a jab, and he also raised his voice in praise of the national hero. Fetching a bottle of rum from my saddlebags, I held it high, which made our rivals' eyes light up. One of the two blacks, a giant of a man, took the bottle and raised it to his mouth. Dennis looked at me anxiously and chose that moment to pick up a little notebook that had fallen on the ground.

As he bent down, one of the mulatto fellows, with whom José had spoken Spanish, began to shout and aimed his pistol at poor Dennis. The young man began to tremble and stammer and wave his arms around, which only made things worse.

From the man's tumult of words, all I could understand was that the book was from Arboleda, and that we were exploiters and enemies. Next to us, the river was rushing over its rocky bed. On the other side, bare rocks rose steeply. The sun was almost gone, casting only the sparsest rays of light on our strange mixed company in those inhospitable Colombian wilds. It was clear that these four would not let us pass without giving rein to their hatred. The intoxicating leaves they had been chewing were making them act irrationally. I exchanged a quick glance with José, who had already drawn his pistol from his belt. The three cordillera Indians had stood a little ways back with their mules throughout the show.

Their broad faces remained expressionless, as if trying to distance themselves from whatever happened next.

Their passive manner was suspicious to me. It could have meant anything. Fear, cowardice, or the fact that they were waiting for an opportunity to get rid of us themselves. But then, with great relief, I saw the Indians come to life. They carried no pistols, but they had machetes, and in the blink of an eye they were holding them in their hands, which brought our adversaries back to their senses. A shot rang out, and Dennis fell to the ground, but then José and I fired simultaneously at the bellowing bandits. The giant dropped the bottle and fell down backward. He tried to rise, but he stumbled and slipped into the river, where the current tore him away. The machete the other black man was wielding flashed in a ray of the setting sun. He was barely a meter from me, but when I tried to fire, my weapon malfunctioned. José fired, and the powerful, dark-skinned fellow froze in place. A round hole gaped in his forehead, and blood poured over his face and nose and into his open mouth.

The Indians drove away the other two with their machetes, wailing with such intensity that it made my hair stand on end.

"Go on, away from here!" I cried, helping Dennis to his feet. His shock was far worse than his injury: the bullet had left a flesh wound on his upper arm, but that was quickly bandaged.

"I can't stand the sight of blood. At least, not my own," he stammered, clearly on the verge of passing out.

"José! Do we still have any rum?" I asked my brave companion, who had risen greatly in my esteem.

"Sí, señor." *The plucky man put away his pistol and took a leather waterskin from his pack, which he quickly uncorked. "Drink, Señor Dennis, drink!"*

Dennis took a hefty swig from the waterskin, swallowed, and coughed, and the color returned instantly to his cheeks. "God, that wasn't rum. What was it?"

José laughed. "Better than rum—cachaça!" He then spoke quickly to the Indians, who gathered and stowed whatever they were able to salvage.

Finally, we made it past that bottleneck and set ourselves up for the night in the relative safety offered by a copse of enormous trees. Not one of us slept well that night, and we took turns on watch, but it seemed the bandits had had enough for the time being.

The next morning, we found ourselves in a scarcely improved situation. When we continued on, it was apparent that a few days earlier there had been a landslide, for the narrow trail that led between the river and the steep, heavily wooded slope was now blocked by fallen trees and boulders. Going around this obstacle or even climbing over it was out of the question, as was turning back, because then we could almost certainly expect another ambush. José stood there frowning and shaking his head, his muscular arms planted on his hips. "Una catástrofe . . ."

Surprisingly, it was our wounded young botanist who spoke up. "I experienced a similar circumstance on an expedition in Peru. We could not surmount the barrier with the animals, and turning back would have meant many days travel, even without armed bandits awaiting us. We must build a raft!"

"My dear Dennis," I replied, "a raft? And how are we supposed to do that?" I surveyed the area. There were certainly enough felled tree trunks lying around, but how were we supposed to hold them together?

Our plant expert climbed up the slope to where he could reach the branch of a tall tree. "We have balsa!"

José slapped his forehead theatrically. "Sí! Balsa! That is what they use to make the big rafts on the Magdalena."

Nodding slowly, the Indians seemed to regret ever joining our unfortunate expedition.

"Balsa is a kind of mallow," our pale botanist lectured. "The branches are as flexible as willow, and the dry wood is lighter than bamboo. We can cut whatever we need with the machetes, and I'm sure our Indian friends know exactly how to weave a raft and seal it with resin. The woven balsa will swell in the water and become watertight, but we'll have to leave the mules here."

I was sorry to leave the animals, but there was no way around it. And, Sir Frederick, it was astonishing. Within a few hours, we had actually built a raft big enough to carry six men and the most vital of our equipage. You can take this as proof that nothing can deflect me from my goal—the Sobralia mystica.

To steer the raft, we had four long poles fashioned from whole saplings. We tied our bags tightly onto a raised section in the center of the raft and wrapped them in blankets. The wild waters of the river would no doubt wash over us and the bags, but at least the medicines, instruments, and papers we carried would be protected. I will spare you the details of our turbulent ride. We were fearful for our lives at several points but stayed on the water as long as we possibly could. Like so, we covered more ground than we would have on foot. After one particularly dangerous rapid, raw and battered, we made it to the shore; by that point, there was little left of the raft.

Before we initially boarded our vessel, we had removed our shoes and stockings and were thus grateful to have at least halfway dry shoes to put on. The idea of marching through the jungle without shoes is not a pleasant one. Dennis had also had his experiences with the voracious little chiggers. As we lay down to sleep that evening, we were thankful that we had not lost the bottles of mustard seed oil, because the greedy bloodsuckers were already closing in on our camp. We had left the mountains behind us, and the vegetation in the jungle was lusher and greener. We traveled for several more days, then had to hack our way through part of the rainforest, but bit by bit we were drawing inexorably closer to the home of the Motilones.

I am writing these lines in a mission station where we have been able to replenish our supplies somewhat. A nun—a raw-boned, pitiable creature—treated Dennis's arm. The bullet wound had become infected, and we feared that gangrene might set in, but the nun had a decoction of herbs that healed the injury superbly.

Rarely have I experienced so much misfortune on a single leg of a journey. I don't want to sound superstitious, but a curse seems to have befallen this expedition, ever since I saw Rudbeck in Barranquilla.

Before I finish this letter, I want to mention another strange incident. The mission station consists of three poor huts and a kind of shed, a hovel really, where animals and a few local people are housed.

It happened just before sunset. The jungle animals began their usual nightly concert, and fireflies were shimmering against the impenetrable green of the forest. It is an incomparable spectacle every night. I was sitting on a tree stump beside the shed, and after ruminating there for a short while, I looked more closely at the forest edge and saw a figure there, chewing. It was an old Indian, and he must have been standing there and observing me for some time. He belonged to the forest tribes, for he wore nothing besides a few strings and a loincloth. But what was so surprising was the chain of leaves that hung over his body. One strangely shaped "leaf" caught my attention, but the light was so poor that it was only from the outline that I could see it was an orchid flower. And it was black, I swear on my life! If I was mistaken, then it was on account of my exhaustion and overexcitement, but I swear it was the flower of a black orchid!

All of this took place in little more than a heartbeat, and after a moment the man had disappeared again into the dark green of the forest.

I hope to be able to report more soon.

Ever faithful,

Your humble and obedient servant,

Derek Tomkins

5.

Winton Park, Northumberland, November 1860

From what Jane had been able to see of Winton Park thus far, the drawing room pleased her most of all. As was usually the case in such houses, residents and guests would gather in the drawing room before dinner and chat over an aperitif until the butler asked them to the table. Floral wallpaper, vibrant landscape paintings, and numerous potted plants lent the long room an airy ambience. One could sense the touch of a delicate female hand in the décor, and Jane studied the collection of small porcelain figures on the tables with interest.

"Very pretty!" said Jane, although she didn't indulge in such decorations herself.

She was rewarded with a smile from Charlotte. The mistress of the house wore a silk dress in muted shades of red and brown, coupled with extravagant pearls. "I brought the little figurines with me from Germany. In my youth, I traveled a great deal with my parents."

With a melancholy expression, she lightly stroked the coquettish figure of a shepherdess holding a lamb in her arms.

"But not anymore? Your husband must travel a great deal for his orchids, though, mustn't he?" Jane was standing by a table on which three pots stood, each home to a flamboyantly colored specimen.

"He still travels a lot, that's true, and at first I traveled with him, but the children take a lot of managing. And he needs his quiet."

By the fireplace stood three armchairs, while a Chinese folding screen concealed a small sofa on which a book lay. In front of the terrace doors was an intimate seating area that seemed made for chatting over a cup of tea. Jane heard the drawing room door open and the patter of children's feet over the wooden floor.

"Mama!" the girl called out, crying piteously. She was the spitting image of her mother, with the same petite build and thin, brown locks.

Charlotte crouched, her silk skirts rustling, and scooped her daughter into her arms, cuddling and kissing her. Planting his feet in a victory pose next to one of the tables with the porcelain figurines, Cedric folded his arms over his chest. Suddenly, Jane heard a whimpering sound, and the governess entered the room, a furry, white lapdog in her arms.

"Cedric, you've been a very bad boy!" she admonished the youngster, who did not seem particularly cowed.

Charlotte straightened, her face anxious. She kept one protective arm around her daughter, who held on tightly to her skirts. "What is the matter, Miss Molan?" She screwed up her nose. "Something smells burned!"

The governess nodded indignantly and held out her hand. Now Jane saw that the little dog's tail was singed. "Cedric soaked a piece of cloth in kerosene and tied it to Pebbles's tail. Then he lit it."

Charlotte looked horrified and turned to her son, who seemed oblivious to any wrongdoing.

"I just wanted to see if it would make him run faster. He didn't want to play," he grumbled.

Jane was speechless, and her thoughts returned to the time her own dog had been hurt, when she had feared for his recovery. But these were not her children, and she would not stick her nose into Charlotte's business.

"A dog feels pain just as we do, Cedric, and if he does not want to play, then you have to accept that. You don't always want to play, either," said Charlotte earnestly.

"But I'm not a dog, and Pebbles is so useless—he can't even hunt. He's just a good-for-nothing little glutton. That's what Father says," the boy replied without so much as a second look at the whimpering dog.

"Go to your room. You're not getting any dinner. We'll talk about this tomorrow," Charlotte ordered, earning a hateful glare from her son.

Charlotte addressed the governess. "Take Pebbles to O'Connor. He'll know how to help him. And it would be best if he held on to him for a few days. The poor thing has suffered enough."

"Yes, my lady. And Elly? Should I take her along, too?" The governess held the dog away from her so that it didn't touch her dress.

"No, she can eat with us. I will put her to bed later myself. Thank you," said Charlotte, dismissing the governess, whose expression betrayed nothing of what she thought of the little episode.

An exemplary employee, thought Jane, but could not stop wondering what was really going through the woman's mind. Melissa Molan's eyes were too intelligent, her movements too calculated and confident. Obedience and humility must have demanded a lot of her.

When Miss Molan had left the drawing room with Cedric and the dog, Charlotte turned to Jane. "I must apologize, Lady Jane. I never wanted you to witness such private affairs. I will have to employ a tutor for Cedric, someone with a firmer hand who can hold him to some limits." She smiled weakly. "My own words, I'm sad to say, seem wasted."

Charlotte then led Jane to the library, its walls covered by floor-to-ceiling bookshelves. The ceiling itself was wood-paneled and the overall impression accordingly dark. In the center of the library stood a large desk on which several books lay open, all of them clearly on the subject of botany. "Plants, and particularly orchids, are my husband's obsession, as you can see. If he isn't in his study poring over the latest discoveries, then he is out in his greenhouse. He's invested a lot of money in it, especially in the irrigation system. I will show you tomorrow. It is really very lovely in there."

Jane listened as Charlotte spoke, mentally filing away interesting details and scraps of information about the residents of the house. She realized that she would find out nothing from Charlotte about any strange happenings, because the woman appeared apprehensive and seemingly afraid of her own husband. From society gatherings, Jane had a vague memory of Sir Frederick as an eccentric, introverted man. Well, she would soon have the opportunity to get to know the fellow better. There was a knock at the door, and the butler bade them enter the dining room.

As in the library, the dining room ceiling was clad in dark wood. Heavy carvings, pointed, arched doorframes, and imposing columns surrounded a table set in the center of the room, large enough to easily seat twelve. Carafes, glasses, and covered bowls stood at the ready on a sideboard, and the room smelled of roast meat and spices. The master of the house was already seated at the head of the table, reading a letter.

He merely glanced up when Charlotte said, "Please, Lady Jane, sit here."

Slowly, Sir Frederick lowered the pages of the letter and stood. He was a tall, lean man with dense blond hair, cut short and streaked with silver. A slightly crooked nose dominated his narrow face, from which gray eyes unabashedly looked Jane over. *As if sizing up a rival,* thought Jane instinctively, pasting on her most polite smile.

"Lady Jane. It is my pleasure to welcome you under our roof! What a happenstance that two of my wife's friends should find their way to our remote hilltop, to what some call a wilderness." Sir Frederick took her hand and kissed it gingerly. "Please sit on my left. You can tell us all about London's vitality and shine a little city light into our modest halls."

When they had all sat down, he frowned at his wife and daughter. "Where is Cedric?"

Charlotte's shoulders immediately sank. In a low voice, she said, "He behaved very badly and has been punished. You must speak to him tomorrow. Things can't go on like this."

"Ceddy burned off Pebbles's tail!" Elly crowed. In her flowery dress, she had to perch on a pillow to be able to reach her plate.

"Speak only when you are spoken to, Eleanor! I am talking to your mother." Elly's eyes instantly filled with tears. Sir Frederick turned back to his wife, who was stroking Elly's hair soothingly. "Is that true?" he asked.

Watching this scene, Jane realized with a pang how much she missed David with his calm manner, always willing to listen to the concerns and needs of his staff, always willing to listen to her, and attentive and loving when he sensed that something was troubling her. The time they had spent together so far had been as intense as it was brief. Oh, of course they argued, and she only knew the side of him he let her see, and he drove her mad when he didn't trust her to look after herself. Though admittedly, there were events in her recent past that had gotten out of hand . . . She sighed. There were so many things that remained unspoken between them, but Jane was absolutely convinced that David would never rebuff his daughter so coldheartedly, should they ever have children.

"My lady?" A young maid was standing beside her, tightly holding the lid of a tureen. "Soup?"

"Yes, thank you." She breathed in the scent of cooked rabbit.

"Bon appetít!" said Sir Frederick.

They ate in silence. The only sounds were the clinking of spoons and the occasional slurp. Jane found the silence oppressive, especially as she was used to talking with David as they ate. Little Eleanor poked at her plate and cast conspiratorial glances at Jane from beneath the hair falling over her face, and Jane could not stop herself from winking at the little girl.

When the soup had been cleared, Sir Frederick turned to her. His fingers drummed impatiently on the table. "Even though you are our guest, I must warn you not to encourage the child to unnecessary silliness. She has to learn to behave appropriately."

Jane smiled. "Of course. It's only that Elly *is* a child, and children are sometimes just silly. That is what makes them so delightful."

"You can think what you like about that, but in my house, you will abide by my rules. If that does not appeal to you, then you are free to leave at any time." He set his mouth in a hard line, and the sharp contours of his jaw became even more pronounced. He was clearly not used to a woman opposing him, and Jane had to allow that it had not been clever to provoke the man like that.

"Please, Frederick, Jane didn't mean anything by it. And our little Elly is so sweet she can wrap anyone around her little finger, isn't that true, my angel?"

The girl wriggled around on her chair and tugged at the large napkin that Charlotte had tied around her neck. Her father looked at her and cleared his throat. "Well, all right. But discipline is the foundation of raising children well, as you perhaps know from your own experience, my lady."

"No, Sir Frederick. I have not yet been granted that particular joy." Jane sipped her wine. "An outstanding claret."

The doors opened, and two maids entered carrying platters of smoked fish and mussels. Eleanor bravely ate a piece of smoked fish, and Jane praised the mussels, which were tossed in butter and spiced with parsley.

"The orchids in the drawing room are exceptionally beautiful," said Jane, dipping her fingers in a water bowl in which a sliver of lemon floated.

Sir Frederick's eyes lit up, assuming an almost fanatical gleam, and Jane leaned back with satisfaction. If you talked to him about his plants, it seemed, all else was forgotten.

"They certainly are, and you have yet to see my newest and rarest specimens. You know, a man has to dedicate all his love and attention to these wonderful creations of nature just to keep them alive in our harsh climate. Oh, and actually growing them yourself is an art! An art to which I have devoted myself for several years now, and may I say, not without success." Sir Frederick placed a hand on the letter that lay beside his glass. "These pages arrived today from South America."

"Where is Mr. Tomkins now? Is he all right?" asked Charlotte. "You know, Lady Jane, Derek Tomkins is a professional orchid hunter who searches for plants exclusively on my husband's behalf."

"Really? How extraordinary! I have no doubt that is an expensive undertaking. When I think of a man sailing across the Atlantic with the sole purpose of picking flowers in the jungle that he then . . . well, that he then packs up *how*, exactly?" Jane wondered.

Sir Frederick raised an eyebrow in amusement. "You have a sense of humor, my esteemed Lady Jane. But believe me when I say that 'picking flowers,' as you call it, is a serious and perilous undertaking. Men kill for special orchids."

His last words caught Jane's attention. "Who would kill for flowers?" she asked.

"Men like Derek Tomkins, Jane," Charlotte explained. "They receive a great deal of money for special plants. What is going on right now can only be called an orchid hunt." She glanced with some distress at her husband.

"You worry far too much, my dear," Sir Frederick replied. "It is simply like all good things in life. The rarer they are, the more they are worth."

"But it is true that Sir Robert's home was broken into, that a servant was shot at, and that someone stole orchids from his hothouse. All that is going too far!" said Charlotte with disgust.

"What does 'shot' mean?" Eleanor asked.

"Pushed, angel. Someone was pushed and fell over," said Charlotte.

"What nonsense you tell the child! She must know what 'shoot' means, don't you, Eleanor?" Sir Frederick said, frowning at his daughter.

The girl nodded rapidly. "O'Connor told me that sometimes you have to shoot animals because they get sick or because we eat them."

"Are you letting her speak to the gamekeeper alone now?" Clearly annoyed, Sir Frederick refilled his wineglass.

Luckily, just then the butler entered with a maid and set tureens of mashed potatoes and gravy on the table. Filets of venison were served on silver platters with preserved cherries. As expensive as the hunt for orchids might be, the household did not seem to be suffering because of it.

After dessert and cheese with a sweet wine rounded off the excellent dinner, Sir Frederick stood up from the table. "I wish you a good night's sleep, my lady, and please also convey my best wishes to Lady Alison. It is truly a tragedy that she is stranded here in her condition, at a time when any woman would naturally prefer to be in her own home."

"She could not be in better hands, I'm sure. Thank you." Jane bowed her head politely, then watched as the tall, lean figure hurried away.

"Now he will go back to his study and bury his nose in a book. Then before he goes to bed, he'll check on his precious plants! Every evening it is the same!" Charlotte complained quietly as she and Jane returned to the drawing room. She pulled on a bell cord, and it wasn't long before the governess appeared.

"Get Elly ready for bed. How are Cedric and Pebbles?" Charlotte asked curtly.

"Cedric is drawing and has not complained. The dog is being treated by Mr. O'Connor, and he will keep him for at least a week. Will that be all, my lady?" Melissa Molan stood rigidly before Charlotte with her chin raised. "If I may be permitted to ask, have you reached a decision about employing a tutor?"

"Not yet. Why? Do you have a recommendation?" Charlotte looked at the governess doubtfully.

"There is someone I remember from my last place of employment. I know that those children are now attending boarding school and that as a result the tutor is seeking a new post." Nonchalantly, Miss Molan turned and regarded the porcelain figurines. "He has experience with . . . willful boys."

"Well, then he should certainly apply. We will review his credentials. Thank you." Charlotte waited until Miss Molan had left them, then turned to Jane. "I really don't like such recommendations. One never knows what relations the staff has with one another, and love affairs among the servants always lead to problems. But to be perfectly frank, Jane, Cedric pushes me to my absolute limits. If the tutor she recommends can rein him in, then he can have whatever little dalliance he wants with Miss Molan, with my blessing."

Seeing a mischievous smile appear in Charlotte's eyes, Jane laughed, but her laughter immediately died as the young mother suddenly pitched forward, only just catching herself on a table edge. The porcelain figurines crashed together and two broke.

Jane quickly put her arm around Charlotte's slim waist and led her to an armchair. "Are you sure you don't want to call for a doctor?"

Charlotte's eyelids fluttered fearfully. "No! It's already passing. My husband sees illness as a weakness that one can master by strength of will."

"That is certainly a charming notion. Now wait here while I fetch the smelling salts and some water." Charlotte's words had not made Sir

Frederick any more endearing to Jane, nor did the governess seem to offer any real support for Charlotte.

When she stepped out of the drawing room into the hall, she saw the butler and a maid whispering in a corner. As if caught kissing, the girl turned red and ran off.

"Do you know where Lady Charlotte's smelling salts are?"

"Of course." The good-looking butler's face betrayed nothing, his demeanor exemplary, and within a minute he returned from an adjoining room with a small vial in his hand. "Is her ladyship unwell?" Something in the man's tone irritated Jane.

"Thank you." She took the vial and hurried back to her hostess.

6.

"My lady!" Alison's maid seemed to have been waiting for Jane, for she instantly rose from a chair in the corridor as Jane approached.

Still mulling over what she'd seen and heard at dinner, Jane looked up in surprise. "Nora! Is Lady Alison all right?"

Nora nodded. Her hair was covered with a white bonnet, and her black dress was trimmed with lace. Alison hated plain clothing. "Yes, my lady. Lady Alison would very much like to speak to you."

Jane heard Charlotte and Frederick's voices. They seemed to be arguing in the library, and she heard the name of their son. "Gladly."

She found Alison dressed in a silk dressing gown, sitting in an armchair by the window of her bedroom. On the table in front of her were the remains of dinner, which Nora now cleared away. Ally's long, blond hair was untied and tumbled over her shoulders, and Jane could not resist the urge to stroke it. "Thomas must love your hair!"

Ally laughed brightly. "You flatterer! But you're right, he does like it when I wear my hair down. Please, sit. Would you like something to drink? I've got a very nice port."

"That sounds like just the thing after an evening like this." Jane fetched the bottle and one glass; because she was expecting, Alison was abstaining from alcohol. "Cheers!" Jane took a large swig. "What a family!"

Propping her chin on her hand, Ally gazed at Jane with a concerned expression on her face. "Isn't it? Have you also noticed the tension in the air here? And Charlotte's attacks? Has she had another one?"

"I am sad to say she has. I suggested calling a doctor, but she doesn't want that. Is she so afraid of Frederick?"

Alison clasped her hands in her lap. "Frederick has changed very much. I never really liked him, but he at least treated her well for a time." It was clearly difficult for Alison to talk about the matter, but she looked her friend in the eye. "But ever since he has become obsessed with his orchids, he's had no patience at all. The slightest noise from the children or the little dog will set him off. I feel so sorry for the poor animal, although I have never been much of a dog lover, unlike you. Those yapping little lapdogs, my God, they are so annoying. But I tell you, I would take Pebbles away with me with no hesitation whatsoever, just to finally give the poor beast some respite from that small devil Cedric."

Jane quickly relayed all that had happened at dinner, and Alison sighed. "Things like that happen all the time, but that isn't why I wanted to talk to you. Jane, I didn't tell you everything in my letter. I was concerned that if David had read it, he would never have let you drive up here at all."

Jane looked at her excitedly. "He didn't want me to come up as it was, but that was mostly because of the weather. Why, have the Halstons got a skeleton in their closet?"

It was intended as a joke, but the expression of deep concern on Alison's face made Jane shudder.

"I fear they do. A very big skeleton!" Alison whispered.

"Ally! And you're still here? I'll send a telegram to Thomas immediately. He has to get you out of here!"

"No, no, listen. When I first arrived, there was a very pretty maid who had been working here only for a few weeks. Her name was Rachel. I remember her very well because there was something foreign about her, and she seemed less easily intimidated than the others. In any case, she went out one night and never came back. She did not leave a note, and no one knows where she was planning to go. It's a mystery!"

Jane's eyes widened. "A criminal mystery." She clapped her hands, then quickly became serious. "Did she take her things with her? Have they questioned the staff? What about her family?"

"Now you sound like a policeman. Oh, I am so happy to have you here, Jane. Charlotte said that Rachel has family in Crookham. They were sent a telegram, but there's been no reply. She abandoned her last position, which does not speak in her favor. Charlotte told me that she had been employed at the Cunninghams' in Devon." Alison rolled her eyes.

"*The* Cunninghams?" Jane knew the reputation of Lord Edward Cunningham's sons. The Cunninghams' country estate near Exeter was renowned for its debauched parties and hunting events.

"That was my reaction, too. She must have had a good reason to run away, because I am sure they paid better than Sir Frederick. He's very tightfisted. Charlotte has to account strictly for every penny, and I feel sorry for Mrs. Gubbins, the housekeeper, who has to arrange the salaries and household expenses with Sir Frederick once a month."

Jane sipped her port, which was sweet and strong. "If she ran away from there, we can assume that she is a decent girl and didn't want one of the Cunninghams to get her pregnant."

Blushing, Alison nodded. "You're always so direct."

"But that's what it comes down to, isn't it? A young woman gets in a family way and loses her position. And if they don't have a family to support them, they can either give the fatherless child away, which could mean bribing an orphanage with money that most of them don't have, or they can sell the child, which many cannot bring themselves to do. Then mother and child end up in the poorhouse or out on the street. Did I leave anything out?" Jane brooded.

"I don't think so. Although it also happens that bastard children are simply killed." Alison ran her hands gently over her swollen belly. "A horrible thought. But Rachel was not pregnant. I would have noticed; I've developed a bit of a sense for that." She grinned. "You, at least, are not expecting."

Jane took a deep breath. "No, and if I were, I'd keep well away from you, simply to stop you from making an ungodly fuss in your glee!"

"Then there's a chance . . . ?" her friend probed carefully.

"You mean?" Jane pursed her lips and slowly said, "Oh, yes, a chance, perhaps, one day . . ." She thought of the passion in David's embrace and of his kisses, which did not stop at her face or breasts. In the beginning, his caresses had shocked her, but he quickly stripped away her modesty and spurred her desire for intimacy, for his touch.

"Not another word, dearest. I understand. But I would not have expected anything else from a man like David. There's a passionate man hiding beneath that cool, reserved façade, isn't there?" Alison gave her friend a sly smile.

Jane cleared her throat. "I never would have thought it possible, you know. I mean, that I would find being close to a man so eminently appealing . . . but we are getting a little off track, aren't we? Rachel was not pregnant, so why did she run away? Did she receive a message?"

Alison raised her eyebrows. "An interesting idea! I don't know."

"Winton Park is certainly remote, and it's not far to the moor proper from here. It is dangerous to stroll around alone out there at any time of the day or night, but it's even more dangerous in the dark. If she left the house at night, then she must have had a very good reason to do so," Jane mused aloud.

"A lover!" Alison squealed.

"The butler! You have noticed how handsome he is, haven't you?"

"Jane, really, don't let David hear you say things like that! But yes . . ." Ally giggled. "I noticed immediately. Oh, and there's a gamekeeper, too. O'Connor. Nora prattles on about him all the time."

"*We* can't start interrogating the men, though. That's a job for Hettie," said Jane with a smirk.

Hettie unpacked the traveling case and smoothed out one of Jane's more festive evening dresses. "Do you think you'll be wearing this one at all, ma'am? From what I've heard here . . ." She clucked her tongue meaningfully.

Wearily pulling combs out of her hair, Jane dropped them on the dressing table in front of her. "No need to build up the drama, Hettie. What have you found out?"

"Well," Hettie began, pulling a crumpled note out of her skirt pocket and unfolding it before Jane's astonished eyes, "to start with, I had a bit of a chat with Nora, but she's terribly shy, you know, and hardly says boo to anyone else in the house. Then I talked to Della, the young, dark-haired maid who does the washing."

Jane's weariness evaporated in a heartbeat. She listened attentively to what Hettie had to report.

"Della's been here two years, she's twenty-two, and she comes from Thwaite in Yorkshire. This is her second post, and she says it's definitely not going to be her last."

"You're so good at this, Hettie! What doesn't she like about it here?" said Jane, patting her maid's arm proudly.

"It might be nothing at all, but as you always say, any detail could prove important. Della doesn't like the housekeeper one little bit. It seems the domestic staff fall into two camps—those on Mrs. Gubbins's side and those for the butler, Mr. Draycroft."

"Mrs. Gubbins?" Jane pondered for a moment. "I haven't met her yet."

"She's away right now visiting relatives, but she'll be back tomorrow. Della says it's been really nice without the old dragon here. The girls all sleep upstairs, under the eaves. They share three to a room. They can't lock the doors, and Mrs. Gubbins combs their rooms regularly and checks that no one's pilfering the silverware," Hettie said.

"Nothing unusual about that. Why doesn't Della want to stay here?" Jane pressed.

"Mainly because of Sir Frederick, I reckon. She finds him peculiar, the way he spends most of his time with his plants, and how he even speaks to them! And strange visitors often stop by. Rather dubious-looking characters, Della says, and she thinks it's strange that a lord would associate with riffraff like that. And she says she knows riffraff when she sees them, because she grew up around people like that."

"Hmm, that certainly is striking. Although I imagine they could be orchid dealers," said Jane thoughtfully.

"D'you think so? I mean, when I remember that shop in London where all the lovely flowers were, and the gentleman who advised us . . ." Hettie trailed off. She waved the crumpled note back and forth.

"Right again. There's more? Go on."

"Mrs. Gubbins is Sir Frederick's right hand. She was the housekeeper for his first wife. She's jealous of the young mistress and the children, because the first Lady Halston couldn't have children. Mrs. Gubbins has a daughter of her own, by the way. She's currently away in India." Jane raised her eyebrows in surprise, but Hettie folded the notepaper again. "I couldn't find out any more because I had to go to dinner and then unpack."

Jane handed Hettie the hairbrush and pulled the pins from her hair, letting her long, chestnut mane fall free. While Hettie gently untangled it and brushed it out, Jane said, "That is very interesting, Hettie. A housekeeper who's jealous of her new mistress. But we still must be suspicious of everyone living under this roof. And apart from that . . ." She sighed. "Apart from that, we don't yet know what is making Charlotte so weak."

Hettie pulled the brush vigorously through Jane's hair. "Poison!"

"That's the last thought I want to entertain. Emotional strain can also wear you down and make you sick. Oh, but I haven't even told you a word about Rachel!"

Hettie listened to Jane's breathless story, then cried out, "Della wanted to say something about Rachel, too, but Mr. Draycroft came along, and then she fell silent."

A pretty maid and an attractive butler—a scenario rife with potential conflict.

The next morning, the sky was still overcast, and the air was foggy and cold. Jane had breakfasted with Alison and was on her way to the drawing room to write a letter to David.

"Good morning, Lady Jane!" Charlotte, coming from the kitchens, greeted Jane with a lackluster smile in the hall.

"Good morning, Lady Charlotte. How are you feeling?" Jane asked.

Charlotte waved off her concern, her petite, delicate hands making the gesture jittery. "Please, don't fuss about my condition. The cold and the fog get to me, but that's always been true. Maybe I should winter in Italy." She laughed softly. "That would be a mad idea, wouldn't it?"

"Why not? It's a very sensible idea if you ask me! If the climate there does you good and you come back recovered and full of vim and vigor, I'm sure your husband would be pleased, too."

Sir Frederick must have heard her last words, because he came out of the library with a frown on his face and met them in the hall. "What's that I hear? What would I be glad about?"

Jane ignored Charlotte's nervous fluttering and said, "About a wife fortifying her constitution in Italy's mild climate."

The tall man, wearing a coarse tweed suit and sturdy shoes, examined Jane through narrowed eyes. "Italy? You're not planning to go off to that execrable land, are you, Charlotte? The place is positively overflowing with artists and other good-for-nothings!"

"Oh, no! Nonsense! That was Lady Jane's idea! I'm very happy here, you know that," Charlotte reassured him emphatically and took his arm.

Jane realized that there was little sense in pursuing the subject further. "Lady Charlotte, is it all right if I compose a letter in the drawing room?"

"Of course! You'll find everything you need there, and then you can leave your letter in the harlequin bowl on the escritoire. Mr. Draycroft will make sure that it is delivered to the post office." Charlotte stroked her husband's sleeve. "We still wanted to talk about Cedric, didn't we?"

"Hmm? Yes, that's right," Sir Frederick murmured reluctantly, and he accompanied his wife into a small sitting room.

The graceful escritoire stood in a corner beside one of the terrace doors, but Jane still needed the light from a gas lamp because the heavy gray clouds let through little of the morning sun. The harlequin figure that decorated the bowl was easy to see, and at least its grin and colorful costume radiated some cheer.

A stack of cut paper and envelopes lay beside a marble tray with pens and ink. Jane saw a handwritten page peeking from beneath a book of poems by Elizabeth Barrett Browning and realized that Charlotte had started her own letter. Jane lifted the book briefly and caught a glimpse of the first line, which read, Honored Mama. It would have been interesting to find out whether Charlotte revealed anything more about her condition to her mother. But then again, the rather formal opening suggested that the mother-daughter relationship was not especially close.

Jane heard someone discreetly clear his throat, and she dropped the book in surprise. Turning around, she discovered the butler standing in the doorway, holding a tray on which an envelope lay.

"Excuse me, my lady, I don't mean to intrude. This telegram has just arrived for you."

Mr. Draycroft wore his dark suit with the aplomb of an aristocrat. His eyes were unwavering, and Jane judged his appraising gaze as arrogant. He had only let his guard down briefly, however, before he immediately reassumed the impenetrable mask of the perfect servant. With a polite bow, he held the tray out to her.

Jane took the telegram. "Thank you."

The butler departed as he had come—without a sound—and Jane tore open the envelope. "David!" she whispered, and read: *Jane. Expecting message. David.*

She reread the spare message, but nothing about the imperious tone changed. Was she supposed to feel flattered that he had sent a telegram so soon? Or should she be indignant at his choice of words? Taking a deep breath, she folded the telegram and tucked it into her skirt pocket. It would be better not to reply in the mood she was in.

7.

Seymour Street, London, November 1860

David sat at the breakfast table and flapped open the morning paper. The rustle seemed to fill the silence of the room, and he stared sullenly at the empty chair opposite him. Disinterestedly chewing a slice of toast, he scanned the headlines: Montgomery revolt on the Missouri; the annual meeting of the Lancashire and Cheshire Mechanics' Institute was coming up; Garibaldi's redshirts were advancing, and many more enthusiastic British volunteers were joining his troops.

Brooding and distracted, David burned his mouth on his hot tea, swore, then turned the page. George Sand was seriously ill; Jane had read a number of her works. David turned a few more pages, pulling up short at a small article, one among many on the page. Crimes were committed every day in London, but had a murder victim ever before been decorated with an orchid?

Orchids! David sniffed and thought of the yellow orchid that Jane had left for him. She had only given him the plant because that tiresome Sir Frederick grew them. Personally, he had little interest in the exotic, strangely formed things. He would choose an English rose over an orchid every time, and roses had the advantage of a captivating fragrance.

He quickly read through the article about the murder. An employee of the highly respected nursery Veitch and Sons had been found dead the previous day in Nepenthes. An inspection of the body had revealed that the man, an orchid specialist, had been strangled with a hemp rope.

Nepenthes? David read on and discovered that it was the name of a hothouse at the firm's place of business. Its special irrigation and heating systems had made it the Mount Olympus of hothouses, according to *The Gardeners' Chronicle*. The article went on to talk about the race to obtain the rarest orchids, and the honor accorded whoever possessed them. David lowered the newspaper. Good and honorable men went to war and lost their lives in the fight for freedom and for the glory of their homeland. But the newspaper fellows wrote about the honor attached to owning a flower! He would wager that not a single one of those effeminate hacks had ever set foot on a battlefield, killed an enemy, or watched a comrade die.

If Jane had not gone to Sir Frederick's mansion in Northumberland, the article would hardly even have caught his eye. But now Jane was spending her days in the house of an orchid collector.

Without finishing his breakfast, he stood and stalked out of the room, taking the newspaper with him. He met Levi in the hall, watering the plants. "Levi, where is Blount?"

"Good morning, sir," the old man answered with his slight accent. "Mr. Blount will be back soon, I believe. He had some business to take care of."

"Hmm. All right, thank you. Oh, Levi . . ."

The man flinched slightly. "Yes, sir?"

"Any news of your family?" David asked.

"No, sir," Levi replied quietly, lowering his eyes. "It's as if there's no one left who knows anything about them."

"Those were bad times, terrible times for you and Josiah. I hope you have managed to settle in here." David observed the mix of expressions that crossed Levi's face. He seemed suddenly to be on guard, for his posture stiffened and he tightly grasped the watering can. "We are very grateful to you, sir, for everything you have done for us."

"That's not what I mean. Are you happy here, or would you prefer to return to your homeland?" They were standing close together in the hall, speaking in lowered voices.

"No, I . . . no, everything is fine." Suddenly, Levi looked directly at David, and David saw so much fear in his eyes that he was ashamed to have put the other man on the spot. "Have I done something wrong?"

"No! I am very satisfied with your work. It's just that sometimes I think that this position doesn't pose much of a challenge to you, and that you might conceivably prefer to do something else."

A cynical smile crossed Levi's face. "What dreams could a man like me still harbor, sir? I am alive and I take care of Josiah, and that is enough, though I dream of more for him."

"He is a smart, endearing lad who will certainly make his mark, provided he doesn't fall in with the wrong crowd. Sometimes, national pride—when misunderstood—has led to the perpetration of cruel deeds and destroyed more than one young life," said David, as he heard the outer door to the servants' wing swing shut.

His face paling a little, Levi shifted his weight nervously from one foot to the other. "I see no danger there, sir. He likes it here in England very much."

"Good, then we understand each other. Ah!"

Blount entered the hall just then, and David quickly bade his friend to follow him into his study. "Close the door, Blount."

Once they were alone, Blount turned to David. "Captain?"

David spread the newspaper on his desk, next to the yellow orchid. He pointed to the article, which bore the fitting headline **Orchid Murder**. “Did you read that?”

Blount, small and wiry and wearing his usual brown suit, nodded. “And I took it upon myself to make some inquiries.”

David nodded encouragingly. “Go on. You have my attention and my confidence.”

Clearing his throat, Blount said, “I immediately thought of Lady Jane’s destination. And because this orchid also came from Veitch and Sons, I took an early stroll down to Chelsea and asked around.”

David glanced at the nursery’s gold emblem on a band around the orchid’s pot.

“The victim was a young employee, Jeremy Korshaw. He’d been with the firm just six months. His absence had been noted late yesterday afternoon, but they only found him in the famous Nepenthes hothouse later in the evening. It seems he worked in there often. If he didn’t strangle himself with that rope, then he was most likely throttled.”

“Anything about his background?”

“None of the gawkers there could help with that, but I’m meeting another of the workers this evening, a chap by the name of Tom who cleans up all the rubbish. Says he’ll be happy to tell me more about Korshaw . . . for a small consideration.”

“Good work, Blount. And you know, I think I should purchase another one of these plants.”

A trace of a smile appeared on his loyal companion’s face. It was rare for Blount to show any emotion at all, but his deeds spoke for themselves. Before leaving the house a short while later, David checked the hall table, but there was still no letter from Jane. Grimly, he slipped on his hat, flipped up the collar of his coat, and stepped into the cold November morning, where a coach awaited him.

His route took him first to the Brompton police station, south of Hyde Park. Just over thirty years earlier, the Metropolitan Police

Act had divided London into seventeen districts, each with its own police station; ever since then, crime rates in the city had been falling. There were many who had little love for the "peelers" and "bobbies," as the uniformed officers had come to be known, but the institution had firmly established itself within the city overall. David Wescott now entered the plain building and was greeted by a young sergeant.

"Good morning, Captain Wescott! You'll be wanting to see Mr. Rooke?"

"That I will, Berwin." David followed the sergeant down a dark corridor. Sergeant Berwin rapped sharply on a door, then ushered David into the tiny office of Superintendent Michael Rooke.

Rooke was about the same height as David, heavily built and with an honest face. His nose had been broken at least twice, and two deep scars marked his chin. In contrast to David, he wore his dark hair short and had a neatly trimmed moustache. The two men knew each other from collaborating on some difficult cases, and they liked each other. An initiative introduced by Sir James Graham meant that a select few plainclothes officers were now able to carry out inquiries as part of a special criminal investigation office. Michael Rooke coordinated his people in secret and had achieved considerable success in solving cases of violent crime.

"David! Always glad to see you! What brings you here today?" Michael greeted him heartily, offering him a chair. The furnishings in the office were spartan, as were the officers' salaries, but Rooke made a tidy sum on the side as a private investigator.

David appreciated Rooke's straightforward manner. He was the kind of man who got right to the point. "Nothing political this time. I'm here about the so-called orchid murder. Have you found out much about the victim?"

With one of his large hands—hands that could break a man's arm with a quick twist—Michael Rooke scratched his chin. "Strange that *you* would be asking me about that. Are you collecting orchids now, too?"

David laughed. "Lord, no! I'm here more on my wife's behalf. She is visiting Sir Frederick Halston and asked me to poke around a little in the milieu."

Michael raised one eyebrow. "Your lady is determined, isn't she . . . and by the way, I still have nothing new to tell you about the whereabouts of the orphans. Australia is far away, and the arm of the law is not long enough."

"Thank you anyway for your efforts, Michael, but my interests currently lie more with these orchid-gathering lunatics. Who in their right mind would pay a small fortune for a few exotic plants that are going to die on him sooner or later?"

"Ha! My sentiments exactly, but you're wrong if you think the collectors are lunatics, my friend. Eccentric, perhaps. But money and prestige are at stake. Sir Frederick is one of the leading collectors; as we speak, he is practically at war with Sir Robert Parks to amass the best orchids. You would be amazed how often hothouses are broken into. The thieves know precisely what they are there to steal because they are carrying out contract burglaries. I suspect that was also the case at Veitch and Sons."

"But what sort of burglar would throttle an employee if he was caught in the act? Wouldn't a knife be the weapon of choice instead? Might it not be something personal? Something to do with Korshaw's life?" David suggested.

"You don't know the details. The killer brought the rope with him, and it was knotted in a special way; it reminded me of sailors' knots. I'm having drawings of the knot done. You can have a look at them tomorrow if you like. In any case, the burglar wanted to send a signal, perhaps a warning to someone."

"Have you already talked to Mr. Veitch?"

"It's early, and I've only just had breakfast. I'll know more by tomorrow," said Rooke.

"Then I'll see you tomorrow."

Back out on the street, the cold November wind and the city's stink were like slaps in the face. Living in London had many advantages, but healthy air was not among them. Human excrement, cadavers, horse dung, slaughterhouse waste, and the dross from tanning factories—everything was disposed of by simply tossing it into the Thames. The rain, meanwhile, washed the refuse from fish markets, hospitals, bone merchants, candlemakers, and dyers into the river. On hot summer days, the pestilential reek that rose from the Thames was unbearable. In winter, the stale air was hemmed in by the blanketing clouds and coal gas and forced into the city's many streets and alleys. David pulled on gloves and returned to the coach; he had instructed the driver to wait for him.

"King's Road, Veitch and Sons," David told the driver before he climbed in.

As the carriage pulled up in front of the nursery a few minutes later, a throng of curious onlookers had already gathered on the footpath and among the trees. A uniformed officer stood squarely in front of the Veitch and Sons entrance, keeping the spectators at a distance with his impressive sideburns and menacing glare.

"Are you a customer, sir, or a friend of this establishment?" the constable asked when David approached.

"A customer, but only if it doesn't cause any inconvenience," David replied politely.

The officer stepped aside. "In you go, sir. Bad news indeed if a death should cripple the business, sir; every customer's welcome. Mr. Veitch is a fine man."

David stepped inside the salesroom and was surprised by the tasteful interior. Hundreds of houseplants were arranged on wooden and marble pedestals; beautiful plants seemingly deserved a correspondingly beautiful setting. It was some minutes before a thin, elderly nurseryman appeared from among the forest of leaves. The green apron he wore over his dark suit bore the company's emblem.

The man's watery gray eyes looked at David, then immediately refocused on the various potted plants, which apparently seemed more in need of his attention. "Good day. One moment . . ."

Like a grasshopper, the man sprang from plant to plant, tugging off an occasional dead leaf, before finally nodding with satisfaction. "Now they are better. They are suffering, you see. Plants have a soul, and they sense if something isn't right. Someone has taken away their friend, and that is painful for them."

"Hmm. You mean Mr. Korshaw?" asked David carefully.

"Did you know him?" the nurseryman said, downcast.

"Not really, but I often bought from him," David lied. "He was very knowledgeable, in contrast to me." He smiled and pointed at a violet orchid. "For me, the color is what matters."

"The color, yes, well . . ." He produced a well-worn notebook from his apron pocket. "What was the name?"

"Wescott. Captain Wescott," said David.

The gardener rapidly leafed through the small book. "I can't find you. He made a note of every customer; we all do, so that we know immediately what someone might prefer when he places an order. What color, captain? Violet, or a vibrant pink? Or perhaps a rich yellow? I have a stunning Eulophia here . . ."

"Not yellow. A dark violet. My wife really loves that color." David followed the man deeper into the store. "So the tragic accident happened in Nepenthes, the holy of holies. Very unfortunate, very unfortunate," Wescott chattered away. "How did Mr. Veitch take it?"

The front door opened, and a woman in a midnight-blue dress entered. She wore a veil, and her jacket was trimmed with expensive fur; everything about her reeked of arrogant impatience.

The nurseryman flinched at the sight of her. "Excuse me, Captain. I'll be back in a moment."

David saw a round face with bright red lips beneath the veil. Too garish altogether, like the rest of her appearance.

The nurseryman greeted her. "Lady Dykson, how nice of you to come by today. I'm very sorry, but our—"

"Where is Korshaw? What are these stories I'm hearing? He *can't* be dead! Unheard of! I demand to be served by Mr. Korshaw alone." With every turn the determined woman made, her skirts swished audibly.

"That is not possible. Please, take a seat. I'll fetch Mr. Veitch for you." The nurseryman looked at David apologetically, then disappeared down a corridor.

"May I introduce myself? Captain Wescott," said David, taking a small bow.

"Oh, I didn't see you there." Lady Dykson fluttered her eyelashes. "Captain."

Wescott knew this kind of woman well, the kind whom neither title nor fortune could save from a lack of grace. "Tell me, my lady, Korshaw was quite healthy, wasn't he? That's how I remember him, at least."

"Of course he was healthy! In the bloom of life, and such a charming young man. He knew more about orchids than anyone else. He had not been here very long at all, and he was one of the most beloved of the nurserymen," Lady Dykson explained.

"Where was he before coming here?"

"He'd just come back from a sea journey, from India, I think. Or was it Granada? Well, wherever it was, he'd been abroad collecting orchids. Imagine that! Someone jaunts off to a tropical wilderness and picks flowers to bring back to England. Isn't that adorable?"

And lucrative, thought David, as he joined in the lady's artificial laughter. "Quite remarkable, as you say. Such strenuous journeys must take a lot out of a man. Perhaps he brought back an illness with him?"

Lady Dykson pursed her scarlet mouth anxiously. "Oh, that would be horrible! But no, he would have been pale or . . . Well, now that you mention it, he didn't seem as stable as usual lately. An illness like that wouldn't be communicable, would it? I mean, one never can say for sure how those terrible tropical diseases spread."

"Don't worry. What killed him is unlikely to be of any danger to you."

"How do you know? Are you a doctor?" Lady Dykson snapped indignantly.

David smiled. "I imagine a rope around one's neck is unlikely to be catching."

It took a moment for his words to sink in, but then Lady Dykson gaped at him in shock and fear.

Fortunately, just then the nurseryman returned, accompanied by his employer, freeing David from the humorless woman's company.

8.

Winton Park, Northumberland, November 1860

After the strains of the long journey the previous day, Jane needed fresh air and exercise, and a walk would perhaps allow her to meet the gamekeeper. If she wanted to understand what was going on at Winton Park, she had to know everyone who lived on the estate. It was perfectly clear that something was troubling Charlotte, but she was keeping her secrets to herself, and not even Alison had been able to get her to loosen her tongue.

"Hettie, where have you been?" Jane was waiting for her maid at the steps leading down to the garden.

"Beg pardon, ma'am, but the cook gave me this when she heard that we wanted to check on Pebbles." Hettie held up a cloth bag that smelled like ham.

"Ham for the little dog?" Jane shook her head as she trotted lightly down the steps.

In front of them lay a broad semicircular lawn bounded by a low boxwood labyrinth and some flower beds. There was a rose garden with a small gazebo that would be perfect for taking tea in summer, and an area to one side that might have been a stage, surrounded by a stone balustrade. Winton Park was huge and offered sufficient lodgings for illustrious visitors, for whom artistic performances would very likely have been on the agenda.

"No, the ham is for Mr. O'Connor. The giblets and the bread are for the dog," Hettie explained.

"And did you ask exactly where Mr. O'Connor's cottage lies?" Jane gazed dispiritedly at the woods in front of her; she did not like the idea of idly wandering around in search of the gamekeeper's cottage.

"We're supposed to follow the middle path until we come to the river. From there we cross a bridge, then take the path that leads straight into the woods. That will take us directly to Mr. O'Connor. Mrs. Elwood says that it sounds further than it is." Hettie hopped along happily beside Jane. "Oh, and we absolutely have to be back before dark. If we get lost, she said, we could end up on the moor."

"Before dark? My goodness, how long does Mrs. Elwood think we'll be strolling around out here?" Jane began to walk faster, casting doubtful looks up at the sky.

"Mrs. Elwood said that it would stay dry, but that the fog could thicken." Hettie hesitated. "Shouldn't we ask someone to go with us?"

Stopping short, Jane put her hands on her hips. The woods were more extensive than she had thought, and one maid had already disappeared. There could, of course, be many reasons for that, but taking an unnecessary risk would be frivolous. "Has the captain bribed you?"

Hettie looked at her wide-eyed. "Bribed me? Why would he do that?"

Jane laughed. "To keep an eye on me, that's why! To stop me doing anything foolhardy!"

"But you never do anything foolhardy, ma'am. I'm the one who does that!" said Hettie with certainty.

Jane was wondering whom she might ask to accompany them, besides Sir Frederick or his wife, when she heard a melodic whistling from the edge of the forest. The woods there were a mix of pines and various deciduous trees, looking lost and melancholy now without their leafy coats. A gust of wind swept through the trees, its whistling blending with the rustling of the pines and the groaning of the knotty trunks. Gray clouds scudded across the sky, and the moor seemed to lurk just beyond the woods. *Moor landscapes can be so beautiful,* thought Jane. But she knew, too, that a single misstep could spell disaster on this treacherous ground.

"There's a man coming, ma'am, and from the way he's dressed . . . ," Hettie began.

"He can only be the gamekeeper," Jane finished her sentence. "We're in luck." Curious, they watched as the slender man in buckskin trousers and a chafed tweed jacket drew nearer. A bag of game was slung across his chest, while a shotgun and a hunting knife completed his outfit. He let out a sharp whistle, and a mottled hound followed at a run.

A cap perched atop his gold-brown hair, which he had tucked lazily behind his ears. As his name suggested, his features were Irish. Wry green eyes took them in, and his broad mouth stretched into an equally broad smile.

"Ma'am." He touched his cap casually in greeting.

An independent man, thought Jane, *who probably does not have an easy time of it here in Sir Frederick's realm.* From the corner of her eye, she saw Hettie giggle shyly, her arms wrapped around the bundled bag that she carried.

"Are you O'Connor, the gamekeeper?" asked Jane crisply.

"One and the same, ma'am. At your service." His eyes maintained their rather disconcerting expression. His words and tone were a little enigmatic, and Jane found herself wondering how many women had taken advantage of his "service." Perhaps even Charlotte? Is that why she was afraid of her husband? Reluctantly, she shook away the thought.

"I am Lady Jane Allen. I will be a guest at Winton Park for the next few days. We wanted to ask after little Pebbles. Hettie, give the man the parcel."

A blushing Hettie handed the man the bag. "Here, sir. Mrs. Elwood sends her greetings. The bread and giblets are for the dog."

He stowed the bundle in his satchel. "I wouldn't have pinched them from him, little lady. I respect animals. Eh, Rohan? Good dog." He fondly scratched the brown-and-black hound, who was rubbing his head against the satchel. "Oh, I know you want that, I know. Later, boy."

"Can I pet him?" Hettie asked.

"He'll let you pet him if he likes you. If he doesn't like you, you'll know it soon enough." O'Connor grinned.

"Pebbles is in your cottage, Mr. O'Connor?" Jane inquired. She wanted to find out more about the gamekeeper.

He looked at her in surprise. "He's there now. Should I go and fetch him already? I said I'd hold onto the poor beggar for a week. I won't let that little rat get his hands on him before that," he said bluntly.

Jane pulled her scarf more tightly around her neck; the wind was biting, and it cut through her clothes. "I assume that by 'little rat' you're referring to Master Cedric?"

O'Connor planted his feet and lifted his chin. "Bet your life on it. And I'm not ashamed to say it." He seemed about to say more but instead pressed his lips together and coolly stared at her.

"No, I haven't come to collect the dog." She held his gaze. "Though it might not be the worst thing to happen to him if he were to run away and find a new home elsewhere."

O'Connor relaxed. "My lady, I would wish him the same, but that would cost me my head, and another creature would have to suffer in this pup's place."

"Running away isn't always a bad solution, though. At least it wasn't for Rachel, don't you think?" It was a shot in the dark.

"Rachel?" His eyebrows narrowed, and one hand went to the strap of his shotgun. "What about her? Has she turned up?"

Before Jane could say another word, Sir Frederick's imperious voice rang out.

"O'Connor!" the lord of the manor bellowed, the man himself out of sight behind a hedge.

The gamekeeper grimaced, then touched his cap. "My lady. Keep an eye on each other. The moor can prove deceptive." He strolled off toward the entrance to the garden.

Jane furrowed her brow. *An inscrutable man, O'Connor.* "Come on, Hettie, let's visit the horses. I have no desire to run into Sir Frederick today." Jane picked up her skirts and hurried down the narrow path sheltered by the trees.

Jane knew that useful information could be gleaned from stable-boys and coachmen, and after a ten-minute march, they reached the stables. It smelled of dung and hay, and they could hear the whinnying and snorting of horses inside. A male voice was speaking softly and reassuringly to the animals.

Entering the stable through the main door, Jane and Hettie found a young man standing inside, cleaning the hooves of a gray mare.

"Hello!" called Hettie. She strolled toward the young man, who turned his head as far as his bent-over stance would allow. "That's a pretty horse. Does she belong to Lady Charlotte?" Hettie went to stroke the horse's flank. The animal had a slender, beautifully formed head. The mare eyed her nervously with its dark eyes.

"D'you know horses? If you don't, better leave her alone. She's flighty and likes to bite." The young man lowered the mare's freshly cleaned front hoof to the floor, then repositioned himself by its hind-quarters. He stroked a hand over the muscular rump and haunches all the way down to the fetlock before lifting a hoof and resting it on his thigh.

"What's her name?" Hettie asked, caressing the horse's soft muzzle.

"Shadow." Hard-trodden muck and small pebbles flicked onto the stone stable floor. "And yours?"

"Hettie," the maid replied. Jane thought it was about time to remind her of the reason they were there, and she stepped closer.

"If that isn't Lady Charlotte's horse, I would love to ride her. Would that be all right, Mr. . . . ?"

"Miles. Just Miles, ma'am."

"Miles, could you have Shadow ready for me in, say, an hour?" Jane observed the stableboy closely. He was not especially tall but was powerfully built, and he spoke with the thick accent typical of the region.

"Ma'am, I would gladly do that, but this horse ain't easy to ride." Miles looked at her doubtfully, further tousling his already disheveled hair. Muscular forearms jutted from his rolled sleeves.

"Who rides her then? I hope to cajole Lady Charlotte into going for a ride together," said Jane with her most charming smile.

"Truth be told, Sir Frederick bought her for the lady, but she and the mare didn't see eye to eye, and the horse is too skittish altogether for him." Miles, abashed, stopped talking, as if realizing he had revealed too much about his employer.

At least two dozen stalls and a stack of hay lined the long walls of the stable. Just opposite, a large black horse was being led out of its stall. Jane noted the even gait of the impressive animal.

"That one's Blandford, Sir Frederick's own, from a noble line. He scooped him up from under the nose of another bidder at auction. Cost him an arm and a leg." Miles grinned. "But the other man's a step ahead when it comes to orchids, or so I've heard." Miles looked around quickly, but there was no one else within earshot. He continued in a low voice. "His lordship spends so much time with his orchids that he hardly has time for anything else. Neglecting that beautiful animal. If I had the say-so around here—"

"But you don't, Miles!" snapped an older man in boots and riding clothes, appearing from another stall. "Get to it and finish up here. The other horses need seeing to as well!"

The man smacked his boots with his riding crop to add some weight to his words and nodded to Jane. "If you'd like to ride one of our horses, ma'am, then I'd ask you to let me know. I'm Gubbins, the stable master."

"In about an hour, I would very much like to take Shadow out for a short ride. Perhaps together with Lady Charlotte," Jane repeated.

Mr. Gubbins wore his beard trimmed short, which emphasized his coarse features. "I'll pick out a gentler beast, ma'am. Shadow's not for you," he replied brusquely.

Taken aback at the man's tone, Jane opened her mouth to respond, but Mr. Gubbins had already turned to Miles. "Moondancer and Ginger, Miles, understood?"

"Yes, Mr. Gubbins," Miles murmured and shifted to Shadow's other hind leg.

"A good day to you, my lady!" said Mr. Gubbins, then stalked away.

Jane exhaled indignantly. "Well, isn't he the polite gentleman!"

"Oh, that was nothing, ma'am," sniffed Miles. "He's only too happy to take a swing with that whip of his, you have my word about that."

"Gubbins . . . is he related to the housekeeper?" Jane wondered aloud.

Miles nodded. "Her husband," he said, then set back to work, diligently scraping the hoof clean. Another stableboy pushed past with a wheelbarrow full of straw.

"Poor Rachel. She was probably scared, and that's why she ran off," said Jane, as if to herself, pulling her gloves smooth.

"Oh, no, ma'am. That ain't it at all." Miles lowered Shadow's hoof, then lightly slapped the mare's rump and stroked her neck. He glanced around, then said quietly, "Rachel was something special. Young and very pretty, and there were several who had their eye on her. Mr. Gubbins, for one!"

Hettie, standing right next to Jane, said, "Well! He's a married man!"

Miles laughed. "Pardon, ma'am, but that ain't ever stopped a man from chasing a fresh skirt!"

"Miles!" came a cry from another stall. "Help me here, damn it!"

On the way back to the house, Cedric came running toward them. He was not wearing a coat, and he appeared to have been crying.

"Cedric, what's the matter?" Jane reached a hand toward the boy, but he dodged her, jumped over a bush, and ran across the grass toward the woods.

A moment later, the governess, her face red with anger, followed in his stead. But her heavy skirts hindered her progress, and she stopped and pressed a hand to her corset, gasping for air. "This boy will be . . . the death of me . . ." Melissa Molan took a few deep breaths until she had recovered enough to speak normally again. "His father scolded him this morning."

They saw the boy glance back just before reaching the steps leading down from the garden. "He'll be out of sight soon," said Jane.

"Oh, no! Cedric!" the governess yelled, and she ran after him again.

Hettie shook her head. "Poor woman. I wouldn't enjoy looking after that boy. Imagine if anything happened to him!"

"Miss Molan will know how to bring him to his senses." Jane watched the scene at the end of the terrace unfold and noticed that although Cedric ran down the steps, he did so at a noticeably slower pace, as if he was waiting for Miss Molan to catch up.

Before long, they saw the governess reappear among the trees, holding Cedric's hand. Now at ease, Jane continued back to the house, where she first paid a visit to her bedridden friend, after dispatching Hettie to the kitchen to find out more about Mrs. Gubbins.

Alison lay on her bed in a light-green robe. Her blond hair fanned across the pillows as if in a painting, but she seemed pale. "Jane! You've been out walking! Oh, I wish I could go riding with you! The landscape here is so beautiful when it isn't foggy." She patted the bedcovers beside her. "Sit and tell me everything."

"Are you sure you're feeling well, Ally?" Jane asked and took her friend's hand. It felt cold.

Alison coughed lightly. "I might have caught a cold. Now I really do feel better lying in bed." She smiled mirthlessly.

Jane told her what she had heard that morning and relayed her thoughts about it all. "I think it's vital that we find out exactly what happened to Rachel. She was very pretty, and popular, too, apparently. Why would a girl like that run away, especially in winter? And all her things are still here, aren't they?"

"I believe so, yes. Nora?" She called for her maid.

"Yes, my lady?" The girl stood at the end of the bed, helplessly staring at the floor.

"Run down to Lady Charlotte and bring her to us!" Alison instructed her.

"I wanted to see if she'd go riding with me," said Jane. "She's so closed off, and from what I've heard, her husband doesn't make it any easier. Has she always been so terrified of Sir Frederick?"

Alison looked at her in surprise and pressed a handkerchief to her nose. "I never had that impression. Quite the contrary, actually. Charlotte seemed very taken with him at the start, which I personally can't understand at all, but I try to keep my nose out of other people's marriages. Frederick was always very serious, and it took him a long time to get over the early death of his first wife, Eunice. She was just twenty-one when she died."

"She isn't in one of those portraits in the stairway, is she?" Jane could not remember seeing the likeness of a young woman.

"No, but Eunice was supposed to have been very beautiful. I think I've seen her picture in Frederick's study. She had black hair, a very light complexion, and large, dark eyes. A classical beauty. Now that you mention it, she probably looked very much like poor Rachel."

"How long has Rachel been missing now?" Jane asked, handing her friend a glass of water as Alison began to cough.

"Almost two weeks." Alison sank back into her pillows.

"And no one has asked after her? Her family lives close by, don't they?"

Alison sighed. "Jane, you know just how it is so often with families like that. They're simply happy when there's one less mouth to feed."

"But that doesn't mean that it *is* like that. They might be crazed with worry and simply don't have the courage to ask about her. I'm going to visit them and ask them myself!" Jane decided.

Ally's eyes widened, and she took Jane's hand. "You always see the good in people. I admire that so much."

There was a knock at the door, and Nora entered with Charlotte. "What is it, Ally? Oh, it's so nice to have you both here!" Charlotte's cheeks were mottled, and she seemed tense, as if she had been very upset recently. "Lady Jane, you—"

"Enough formalities, Charlotte," Alison interrupted her with a laugh. "No more 'Lady-this' and 'Lady-that.' You too, Jane, or I can't talk to either of you anymore!"

Jane and Charlotte embraced and kissed each other on the cheek. "My dear Jane, what must you think of me?"

"That you're the cousin of my best friend in the world, and because of that, you already have a place in my heart," said Jane. "We've been sitting here worrying about Rachel, the poor girl. Charlotte, did she actually leave her things behind?"

Charlotte was clearly taken by surprise. "Rachel? What do you want with her? Young things like her run away all the time; they have love affairs and I don't know what else. She wasn't with us very long, but yes, she did leave all of her things here. I had one of the servants pack them up. In case she comes back, she can take her things with her and start searching for a new position."

"But that makes no sense! Why would she leave all of her possessions behind?" Jane said. "She already has so little, and I'm sure she valued her clothes, in any case!"

Ally coughed. "I agree, but I'm tired. Go ride for a while together! Charlotte, it will do you good."

Charlotte leaned over Ally and placed a hand on her forehead. "You're feverish, Ally! I will have the kitchen staff make you some tea using my herbs; meanwhile, you should get under your blankets and keep warm. Laura shall bring you some hot stones, and I have a copper pan, too, which will keep the water warm longer."

"Oh, it's just a little sniffle," said Ally.

"You're pregnant! You can't take anything lightly in your condition. Jane, I can't come along with you, but Frederick loves to go out riding!"

9.

As it turned out, Sir Frederick had other business to attend to and thus did not have time to accompany Jane. He would ride later by himself and sent O'Connor to escort Jane instead. Now the gamekeeper stood in front of the stables with two saddled horses at the ready. His dog ran around them excitedly, and Jane felt a remorseful stab inside. She missed Rufus and the rides she took with David. O'Connor helped her onto the sidesaddle. She never rode sidesaddle in Cornwall, but Sir Frederick would hardly tolerate such unseemly behavior, so Jane resigned herself to the situation and clucked her tongue to rouse Moondancer to a walk. The brown mare started to move, and O'Connor, riding next to her on a black thoroughbred, asked, "And where would the lady like to ride?"

"Out onto the moor! Earlier you said that I should take care. Why?" The horses walked along the gravel paths.

"One of my responsibilities is to make sure that nothing happens to Winton Park's guests. You don't know your way around here." He was a good rider and brought his horse up to a trot with a little pressure from his legs.

At first, Jane had to get used to the mare she was riding, but the patient beast soon easily followed the lead set by O'Connor's horse. Riding side by side along a path bordering the forest, Jane breathed in the cool, fresh air. The River Coquet meandered between the hills, flowing at a leisurely pace. The river was well populated with fish, and the forests offered rich hunting opportunities, both indications that Sir Frederick was one of the wealthiest landowners in Northumberland. *Though one might not guess it from looking at Winton Park,* thought Jane.

"It's true that I don't know my way around here, Mr. O'Connor, but I learn fast. Rachel's disappearance strikes me as a mystery. Why isn't anyone looking into it?" Jane knew nothing about O'Connor, but of all the people she had met so far at Winton Park, he seemed to be one of the few who were not afraid of Sir Frederick.

"My lady, I'm just the gamekeeper, no more. You're asking the wrong man. The moor begins around the next curve. I'll ride in front, and you follow. Give Moondancer a slack rein; the animals have better instincts than you and I."

The fog had thinned, and the hilly landscape spread out before them. The forest retreated, giving way to the grasses and low bushes more typical of the marshy regions. Only an occasional birch or pine was rooted in the moor's acidic soil. The hills were picturesque and no doubt even lovelier in summer, but Jane still preferred the raw coastal landscape of Cornwall.

For the next half hour, they rode in silence, Jane following O'Connor. She took pleasure in the horse's movements and the smells and sounds of the natural world around her. The track they were following grew ever narrower, with muddy earth on both sides. "I would not like to have to navigate these parts at night."

"That's something to be avoided to be sure, my lady," said O'Connor, reining in his horse at a fork in the path.

"What's that up ahead?" asked Jane, who had spotted a small building in the middle of the moor.

"A hunter's hut, used only in the summer. All of this belongs to Sir Frederick. We should turn back, my lady. There's going to be rain."

The sky had turned dark, and wet weather was certainly in the offing. "No one would hide there, would they?"

"In that hut?" O'Connor asked in disbelief. "I come by this way regularly, and I've never seen a stranger there. Rohan would let me know right off if someone was nearby."

At the mention of his name, the hunting dog pricked up his ears and looked at his master.

They spoke little on the way back. As O'Connor helped her dismount, he said, "The Gubbinses have been here half an eternity. If there's anyone around here who knows what's going on, I'd not look past them."

"Thank you, Mr. O'Connor."

He looked at her with something close to sympathy. "For what? I'm only doing my job." He wandered off, leading the horses by their reins.

Jane knocked muddy earth from her boots with her riding crop. Beneath her long, black skirt, she wore close-fitting stockings that protected her from the cold. The elegant black hat she wore, like the sidesaddle, was another concession to the rules of decency. But the dagger David had given her certainly was not. He had trained her how to handle the effective little weapon, showing her how to defend herself with it. Jane smiled to herself. If Sir Frederick knew what she was keeping concealed in her boot . . .

"Ah, Lady Jane! I trust your excursion was an enjoyable one?"

Speak of the devil, thought Jane, this time smiling at Sir Frederick. "It was glorious! I must congratulate you on maintaining such a wonderful estate, Sir Frederick. The views across the forest and moor are exceptional."

Her host was also dressed for riding, and Miles was just leading his regal steed back to the stables to unsaddle it. "Aren't they? I would gladly have given you a tour of it myself, but O'Connor is a reliable man. Or did you have some grounds for complaint?"

"Most certainly not. He is cautious and had an eye to my safety the entire time. I fear I tend to be rather impulsive!" Jane said with a laugh.

The trace of a smile crossed the man's gaunt face; he was at least half a head taller than David. "Unbridled emotional actions are in a woman's nature. Charlotte, I'm happy to say, is among the more sedate of your gender."

Jane cleared her throat. "You said you wanted to show me your hothouse? I've heard so very much about it. Even in London, they extol the depth of your knowledge and the extraordinary quality of your orchids."

Flattered, Sir Frederick raised his eyebrows. "Is that so? Well, I suppose I have carved out a certain reputation for myself. Why not take a look now? After you, my lady."

The hothouse was situated on the opposite side of the manor, behind an enormous elm tree, and in contrast to Veitch and Sons' Nepenthes, it was an architectural gem. The steel-beam-and-glass construction on a solid foundation looked to Jane like a miniature version of London's Crystal Palace. So this was how Sir Frederick was spending every penny. He opened the door and ushered Jane inside like a monarch granting a special guest a tour of his treasure chamber.

"Please feel free to doff your hat and gloves. This is the East India section, and it is kept particularly warm." He had already removed those items himself, leaving them on a table in the entrance area.

Jane gazed around in genuine admiration; the place reminded her of her childhood in India. The smells and the warmth were comforting, and in the dense, green splendor the brightly colored orchids positively glowed. It was an incomparable spectacle beneath the building's glass canopy. The irrigation and ventilation systems hummed and droned in the background, there was the sound of splashing water, and two gardeners in green aprons darted around busily among the plants.

"My God, this is magnificent!"

"It is, isn't it?" Sir Frederick's eyes gleamed, and he checked the leaves of a plant as they walked. "Did you know that the orchid dates back to Greek mythology? Orchis, the son of a nymph and a satyr, fell in love with a priestess of Dionysos. Orchis tried to have his way with the priestess by force, but she called on the wild animals to help her, and they killed Orchis. When the priestess saw him dead at her feet, she regretted her act and begged the gods to restore Orchis to life. The gods heard her and transformed him into an orchid."

Awestruck by the burgeoning life all around her, for a moment Jane could almost imagine the Greek story was true. The flowers there were not simply lined up on display as they had been in the nursery in London but were thriving among the palms and ferns. In the center of the hothouse stood a tall and very exotic tree, reaching toward the light with its twining network of branches—or were they roots?

"Orchids are the most astoundingly adaptive plants in the entire plant kingdom. From their roots, one can ascertain precisely what type of region they originated from," Sir Frederick lectured. "We are not even close to grasping all there is to know about these queens among flora, but we are collecting data, and, of course, the plants themselves to try to understand them in their tremendous variety. Look here. Thin roots and soft foliage indicate that this orchid lives in a cloud forest. It is dependent on humid air and the formation of dew. Orchids from dry regions have firm leaves and thick roots to store water."

Jane discovered a small orchid with a cluster of closely spaced white flowers with purple stripes radiating outward. "Where does this orchid come from?"

"Oh, that is an *Encyclia radiata*, a rather demanding species; they live in South America and Mexico. But here, this is *Phalaenopsis aphrodite*! White as snow on the outside, then unfurling to reveal her delicate, vulnerable innermost parts, as yellow as the yolk of an egg." Sir Frederick lovingly gazed at the blooms.

"Not even Veitch and Sons have more beautiful plants!" Jane looked around. "And their hothouse isn't really—"

"You've been there? Have you read the news?" Sir Frederick interrupted her.

"No. What news?"

"An employee of Veitch and Sons was found dead in Nepenthes! Plants are extremely sensitive . . ." With his long fingers, Sir Frederick plucked at the leaves of an orchid.

Shocked at the sudden revelation, Jane took a step backward, knocking over a pitcher from a shelf. It shattered as it landed on the stone floor. "How horrible!"

"Come, let the workers take care of that." Sir Frederick led her onward through the green depths of his hothouse. "I buy regularly from Veitch, although I have my own man in the field searching for special plants. One must stay among the leaders of the hunt."

They stopped before a magnificent white orchid with five finger-shaped petals that appeared almost frayed.

"Look at this. The labellum protrudes like a tongue painted in violet and yellow."

Jane gathered that the lowest petal, which looked like a lip, had to be the labellum.

"This is *Cattleya dominiana*, the first successful crossbred orchid created by a human hand. Such crossbreeds are also known as hybrids, and the man who created it was John Dominy at the Veitch nursery. This new flower bloomed for the first time last year. Dominy created it by crossing two Brazilian plants; it was an absolute sensation! It is hard enough to get orchids to bloom here at all."

"I hope it wasn't this Mr. Dominy who died?"

"If it had been, they would certainly have mentioned his name in the newspaper. But please understand, my lady, there is much more at stake here than the breeding of plants. We are pioneers in the botanical field! There are so many secrets waiting to be uncovered in the world of orchids. There are species that are as rare as rubies and as beautiful as what we see in our dreams . . ."

Jane looked at the orchid and tried to imagine how it was possible to breed a new flower from two different plants. "Where is your man in the field right now?"

"Colombia, or New Granada, or whatever it is called these days; it depends on which of those savages is in power. Tomkins is an experienced orchid hunter and has already sent me many wonderful plants. But one still eludes him . . ." With a frown, Frederick Halston walked on.

Jane pushed back a palm frond that was obstructing their path. It was slowly getting too warm in the hothouse, and the humidity was becoming uncomfortable. "What could you possibly still lack?"

Sir Frederick wheeled around to face her, glaring at her with a strange, almost crazed expression. "The black orchid!"

"Sir Frederick!" Jane heard Mr. Draycroft's voice, and the butler joined them, holding a letter.

"I won't trouble you for your time any longer. Thank you!" Jane said and hurriedly retraced their footsteps out of the hothouse.

Reentering the manor house, she checked the large grandfather clock in the hall. It was already past midday, and her stomach felt empty. She turned and saw an older woman in a snug-fitting black dress fussing about; the woman's expression was stern, and a collection of keys dangled from her waist. Jane realized that she was looking at Mrs. Gubbins. The housekeeper seemed to be in the process of checking whether the place had been kept properly clean in her absence.

"My lady," she said politely, bowing her head at the sight of Jane. "I am Mrs. Gubbins, and I am accountable for the household. If there is anything you wish for, please come to me. Has everything been to your satisfaction so far?"

"That is very nice of you, and thank you, I have been well attended to since my arrival. Would it be possible to have a light lunch sent up to me?" The housekeeper was slim and had no doubt been very attractive in her youth, but now she looked careworn. Deep lines had carved their way into the skin on either side of her mouth, and a crease on her forehead mirrored inner disquiet.

"Very well, my lady."

An excited Hettie was already waiting for Jane in her room. "Ma'am, there you are! I was getting worried!"

Jane tossed her hat and gloves onto the bed then sat in an armchair. Hettie went to unlace Jane's boots.

"Where did you go riding? And with whom? And how was it? And—"

"Hettie! One thing at a time. How is Alison?"

"Lady Charlotte went to a lot of trouble on her behalf and seems to know much about herbs and medicinal concoctions. Lady Alison is resting now, and her fever has not gone up at all. Nora says that both Miles and Mr. Draycroft had their eye on Rachel. Oh, and that Sir Frederick was seen with her in the hothouse!"

Hettie eased the first boot from Jane's foot.

"That is definitely interesting, but one shouldn't go drawing conclusions too hastily." Jane told Hettie about her ride with O'Connor and her visit to the hothouse. "I think Sir Frederick shows practically every visitor his orchids! He is positively obsessed with those flowers! And, oh . . ." She told Hettie about the dreadful event at the Veitch and Sons nursery.

Hettie clapped a hand over her mouth. "Good gracious! And we were just there!"

There was a knock at the door just then, and a maid entered with a tray bearing tea, sandwiches, and warm apple crumble. Hettie breathed in the aroma of the delicious dessert.

"Mrs. Gubbins is back, too!" said Hettie a short while later, polishing off the last morsels of apple crumble.

"I've already met her. Where was she?"

"Visiting her mother, who lives close to York. She's been ill. Della told me that Mrs. Gubbins didn't like Rachel, who apparently had gypsy blood, which Mrs. Gubbins felt would only bring calamity."

"Gypsy blood? Hettie, we have to visit Rachel's family, but I must send a telegram first."

10.

London, November 1860

"Good morning, sir. Would you like anything in particular for breakfast?"

The voice was unfamiliar, and David, still sleepy, looked up at a face he did not immediately recognize. It took him a moment to remember that he had joined a card game the night before, had drunk too much, and so had stayed in the club. "Ham and scrambled eggs. Toast and tea."

"Very good, sir. They are drawing a bath for you right now." The butler silently closed the door behind him.

He was not proud of the previous evening, for he had drunk more than was good for him and had gambled away more money than he could really afford. Normally, he calculated precisely how much he could afford to lose and left the table when he reached his limit. But some devil had been riding his shoulder, whispering in his ear that she had left him alone and that it was his right to do damned well whatever he wished. When he lifted his head and the hammering started to make the anvil ring inside his skull, he groaned and closed his eyes again. His tongue felt furry, and his stomach was far from happy.

It was the first time he had felt like this since he had been married. A smile crept into the corners of his mouth. Whatever initial misgivings he may have had about his marriage, that headstrong, independent woman had swept them all aside with her impulsive ways. Her ready wit and her passion for everything she did drove him mad, but also mad with . . . He hesitated. So far, both of them had avoided speaking about their feelings. No, he would not let himself be turned into a sentimental fool.

He swung his long, powerful legs resolutely over the side of the bed and stood, breathing deeply to settle the rebellion in his stomach. He knew that a decent breakfast would make the world seem like a friendlier place.

A little while later, his hair still wet from a refreshing bath, he sat in shirt and trousers at a table in front of the window. He had a good view of St. James Street, where he could see night owls shamefacedly attempting to hail a coach, trying to get home as discreetly as possible. Very likely they were going home to face a wife who, like them, had her own life to lead. A wife who would politely welcome them home, not asking where they had been and what they had done, and who expected the same courtesy in return. These were the kind of couples who appeared together as expected at social functions, but who had little to say to each other otherwise. It was exactly the kind of life that he had supposed for himself, because he had not been prepared to allow another human being to get as close to him . . . as Jane had. Yet she had turned everything upside down.

He ate the last mouthful of breakfast. Brooks's was a second home to many gentlemen, and not without reason. Those who ran the club knew exactly how to tend to the members' well-being, but he still would have preferred to have eaten at his house on Seymour Street, to share the newspaper with Jane, and to talk about the latest developments in China or the everyday concerns of the household with her.

There was a knock at the door, and the butler brought in a telegram and a message. David opened the telegram and pulled out the thin strips of paper inside. Jane's brief report about her research was not revelatory, but what she wrote about the inhabitants and staff of the estate did little to reassure him. Knowing Jane, she was probably already on her way to Crookham to question the family of the maid who had disappeared. Alison was ill and Charlotte continued to suffer from dizzy spells. He was not to worry . . . My love, Jane.

He smoothed out the strips of paper and leaned back. Maybe it was time to set one or two things straight between them.

The message, from Michael Rooke, was an invitation to meet him at the police station.

When he got to the station, Rooke was standing in the corridor talking with a policeman. Upon seeing David enter, he dismissed the other man with a jovial thump on the shoulder, then turned to the captain.

"Good morning, David!"

"Michael!" The men shook hands and went into Michael's office.

"What a night! We had a fight at Madame Velmont's place in St. Giles." Rooke took his seat opposite David and ran his hands through his hair. Dark shadows under his eyes bore witness to a mostly sleepless night, and his clothes were so rumpled and creased that it looked as if he had not had time to change them from the previous day.

"Just a fight?" Madame Velmont's brothel was located in one of the city's most disreputable quarters, but its customers came from every walk of life and every layer of society. If Rooke had been personally called there, it must have had something to do with an important customer, someone who did not want to find himself caught in a scandal.

Rooke snorted. "It's the same old story. Rupert, the son of Sir Robert Parks, went on a little bender last night, then found he could not pay. Not the first time that had happened . . . so Madame Velmont threw him out and banned him from the establishment."

"I wouldn't want to be in Rupert's place. Sir Robert can be an unpleasant character . . . but is that why you called me here?"

"We've done some poking around in young Korshaw's past, and we stumbled across a number of inconsistencies. Jeremy Korshaw had been with Veitch for six months. Veitch's nerves, by the way, are at a breaking point, and I don't know whether it's Korshaw's death that is affecting him most or the loss of several extremely valuable orchids that he was planning to sell in an upcoming auction." As he spoke, Rooke toyed with a pen that lay atop a stack of files.

"As a businessman, his first thoughts are probably for his losses, though I don't want to do the man an injustice," said David tersely.

"Veitch's employees have all been there a long time and seem very satisfied, but with Korshaw, it seems that Veitch had dropped a fox in among the hens."

"How so?" asked David curiously.

"Before Veitch, Korshaw spent a year unemployed, and according to Veitch, he had kept his head above water using his savings and an inheritance. From 1854 to 1858, Korshaw worked in India, Mexico, and Colombia as an orchid hunter."

"An orchid hunter? Who was he working for?"

"Various and sundry individuals. We examined his apartment in Fulham. He lived a spartan life and had just a basic furnished room in the home of an old seaman's widow. For a man who had traveled so far and wide, there was little that pointed to the years he had spent abroad. If I had bumbled around those places for so long, I would have certainly brought home an exotic souvenir or two."

"Maybe he was running out of money?"

Rooke nodded. "His landlady did not speak highly of him. He owed her two weeks rent. I haven't had the time to go through all his papers, but among his earlier employers was a German orchid collector . . ." Rooke rummaged through the papers lying on his desk. "Ah, here it is. The man's name was Sander. From what I've heard, he was an expert, really top of his class. Then there were three London nurseries, Veitch among them, and a customer in Northumberland."

"Northumberland? You're talking about Sir Frederick Halston, aren't you?"

"Oh, that's right, your wife is visiting Sir Frederick as we speak." Rooke dug around in the stack of papers some more, then shook his head. "I can't confirm that. All we have here are delivery dates and 'F.H., Northumberland' as the consignee. But I've got a man checking names. We'll know more soon enough."

"Is Sir Robert among Korshaw's clients? He's certainly rich enough, after all, and I know he likes nothing more than to trump others, whether in a game of cards or at auctions. You yourself mentioned that he and Sir Frederick were caught up in a competition to see which of them could display the most beautiful orchids."

Rooke looked hard at David. "Are you keeping something from me?"

David sighed. "Jane drove up to Winton Park to keep her friend, Lady Alison, company. Alison is afraid for her cousin, Charlotte." He briefly outlined the maid's disappearance.

"I don't know any more than you do. I can think of a thousand reasons why a maid would vanish. Usually there's a love affair involved."

Rooke's brow furrowed as he delved deeper into the file. "Veitch has business connections to quite a few renowned orchid collectors: Robert Warner, Wentworth Buller, Lord Cunningham, and John Day, to name a few. Even if Parks and Halston are on their books, it proves nothing. These are men of impeccable reputation, not the kind I can simply walk up to and ask if they dispatched an assassin to steal a flower."

"Pity." David grinned. "How much did you say the orchids were worth? The ones that were stolen?"

"I'll spare you the genus and species, but a single specimen could well have fetched fifty pounds at auction. Lose half a dozen of them, and it's a major financial blow."

"So it's all about money. Is there anything more about Korshaw?"

Sergeant Berwin put his head around the door, and Rooke glanced up at him.

"Sir, there's a young woman here who says she wants to speak to you and won't be put off."

"What kind of young woman, Berwin?" asked Rooke.

"Not that kind. Seems a decent sort. She's from Ilford and wants money she claims Korshaw owed her."

"Bring her in."

"Yes, sir."

David stood and made to don his hat, but Rooke signaled for him to stay. "This could be interesting. Like I said, a fox in the henhouse. It seems that Korshaw had gotten into some trouble with his clients, withholding orders to drive up the price, that sort of thing. Ah, thank you, Berwin."

David leaned against a shelf along the wall, and Rooke greeted the new arrival. The young woman did not look like a prostitute. Her dark dress was simple and tattered, her boots and woolen shawl patched. She wore a scarf over her head and gloves with the fingers cut off. Her work-worn hands, pale face, and deep-set eyes bore witness to a life of poor food and trouble.

"Please have a seat, Mrs. . . . ?" Rooke pulled out a chair for her. "Berwin, bring us tea and a piece of cake."

The sergeant, who had been waiting at the door, disappeared into the corridor. The woman looked around anxiously, shooting David a glare, then perched carefully on the front edge of the chair. "It's 'Miss.' Miss Etta Ramsey. By rights, I ought to have been Mrs. Korshaw, but that two-faced liar duped me!"

David looked the woman over as she talked. He guessed she was in her midtwenties, and her red, cracked fingertips suggested that whatever she did for work involved water or lye; perhaps she was employed in a laundry or as a kitchen hand. What would a well-read, well-traveled man want with a young woman as ordinary as Etta Ramsey?

"Miss Ramsey, how did you hear about Korshaw's death, and why are you here?" Rooke stood with his back to the window, resting his hands on the sill.

"I read about it in the paper and thought straight off it had to be my Jeremy who'd got himself killed." Etta tugged at her gloves and stared at the toes of her boots. "I never had such a fine gentleman interested in me before. That sort o' thing never happens to girls like me. But he told me I was something special and that he wanted a wife who could work and keep house for him. And that I can! I can work for two!"

Berwin returned with a small tray holding a pot of tea and a plate with a slice of fruitcake on it. Etta stared hungrily at the cake, and Rooke said, "Please help yourself. So, you've come all the way from Ilford, have you?"

The woman hastily swallowed a mouthful of cake. "Yes, sir, all the way from Ilford. I had to leave early to come with the omnibus and had to sit outside at that, 'cause that was the only seat left."

Omnibuses were large coaches drawn by two or three horses that followed specified routes through London. The passengers sat crammed together on wooden seats inside and on top; those sitting on the roof were exposed to the elements. They cost little to ride and were very popular.

"Please tell us how you came to know Korshaw," Rooke encouraged her, once she was finished with the cake.

"Thank you very much," she said, a little color returning to her cheeks from the food and tea. "In my position on Grosvenor Square, I worked in the kitchen and in the herb garden. I know about herbs, learned it from my parents. They live in Ilford, too."

Rooke and David listened patiently, for Etta's connection to Korshaw was more than coincidental.

"Mr. Korshaw delivered flowers there all the time, and sometimes he spoke to me and asked me about the flowers in his lordship's house. They kept a small hothouse in the garden, and 'cause I knew my way around plants I was sometimes allowed to help clean it up. His lordship said I had a bit of a green thumb, and that was the only reason why I was allowed in. That hothouse was like a holy place for him."

"Uh, Miss Ramsey, where exactly were you, or are you now, employed?" asked Rooke.

"At Lord Cunningham's, sir. I was not happy to leave there, but my parents needed me, and so I live with them now in their house in Ilford. We have a garden there, too, and I tend to that." Etta Ramsey ran a finger along the edge of the scarf on her head. She had ash-blond hair and a mousy face.

"Cunningham!" David could not help himself. Obviously, Korshaw had used her to find out about Lord Cunningham's orchids, then dropped her as soon as she left her post in the house.

"Mr. Korshaw was so kind and gentle, and he brought me little gifts sometimes. Twice he took me out to a restaurant, and that's when he told me he was looking for a hardworking woman like me for his wife. But then I got the message that I had to go to my parents' house. His lordship was very nice and understanding and paid me an extra month's wages, and when I told Mr. Korshaw, he asked me for the money so's he could make preparations for our wedding."

David felt sorry for the woman. Fraudulent young Korshaw had swindled her out of the little severance she had worked hard to earn. And, what was perhaps worse, Korshaw had destroyed her dreams of a better life. She could expect nothing from the dead man's estate. His outstanding rent would be paid first, and then there were burial costs. Even if the sale of Korshaw's possessions brought any profit, Etta

Ramsey, without so much as a promissory note from Korshaw, would not have claim to any of it.

After the deeply disappointed Miss Ramsey left, Rooke said, "Who would have thought a few orchids could cause so much misery?"

David nodded pensively. Of all the places Jane could be a guest, she was staying in the house of an orchid collector. He had to get home immediately and find out what Blount had uncovered.

Colombia, October 6, 1860

Dear Sir Frederick,

I cannot say with certainty precisely where we are at this moment. The mission station lay on the edge of the rainforest, and we have now ventured into the jungle. I am writing now to stave off insanity, for this forest is so dense and wet that I long to see the sky. It is as if I am wandering through a cave deep inside a mountain.

You may, of course, reply that I have been in rainforests many times, but this particular forest seems endless, its canopy so dense that barely a gleam of sunlight makes it through. On the other hand, that same canopy wards off the rain that usually falls at midday and in the afternoons. There is a proliferation of foliage and vines all around, and the sounds here envelop you as if you are trapped in an exotic cocoon. Parasitic growths are everywhere, and everything is so intertwined that there is a great danger of mistaking the flowers, fruits, and foliage of the various plants.

Dennis is in heaven. He fills his vascula with insects and exotic plants, things even I have never seen before. I know your only interest lies with orchids, but the sheer beauty of the mosses, lichens, and trees we are seeing here takes my breath away.

Please excuse my ravings; I can only blame the cachaça that sweetens my nights. José remains as loyal as ever, slashing the way clear for us with his bush knife. I am sure you remember my last letter, in which I wrote about the strange encounter with the Indian at the mission station? It seemed to me a sign from heaven that I should continue my search for the black orchid. I know well that this legendary orchid is your heart's desire, so I have decided to follow the secretive Indians into the rainforest, although I must confess that I use "follow" euphemistically, for the inhabitants of the forest leave no traces. The only basis for my explorations are the stories told by the Indians and Sister Leonella at the mission.

The morning after seeing the old Indian, I talked with the good sister. She did not seem surprised when I told her about the encounter.

She said to me: "Do you know, Mr. Tomkins, I have been serving God for as long as I can remember. Before my order sent me to this continent, I was active in southeast Asia, but when I came to this tiny mission, here in the midst of all this wild nature, I felt that I was out of place." The sister looked at me, and I saw in her eyes a mélange of despair, resignation, and fear.

"This rainforest belongs to the creatures that live in it, that live with it, and that respect it. I cannot speak so openly with Pater Antonio. He would call my words blasphemy, but I do not doubt in God!"

The good woman wrung her bony hands, her eyes skipping between me and the station and the rainforest. She wore the habit of a Carmelite nun, and it was clear she took her divine calling very seriously. I would go so far as to say that she truly lived it, and for this reason I attach great weight to her words. "No one would ever doubt that, Sister," I said, attempting to reassure her.

Her careworn face relaxed a little. It may be that she was sick. Anyone who lives for as long as she has in the tropics will be struck by fever, and many suffer problems with their heart.

"You are not like other plant hunters, Mr. Tomkins," she said. "Those men are brutal good-for-nothings in both thought and deed. You, however, understand the land and its people."

Her words were flattering, even though I fear the devout woman saw too much good in me. I may be a philanthropist of sorts, but my work is of utmost importance to me. If I had put my philanthropic leanings ahead of my business decisions, well, there are some orchids that would never have been shipped to England . . .

"I do my best, Sister Leonella," was my reserved reaction.

"I am not innocent, Mr. Tomkins. By accepting the habit, we do not lose our understanding of the ways of the world. On the contrary, with fewer distractions and worldly cares, our view can become clearer, and you may

take my word that any lay sister would have seen the evil resident in the eyes of Mr. Rudbeck."

I sat bolt upright, as if bitten by an ant. "Rudbeck? Where did you meet that man?"

The good sister nodded thoughtfully and poured water from a pitcher into two cups. She handed one to me. "Here. Drink."

We were sitting on a wooden bench in front of the mission house in the early hours of the morning. The first rays of sun crept over the forest canopy and lit the clearing that surrounded the tiny station in the middle of nowhere. It took an inordinate amount of work to maintain the clearing. New shoots and invading tendrils had to be removed daily. If there was no one there to stand against the incursions of nature, then the forest would have quickly reclaimed what truly belonged to it.

"Mr. Rudbeck and his men spent a night here a week ago before moving on." The sister folded her hands in her lap. "Bad master, bad servants. I heard them boasting about how they had molested a young Indian girl. She was a member of one of the forest tribes, if I understood them correctly. The poor soul managed to flee, but I would not like to find out what became of her."

Such atrocities are often practiced against the Indians. Many of them come from peaceful tribes that do not defend themselves. Those of us who come as intruders are met by these simple creatures with a naïve openness that can easily spell their doom. But that is the law of the wild. The strong survive.

"Ever since, the old Indian has been sitting at the edge of the forest every night, staring at us. Sometimes

I can't see him, but I know he is there. The Indians can make themselves invisible."

I did not know what to make of it. Was the old man trying to warn us? Or was he waiting for Rudbeck to return so that he could kill him? I must admit that I know little of the customs of these tribes.

"Where did Rudbeck go? Did he say what he was planning?" I asked.

"They talked about the Motilone Indians, and that they are said to be the protectors of a mystical flower. When Rudbeck and his men left us, they headed toward the northwest." The nun spoke quietly, all the while observing a movement in the grass right in front of us. "Keep your feet still. The snake is after the rats that live beneath our house."

A moment later, a sizeable red-brown snake slipped quickly by our feet and disappeared into a gap between wood and earth. I later described the reptile, which was decorated with a lovely pattern, to Dennis, who was shocked to discover that a poisonous lancehead had slithered so close to me.

The nun showed me where Rudbeck and his men had hacked their way into the rainforest. For this reason, I have temporarily abandoned my plan to find the Motilones and their holy orchid. If Rudbeck succeeds in finding it before I do, the Motilones will want nothing more to do with whites like me. I am well aware that I stare death in the eye every day I am out here. I am not afraid of a bullet, or of drowning in river rapids, or of dying from a snakebite. But what I do fear is a horde of furious wildmen who would bury me in an anthill or press bamboo stakes through my limbs to satisfy their thirst for revenge.

"Do you also envisage stealing away the holy flower of the Motilones?" asked Sister Leonella bluntly.

"Uh, well, not stealing, and they would hardly be likely to give it to me, so I was thinking more of buying one," I stammered.

"That orchid is like a holy relic to the Motilones," she said. "Would you go into a church and purchase the bones of a saint?"

The nun's habit and her frail appearance belied Sister Leonella's sharp perceptions.

"Of course not! But our relics don't grow on trees, nor can they be replaced. If the Indians were prepared to hand over one or two little plants in exchange for fair compensation, then in a few weeks they would not notice that an orchid was missing. Everything grows so fast here. You can practically stand back and watch!" I defended myself.

The sister poured the rest of the water from the pitcher into a cloth and dabbed at her forehead. The higher the sun climbed, the more oppressive the heat became. "What value does money hold for an Indian? They use it to buy cachaça and betray their own traditions. We are taking away their dignity, Mr. Tomkins. That's what we are doing."

I must admit that her words, plainspoken as they were, affected me deeply. Though I know that if I don't get my hands on the holy orchid, someone else will come along and simply steal it. And people like Mungo suffer from far fewer scruples than I do.

"Sister, that is all well and good, but I have a contract and am paid for finding orchids and shipping

them to England. There is nothing wrong with that. The English, after all, are happy to see the beauty of these flowers. No one but the monkeys and parrots would ever see them otherwise. I don't necessarily have to retrieve a holy specimen, the theft of which would doom me to hell. The black orchid the old Indian wears around his neck would do just as well."

"Black? I've never heard a word about a black flower. How can something like that exist? Black! I don't believe that. But the old Indian you speak of belongs to a tribe that lives in the forest to the southwest. A three-day march in that direction leads to waterfalls that are said to be quite marvelous, but the tribe is especially shy and no one knows much about them."

"Indians love magical sites, and that includes waterfalls. Maybe we'll have some luck there. If not, we'll certainly find orchids close by," I replied, and the decision as to what route we would follow was made. That is how things work out here. One makes plans that the events of the next day render null and void. Very often, too, our maps are simply wrong. I rely more on my own sense of orientation and on the stars. I have always come through best that way.

Tonight we are camping in the middle of the jungle, and I am lying beside Dennis in the tent. We have sealed every chink and cranny as much as possible, but there is always some insect that manages to creep inside and tries to suck our blood. The wound on Dennis's arm has become infected again; he fell and tore the bandage off the wound in the process, and some muck got into it. The poor chap is feverish, and I can only hope that he will be much improved by tomorrow morning. We cannot leave him behind alone, but at the same time it would be a shame not to be able to move on tomorrow, for the waterfalls are close enough for us to hear.

José suggested that we rinse out Dennis's wound with cachaça, since that terrible stuff seems to work on flesh wounds. Indeed, this morning, Dennis was completely lucid and fit enough to march on with us. But will he ever again seek his luck as an adventurer in the wilderness after this experience? I've been traveling the world for so many years and have come to realize that there are various kinds of researchers and adventurers. I once stumbled upon a couple doing research in Africa, a husband and wife team. I have never before or since met such a resolute woman. She carried baskets just like the men did, and she had no fear of reptiles or other things that most women generally seem to view as cause for hysterics.

Our dear Dennis—for I have taken the young man very much into my heart—has a strong will but a body prone to fevers and other diseases that does not recover well. If both of us survive this adventure, I will do my utmost to put him on a ship bound for home. But until that time, we battle on together through the rainforest, in search of exotic plants.

Today, around noon, we reached a clearing near the bank of the river. The rush and roar of the waterfalls was so close and so tempting that we would have liked nothing more than to peel off our sweat-soaked clothes and take a refreshing dip. I was on the verge of doing just that when one of the Indian bearers cried, "Caimans, señor, caimans!"

All at once, our camp became frenzied, and everyone jumped to their feet to see the creatures that were causing all this commotion. José had drawn my attention many times to traces of these large animals, which liked to doze on the riverbanks. On the sandy shore, one can easily make out the impressions left by their scaly bellies and claws. But because the Indians are afraid of alligators, we've always kept these observations to ourselves. Now, however, five impressive specimens lay on the riverbank. The animals are, in fact, not especially aggressive, but one should still avoid provoking them. So we retreated, waited out the midday rain, then sought a spot on the shore uninhabited by caimans, where we filled our water bottles without the risk of losing a hand in the process.

I hope very much that the consignment I shipped before my departure has arrived safely ahead of this missive. The shipment contained a number of fine examples of Bulbophyllum and Grobya. The latter in particular should develop into quite a magnificent specimen with many eye-catching petals and a helmet-shaped dorsal sepal. I cannot recall that this species has ever been brought to flower in England.

I remain,
Your humble servant,
Derek Tomkins

11.

Crookham, Cheviot Hills, November 1860

The coach slowed, and Jane looked out the window. The landscape here was ancient and broad, wild and harsh and only sparsely settled . . . and vaguely repellent. Small farmsteads lay dotted about that survived off cattle and sheep breeding. From Allenton, they'd taken the main road out of town to reach Crookham. Directly to the north of Allenton, the moor and the eponymous Cheviot Hills made passage impossible. The long-contested Scottish border and the River Tweed were not far away, and the remains of Roman encampments could be found all around the area.

Hettie was fascinated by these sites, and Jane had had no objections to occasionally stopping the coach and taking short jaunts on foot to look at the old ruins together. Jane had waited a day to be sure that Alison had not come down with a serious illness. When Alison began feeling unwell, Charlotte immediately sent for Dr. Cribb, an experienced physician in his middle years and a man whose manner naturally inspired confidence. But luck was with Jane's friend, and apart from a sniffle and a light cough, she did not get any worse.

Jane had asked Dr. Cribb to be patient and stay on for a few days, not just for Alison but also because Jane hoped Charlotte might let the doctor examine her. Indeed, Charlotte seemed very pale and peaked, but she blamed it on the cold, wet November weather. It had grown considerably cooler, and there was a good chance that snow would fall the next day, the first of December.

"Can you taste that, too, ma'am?"

Hettie's voice dragged Jane back to the moment. "What's that, Hettie?"

"The winter wind. Back home, we say the air tastes like snow, and it truly does. And it's even colder here than in Winton Park, though we can't be more than thirty miles north." Hettie wrapped her shawl higher and stamped her feet. "Whew, it'll freeze your bones, it will!"

"Well, we've arrived. At least the guesthouse looks respectable." The coach drove through an arched gate into a courtyard ringed by low stone buildings.

Crates and bales of hay were stored under cover along one side of the courtyard, in front of a stable. On the other side, a farrier was at work, shoeing horses and trimming their hooves. The building in the middle combined a restaurant and a travelers' hostel. Everything looked plain but in good condition. They could rent a basic but clean room for a night, and if the evening meal delivered on the promises of the delicious smells drifting from the kitchen, they could certainly have done worse for themselves.

The proprietor of the guesthouse was a red-faced man as round as a cartwheel. He stood in the courtyard with his hands propped on his hips, overseeing the unloading of their luggage and telling the stablehands what to do. "Is there anything else you wish for, my lady?" he asked when Jane approached him.

"I would like to visit the Bertram family. They live here in Crookham."

The proprietor frowned. "Bertram? That's a whole clan, my lady. Most of 'em keep sheep, and the rest fish the rivers. Sally's the daughter of Willis

Bertram, and she works for me in the restaurant. No one else wanted her in their employ because her mother's Romany. What do you want with 'em?"

"Can I talk to her?" Jane asked, ignoring their host's question.

"Of course, there she is now. Oy, Sally, over here!" the man called to a young girl carrying a wash basket across the courtyard.

The girl hurriedly set the basket down, smoothed out her white apron, and trotted over to them. She was rather short, probably no older than sixteen. Her face was very pretty, and her bonnet couldn't contain all her pitch-black hair. *A Romany trait, just like her dark eyes,* thought Jane, and she smiled at the shy young woman.

"Hello, Sally. I'm Lady Jane Allen, and I'm looking for Rachel Bertram's family. Do you know her?"

Sally stared at her wide-eyed. "She's my sister! What's wrong with her? Is she all right?"

"That's what we're trying to find out, Sally. So you haven't seen her lately?"

"No, my lady. Rachel hasn't been back to Crookham since she started workin' with them fine folks. Nor would I if—"

She didn't get any further, because the proprietor snorted loudly and said, "Ungrateful little slattern! No one'd take you on, but here I give you work and you're no better than your tramp of a sister. You're all the same, you pack of gypsies!"

Sally's eyes flashed angrily, and she swallowed hard, then said, "Is there anything else, my lady?"

"Where can I find your family?"

"Down the street. The little house with the sheep barn."

"Thank you, Sally."

The girl curtsied and ran back to her wash basket, the proprietor shooting her a look full of daggers.

Jane and Hettie set off immediately to visit the Bertram house, wanting to get back to the guesthouse—with the lilting name of "Blue Bell"—before dark and in time for dinner.

The Bertram house lay some distance from the street and could only be reached through a closed gate and down a long, narrow path. Behind the house flowed the River Till, and sheep grazed around the impoverished house. The barn was little more than a ramshackle lean-to, crookedly built and so low that an adult could not possibly stand upright inside it.

Hardly had they touched the door when a black-and-white guard dog came dashing toward them, snarling threateningly. A second dog approached from the side of the house, barking furiously. It wasn't long before Jane heard a whistle, and although the dogs fell silent, they maintained their threatening attitude. A powerful-looking man with gray, shoulder-length hair marched around the corner of the house, his hands smeared with blood as he wiped a knife on his trousers.

"Oh, no. He's probably just slaughtered a sheep, ma'am," whispered Hettie, who came from the country herself.

"No wonder Rachel didn't want to return," Jane replied just as quietly, then said loudly, "Mr. Bertram?"

The man slowed his pace along the path and stopped a few feet short of the gate, the dogs like two guards in front of him. "What if I am?" he growled unpleasantly.

"Then you're Rachel's father?" Behind the man, Jane saw the door of the house open and a small, dark-haired woman step out. Even at that distance, the similarity to dark-haired Sally was unmistakable. The woman moved with a proud, erect posture and wore a scarf wrapped around her head and shoulders.

"Has she run off? What d'you want? She ain't here. Or d'you think somebody'd come back to this place of their own accord?" the man snapped.

The sound of men's voices carried from the barn, and Mr. Bertram turned around nervously. "Leave us in peace. I've got enough troubles for havin' a Roma for a wife."

"I don't want to cause you any inconvenience, Mr. Bertram. I would like to help you, in fact. Your daughter vanished about two weeks ago. They are worried about her at Winton Park. Rachel did not take any of her things with her. She just went out one night and didn't return. Do you find that normal?"

The man stepped closer to the gate, and Jane could see the lines in his weathered face, the markings of a struggle to simply survive. In a voice filled with bitterness, he said, "What I find or not makes no difference. If you're poor, you've no rights. That's how I see it. We had a telegram. Ha, a telegram! Sir Frederick wanted to know if Rachel was here with us. No, she ain't. And if she shows up here, I'll send her back. Now leave us in peace!"

Mr. Bertram whistled softly, and his dogs turned and followed him to the house. Hettie wanted to leave because the weather had chilled considerably, but Jane stayed put. "No, wait. I think Rachel's mother wants to tell us something. I saw her earlier."

As dusk began to settle, the path up to the house faded in the shadows of day's end. They had to wait for some time. Old Mr. Bertram had disappeared behind the house again, and the voices of the men grew louder. They were probably dividing up the sheep and celebrating the slaughter. Finally, Jane saw a small figure sweep silently along the path until she reached the gate.

"I'm Rachel's mother, Zenada," murmured the woman that Jane had noticed earlier. In her youth, she must have been very beautiful indeed, and there was still a trace of loveliness in her eyes. But lines were now engraved around her mouth and eyes, every one a witness to a lifetime of struggle and intolerance.

"We're looking for your daughter, Rachel. Do you have any idea where she might have gone, madam? I'm Lady Jane Allen, a friend of Lady Charlotte's."

Jane felt the gypsy woman's piercing gaze fall on her. "You are a good person," Zenada said plainly, taking a letter out of her skirt. "Here.

I received this from my daughter four weeks ago. My husband does not know about it. He's afraid . . . we've gone through too much."

The woman's hands were warm, and they squeezed Jane's as she held the letter. "And if you find her body, tell me. I know she is dead."

A shudder ran through Jane. "How do you know that?" she whispered.

A sad, tight smile played across Zenada's lips. "I'm her mother. When she died, I felt her pain. And her fear."

"Zenada!" her husband bellowed.

The woman flinched, gathered up her dress, and ran back to the house in the failing light.

Hettie was trembling with curiosity, but Jane kept the letter in her bag until they were alone in their room in the Blue Bell. The room contained two narrow beds, a wardrobe, and a table with two chairs. Hettie lit the oil lamp on the table; with its beige glass shade, it cast just enough light to illuminate the room. After removing her gloves and her coat, Jane sat on one of the chairs and took the crumpled envelope from her bag. She could tell that it had been unfolded many times.

"That Zenada seemed a bit spooky, ma'am," said Hettie.

Jane shook her head. "Why? She's a mother, and she's also Romany. Roma women often possess a sixth sense, an instinct for the supernatural."

"Do you believe those fortune-tellers at the markets, too? Not me!" said Hettie.

Smiling, Jane replied, "There are many things between heaven and earth that we don't understand. I don't believe in crystal balls, but I do believe that there are people with special sensory gifts." She quickly read the clearly hastily penned lines, with scattered Roma phrases mixed in. "Oh, well, if that doesn't . . ."

"What does it say?" Still holding her coat in her arms, Hettie looked at Jane excitedly.

Dearest Mama,

My heart aches, and I miss you and Baba so much! But as dearly as I want to come and visit, Mrs. Gubbins will not allow me a weekend free. She says I'm not entitled. But I will come and visit you at Christmas; then she can't tell me no, and you can make your delicious salmaia*!*

Mrs. Gubbins is a dragon who stands guard over the memory of the first Lady Halston, destroying anything that might muddy it. She can't stand the idea that I look so much like the deceased woman. Sometimes, Sir Frederick calls for me and then simply makes me wait in the room. He looks at me so strangely, but he doesn't do anything. He just looks at me, then sends me away again. He is a serious, stern man, always in his hothouse or brooding over books about plants.

Mama, what is it about these orchids? Lord Cunningham was just as obsessed with those exotic plants. One evening, Sir Frederick sent for me, and I stood in the library as bidden and waited, but he wasn't there. While I was standing around, some papers lying on a desk caught my eye. They were lists with drawings of orchids that had complicated names and extraordinary prices. Mama! So much money for a flower! We could live for a year on that much money!

Suddenly, a side door opened, and the governess came in so fast that it seemed the devil himself were after her. She jumped when she saw me, then hissed: "What are you staring at. Go to your work!"

"I'm supposed to wait here, miss," I answered politely, but she'd already left. Not a minute later, Mrs. Gubbins came in with a tray, and she snapped at me, "What are you doing here?"

But then Sir Frederick himself came and said that though he had called for me, the matter had sorted itself out. I went straight to the laundry and folded the dry washing. There are so many secrets in this house, Mama. Sometimes I hear Lady Charlotte crying—she is very sick and weak.

As pushy and loud as Lord Cunningham's son was, I could always avoid him, but there are things going on here . . . Baba would say that evil dwells here.

Del tuha, *God protect you!*

Rachel

P.S. Don't show this letter to Papa, or he will worry and think I'm going to lose another position.

Jane, shaken, lowered the letter and looked at her maid. "Poor Rachel was scared of someone, that much is certain!"

"But scared of whom?" Hettie murmured. "And where is she now?"

As it turned out, the latter question would be answered faster than the women would have liked. The next morning, they left the guesthouse early. The horses had rested overnight, and Jane and Hettie were seated in the coach by sunrise. The return journey was interrupted only to briefly feed and rest the horses, and as they drove up the lane to Winton Park, the first flakes of snow whirled from the sky.

When a servant opened the coach door for them and they stepped out into the courtyard, Jane looked up and closed her eyes, letting the tiny crystals of ice settle on her face. "Snow to start December," she said to herself.

But she was a little concerned: if it really did start to snow heavily, then they would be trapped at Winton Park, an outcome that Jane did not like the thought of for many reasons. Her concern only deepened when she saw Draycroft, the butler, standing at the top of the steps, his face grim and stiff.

"My lady, I trust you had a good trip?" Draycroft signaled two servants to collect the luggage.

"I did, thank you. But has something happened, Mr. Draycroft?"

The butler cleared his throat. "The maid who disappeared two weeks hence has been found."

"She's been found?" Jane's voice trembled; it seemed that Zenada's prophecy had proved correct.

"Yes, my lady. Drowned. In the moor. Please, come inside."

Behind her, Jane heard Hettie's breath catch, but her maid said nothing. It was rare for Hettie to be at a loss for words.

12.

Winton Park, Northumberland, December 1860

Their weariness from the journey disappeared in an instant. Jane was on the alert, her mind focused, and she unbuttoned her coat as she climbed the steps.

"Mr. Draycroft, please show me to Sir Frederick at once!" Jane ordered. "Hettie, you take care of our things."

"My lady, I'm sorry, he is . . . well, in . . ." The butler was clearly having difficulty finding the right words. "Please follow me."

"I'm not squeamish, believe me." Holding her head high, she determinedly followed Draycroft as he led her through the kitchens. From there, they went down a set of steps into a vaulted cellar complex, where the household's food was stored in various rooms. Apples and potatoes were kept in large sacks; rice, flour, and jars of preserved fruits and marinated vegetables sat on shelves; and there were pantries for game. The smokers were outside, but hams and sausages hung in the cellars in readiness for the long winter. In earlier times, these same vaults had no doubt held prisoners awaiting their final fate. "How are Lady Charlotte and Lady Alison?" Jane asked the butler.

"They are well. Please wait here." Draycroft gestured toward a bench standing alongside a whitewashed wall.

The floor was made of large, coarse stones, and iron rings were set into one wall; Jane did not like to think about what they may have been used for in the past.

"My dear Lady Jane!" A moment later, Sir Frederick appeared from one of the cellar rooms, followed by Draycroft. "Such a tragic piece of news to digest the moment you return. Please, we can talk upstairs. Draycroft, really, why did you bring Lady Jane down here at all? This is no place for a woman's sensitive disposition."

Jane stayed where she was and peered over Sir Frederick's shoulder. "Is that where the poor girl is lying? I spoke to her mother in Crookham. Would it be asking too much to see her?"

Her host's expression froze. "You were in Crookham? I thought you were going to visit Berwick at the coast?"

"It was on my way, and as it turned out, Rachel's parents were home," Jane replied. She moved as if to pass him, but he stepped uncompromisingly in her path.

"That is no sight for a lady!" he thundered.

The heavy wooden door behind him swung open with a creak, and Dr. Cribb stepped out. He looked pale and exhausted and was carrying his doctor's bag. "Oh, my lady, this is not an opportune moment." Wearily, he wiped the back of his hand across his forehead.

Jane could see that she wasn't going to make further progress into the room, but that did not mean she was going to give up. The entire story stank to high heaven! "The poor girl! Did you know, Doctor, that a similar tragic story played out at Rosewood Hall at the start of the year?"

Sir Frederick led the way back upstairs, and Jane walked alongside Dr. Cribb, giving him a brief account of the events surrounding the orphan girl at Rosewood Hall. The doctor gazed at her with surprise and admiration.

"My lady, I must say I'm impressed at your courage and willingness to help. Still, I would not advise you to view the young woman's body."

Jane lowered her voice and slowed down, and the doctor slowed down with her. "The girl was scared, Doctor. Are there any signs that it was not an accident?"

The doctor's brow furrowed. He had bushy, gray sideburns that brushed the corners of his mouth and made him look older than he probably was. Jane could not understand the new fashion for beards and found most of the hirsute creations of the day laughable.

"I should probably not be telling you this, but there is, in fact, a wound to the head. It might have come from a fall. It may be that the girl ran in the darkness, stumbled, fell, landed badly, and . . . that was that. One does not always have to assume the worst, my lady."

"Have the police been informed?"

"No, nor will they be. There is no serious evidence that this was anything other than an accidental death." Dr. Cribb stopped walking and looked intently at Jane in the dim light. "You would do best to stay out of this, my lady. This is not your house and not your maid. Sir Frederick can become very unpleasant when someone pokes their nose into his affairs."

"And if a crime has been committed? Are we supposed to leave it unatoned, just because Rachel was half Roma and came from a poor family?"

"Where are you, Cribb? My lady?" Sir Frederick had stopped, turned, and walked a few steps toward them. "Is there a problem?"

Jane hesitated, but the doctor quickly said, "No, everything is fine. My lady feels a little weak, that's all. A bowl of soup and you will soon be as right as ninepence, won't you?"

"Yes, Doctor," Jane replied.

Sir Frederick looked at her skeptically.

Once upstairs, Jane went straight to her room, where Hettie was waiting for her. "Ma'am! Did you see her corpse?"

Jane had Hettie help her out of her coat, then pulled off her gloves. "No, they would not let me in. But Dr. Cribb told me that Rachel had a head wound. He—and Sir Frederick, too, of course—assume that Rachel stumbled and fell. That it was an accident."

"But she was so afraid of something here!" Hettie cried and handed Jane a damp cloth to wipe her face. "And she was found a long way from here, near a lonely hut!"

"Where exactly was Rachel found? And who found her?"

"I heard from Gladys, Lady Charlotte's maid, that O'Connor found her."

"Gladys, you say?" Lady Charlotte's maid was a quiet, unprepossessing woman who stayed in her mistress's shadow.

So the gamekeeper had returned to the hut on the moor after they had ridden there to find out for certain that Rachel was not hiding inside. *If only the girl* had *sought refuge there,* thought Jane. What Rachel had written to her mother was not reason enough to explain her death, though. More must have happened. What had she seen or heard?

"Yes, ma'am. Gladys heard O'Connor and Sir Frederick arguing when he and two other men brought the body back on a cart."

"Interesting, very interesting . . . and how is Charlotte?"

"Oh, I almost forgot. Gladys hasn't been Lady Charlotte's maid for long, but she says she could have landed worse. Her mistress is decent enough, but often very moody, especially when she gets her dizzy spells and headaches. Just after we left, Lady Charlotte fell ill again. And unfortunately she was outside with the children when the cart carrying the body arrived, so she saw everything. Since then she's been hiding in her room, beside herself."

"I need to put on a fresh dress," said Jane. "Then I'll pay Charlotte a visit."

It took a lot of knocking before she heard any movement from inside Charlotte's room. Finally, there was a rustling on the other side of the door, which then opened a crack. "My lady does not wish to be disturbed," said Gladys in a hoarse whisper.

The maid's thin face was marked by faded pox scars. Her pale-blue eyes looked both frightened and alert, and Jane suspected that more lay behind Gladys's nondescript appearance than she would admit. "Please tell Lady Charlotte that I wish to speak to her urgently."

"Yes, my lady." Gladys left the door ajar, and Jane heard a whispered exchange between Charlotte and the maid.

"Jane! Come in!" Charlotte called from inside.

Gathering up her dark-green dress, Jane walked in past a screen, where she found Lady Alison's cousin lying on a day bed in front of the fireplace. Everything about her, from the way she held herself to the look of suffering on her face, was a picture of despair. But there was nothing theatrical about it; Charlotte looked seriously ill. Jane could not tell if it was her body or her soul that was more in distress.

Jane went over and took Charlotte's small, cool hand in her own. "Oh, my dear, what is happening with you?"

Her skin, already so pale, had taken on a grayish tone, and her breathing was shallow and irregular. Jane felt her pulse, which seemed to be skipping.

"Nothing. It will be gone again in a moment. It was simply the sight of that poor soul. Rachel was a beautiful girl, so young, so full of life. This accursed moor sucks the life out of everything close to it." After speaking so quickly, Charlotte broke into a wheezing cough. A long strand of red-brown hair fell across her forehead and curled at her neck. Jane could clearly see the veins beneath her thin skin.

"Oh, Charlotte, don't say that. I . . . Gladys, would you please bring us a strong cup of tea and two glasses of port?"

She waited until she heard the door latch click. "Listen to me, Charlotte. Rachel did not simply have an accident. She ran away from someone or something because she was scared! I've been to see her parents. I did not learn much from her father, but her mother showed me a letter that Rachel had sent. In the letter, she wrote very clearly that she was afraid of something in this house. Charlotte, please, do you know any more? Are you also afraid?"

Charlotte repeatedly and anxiously glanced toward the door. "No, no! Why would I be? It's just the air, the moor, that's making me sick and giving me nightmares. I have to learn to control my hysteria. Dr. Cribb says the same."

"Nightmares? What kind of nightmares?" Jane asked, stroking Charlotte's hand. She noticed that Charlotte's pupils were unnaturally wide. "Did the doctor give you any medicine?"

Sighing, Charlotte lay back against the pillows, her lilac-colored dress cascading over the side of the bed. She appeared almost ethereally delicate, like a painting in a museum. "Laudanum . . . but that doesn't make me sick, if that's what you mean. It just calms my nerves, which is good."

A little blue bottle sealed with a cork stood on a side table. Beside the bottle lay a teaspoon. Jane, who remembered Lord Hargraves's morphine-addicted sister Violet only too well, said, "Be careful with that, Charlotte."

"Jane, your concern is lovely, but I know what I am doing." She sounded irritated. "I would like to rest now."

"Of course, but you can't shut your eyes against reality indefinitely." Jane stood up, but Charlotte grasped her by the wrist.

"What makes you say that?"

"Think about it! Rachel was afraid. She was a pretty girl who did not balk at leaving her position with the Cunninghams, although she would have known perfectly well that it would have been difficult to find another post after that. But she was defending herself from the advances of Cunningham's son, who is a notorious philanderer. That in itself I find admirable, but you have to keep in mind that she was also half-Roma!"

"Roma? I did not know that." Charlotte was having trouble focusing her eyes, because the opiate was beginning to take hold. Her hand dropped slackly to her side.

"Her mother, Zenada, is Romany. If Rachel was anything like her mother, then she had a solid moral center along with a strong will. Someone like that does not go around saying she is scared, not without reason. Do you understand? She was not some hysterical kitchen maid throwing herself at whatever man came along."

"Zenada . . . the things you know, Jane. That's a nice name. It sounds so exotic . . . but I'm tired. Let me sleep." Charlotte's eyes drifted shut, though she fought to keep them open.

"What is it you're afraid of, Charlotte?" asked Jane softly, not expecting an answer.

"Of . . . ," Charlotte murmured before nodding off completely.

Jane sighed and gazed at the numbed, sleeping form before her, patting her small hand. "Of whom, Charlotte?"

When Gladys returned with the tea, Jane drank a mouthful, sipped at her port, then excused herself.

She next visited Alison, who was waiting for her. Despite her reddened nose and a light cough, her pregnant friend looked radiant. Jane immediately embraced her.

"Jane, tell me everything! I'm dying of curiosity!"

Obliging, when Jane came to the part about Rachel's death and her doubts about the course of events surrounding it, Alison nodded. "That isn't normal! But perhaps she had a lover after all? She might have been pregnant and he didn't want to marry her."

"That would certainly have been possible, but the letter she wrote to Zenada doesn't make it sound like that was the case . . . I'm going to speak with the stablehand again. He knew more about Gubbins."

"Mrs. Gubbins was completely infatuated with Eunice, but would she hold a grudge against Charlotte for that? I don't think so."

Nora, who was sitting in a corner mending a seam on a blouse, glanced up. "Excuse me, my lady, but Della said that Mrs. Gubbins has a picture of the late mistress hanging in her room."

"Really? And what does Mrs. Gubbins have to say about Lady Charlotte?" Jane asked.

"As far as I know, all she says sometimes is that the first Lady Halston could make Sir Frederick laugh nonstop and that she was very popular at parties and gatherings." Nora looked down and focused again on her sewing.

"Thank you, Nora," said Ally, who then leaned forward so that only Jane could hear her. "You don't think that Mrs. Gubbins is . . . poisoning Charlotte?"

When she said "poisoning" almost inaudibly, Jane took a deep breath. "That would be terrible, and how would she manage it, anyway? No. Besides, it would have to be somebody who is around her constantly."

"Gladys?" Ally said automatically, lifting one hand to her heart.

Jane was reluctant to suspect someone of such a perfidious act without solid evidence. "Would Gladys have a motive? That's the crux of the matter. Who would consider Charlotte an obstacle?"

"Nobody! She is such a lovely person and always has been. She wouldn't hurt a fly. Really, just look at her son—he runs rings around her!" Perched on the edge of her bed, Alison was no longer whispering.

"Her husband?" Jane wondered aloud.

"Oh, all Frederick thinks about are his precious orchids. Charlotte gave him an heir, and that's all that mattered to him. Besides, he's not the kind of man to go looking for love affairs, and Charlotte brought a large inheritance with her."

"An inheritance that Frederick may be spending on expensive orchids." Jane helped her friend to her feet.

"Which is no reason to rid himself of her!" Alison pressed her hands into the small of her back, pushing her swollen belly out. "I am truly happy to be bearing this child, but I will be especially glad to hold it in my arms. It's damned heavy!"

"Then it will be a boy," said Jane.

"Anything but twins again." Alison grinned.

A gong rang from below. "Dinner. A pity that you can't come along, Ally, but it looks like we'll have Dr. Cribb in your place."

"Jane," Alison said, her voice earnest, "you do think something about Charlotte isn't right, don't you? I haven't just been imagining it?"

"No, Ally, definitely not." She kissed her friend on the cheek and left the room.

Dinner was a quiet, uneventful affair. Neither Sir Frederick nor Dr. Cribb mentioned the dead maid, and Charlotte sat as silently as a waxwork figure, poking at her food with no appetite.

"Where are the children this evening?" Jane asked as the cheese was being served.

"Miss Molan is eating with them. Cedric didn't complete his arithmetic," said Charlotte disinterestedly.

"Which is precisely why it's time for him to go off to a decent school." Sir Frederick set down his glass with a loud clang. "Loughborough in Leicestershire is an outstanding institution and will make a proper young man out of him. He'll be heir to Winton Park one day, after all!"

"He is still only a little boy, and if he has a tutor here at home, then he can stay with us another year." Charlotte's voice tightened. "Miss Molan has already recommended someone, and he is presently on his way here to introduce himself."

Dr. Cribb came to Charlotte's aid. "A male teacher is exactly what the boy lacks. Cedric is intelligent and is trying to test limits. Everything he learns here will serve to make him stronger and will make life easier for him at school."

Sir Frederick twisted his mouth disparagingly, drank a mouthful of wine, and said, "Let's meet the man and then decide."

Jane woke in the night because she thought she heard someone crying. Throwing back her blanket, she slipped into her robe and tiptoed barefoot across the room. Carefully, she cracked open the door and peered down the hallway. Everything was dark. Feeling her way along the wall, she crept down the corridor, following the muffled sobs. She left the guest wing, slid along a banister, and stopped at the entrance to the family wing. The sobbing was clearly coming from Charlotte's room. Suddenly, Jane heard a dull thud, like someone had fallen to the floor, and the sobbing abruptly stopped.

Jane waited, wondering what she ought to do. Then came a suppressed scream, and steps approached the door from inside Charlotte's room. Jane darted back into the guest wing and pretended that she was just leaving her own room as Gladys stepped out of her mistress's chamber.

"Can I help with anything, Gladys?" Jane called, but Sir Frederick appeared at that moment from the room next door to Charlotte's.

"Fetch Dr. Cribb, Gladys, and be quick about it!" he snapped. When he saw Jane, he muttered grimly, "Go back to bed. This has nothing to do with you."

With a few short strides, he reached the end of the corridor and slammed the door shut that marked the entrance to the family wing.

The next morning, before breakfast, Jane drafted a telegram to David.

13.

Winton Park, Northumberland, December 1860

The northbound train was a considerable improvement over making the trip by horse and coach. David had read up on the subject of orchid breeding during the voyage. When he finally met Sir Frederick, he at least wanted to be able to keep up his side of the conversation. Pushing *The Gardeners' Chronicle* into his bag, he wondered how an orchid keeper looked after his plants in the winter.

A bitter wind rose to meet David when he reached the station at Durham. On the platform, a chestnut seller touted his wares, and a gaudily made-up woman touted herself. David had no interest in either. It was early in the afternoon, and he wanted to continue his journey without pause. Several coaches were lined up along the street, but many of the horses did not look as if they could make it all the way to Allenton. One young coachman and his obviously well-tended vehicle caught David's eye. After negotiating a price with the man, David had his bags loaded aboard.

During the drive, David returned to his study of orchids, beginning to understand why it was so difficult to get the exotic plants to bloom in

England. It had taken years for growers to discover what temperatures and how much moisture the plants needed—and when. Apart from a few aristocrats, it was the businessman John Day who had made a name for himself in London with his unusual flowers. Sir Frederick was mentioned in a number of articles, but the recognition that he was no doubt seeking had so far eluded him.

David thought of Korshaw and his customers, trying to envision the world of orchid lovers. How far would someone go to possess a true rarity? Korshaw, for one, had seduced the naïve Etta Ramsey simply to find out what Cunningham was doing in his hothouse. Veitch had shook his head and said that such people were utterly mad! Veitch was a respectable businessman and knew exactly which orchids would bring in the biggest profits at auction, but he was also enough of a realist to understand that new plants were being imported all the time, and that orchids would soon be accessible to those besides the very rich.

David had asked Blount to investigate Cunningham since Rachel had been employed with him; the girl seemed to be the key to whatever was going on at Winton Park. At first, when Jane had telegraphed him to say that Rachel's death was probably no accident, he had been furious. That was so typical of Jane! She wanted to help and paid no heed to the possible danger she was putting herself in. But he had to grant her that she could not have foretold this turn of events.

It was already dark when the coach turned into the courtyard at Winton Park. The wheels rattled loudly across the stones, rolling to a stop on the gravel in front of the entrance. He leaned back, gazing up at the Jacobean walls. A lantern hung over the front door, and several windows were lit. Somber, Thomas had said of the place, and that's exactly what it was. After David paid the coachman, the butler came down the steps to meet him.

"Good evening, sir. We were not expecting any visitors. Who may I say is here?"

David noted politely, "Captain Wescott."

"Very good, Captain. I will have your bags brought inside momentarily." The butler bowed and led the way with measured steps.

David stepped inside the main hallway and glanced at the large grandfather clock. It was already eleven o'clock. No wonder the house was so quiet. But still, as he stood at the base of the stairs, he listened carefully, hoping to hear Jane's voice.

"Captain, Sir Frederick is in his hothouse, and Lady Charlotte has already retired for the evening. If I may, I will have the staff prepare a chamber and something for you to eat," the butler suggested.

"Thank you. Could you take me to the room of my wife, Lady Jane?"

Without showing the slightest sign of surprise, the butler nodded and led David upstairs to the second floor. Wescott noticed the prominently placed Halston crest and the fancy wood paneling, but other similarly old families had far more magnificently adorned houses. Clearly, Sir Frederick invested his fortune not in valuable paintings or sculptures—as Thomas did, and he was a rare visitor to the upper house of Parliament. Only when it was absolutely necessary and unavoidable did he appear for parliamentary gatherings, but he was more often noted by his absence. David did not even know who might be counted among Halston's close allies. Sir Robert Parks and Lord Cunningham were rivals, and they were far more famous as orchid collectors, though they continued to be influential members of London society. Cunningham was certainly getting on in years, but he was still a true socialite and an infamous philanderer. His son, regrettably, was proof that the apple never falls far from the tree.

They encountered nobody on their way upstairs or down a wide corridor, but David heard women's voices. He recognized Alison's bright laugh and was relieved that she was well.

The butler stopped in front of a door and knocked. After a moment, Hettie's round face appeared. "Oh, it's the captain!" she called, smiling broadly. "This is a surprise! I'll fetch your wife!"

Before David or the butler could utter a word, Hettie charged past them and disappeared into the room opposite. A muffled cry of joy rang out, the door flew open, and Jane fell into David's arms. The butler discreetly departed.

Jane pressed herself to him and buried her face in his neck. "David!" she sobbed.

Stroking her hair, he murmured, "Jane, come, let's go into your room, and you can tell me everything."

Once the door was closed behind them, he threw his gloves and coat over a chair and took Jane in his arms, kissing her passionately and discovering that her lips had lost none of their sweetness. Then he took her by the hand and led her to an armchair by the fireplace. Pulling up a chair, he sat across from her, close enough to take her hands in his.

"I'm so happy you're here, David!" said Jane, looking at him through teary eyes. "I was afraid something terrible had happened to Charlotte last night."

"What happened?"

"I don't know." Jane squeezed his hands. "Sir Frederick and Dr. Cribb haven't let anyone in to see her. She wasn't well before so the doctor prescribed her laudanum. Then I heard someone fall down during the night and cry out, and—"

"You heard that from here?" asked David doubtfully; the doors were solid and the family's rooms no doubt some distance away.

Jane removed her hands from his and wiped her cheeks dry. "I was on my way to the kitchen and just happened to pass by Charlotte's room."

Raising one eyebrow, he was unable to suppress a smile. "Coincidentally, in the middle of the night, you went creeping around another person's home?"

"Well . . . all right, I wanted to go down to the cellars to see Rachel's body. Because of the head wound?" She looked at him so earnestly that he could not help but laugh. "Are you laughing at me?"

Shaking his head, he leaned forward and quickly kissed her. "No, I simply find you completely incorrigible and irresistible. Name one lady, apart from yourself, who would even think about looking at a corpse in the dead of night?"

Jane smiled, then lifted her hands to her slightly disheveled hair.

"Pointless," he said, shaking his head.

"Excuse me?"

Lightning fast, he pulled a hairpin out of her carefully arranged hair and tossed it behind him. "What are you going to do about that?"

Another hairpin flew to the floor, and Jane stood up. "I'm going to tell Hettie that I won't need her anymore tonight."

When she returned from the adjoining room, he was unbuttoning his shirt.

"Did you come with Blount?"

"No, he's taking care of a few things for me in London, but we can discuss that tomorrow."

Her eyes gazed into his as she helped him untie his neckerchief. "And what are we going to discuss now?"

"We're not going to talk at all now, Jane." When his lips touched her neck, nothing escaped her mouth but a sigh.

It took a moment for David to realize where he was. Jane's chestnut hair was splayed over his chest and arm, and her body was still entwined with his. He swept a strand of hair out of her face and looked at her, relaxed in sleep. Yes, she meant far more to him than he had ever imagined possible. If anyone ever did anything to hurt her, he would follow them into hell to take revenge.

His father had been wrong. Love was not a disease for fools. Love did not destroy. It healed. He glanced out the window, where the morning sun was rising over the woods and hills. His father's hate had poisoned David's heart for so many years, hardening it against any emotion. He had passed through so many battlefields without finding redemption, and then fate had thrown this unconventional woman into his arms.

He felt movement, and Jane stretched and opened her eyes. "You're still here."

"Yes, my darling, and now I want you to tell me everything you've discovered about the dead maid."

Instantly, Jane was awake. She summarized all that she had been through. "Zenada gave me the letter because she thinks, as I do, that Rachel met her murderer here!"

"Those are strong words, Jane. And it was Cribb who told you about the wound on her head? He certainly would not have done so if he were conspiring with Sir Frederick in some ugliness. I think we can rule out the doctor."

"Good. But not Sir Frederick?" She stroked his chest.

"There's nothing either for or against him. Listen, if you keep doing that, I'll lose my concentration."

"She's still here."

"Who?" He held onto her hand tightly as it reached his navel.

"Rachel. She's going to be buried today."

"Jane, let's get up. I want to take a look at her. Cribb will allow me. After all, I'm officially involved in a police investigation."

"What? You didn't come here for my sake?"

"Of course I did! I'm only on this whole damned case because of your orchids."

Jane sat up suddenly. "My orchids? Ally asked me to come here!"

Taking a deep breath, he rested a hand behind his head. "Either way, an orchid gardener named Korshaw has been murdered. Korshaw worked at Veitch and Sons. Thank you for the orchid, by the way."

"Korshaw? I wonder if that was the man who served me? A coincidence? My God," said Jane, turning over, her hair veiling her body.

"He was responsible for sales, so I imagine you dealt with him." David explained to her what he knew about Korshaw and his jilted fiancée.

"At Cunningham's? Rachel was also employed there. Oh, David, what are we going to do now?"

"There are several possibilities . . ."

While Jane was still in the bath, David used the early morning hours to get an overview of the situation for himself. Out in the corridor, he was met with a wall of cold air that confirmed the dramatic drop in temperature in the last twenty-four hours. New snow covered the grounds, reaffirming his conviction that they were in for an early and hard winter.

On the landing between the guest and family wings of the house, he encountered a rather plain young woman whose black dress indicated her status as a lady's maid. She carried a tray on which a small empty medicine bottle and two glasses perched. Because he already knew Hettie and Nora, he guessed that this must be Lady Charlotte's maid. "Good morning, miss," he greeted her pleasantly.

"Good morning, sir," she replied quietly.

"How is Lady Charlotte this morning? Excuse me—Captain Wescott, at your service."

"Gladys, sir." She swallowed, and the tray began to tremble in her hands. "Not very well. I'm going for the doctor."

From a room farther along, he heard a child crying and another yelling angrily. A door flew open, and a woman exited, dragging a howling boy behind her. She then opened another door, pushed the boy inside, and turned the lock from the outside. "You will calm yourself down, Cedric!" she said sharply.

"That's Miss Molan, the governess, sir." Gladys steadied the tray with both hands, but the glasses still tinkled against each other.

When Melissa Molan saw David, she stood up straight and stared at him defiantly. Turning on her heel, she returned to the children's room. *A self-confident young woman,* David noted. And clearly one who was used to being around men, in contrast to shy Gladys, who was flustered by David's very presence.

"Mr. Draycroft!" Gladys suddenly cried and she stumbled forward.

David instinctively grabbed her by the arm, preventing her from falling down the stairs. The tray and everything on it, however, clattered onto the stairs. The butler picked up the fallen items.

"Good morning, Captain. The dining room is the first door on the left at the bottom of the stairs." He seemed to be waiting for David to release the maid's arm.

"All right?" David asked Gladys.

"Yes, thank you, sir. Mr. Draycroft, we need the doctor for my lady. Is there still any laudanum left?" Gladys asked.

"Mrs. Gubbins keeps some in the medicine cabinet. I'll have it brought up. Go to milady, Gladys," Draycroft ordered, and the maid obediently left. After straightening his neckerchief and vest, David continued down to the dining room, where he found his host already at breakfast.

"Ah, our unexpected guest from last night. Captain Wescott!" Sir Frederick stood up and shook David's hand, offering him a chair at the table. Apart from them, only a male servant was in attendance, serving the food.

After the usual exchange of pleasantries, Sir Frederick asked, "Have you come to collect your wife?"

Setting down his cup, David gestured toward the morning newspaper on the table beside Sir Frederick. "Perhaps you read that an employee of Veitch and Sons was murdered. You're familiar with the firm, I assume?"

"But of course! Every orchid grower of any standing knows Veitch." Sir Frederick narrowed his eyes, and his expression became unfriendly. "Why do you ask?"

"Well, as things have turned out, I am working with Superintendent Michael Rooke on the case as an advisor. A number of nasty circumstances are involved that have turned a simple break-in into a far more serious matter." David nodded when the servant brought him a plate of scrambled eggs and ham.

Sir Frederick pursed his lips. "You've piqued my curiosity. I gather this Rooke and his bobbies want to find out what's behind it all—I beg your pardon—with your help, of course."

An arrogant snob, David thought, but continued unmoved. "There is no doubt that our country is in need of new institutions to fight crime. Who better to do that than veterans and those who come from the streets and know the environment in which they will need to investigate?"

"Bah! Good money down the drain! We have more than enough first-rate minds among the aristocracy. What will we have become when the plebs can interrogate the nobles!" said Sir Frederick in disgust.

"If by first-rate minds, you are referring to people like Lord Lucan, who sent hundreds of fine soldiers to a senseless death, then I hold little hope for a functioning executive branch." David chose his words carefully; he knew that Sir Frederick hadn't served. The Battle of Balaclava was widely discussed, certainly after Lord Lucan's trial if not before.

"Oh, Lucan knew what he was doing. It's easy to cast judgment after the fact! An experienced officer like him!" Sir Frederick sniffed.

"I was there." David cut a piece of ham, savoring its taste.

"Humph." Sir Frederick threw his napkin on the table. "Any more questions? Business calls."

"Did you ever deal directly with Korshaw?"

"Once or twice. I mainly dealt directly with Mr. Veitch."

"What do you think of Lord Cunningham?"

Sir Frederick looked at him in surprise. "Cunningham? He has an outstanding reputation. His orchids are among the best in the land."

"Your deceased maid was employed at Cunningham's before she came here. Did that have any bearing on your decision to take her on?"

"Mrs. Gubbins carries out interviews with prospective staff. Do you seriously think I would question a maid about her previous employer?"

Indeed, David could not imagine such a self-righteous, arrogant man trying to worm confidential information out of anyone, much less a servant, but a man was capable of taking on unusual roles in certain circumstances. Unseen depths might lurk beneath a glossy surface.

"It would be only natural for a man to want to find out how his competitors work, which orchids have been ordered, or what particular growing methods succeeded. After doing a little research on my own, I now have the highest respect for orchid growers. One can see it almost as a science, especially when it comes to watering systems, and the humidity and temperature that have to be maintained in the greenhouses." David had calculated correctly. At the mention of Sir Frederick's great passion, the lord of the manor instantly forgot his wounded vanity.

"It takes years of experience with these plants to get them to flower in our latitudes. Personally, I focus on the breeding of hybrids, which demands a very scientific approach indeed. Believe me, Captain, if there is ever anything I want to know, then I will talk to Cunningham myself."

14.

David had joined Jane for a cup of tea while she ate breakfast, then both of them had changed to go out riding. Before heading to the stables, however, Jane had a stop she wanted to make. They left the house through the main entrance.

Outside, David hesitated. "Do you know how we can get down to the cellars through the staff entrance?"

Jane giggled. "Don't tell me you've developed an interest in Jacobean architecture?"

The cold air froze their breath, and the thin layer of snow crunched underfoot. Turning up the fur-lined collar of his coat, David tapped at his boots with his riding crop as he walked. "It's a side of me you haven't seen before. I'm always trying to surprise you."

She hooked her arm in his and grinned. "And you're doing an excellent job of it."

A coach rolled into the courtyard, and Dr. Cribb immediately jumped out. "Good morning," he shouted as he ran up the steps to the house.

David waved, then drew Jane away. "This is our chance. Everyone is focused on Lady Charlotte. Come on!"

Moving quickly around the outside of the house, they headed for the stairs that led down to the servants' wing. Della stood at the top of the stairs, hurriedly stuffing a piece of bread into her mouth. Still chewing, she disappeared back into the kitchen. She had not seen them.

"Here?" David asked.

"I think there's a stairway to the cellars through there. But what if it's locked?"

Her husband grinned and patted his jacket pocket. "I'm prepared."

They trotted down the steps; the door into the vaulted cellars was open, and they slipped inside. Just enough light fell through two small barred windows to show them the way. Jane stopped in front of the third door beneath the ancient arches. At the other end of the passage, they could hear the sounds of the kitchen, but there was no one else in sight.

David tried to turn the heavy iron door handle, which creaked but did not give. Reaching into his jacket, he took out a strangely formed hook; after a few seconds of twisting it within the door lock, he turned the handle again. This time, the door opened. "You keep watch. I'll check the dead girl."

"No, I—"

But she got no further. David kissed her, then held her face in his hands. "Please."

There was enough insistence in that one word for Jane to swallow her objections and nod. David disappeared through the heavy cellar door, and Jane stood and listened for the sound of anyone approaching. Before long, she heard a door to the kitchen open; there was a crashing sound, someone cursed, and footsteps headed in her direction. Jane pressed herself beneath the door arch, which allowed her just enough room. The cellar walls were almost three feet thick, and the doors were set into the stonework at the same depth.

A man's heavy steps came closer and closer, stopping just before they reached Jane's hiding place. She heard the sound of a crate being set down, then another curse, then someone shuffled away. Jane waited a moment longer, then scratched at the door. "David!"

The door to the kitchens opened again. Jane recognized the butler's voice.

"David! Hurry up!" She peeked around the corner at the butler, who seemed to be waiting for someone. Then she heard Sir Frederick's voice.

Finally, the door opened and David slipped through. Taking Jane's hand in his, they retreated the same way they had come. Only when they were out of earshot did he stop and look at her.

"Well? What did you see?" Jane asked breathlessly.

"The woman had been lying in the moor for two weeks. Be glad you were spared the sight. There was a head wound, yes. But whether it came from a blow or from a fall is almost impossible to tell. I'm not a coroner and can only speak from my own experience." He ran his hands through his hair and put on his hat. "Come, show me the stables."

Along the way, they stood on the uppermost terrace of the garden, gazing out over the edge of the forest. "The woods are bisected by the river," Jane explained. "The moor starts down that way. Maybe O'Connor has time to lead us there. In any case, I can find the way myself, at least as far as the moor."

"No doubt. I'd like to see the place the girl was found. Here, look at this." He pulled a soiled, folded letter out of his pocket and handed it to her.

They continued slowly, side by side, along the path to the stables, passing boxwood hedges and bare deciduous trees.

"That's why you took so long!" Jane unfolded the letter and carefully examined a discolored page. The words were blurred by water and barely readable.

Tonight . . . midnight . . . the hunter's hut . . . moor . . . Love . . .

The last word was so blurred that it was completely indecipherable. "Oh, that's annoying. Who could have written this?"

Taking the letter from Jane, he studied the handwriting. "A very fluid hand, but that's about all I can say."

They had arrived at the stables. One of the stablehands was leading two horses padded with blankets across the yard. Jane recognized him as the young man she had spoken to before. A young groom was saddling a pony just inside the stable. David put the letter in his pocket. "Perhaps one of those fellows?"

Jane shrugged. "Maybe Miles? No, he seemed friendly enough to me."

"No reason to rule him out," David said and waved the young man over.

"Whoa, easy, easy," Miles said gently to the light-colored mare he was leading. "Good morning, sir."

Jane stroked the muzzle of the other horse. "Moondancer, aren't you a beauty. Yes, we know each other, don't we? Miles, this is my husband, Captain Wescott."

"Captain! I would have gladly joined the army, except I can't stand to see horses used as cannon fodder." The young man was wearing a threadbare tweed jacket over a shirt and checked vest. His cheeks and hands were red from the cold, but it didn't seem to bother him in the slightest.

"Seeing a horse die on the battlefield is no pretty sight, I'll grant you that. Are you from this area?" Petting the nervous horse's nose, David murmured comforting sounds.

"Aye, I am, and it's good to have family not far away. When my girl finally says yes, I'll keep my job here, and she can live with my parents," he explained.

"Miles!" someone bellowed from the stable, and Jane flinched.

"Ugh, that's Mr. Gubbins," Jane said. "Terrible man. Didn't you say he'd had his eye on Rachel?"

Scruffy, red-blond hair stuck out from beneath Miles's cap, and the young man looked Jane in the eye when he said, "Yes. I'll stand by that, my lady, but I have to go now. Did you want to go out riding?"

"Yes, if Mr. O'Connor is available? He must know the lands around here," said David.

"In this kind of weather, he's usually out in the woods checking on the feeding sites for the wild game." Miles led the horses into the stable, where Mr. Gubbins was waiting for him with a dour expression on his face.

"I think we can safely cross Miles off our list," David said. "But let's ask dear Mr. Gubbins for his help."

When they approached Mr. Gubbins inside the stable, he said, "If you can be patient for an hour, I'll send someone out to fetch O'Connor."

"Who's the pony for? Little Cedric?" Jane asked.

"The boy is afraid of horses. That's something we have to cure him of, though; as master of Winton Park, he has to be able to hold his own in the saddle. We're famous for our hunts, you know," Mr. Gubbins said proudly.

Then Jane heard the boy screaming in protest. "No! I don't want to! Noooo!"

The boy's shrill, grating shrieks grew ever louder, until Miss Molan appeared with Cedric at the stable door. She looked just as sure of herself as she had at their first meeting. Holding tightly on to the boy's wrist, she kept her grip firm as they approached the pony, stopping near Jane and David.

"Good day, my lady," Miss Molan greeted Jane tepidly, but her eyes brightened when she saw David.

"Cedric, what did we agree earlier?" she said to the boy, whose little face was livid.

Cedric swallowed, opened his clenched hands, and said, "After I've gone for a ride on the pony, I can see the rabbits."

"Good boy. Now go to the pony and talk to him so that he gets to know you," Miss Molan suggested.

"It doesn't need to know me. It only needs to carry me." The boy stamped over to the piebald pony, which was being held by the young groom. "Help me up!" Cedric ordered the groom, without looking at him.

Jane watched the inconsiderate boy.

"Miss Molan, we're trying to shed some light on Rachel's accident. Would you know who her friends were here? Did she have an admirer?" David asked quietly.

Without taking her eye off her charge, who now sat stiffly, concentrating hard, his hands grasping the pony's mane as it was walked around the interior of the stable, Miss Molan replied, "She hadn't been here long. Ask the other maids. I had nothing to do with her."

"Maybe you saw something? Had she perhaps spent an inordinate amount of time talking with a particular male staff member?" David tried again.

"Does Sir Frederick know that you are interrogating us?" Miss Molan asked.

"Of course. And it is entirely in his interest to banish any shadow of a doubt hanging over the poor girl's death. It should also be in your interest to help us do that." His expression was inscrutable, but there was an edge to his tone.

"Naturally, but I observed nothing unusual. You can see for yourself that I am kept permanently busy with Cedric."

Jane looked on as the boy was lifted off the back of the pony. He ran toward them with a triumphant smile. "How nice that he at least likes rabbits," she said.

"Yes, he thinks they're delicious. He wants to watch one being slaughtered, and Sir Frederick gave his permission." Miss Molan took Cedric by the hand. "Come on, then. A promise is a promise."

Jane and David stood still for several seconds, saying nothing.

Finally, Jane asked, "Is that normal?"

"I couldn't say. It wasn't at the boarding school where I grew up, certainly, and my father never said a word to me, let alone actually showed me anything." David cleared his throat. "It's getting colder out. Let's drink some tea in the house and wait for O'Connor there."

"What do we do with the letter?" Jane asked. She had put her arm through David's again. "Sir Frederick doesn't want a police investigation."

"Hmm. My only authority is as an advisor for Rooke. I'm not on official business, so to speak. Jane, do you remember the big bank scandal four years ago?"

"You mean when the high and mighty directors of the Royal British Bank were caught? That was all over the papers. Those pompous old men were so puritanical, starting every meeting with a prayer! At the same time, they were secretly living in complete luxury, financed by tricky bookkeeping and misappropriated deposits." She looked curiously at her husband.

"Precisely. There are many people like that, and when it comes to the black market trade in goods from the colonies, the whole enterprise stinks to high heaven. It's all about exploitation and fraud. We're on the trail of a consortium that sends ships overseas and to the colonies, then manipulates the prices of certain goods, like rice and tea. I can't tell you any more than that, but somehow, I suspect that Korshaw was mixed up with those people. Orchids are a luxury item, and high profits are to be had."

"You make it sound as if important men are tangled up in it. The kind of men one can't simply drag in front of a judge . . ."

"That's exactly it, Jane. Sir Frederick hasn't yet appeared in the circle of suspects, and that doesn't surprise me because he really isn't the kind of man . . . But one can never know for certain."

They had reached the stairs below the main entrance. "Someone more like Cunningham?" Jane said. "Someone with a flamboyant life-style whose sons are even more debauched than the father?"

David nodded. "And how does Rachel fit into that?"

In the hallway, they met Gladys, about to go upstairs and carrying a laden tray covered with a cloth.

"Oh, Gladys! May I come along? I'd like to offer Lady Charlotte some company." Jane glanced at David, her eyes entreating him to understand.

"I'll be in the library," he said.

Jane went upstairs alongside the maid, who kept her eyes shyly on the tray. "What did Dr. Cribb say?"

"Oh, my lady, I can't say anything about that." The tray rattled a little. Gladys seemed nervous.

Standing outside Charlotte's room, Jane heard a child's clear laughter, and when she entered she was pleased to see Eleanor playing with her dolls on the carpet in front of the fire. Against all expectation, Charlotte was dressed and reclining on a sofa. Yet her skin appeared waxen, and there were worrying blue rings beneath her eyes. When Jane drew closer, she saw that Charlotte's lips were cracked.

"My dear, I'm so relieved to see you up and about with your daughter!" said Jane effusively.

"Come sit by me," said Charlotte, patting the sofa beside her. "It's nice of you to come visit a broody old hen like me. It really isn't usual for me to withdraw in this way. I very much enjoy being with my children, which is why I would also prefer for Cedric to stay here as long as he can. Until a year ago, he was a very sickly child. It seemed he was always coughing, and several times we thought we would lose him."

"How old is he? Seven?" That was the usual age at which boys were sent off to boarding school.

"Doesn't he have the face of an angel? I know he isn't an easy child."

A serious understatement, thought Jane.

"But I probably spoiled him too much. Even Frederick let him get away with a great deal, although my husband is otherwise quite strict and very careful about bringing the children up correctly," Charlotte continued, unusually chatty.

Gladys set the tray down on a small table and lifted the cloth to reveal a bowl of porridge and a jar of honey, but Charlotte waved off the food.

"Are you sure you won't eat anything?" asked Jane. "You gave us all such a fright last night."

"Really, it was nothing. I have dizzy spells now and then, but they pass quickly enough. Doctor Cribb has prescribed laudanum and a strong tonic. Look at me, I'm feeling much better today."

Jane was not at all convinced. Whatever was in the tonic made Charlotte euphoric, but she did not look healthy.

"Come here, my darling!" Charlotte reached out to her daughter, who was holding her doll out toward her mother.

"Lula wants to see Pebbles, Mama!" the girl said, looking charming in her lace-trimmed powder-blue dress.

"Pebbles is unwell and needs some peace and quiet, sweetheart. He'll be back in a few days."

"Look." Eleanor extracted a sticky, brown candy from her skirt pocket. "This is from Miss Molan. I get one if I've been good. I've got lots, but Cedric doesn't."

Charlotte took the candy and put it on the tray. "Gladys! Wipe her hands and put a new dress on her!"

"No!" Eleanor cried as Gladys led her out of the room.

"David arrived unexpectedly last night, Charlotte. Will you join us for afternoon tea?"

"Ah, that's why you look so happy, Jane." Sighing, she laid her head against the back of the sofa. "The tutor is expected today. I have to be back on my feet by then, or Frederick will simply send him away."

Jane stood up. "So I will see you for tea later, and you can meet David then. We still want to go out riding."

"I don't enjoy riding very much, nor does Cedric, which is something he inherited from me. But he has to learn. A lord has to cut a good figure in the saddle!" Charlotte's eyelids were growing heavy, and she seemed to be having difficulty keeping her thoughts straight. "Your husband, of course. That's . . . nice . . ."

And with that, Charlotte nodded off. Jane stroked her cheek and murmured, "Sleep yourself well again."

She doubted that Charlotte could do that, however. Jane cautiously sniffed the dusty candy lying on the tray, then touched a moistened finger to it. She lifted her finger to her mouth. It tasted of caramel and was very sweet. Charlotte's two medicine bottles stood on a raised table. "Laudanum, Tincture of Opium" read one label. "Heart Tonic" read the other. Jane smelled both bottles but noticed nothing untoward. Whatever was making Charlotte sick was hiding somewhere else.

15.

Thirl Moor, Cheviot Hills, Northumberland, December 1860

As they left the woods, the frosty wind lashed fiercely at their faces. O'Connor had ridden in the lead the entire time, saying nothing. Just before they started along the path leading into the moor, he pulled up his horse.

"Stay behind me. The horses know where to tread. Give them a free rein." O'Connor turned and gazed out over the windswept, wintry moor through which the narrow path led to the hunter's hut. A buzzard circled overhead in the distance, then dove earthward.

"Mr. O'Connor," Jane asked before they set off again, "how did you happen to find the girl's body?"

The gamekeeper rubbed his stubbly cheeks. "It was what you said on our last ride, my lady, that prompted me to come out here for a thorough search. A day or two later and there would have been nothing left to find. A scrap of her dress had got caught in some roots. I'll show you."

"So you also searched the woods?" David asked from behind, keeping his horse close to Jane's as they rode on.

"Aye. I searched all the places that the people hereabouts like to use for their little trysts, and I also followed the river to the place the current sometimes deposits drowned animals. Between Christmas and the New Year, Sir Frederick puts on a hunt. It's always a big affair. I had to check all the huts anyway in preparation for it."

The horses walked the frozen path. A thin frost covered the bushes and grass, and they could see crackly pieces of ice forming on the water, but the dark, swampy patches shimmered treacherously. A heavy silence hung over the land, and the snorting of the horses and the far-off cry of a bird sounded intrusive.

"How could she possibly have come out here at night by herself?" Jane wondered aloud.

"She was a Romany girl. They can find their way wherever they are. They've got the sight of cats and can sense direction like migratory birds," said O'Connor.

The midday sun provided little warmth, and the milky sky encased the moor in a hazy cocoon. Finally, O'Connor drew up his horse. "Here's where the body was."

He pointed to a place by the side of the path where crooked roots protruded from the morass. David dismounted and examined the spot more closely. Jane stayed on her horse. Her limbs had turned to stone at the horrible realization that this was where the girl had been swallowed by the moor.

"Did you check the hut?"

"I did," said O'Connor. "It was locked, as it ought to have been. There might have been some footprints by the door, but it had rained and I couldn't have said how big they were."

"Then someone really had been waiting for Rachel. Would you agree, O'Connor?" David poked around in the grass, then took a few steps toward the hut.

"I'll don't think I'll get into that, Captain. I don't want any trouble, if you know what I mean."

"Sometimes you're already in the middle of something. You just don't know it yet," remarked David. He slowly circled the hut.

O'Connor, nettled, turned on him. "Trying to pin something on me, is that it? Would I be so stupid as to go and find her body if I was the one who'd thrown her in?" David looked back at O'Connor but didn't say anything. The gamekeeper's anger was growing. "Are you done sniffing around? My dog does the job better in any case. It was he that found the scrap in the roots."

David had finished going around the hut, his eyes examining the ground. "Thank you for your time, Mr. O'Connor. It's been very informative."

Jane had changed for afternoon tea. Wearing a rust-brown dress—it was made of outrageously expensive silk that was so soft and shiny she had been persuaded to buy it—she went up to Alison's room. David wanted to look in on Alison briefly, too, before they went down to tea together.

Alison appeared rather drained. "Ally, are you all right? Has your cold come back?" Jane asked, hurrying over to where her friend lay on the daybed.

"Jane, how nice of you to come by! I don't have to play at being the suffering expectant mother today, because I've actually been having some early labor pains. I feel as if I've been run over by a milk cart."

"No! Has Dr. Cribb already been to see you? You haven't had any bleeding, have you?"

"No. Cribb was here and prescribed laudanum for me, but I don't like that stuff at all. It makes me woozy, and I don't have any control over my body. I want to feel the life inside me, not anesthetize it."

A new contraction shook Alison, who closed her eyes and took short, sharp breaths. Jane held her hand and kissed her friend's forehead. After a few moments, Alison relaxed but kept her eyes closed. She whispered, "Why don't you tell me what you and David have been up to? Nora was very enthusiastic when she told me he was here. Your dear husband's mere presence seems to be breaking hearts in droves."

Jane smiled at that, then told Alison about their excursion with O'Connor and how Cedric was so afraid of horses. "I'm trying hard, Ally, but I can't bring myself to say I like the boy."

"He was sick for a long time, then spoiled rotten. One ought to keep that in mind, and his father is not what you'd call a model of paternal warmth, after all. How is Charlotte?" Alison had opened her eyes again, and the color was returning to her face.

"She's hiding something. That terrible bout last night and her dizzy spells—it isn't normal at all. Could she be taking too much laudanum? Has she always been so prone to illness?"

Just then, Nora showed David into the room. The maid could hardly take her eyes off David and stumbled as she backed out of the room.

"No, not at all! Oh, David, how lovely to see you!" Ally sat up in bed. "I look like a blubbery walrus, but as far as I can tell, my little menace here wants to see the light of the world as soon as he can."

All three talked animatedly about events at the house, and Alison said, "Poor Rachel! What about the butler? Have you questioned him yet? It would have been easy for him to lure Rachel out there."

"Let's assume it was a rendezvous. Then why did Rachel have to die?" Jane wondered.

David sighed. "An unwanted child is often reason enough for such 'accidents.'"

"Was she pregnant?" Alison automatically placed a hand on her stomach.

"I don't think so. Theoretically, an autopsy should have been done, but Sir Frederick did not allow that, and until we can produce a lover, we have no motive. My own suspicions are tending more toward the Cunninghams and their orchids." David took Jane's hand. "Darling, we should go down for tea."

"David!" Ally said, keeping them a moment longer. "That would mean that Sir Frederick—"

"Not necessarily, Ally." David patted his jacket. "Which reminds me of a telegram I just received from Blount. I have to leave tomorrow."

"No!" Jane could not suppress a cry. She felt David's hand on her back.

"Blount has been looking into Korshaw's past, and Rooke needs me. But I'll return as soon as I can," he promised.

The following morning was even colder, and Jane put on her fur-lined coat to accompany David to the waiting carriage.

"Take care of yourself, Jane," he said and stroked her cheek. "No wandering around at night. I'll send you a telegram as soon as I find out anything new."

"If I can't help Charlotte, then I'll come home and bring Alison with me," said Jane. "It's just that Charlotte isn't doing very well at the moment."

"You have a generous heart, Jane. I hope Charlotte deserves the effort you're making."

Over the course of that day, Jane thought often of David's words and considered Charlotte's behavior in another light. Ally loved her cousin and did not have the necessary emotional distance to get to the bottom of how Charlotte was acting. Did she have the right to distrust Alison's friend, however, when she herself did not know what was making her so ill?

That afternoon, Jane wandered into the green drawing room and looked at the porcelain figurines. The sweet faces and endearing animals were the friendliest things in that gloomy house. Maybe Charlotte felt the same way? Maybe that was why she found some consolation in those little works of art? Holding a little shepherdess and lamb figurine, Jane jumped when loud voices suddenly sounded outside the library door.

"No, Charlotte! Stop behaving so hysterically!" She heard Sir Frederick's sharp voice. "Mr. Hartman was not the right man for the job, and I am going to send Cedric to boarding school. That is my final decision."

There was the sound of subdued crying, and Jane, still holding the porcelain figurine, retreated to a secluded corner of the room in case the doors opened.

"You grant me nothing! Nothing! You've got your accursed orchids, but I have only my children, and now you're taking them away from me, too!" Charlotte sobbed.

"Just look at yourself!" Sir Frederick snapped. "You're not in any condition to raise our children. If it wasn't for Miss Molan, Cedric wouldn't even be able to get on a horse. She at least has what it takes to assert herself with the boy. My God, if it weren't for your dowry, I never would have married you anyway."

"Without my dowry, you wouldn't be able to buy all your expensive orchids!" Charlotte threw back at him, but her voice sounded fragile, and Jane thought she could hear suppressed sobbing punctuating her words.

"You know nothing about the state of my finances, you stupid woman!" Sir Frederick shouted. "What have I done to deserve this? If only my dear Eunice had not died so young."

In utter disbelief, Jane stood rooted to the spot, still holding the porcelain figure tightly in both hands. Then the door swung open and Mrs. Gubbins entered. The housekeeper seemed to have heard the argument between her employers as well, and her mouth was twisted contemptuously—as if agreeing with Sir Frederick's words.

"Do you have a particular wish for dinner this evening, my lady?" Mrs. Gubbins asked calmly.

Jane turned the figurine in her hands around, then set it down on the table. "Very pretty . . . no, thank you. I'll eat almost anything."

Mrs. Gubbins went to hold the door open, as if expecting Jane to leave the room with her. As slowly as possible, Jane acceded to the woman's unspoken demand, then managed to surprise her by asking, "When will Rachel's burial be?"

Out in the hall, Mrs. Gubbins replied, "The day after tomorrow. The girl's family has been sent a message. It is only right and proper that they attend. Death absolves one of all sins."

"Why do you say that? Had Rachel sinned?"

With her hair pulled back in a tight bun, her collar buttoned to her chin, and her black dress, there was something crowlike about the housekeeper's appearance. "I was only speaking generally, my lady, if I may. The girl was half-Roma and turned men's heads with the way she looked."

"That does not mean she did anything wrong. Perhaps someone was trying to seduce her."

Mrs. Gubbins lifted her chin. "Is it not a sin to submit to the temptations of the flesh?"

A bigoted moralistic sentry as a housekeeper who favored the deceased Lady Halston—what a heavy burden indeed for Charlotte, who seemed to have neither the strength nor the skill to assert herself against Sir Frederick.

"I find excessive adherence to such imperatives unhealthy, Mrs. Gubbins," said Jane, and she turned on her heel and left the housekeeper standing there.

After those disagreeable episodes, Jane needed some fresh air; in any case, a stroll outside before dinner would do her good. As she left the house with Hettie a short time later, the sun had already set. Jane buried her hands in her coat pockets as they wandered slowly along the frozen paths. Their breath hung like white fog in the evening air.

"I haven't been in this kind of cold for a long time, ma'am." Hettie pointed toward the yard outside the kitchen, where stairs led down to the cellars. "Is that where you explored with the captain?"

"Yes, and any burglar could also easily get inside there. Wait, do you hear that? That's Miss Molan!" Jane stopped and pulled Hettie with her behind a hedge.

"I'm so sorry, Walter!" they heard Miss Molan say.

Jane peered through the hedge and saw the governess holding a man's arm in a very familiar manner, the two of them climbing the steps from the kitchen yard up to the garden.

The kitchen door was open, exuding the scent of fried fish, game, and herbs, and Jane could see that kitchen staff were scurrying around, preparing the evening meal.

"Mr. Hartman!" Draycroft suddenly appeared at the kitchen door but did not venture outside.

Miss Molan's companion extracted his arm, patted her hand, then turned to Draycroft. "Yes?"

"Your papers. You've forgotten your papers," Mr. Draycroft said as he handed the man a thin file.

"Thank you very much."

"That must be the tutor that Miss Molan recommended," whispered Hettie, standing close to Jane.

"I daresay. And I believe our Miss Molan's interest is more than just professional," Jane murmured.

"Hmm. But he's not allowed to stay?"

"No. Shh!" Jane raised a gloved hand.

Stuffing the thin file into his coat pocket, Mr. Hartman returned to Miss Molan, who was waiting at the steps. Jane could not make out much of Hartman's face in the dark, but she did see that he wore a moustache. He seemed to be of average height, rather stocky, and his clothes looked dignified enough.

"Lissy, don't go blaming yourself, please. I'll take a room in Allenton, and we can talk everything through there. There is too much going on here," said Hartman, nodding toward a young kitchen boy carting out a box filled with rubbish.

Melissa Molan was standing close to Hartman, who took her hands in his and kissed her lightly on the cheek. She murmured something in his ear.

"What did she say? I couldn't hear," whispered Hettie in turn.

"Neither could I," Jane answered. Miss Molan turned back to the house, and Hartman walked away along the path.

"Is that her lover?" Hettie bit her lips excitedly.

"It's possible, but frankly, I would have thought of Miss Molan as being more calculating when it came to her choice of a man. A tutor is not what I would call a step up. Well, one can always be mistaken. Let's finish our walk and go in for dinner."

Just before they entered the dining room, they saw Miss Molan cross the hall, followed by a girl carrying a tray.

"Miss Molan!" said Jane with a smile.

"Della, wait. The children should not start without me," Miss Molan instructed the maid, then turned to Jane. "Yes?"

"Will Cedric have a tutor now?" asked Jane innocently.

A shadow briefly crossed the governess's face. "I'm afraid that Sir Frederick has decided against it. Mr. Hartman would be an excellent teacher, but what can I do? Now the boy will go to boarding school, and I doubt very much that he will be better off there."

"Do you mean he won't be able to watch rabbits being butchered?" Jane said sarcastically.

"Death is part of life, my lady. We have to kill to eat. I must say that I cannot fully comprehend your sensitivities. The children in my care have always learned young that life has its cruel side, and this knowledge has harmed none of them. On the contrary, in fact, it enriches them."

"Well, Miss Molan, I would not think of criticizing your methods. That would be a task for Lady Charlotte. May I ask where you worked before coming to Winton Park? Were you perhaps abroad? You have made an exceptionally cultivated impression on me."

The governess raised her chin slightly and briefly narrowed her eyes. "So far, I'm afraid, a period abroad has not been my fortune, but I will accept your compliment as a tribute to my own outstanding teacher. Thank you, my lady."

Mr. Draycroft came out of the kitchen just then. Ignoring Miss Molan, who quickly left, he bowed slightly toward Jane. "Dinner is served, my lady."

16.

London, December 1860

The city smelled fetid, and it was so cold that the Thames had begun to freeze. As David rode through London, he saw not only the impressive façades of grand houses; not only the wide windows of the shops along Regent Street, offering delicacies from around the world, silk and velvet fabrics, jewels, and exotic stuffed birds; but also the workaday miseries of the poor in the dark alleys, far from the city's shine. In cold weather, the poorhouses and workhouses were bursting at the seams. The mud larks waded out day after day, up to their hips in the filth and sewage, scavenging whatever they might be able to sell—a piece of iron, a length of old rope, a chunk of coal. Often enough, the scavengers cut their feet on broken glass or sharp metal, and a fatal infection could follow.

When David stepped into the police station at Brompton that morning, the stench of the Thames rose to meet him, and he coughed and covered his nose.

"Good morning to you, Captain. A horrible stink, ain't it? Comes from our guest here! Hey, you just going to sit there, you little rat?"

Sergeant Berwin snapped at a boy dressed in rags who was sitting on a chair against the wall.

The boy shivered. His arms and legs were so thin that David could practically see his bones. Sad, sunken eyes stared bleakly back.

"One of our mud larks has figured out that stealing's a better game. Gets him into the pen, eh? Ain't that it? You'd rather be behind bars and fed three times a day than perish out in that stinking brew, wouldn't you?" The officer knew his clientele, but at the same time he was sympathetic to their plight. He turned to David. "Can't say I blame him. He's pinched an apple and earned himself three weeks as punishment," he said with a wink.

The boy looked at them with some fear, but his hands were clasped together gratefully.

Rooke shouted from the other end of the corridor, "David! We're waiting for you!"

"I'll be right there." Something about the boy moved David, and he said, "What's your name, lad?"

"Myron," the boy replied hoarsely, his eyes fixed on his filthy hands.

"Do you know your way around the city?"

Myron nodded.

"Good, then you can run errands for me. Unless you've got something better to do?" David saw a little light flicker in the poor creature's eyes.

"What's the pay?"

"Depending on the distance, a penny or more. You'll get three meals a day, and I think we can find a place for you to sleep. Sound fair?"

The boy looked up from his hands in disbelief. "Yes, sir."

"Good. Sergeant Berwin will tell you where to find me. That issue with the apple . . . no doubt that was a misunderstanding. I'm sure that can be sorted out, can't it, Sergeant?"

The policeman rolled his eyes. "Captain, a heart as soft as yours don't always pay off. They'll lie as soon as open their mouths, and best don't forget it. But if you want him, he's yours."

David left them and walked down the corridor, feeling the boy's eyes on his back as he went.

As he stepped into Rooke's office, the policeman greeted him with a shake of the head. "What do you want with that little imp? Light-fingered rogues, the lot of them. Doesn't matter how young they are. Don't let them pull the wool over your eyes. There's always a big brother somewhere that they owe; then they'll help themselves to your belongings."

"We shall see. So far, my experiences with people I've helped have been good." David thought of Levi and hoped that he had not deceived himself when he'd taken the musician into his house.

Rooke sat behind his desk. "Tea? Something stronger?"

"No, thank you. I'm curious about what you've found out." Without taking off his coat, David sat down. "It's cold in here! How do you bear it?"

Rooke smoothly lifted a bottle of whisky from the floor behind his desk. "One ought not to underestimate the warmth from within."

Both men laughed, but Rooke immediately grew serious again. "I've got something for you, David." He pushed a note across the desk. A name and address were coarsely scribbled on it.

"Bill Pedley, Seven Bells, St. Giles," David read aloud.

Rooke ran a hand over his close-cropped hair. "I have neither the means nor the right men to follow up on that, but I believe you might be successful. The man was once a soldier, lost a leg in India, war wound. Bill was supposed to have been friends with Korshaw in India, according to our informant. Anything more than that is up to you."

St. Giles was one of the most dangerous districts of London, a meeting point for the underworld, where criminals holed up in dingy, stinking alleyways behind the façades of once-splendid buildings. Crime rates there were higher than in any other part of London, and violent crimes were the order of the day. St. Giles was also notorious for its numerous gin distilleries and brothels. Most of the distilleries operated illegally because licenses were either too expensive or simply impossible to obtain. Illicit alcohol, however, continued to be a favorite among the poor, but turpentine was sometimes added, and consumption could lead to death. At the same time, men from all walks of society visited St. Giles in search of danger and thrills.

"Seven Bells, isn't that one of the illegal gin stills? Who does that belong to these days?" David asked.

"Officially, they run a clean operation, but everyone knows what goes on there. A man named Big John is in charge; he stages illegal dog-fights there." Rooke grimly drummed his fingers on the table. Dogfights had been banned since 1835, but rat-baiting—dogs killing rats—was still a popular sport among bettors. "We've almost caught him many times, but he's always warned in advance. He's being protected by someone, someone with a lot of money. I'm certain that Seven Bells doesn't belong to Big John but rather to some influential businessman, or maybe to one of those fine gentlemen in the House of Lords."

"I understand. I'll go and ask Bill a few questions. Any news on Cunningham or Sir Robert?"

"Those men don't talk to me. Perhaps with you, being part of higher society, it'll be different. What's the story with your father, the—"

David's expression caused Rooke to fall silent.

"Excuse me. I just thought . . ."

"I'll take care of Bill, and I'll talk to the two men at their clubs. If you have nothing else for me . . ." David stood.

Rooke also stood, and the two men shook hands. "Nothing, I'm sorry to say. How is your wife?"

"Still in Winton Park, keeping Lady Alison and Alison's cousin Charlotte company. The maid I told you about, the one who disappeared, she was found dead out on the moor. Not an accident, either, from what I can tell. She used to be in Cunningham's employ." David looked thoughtfully at Rooke.

"That doesn't necessarily mean anything. Or do you suspect there's a connection to Korshaw or the orchids?"

David shook his head. "I might be seeing connections where none exist. Well, we'll see if Bill can help us with that."

A colorful assortment of prostitutes, criminals, beggars, and gentlemen prowled the nocturnal streets of St. Giles. The narrow alleys were divided among the district's gangs, and anyone finding himself in the no-man's-land between claimed areas could easily fall victim to a wayward knife. It was achingly cold that December night, yet the gaudily made-up women still crowded the public houses, offering their bodies to whoever was willing to pay.

David and Blount had donned their oldest suits and coats, underneath which each kept a revolver and a knife within easy reach. Even in their worn-out coats, however, they still looked more respectable than most of the shadowy figures that populated the dingy lanes. A dark-haired girl moved away from the corner of a building and sashayed toward them.

"Well, well, who do we have here? Lookin' for somethin' special, boys? I can show you heaven here on earth!" The prostitute thrust her ample cleavage forward. Her milky breasts were barely covered by tattered lace, and beneath a thick layer of white powder were red spots that reached to her neck.

"Diseased old . . . ," Blount grumbled.

But David took a shilling from his pocket and held it out to the woman. "Are we heading the right way for Seven Bells?"

Quick as a striking snake, the woman snatched the coin and deposited it between her breasts. Rotten teeth appeared as she smirked. "Ooh, ain't you polite . . . and pretty, to boot. What's a man like you want in a rat hole like that?"

"Answer, or do you want me to take the coin back?" Blount hissed.

But the woman was not about to be intimidated. She was as tall as Blount and had no doubt seen and experienced the full gamut of misery and violence. "C'mon then, lad! Come and get it!" She tried to push close to Blount, but he quickly stepped back.

"Keep away from me!" he growled, scanning their surroundings. Two men in dark coats were slowly approaching them. "Captain!" he said.

David turned sideways to keep the men in his line of sight, his hand reaching inside his coat for his revolver. As he did, the men changed their route and disappeared into a side alley.

Not missing a thing, the prostitute clucked her tongue. "Cap'n, is it? You'll find the Seven Bells if you turn into Church Street up ahead. There's an alley to the right, then knock on the green door between two houses."

"Thank you," said David, earning a smile.

"You know where I am. Always at your service, my pretty cap'n!" the prostitute cooed, pulling her shawl around her shoulders.

Blount and David rapidly kept walking, ready for an attack at any moment, but they reached the green door without incident. A small sign depicting seven bells, barely visible from the street, had been attached above the door knocker. The place had a mysterious air about it, a sense of the forbidden, and Blount had hardly clacked the iron knocker against the door before three young men appeared behind them.

Their elegant clothes betrayed their class, and their upper-crust accents and foolish affectations confirmed it. "Shh, gentlemen!" one of them said. "Not so loud. Use the secret knock, or they won't let us in—and that would spoil our fun!"

It was clear that the men were drunk, and David already knew they would lose anything of value in their pockets before the night was over.

Secret knock or not, the door opened, and a heavily built man with a shaved head bade them enter. He seemed to know the three young men, because he grinned when he saw them. "You're just in time, gentlemen. The big fight starts at midnight. Still time to place a bet."

The three men walked in, swaying and joshing around, passing through a dimly lit inner yard that stank of vomit and kitchen waste. Two-story buildings enclosed the yard on all sides. Light shone from several top-floor windows, and an open door led down to a kitchen. Cutlery clattered and someone shouted, "Bring me the rice pot, you lummox!"

From a large barroom beside the kitchen came the sounds of music and laughter, dice cups clacking, and a woman singing loudly off-key. Beneath this hodgepodge of sounds, however, David could make out another sound, a kind of squealing or squeaking. Next he heard dogs barking, only to fall silent again, and he knew what that meant: the big draw that night would begin soon.

"Rats!" Blount muttered as they followed the three men and the doorman to the building opposite where they'd entered.

"What's your pleasure tonight, gentlemen?" the doorman asked David and Blount. "Dice? Gambling? Women? We've got something to suit every taste!" the doorman boasted, not without pride.

Ahead of them, the three men swayed through the door of the teeming bar and threw their arms in the air enthusiastically. "There she is! I told you she was waiting for you."

A young prostitute sidled up to the three men, managing to cast David a lascivious look in the process. Stretching far into the depths of the building, the room was divided into screened-off sections. The furnishings were shabby, and the place was rancid with the vapors emitted by people who drank too much, washed too little, and broke out in a fearful sweat when they lost their money at the gambling tables. In one corner, a trio of musicians did what they could, though they were all but drowned out by the noise of the place.

Blount pointed to a table set against the wall, opposite the musicians. "Big John."

As they had learned from Rooke, the man had earned his name not because he was especially tall but because of his enormous strength. He had worked on the docks—and as a street fighter—for many years before he started organizing fights himself, pulling the strings in the background. The doorman who had escorted them inside briefly made eye contact with Big John, then turned to David and Blount. "So what's it to be?"

"Dice." David scanned the swarm of pleasure seekers, seeking out a man with a military bearing and a limp. Once a soldier, always a soldier; that particular bearing was not shaken off easily.

"You'll find three tables back there, by the red screens. Payment up front, no credit. If you want to forget, there are rooms farther back with water pipes to smoke."

"Just water pipes?" Blount said with a sarcastic edge.

Again, the doorman caught his boss's eye, then replied curtly, "Look around. Anything you want, ask the girls."

It had not escaped David that Big John was keeping an eye on them, but they had never crossed paths before. The erstwhile street fighter had a long, angular face with striking, pale-gray eyes and conspicuous, fleshy ears that had been lacerated by the bites of his opponents. It was said that for every bite he suffered, he took a piece of his rival's ear for himself.

"We should find Bill Pedley fast, Captain. I don't like the look Big John is giving us one bit," Blount said in a low voice.

"I'll go shoot dice. You have a drink and flirt with one of the girls," David said, heading over to the gambling tables.

A minute later, he was standing in the midst of drunken gamblers who couldn't see that they were being swindled left and right. The dice were loaded, but David did not say anything, instead gambling and chatting loudly to those around him, dropping comments about his old regiment and the time he'd spent in India. After an hour, his purse was considerably lighter, and there was still no sign of Pedley, nor had anyone mentioned his name, so David gave up and sat at a small table. He did not want to risk embarrassing Pedley in front of Big John, for whatever the soldier could tell him was certainly not for the ears of the sinister muscleman who ruled that little roost.

Blount had been no more successful. Visibly tense, and with a furrowed brow and alcohol on his breath, he joined David at his table. "Captain, I think we can forget about this for tonight. The girls would rather bite off their own tongues than say anything that might get them in trouble, and I don't think I can down any more beer."

Outside, a dog howled. "The fighting's about to start. These things are as brutal as the crowd that watches them," said David in disgust, standing up.

Many of the customers headed for the door. The three young men they had met earlier were among the first to make it outside. "Twenty pounds says Zeus wins tonight!" said one of them, the soft, worn lines of his face making him look much older than he probably was.

The others laughed. "Then you'd be out of the woods, Clifford. Otherwise you'll have to hope that Bill gives you an extension."

"As long as I'm not beholden to Big John."

David stopped in his tracks. "Clifford? That must be the younger Cunningham son."

"Do you know the others?" Blount asked quietly as they followed the men.

"No. Look there. *That* is the pit?" said David in surprise.

Out in the yard stood a dimly lit fighting arena that had been assembled from wooden planks. The goal was to see how long it would take a dog to kill the rats trapped inside. The floor was usually fashioned from wooden planks with all the corners sealed to stop the rats from escaping, but here a stone floor was covered with absorbent wood shavings to soak up the blood.

Already standing side by side at the pit, the three young men leaned their elbows on the wooden sides. Clifford Cunningham looked around nervously. "Where the devil is Bill?"

Other customers were still streaming into the yard, and David used the chaos to sidle up to Clifford, clapping him jauntily on the shoulder. "Clifford, old boy, isn't this a surprise! Long time, no see. How have you been?"

Clifford Cunningham seemed startled by the unexpected contact and looked David over suspiciously. His alcohol-muddled brain seemed to be struggling to remember the name of this man. He took in David's shabby suit and raised one bejeweled hand affectedly. "Have we met?"

David grinned broadly. "I should say so. We played cards at the same table in the club and had a little chat at Lord Russell's garden party. I helped you out there . . . so to speak. Captain Wescott!"

"Oh, of course!" Clifford lied, obviously embarrassed he didn't recognize David, who had invented the whole story.

"This is our first time at the Seven Bells. Which dog will do the most rats? Care to share a tip?" David asked conspiratorially.

Clifford glanced at his friends, who were gazing fixedly at the far wall of the building, where men were milling around dog cages. "Zeus, a Staffordshire terrier. He's the favorite. Unbeaten in ten fights. Bloodthirsty little bastard that bites whatever's in front of him! But not rats, oh no . . ." Clifford raised his eyebrows tellingly.

David let out a soft whistle. "Dogfights? I have to place my bet with Bill, right?"

Clifford fumbled nervously inside his vest, ostensibly looking for money. "If you've already given me a loan once, couldn't you help me again today? Only ten pounds, that's all! I'll win, you can count on it. Then you'll get back double your money."

David produced a ten-pound banknote and handed it to Clifford. "I want to meet Bill."

Tugging David by the sleeve, Clifford pulled him along with him to the cages, where several men were busy preparing the dogs, which were snarling and throwing themselves at the bars of their prisons. In the half darkness stood a smallish man, his unnaturally lopsided posture revealing him to be the man David was looking for.

"What do you want, Clifford?" the man asked. "No money, no bets." His voice was hoarse and emotionless.

David scrutinized the former soldier, a gaunt man with a hard face dominated by a large nose. A deep scar, perhaps made by a saber slash, traced across his nose and went as far as his ear.

"Here's thirty pounds. Zeus'll win, I know it, and then I'm even again. Bill, this is Captain Wescott. He wants to bet, too." Clifford spoke rapidly, pressing the banknotes into Pedley's outstretched hand.

"Captain, eh? I served in India under Governor-General Dalhousie. I was at the annexation of the Punjab, and I fought in the Burmese war. Lost my leg in the occupation of Shwedagon Pagoda. Where did you serve, Captain?" Bill Pedley straightened up proudly, supporting himself on a walking stick.

"First in India, then Crimea. Balaclava," said David.

Pedley's eyes lit up with respect. "I remember you! You spoke out against Lucan in court. Well done! How much were you wanting to wager?"

"Today I just want to watch. Could we talk later? Privately?" David asked. He had to raise his voice above the rising din. The crowd was baying for blood, the dogs were barking and howling, and the men had trouble holding the animals on their leashes.

"Why? What do you want from me, Captain?" Pedley hobbled out of his corner and signaled to the men restraining the dogs.

David leaned close to Pedley's ear. "Korshaw."

"In my office behind the cages, after the fight," Pedley growled.

What David and Blount then witnessed in the arena would have brought any man with half a heart to tears. Several times, David had to close his eyes to block the sight of the vicious curs being goaded against each other. At the end of the cruel spectacle, the wood shavings were soaked with the blood of the losing dog, its owner putting it out of its misery with a bullet. Zeus found his place in Olympus that night.

Colombia, mid-October 1860

Dear Sir Frederick,

After the encounter with the caimans, we fell into an Indian ambush and lost two bearers. I cannot say whether they were the same Indians that I saw at the mission station. The little devils shot at us with poison arrows, and we can count ourselves lucky to have survived at all. Thinking back on it now, they probably wanted no more than to drive us out of their territory.

Who can blame them? There are far too many orchid hunters whose methods can only be described as despicable, and who, at the merest suspicion that a certain tree might house the valuable plants, will have the entire tree felled. And if they don't cut it down, then they cut off all the branches and leave dying plants behind. My worthy lord, I know of collectors who gather thirty or forty plants in a week by such ruthless methods, counting themselves satisfied come Sunday. Behind them are patches of forest once rich in orchids, now ravaged, not even fostering any timber of value.

The Indians were certainly successful in driving us back. We were forced to leave the dead bearers behind in the jungle, along with much of our equipment. Dennis is too weak to carry any more than his satchel and the baskets, but I was at least able to save the instruments and drawings. The conditions are stacked so much against us now, I have called off our search for the black orchid.

We have therefore left the jungle and returned to our original route, in search of the Motilone Indians. We came to a village on the edge of the Sierra de Perijá, the northern cordillera, and discovered that the Motilones had a settlement on the other side of the mountains, on Lake Maracaibo. This means that once again we have to pass through warring regions and, worse, cross those accursed mountains one more time.

Passing through these different climatic zones multiple times in a few weeks takes its toll on the body. In the lowlands, we have the tierra caliente, *then the milder* tierra templada *up to an altitude of perhaps six thousand feet, and above that the cold* tierra fria. *Then one has to add the effects of wind and rain that seem to afflict us whenever we traverse those narrow mule tracks in the mountains.*

We found acceptable accommodations in our village at the foot of the cordilleras. The horror of what we had so recently experienced in the jungle was still with us. Dennis had a new attack of fever, and I wanted to send him to the nearest harbor, but there is no one here who could take him with them. The route over the mountains seems a more likely course of action than trying to navigate the river delta alone, where the usual dangers of the tropics would be waiting for him.

Strangely enough, we are not the only white men to have stopped here in recent days. If I am to believe the descriptions of the local people, then Mungo Rudbeck has also been here! Can you believe it? First he beats us to the mission station, and now he has apparently decided to take the same detour to find the Motilone Indians. Where else could he possibly be headed? And was he also attacked by the hostile Indians in the jungle and driven out? Why didn't they kill him with their poison arrows . . . then I would at least have one less thing to worry about. Please forgive my un-Christian thoughts, but here in the wilderness it is difficult to adhere to the moral standards we know otherwise.

In these far-reaching and hostile territories, where neither animal nor human nor nature itself is well-disposed toward outsiders, one finds oneself thinking the most horrible things. Sometimes, hell seems a place like the jungle, or perhaps like the wild, caiman-filled river, where the beasts wait for your raft to fall apart beneath you so that they can satisfy their eternal hunger. You may not want to know at all how I feel inside, but writing these things helps me keep my sanity. So please excuse me, as your faithful orchid hunter, when I report on the misgivings from which I suffer, and which at times make my days unbearably long.

Particularly torturous is the fact that the black orchid is practically within reach. I am certain that I was not imagining what I saw that evening at the mission station. The necklace the old Indian wore included a black orchid! Once I have successfully secured the Sobralia mystica *and brought it safely to Maracaibo, I will assemble a stronger crew and venture back into the territory of those antagonistic Indians! To allow me to do that, I ask you to transfer an amount of two hundred pounds to the El Mirador in Maracaibo. I cannot contrive such an undertaking without suitable equipment and arms. If I find no money waiting, then I will board the next ship back to England. I expect our expedition over the cordillera to the Motilones to take two weeks.*

The ascent took us three days. José remains with us and is a great help. Dennis is a fine companion, and it would have pained me to lose that intelligent young man. He positively flourishes here in the mountains. The climate is considerably more pleasant than in the jungle, although we are well aware that we will soon be confronted again with the damp heat of the lowlands. Two mules and four bearers are now traveling with us, putting a strain on my financial reserves. The men are stoic cordillera Indians with broad faces. They keep to themselves, saying little, and our agreement is that they are only to accompany us as far as the Motilone territory. We will need to find new bearers there.

These tight-lipped mountain goats, as I call the Indians—for they climb these dizzyingly steep crags with an inborn surefootedness—are our guides along the centuries-old paths. Generations of wanderers have formed these routes, although they remain barely visible. We have walked alongside deep ravines and sheer cliffs, and at times the trail has been so precipitous as to make me feel faint. At one point, our path took us alongside a wild mountain stream between ever-steeper walls of red sandstone and white limestone.

Many times, we found ourselves on paths no more than a yard across, gazing into gorges thousands of feet deep! The mules, however, are as unlikely to stumble as the cordillera Indians. I have learned that one must simply give the beasts a free rein, for they know best of all where to put their feet.

On the fourth morning, we broke camp early, and the sun flooded the plains of the llanos, as they call the rich alluvial lowlands here in Venezuela. It wasn't long before we finally reached the pass through the High Sierra. A cold wind constantly blows there, and we wrapped ourselves in our ponchos. The rocky range divides the lowlands of the Río Magdalena from the lowlands around Maracaibo Lake like a gigantic wall. And let me tell you, my dear Sir Frederick, the view from the top was sublime!

Using the telescope, I surveyed the glorious natural spectacle unfolding before me. It was a hazy morning, and the horizon blurred in the distance. Somewhere in that direction lay the southern shore of Lake Maracaibo.

"From here, it is at least sixty miles to the shore," I said to Dennis. He was standing beside me, and I handed him the telescope.

The Indians had made themselves comfortable in the shade of a rocky wall and were chewing on jerky. They had no interest in pretty views. They knew all those wilds, they lived inside them, and the kind of idleness we know—when, for example, we pick up a sketch pad and attempt to capture what we see—was alien to them. If I myself had a single iota of artistic talent, I would have set up my easel there and then and dipped my brush in all of the magnificent colors before my eyes.

"Look! Could it be? There, on that outcrop. Yes, there's a white man!" Dennis became immediately excited and handed me the telescope, pointing down the mountainside.

I aimed the glass at a rocky ridge below. "Damn him!" I could not help but mutter.

None other than Mungo Rudbeck was standing there, and just then, he turned around. Our eyes met, although he could certainly not have seen me, but perhaps my spectacle lenses had caught the sunlight.

"Is it him?" Dennis leaned forward, and his boots slipped from the rock. I grabbed his arm.

"He is not worth breaking your neck over." I knew that Mungo had at least two dead rivals on his conscience—if he could be said to have a conscience—but I kept that thought to myself so as not to trouble Dennis. We have to move with the utmost caution in our dealings with such a ruthless hunter. I can only hope that, in his cruelty, he does not maltreat the Motilones. On the other hand, doing so might not be such a bad idea, for then they would surely not show him their holy orchid.

Until I have more news to relate, I remain,

Your faithful servant,

Derek Tomkins

17.

Winton Park, Northumberland, December 1860

Jane entered the dining room with Charlotte, who had clearly gone to great trouble with her clothes. But even her fabulous midnight-blue dress and sparkling jewels could not brighten her tired eyes and pallid skin.

"Charlotte, my dear, don't you think you ought to lie down? You look so . . . ," Jane whispered, squeezing the pitiable woman's hand.

"I'm fine," said Charlotte, taking back her hand. She went to the seat at her husband's right. Sir Frederick was standing and waiting for the women to be seated.

Holding a letter in his hands, Sir Frederick seemed to be pondering something and greeted the women with an absent, "Good evening."

The table was set for four people. "Are we expecting another guest?" Jane asked, sipping a little wine.

"Pardon?" Sir Frederick glanced up. "Oh, excuse me, only our good Dr. Cribb. He should arrive any minute . . . he'll be staying overnight. But please, let's begin."

The butler supervised the serving of the oxtail soup. Their tardy dinner guest arrived just as the fried oysters were being brought to the table.

"Please excuse my lateness. I was delayed in Allenton with two cases. A red-hot iron fell on the blacksmith's foot, and the Gladstaines lost their youngest. A sudden death." Dr. Cribb sat down beside Jane, seeming happy to finally drink a glass of wine.

"A girl or a boy?" Jane asked.

"A girl. Delicate little thing. I don't know why, but it happens from time to time. The children suffocate in their sleep and no one can do anything about it." The doctor held his drained glass up to the butler, who refilled it with red wine.

Holding a napkin to her mouth, Charlotte suppressed a sob. "How terrible! Those poor parents. Do we know the Gladstaines?"

Sir Frederick raised his head and frowned in annoyance. "They are villagers, Charlotte. Why would we know them? Pull yourself together."

"But a tender, lonely little soul has passed on. Oh, God, when I think of our own little angels . . . Dr. Cribb, who are the Gladstaines, and do they have enough money for a white coffin and ostrich feathers? That would be the least we could do." Charlotte was more upset than Jane had ever seen her before. Jane doubted very much whether the parents' pain would be lessened by wealthy people adding white ostrich feathers to their children's graves.

"My lady, they are not well off. They are simple workers." Cribb pried an oyster out of its shell.

"Then I will have white ostrich feathers and a white dress sent to them for their daughter's funeral," Charlotte said with resolve.

Suddenly, there was a loud crash behind Charlotte, and glass shattered. She let out a sharp cry and her hands flew to her throat.

"It was just a picture, Charlotte. Please, calm down!" Sir Frederick looked over at the sideboard, on which a still life of flowers had fallen, knocking over plates and glasses as it did so. The nail that had held it up hung halfway out of the wall. "Draycroft, take care of that quickly and quietly."

The butler nodded and brought in two maids, who set to work clearing away the debris. Sensing what was coming next, Jane watched Charlotte, and Charlotte did indeed set aside her napkin with shaking fingers.

Her lips quivering, and speaking in a hoarse whisper, she said, "A picture fell from the wall just as we were talking about the child's death. Don't you see what this means?"

Sir Frederick's expression clouded. He smacked the flat of his hand vigorously against the table. "Enough, Charlotte. I don't want to hear a word of your superstitious gibberish!"

But Charlotte looked right through him, her eyes gazing at another world that only she could see. "No, no, someone will die. One of us is next. I have to go to the children!"

She suddenly stood up, knocking over her chair, and ran from the room. Sir Frederick, who gave no sign of following his wife, calmly turned to the doctor. "Would you check on her, please?"

The doctor was already on his feet. "Of course, sir."

Jane had no doubt that Charlotte would not accept her help. What was she supposed to say, anyway? She was not superstitious and put little store in the kind of dubious wisdom that said, for example, that an owl seen in daylight foretold an imminent death, as did a single snowflake in the garden or a bird pecking at your window.

"My lady, what must you think of us? But that *is* why you're here, isn't it? To study us?" Sir Frederick held the carafe of wine in one hand. "Wine?"

"Please." She watched as the crimson liquid filled her glass.

Sir Frederick set the carafe on the white tablecloth. A drop of the wine ran down over the carafe's bulbous body and stained the cloth red.

"What do think that signifies? Another death?" He ran one finger around the rim of his glass.

"Red on white? Like red and white flowers, which should never appear together in the same vase? No, Sir Frederick, I believe only in what I can see and understand. I grew up in the countryside, and as a result I have rather a practical outlook on life. And you?"

The tinkling of glass accompanied the cleaning up going on behind Sir Frederick.

Her host picked up the letter he'd been reading before dinner. "I cannot claim to talk much with women. They tend to be irrational and are generally incapable of logical thinking, but you appear remarkably disciplined, my lady."

Jane raised her eyebrows in amusement. "Coming from you, I guess I should take that as a compliment, but I do not want to seem presumptuous."

"So, my lady, what is it you hope to find here? Since you have been here, you've been sniffing around my servants, asking questions about the disappearance and now the tragic death of the maid from Crookham."

"Is it so hard to understand that one might wonder what happened to the poor girl? I came here because Alison asked me to. She herself was already concerned about Rachel. I simply did a good friend a favor," Jane said, and smiled sweetly.

"Lady Alison. Yes, that was an unfortunate turn of events. I feel very sorry for her, please believe me. What woman would want to be confined to bed so far from home and family in that, uh, condition?" He was clearly uncomfortable talking about women's matters. "You asked me where I obtain my orchids. Well, here is a letter from the orchid hunter I commissioned. For the last several months, Derek Tomkins has been in South America, or more precisely, in Colombia."

"That must be extremely expensive, sending someone off on such a journey, searching for rare flowers in foreign lands. And not the safest journey, either."

"Men like Tomkins thrive on danger and adventure. When I read his letters, I feel myself cast back to a time in which I myself traveled widely." Sir Frederick handed her the letter. "Please. Read it if you like."

Jane did not have to be asked twice. Taking the letter, she read what the orchid hunter had written about the cordilleras and hostile Indians in the jungle. "A black orchid? Are there really black flowers? I thought that was impossible?"

"But why? We have berries that are black. Why shouldn't flowers also produce such a color?" He reached for the pages, and she handed them back.

"And what if Tomkins made a mistake, and the Indian was not wearing a black orchid after all?"

"A man like Tomkins doesn't make mistakes. He has a reputation to protect, and besides, I will pay him handsomely if he brings me the black orchid. With an orchid like that, I would win every prize there is. It would be a gift fit for a queen."

"If I were superstitious, I would say that a black flower would be a harbinger of misfortune," Jane said with a small smile.

Sir Frederick looked at her with an unfathomable expression. "Are we not all responsible for our own fortunes or misfortunes?"

"And what about curses? Do you believe in those? There are items of jewelry—blue diamonds, for example—that are said to bring down catastrophe on their owners."

"Well, I'm just going to have to risk an old Indian putting a curse on me because I've had my man steal his orchid." For the first time, his lips curled slightly in amusement. "For a woman, your thinking actually seems quite rational."

Jane swallowed a sarcastic reply; the pompous man was so enamored of himself that he actually believed women devoid of intellect. He was probably one of those men who asserted that studying at university would make a woman sick. *But one day,* thought Jane, *one day the tide will turn.*

Sir Frederick turned and addressed the butler. "When *will* the next course be served? Draycroft, fetch the doctor."

The main course was a game dish, and then came cheese and brandy pudding for dessert. The doctor ate heartily and drank his fill of the wine. By the time the port was served, his cheeks were red and his speech was starting to slur. "My compliments to your chef, Sir Frederick! I haven't had such good brandy pudding for many a year."

"Such a pity that Charlotte had to abandon us. How is she, Doctor?" Jane laid her napkin aside. "Could I go cheer her up?"

"Peace and quiet and sleep are what she needs for now. She was very upset indeed about her son. When is Cedric supposed to leave for boarding school?" Dr. Cribb licked the port from his lips.

"In the new year. And my wife's hysterical behavior will not alter that one bit. The boy needs a firm hand, but Charlotte will still have Eleanor, whom she can spoil all she likes. Doctor, I would like to discuss something with you." Sir Frederick stood and the two guests followed his lead. "Lady Jane, it was my pleasure. I wish you a comfortable night's sleep."

"Pardon me," she said, her skirts rustling. "The funeral is tomorrow. When will the ceremony begin?"

"At ten. But we shall not be attending," said Sir Frederick, his tone level.

Jane smiled gently. "I will be. Good night."

18.

London, December 1860

David could not have said if it was the crowd baying at the bloody carnage of the dogfight or the suffering of the dogs sacrificed for the greed of their owners that troubled him more. He returned to the bar-room, threw down a whisky, then went back to the yard where Blount was waiting for him.

Blount, his loyal companion, rarely lost his composure and never his control. "Captain, Clifford and his friends have just left. He was very upset; he's deeper in debt to Bill now than ever before. He may try to tap his father for money, I don't know."

David pushed his hands into his coat pockets. Now that most of the crowd had left the yard, the chill in the air was more evident. The arena had been dismantled as quickly as it had been set up, and all that was left as witness to the slaughter was a pile of blood-soaked wood shavings.

"Most likely Cunningham will pay off Clifford's debts. He's a gambler and womanizer himself, so it would be odd if he didn't help his son out. Having said that, I know nothing about the state of Cunningham's finances—which would be good to know. So this is where Bill's office is supposed to be? It smells like a cesspool."

"It's the rats, Captain." Blount pointed to a dark corner where stacked wooden cages held hundreds of squirming, squeaking rats. Behind the cages lay piles of rodent corpses killed by the dogs.

"I wouldn't be surprised if the plague broke out around here." David pressed his scarf to his mouth and pushed open a door leading to a short corridor and some stairs. Light was shining from inside a door to their right.

"Captain? I'm in here," Bill Pedley called. "Come in, and close the door."

Blount pushed the door to the courtyard closed with his foot and looked around, but apart from them there was no one in sight. From the floor above came the unmistakable sounds of prostitutes and their clients.

"Charming place," Blount muttered.

David let out a small cough and entered the room that Pedley had grandly called his office, but which was really little more than a large storeroom. There was room for a table and two chairs and a tall cupboard, and in a corner stood a chest wrapped with iron bands, probably where Pedley kept his take.

The military veteran was sitting behind the desk, where papers and account books were piled. "Even in my field, accounts must be kept. So, Captain, what can I do for you? Keep it short. And if Big John puts his head in, my lips are sealed."

Fair enough, thought David. "I've heard you knew Korshaw. I want to know all about the man."

Leaning back in his chair, Pedley crossed his hands over his chest. In the oil lamp's flickering light, the notch across his nose appeared even more furrowed. "So you work for the police, Captain? A backward step, isn't it? From war hero to police spy?"

David ignored the insult. "There's more going on here than the death of the gardener, or do I have that wrong?"

Pedley leaned forward and motioned David closer. "Far, far more. Korshaw was a miserable little rat who double-crossed everyone. Every time he opened his mouth, a lie came out. Nothing new . . . he was already that way in Madras."

David stood, planting his hands on the table, leaning forward to catch Pedley's hoarse whisper. Blount was watching the front door and corridor. "Madras? What was he doing there? Was he a plant hunter?"

"Him? Ha!" Pedley laughed drily. "He'd never have risked his neck in the jungle, the cowardly, scheming cur. No, he was an agent for the East India Company. He did business with the locals and sold what he got to the English. He made money at both ends and was not above letting a deal fall through at the last minute if he'd worked out a better one with someone else."

"Why would a man like that return to London and take a job in a plant nursery?"

The veteran twisted his thin lips in a harsh grin. "The higher you fly, the farther you fall. I don't know for sure what happened at the nursery. He apparently left India before the Sepoy Rebellion, and it was probably good that he did, or sooner or later he would have ended up feeding the crocodiles there. When I met him in Madras, his star was already fading, and I'd already lost my leg. He became acquainted with an English couple who wanted to go to Burma. The man, who'd also been a soldier, wanted to try his hand at collecting plants, and that was Korshaw's introduction to orchids."

Blount stepped outside, then quickly returned. "We've got company."

"Who were the English couple? Do you remember their names? Did Korshaw go to Burma with them?" David asked rapidly.

"They were traveling by ship from Calcutta to Bassein. I remember that clearly enough, because I toyed with the idea myself, but my leg was giving me trouble. Hunting for orchids in Burma sounded like a lucrative business, although I didn't see Korshaw as an adventurer. But he went ahead with it anyway . . ."

The sound of several voices came from the corridor, and Pedley said, "I'll take a look in my papers at home. I've still got a letter from Korshaw that he sent from Burma. I know he wrote about the English couple in it."

David gave him his card, and Pedley immediately stashed it in his jacket pocket. "So, that's that," Pedley said, louder. "Same place next week, gentlemen."

"You don't live here, do you?" David whispered.

"God forbid. Queen Street 21."

The door flew open and Big John stalked in, followed by his doorman. "What's goin' on here? Have these gentlemen not paid what they owe?"

"On the contrary. They're here for the first time, and I'm sure they will soon count among our regulars. Thank you, gents!" Pedley nodded, a signal for David and Blount to leave.

Close up, Big John's muscle-packed shoulders were even more impressive. Likewise, the doorman was not someone David would pick a fight with. Only when they were back in the dark alley did David and Blount breathe more freely again.

"I don't like that one bit, Captain. Not one bit!" Blount had his revolver drawn, his eyes scanning their surroundings.

The doorways and windows of the buildings were dark on all sides, and the gas lantern on the main street down the way was the only source of light. They listened to the murmurings of the city around them, a motley of human and animal sounds muffled by the mantle of night. A rat scuttled through the filth underfoot, and another crawled up the wall of a house. The men could see their breath in the cold air as clearly as the columns of smoke rising from the chimneys. Somewhere, a woman cried, and a child whimpered.

"We'll look for a coach. I recall a stand two streets ahead," said David as they continued toward the main street.

But this was not Grosvenor Square. It was St. Giles, a quarter of London forgotten by God. Anyone out after midnight did not hesitate long.

Both men heard the sounds at the same time. Without a word, they positioned themselves back to back and planted their feet. The noises might easily have been dismissed as the scrabbling of rats, but the closer they came, the more clearly they could be heard as shoes on cobblestones.

David held his knife in his left hand, his revolver in his right. "How many?"

"Three," Blount whispered. "Two on my side, one coming your way . . ."

There was a dull scrape, and someone jumped onto a ledge above their heads, preparing to attack from above. With no time left to think, Blount fired his revolver at the first attacker. A second shot rang out, and a third. A hot pain jolted through David's arm and knocked the revolver out of his hand. Gritting his teeth, David gripped his knife tighter and waited for the dark figure stealthily advancing on him. He was a soldier, experienced in open battle. He hated snipers and ambushes, and these fighters were accomplished in that kind of fighting. His attacker dodged back and forth without a word. A blade flashed, and David instinctively parried.

His wounded right arm slowed his reactions, and he felt blood trickling into his hand. Blount snarled, letting out a triumphant curse. David heard a choking groan but was struggling to defend himself from the agile, catlike motions of his own attacker; finally he managed a strike to the man's gut and felt his blade sink deep into his enemy's body. Teeth flashed and a hoarse voice uttered, "*Urod!*" before the men melted away into the darkness and the whole horrific episode was over.

David and Blount stood side by side, breathing heavily, listening for further sounds in the darkness, then finally propping their hands on their thighs, exhausted. “Damn it! Someone wanted to teach us a lesson, Captain.”

David nodded and groaned as he moved his arm.

“One of those mongrels shot you!” After collecting the weapons on the ground and pushing them into his belt, Blount urged David forward. “We have to get out of here. They might try again.”

The entire attack had lasted a matter of two or three minutes, and no faces had appeared at any of the windows around them. Even the gunshots had not lured the curious out of their houses. There was so much misery and crime in St. Giles that the inhabitants were busy simply trying to survive. Taking time to look after the lives of others was a luxury they did not have. All the same, David and Blount felt eyes on them as they walked to the main street, continuing along the road until they found a coach whose driver was prepared—for what he termed an exorbitant “night fee”—to drive them.

Sitting in the half-open hansom cab, Blount wanted to check David’s arm, but David demurred. “It will see me home.”

Blount persisted. “I could at least bandage it, Captain.” Still feeling blood flowing over his hand, David finally assented, pushing off his coat. A stab of pain made him draw a sharp breath.

With practiced movements, Blount cut open David’s shirt and bound the deep bullet wound with the remnants of the sleeve. David shivered. The frosty night air was draining the warmth from his body, already weakened by blood loss. “Thank you, Blount . . . they were Russians.”

“Yes, and I don’t even have to ask Levi for a translation.” “Urod” was a word they knew from the Crimean War that meant something like “bastard.”

“Do you suppose it was Big John? Bill?” David wrapped his coat around himself. The coach bumped loudly over the empty night streets, glittering in the lamplight.

“Because we were asking about Korshaw? Unlikely.”

The hansom cab went down the length of Oxford Street as far as Orchard Street, turning there and arriving at David's house in Seymour Street minutes later. David climbed out with relief, letting Blount pay the driver, and was met at the door by an anxious-looking Levi.

"Oy, dear Lord, what's happened to you? Should I call a doctor?"

"No, no. They do more damage than good. Blount will tell you what's needed. Put some water on." Going into the small living room, David let his coat fall to the floor and sank into an armchair.

It wasn't long before Blount came in, followed by Levi and Ruth, the cook. Ruth carried a tray of clean towels, two knives, a pair of tweezers, needles and thread, and a whisky bottle. "I'll fetch the water. It must be hot enough by now, sir."

She looked sympathetically at David then hurried away. A shadow hovered about the doorway. The street urchin, Myron, had apparently followed Ruth from the kitchen, where he liked to curl up on the bench beside the stove to sleep.

When Blount spotted the young boy, he dragged him in by his ear. "What are you doing here, boy? Looking for something to pinch?"

"No, sir, no!" Myron cried. "I'd never do that. The captain rescued me and took me in. No one was ever so nice to me!"

"Leave him alone," David growled between clenched teeth. Then he groaned, because even the slightest movement sent a shock of pain through his arm and shoulder.

"Laudanum, Captain?" Blount asked, rolling up his sleeves.

"No. I hate that stuff. Give me the whisky bottle; that will have to do." David took several large swigs then leaned back in the armchair. "Get started. You know what to do."

As expected, the bullet was still in the wound. David trusted Blount's skills as a field surgeon, which he had proven more than once. When the bullet was out and the wound cleaned, Blount picked up the needle and thread.

"This is unavoidable, Captain. Laudanum after all?"

David swallowed more whisky and shook his head. "Come on, let's get it over with."

The cook stood on David's other side, wiping his forehead with a damp cloth. Levi collected the bloody clothes and rags and laid out David's dressing gown. David knew that he could count himself lucky to have servants who were not only obedient but also devoted to him, but he missed Jane. With the second stitch, David closed his eyes, gripped an arm of the chair, and swore to himself that he would be more careful in the future. How could he lecture Jane about her frivolous undertakings if he let himself fall into traps like that, like a beginner?

Abruptly, he opened his eyes, reaching again for the bottle. "That was a trap, Blount!"

His loyal companion tied off the threads and bandaged the wound. He examined his handiwork with satisfaction. "We should consult a doctor tomorrow about the possibility of gangrene, Captain. A trap? What do you mean?"

"Thank you for that." David exhaled and allowed Levi to help him into his dressing gown. "Rooke sent us in there after getting a lead. What if that was exactly what they had been hoping for?"

"Who are 'they'?" Blount washed his blood-smeared hands in a bowl then dried them.

"If only I knew, but I can't think clearly anymore. Tomorrow, Blount. Let's get to bed now." Out in the hall, the clock struck four times.

"Good night, sir," said Ruth. "We are very happy to have you back again. Can I make you a hot drink or bring you something to eat?"

But David only murmured good night as he trudged toward the stairs.

19.

Winton Park, Northumberland, December 1860

Jane was already dressed and adjusting the black veil on her hat when a bloodcurdling scream filled the house, making the fine hairs on her neck stand on end.

Hettie, also wearing black, had been brushing off Jane's coat, but stopped abruptly when the scream rang out. "Good God, what was that?"

"Ally!" Her thoughts turning first to her friend, Jane ran out of the room, followed closely by Hettie. Out in the corridor, she saw Ally's maid looking around in alarm, which unsettled Jane.

"What was that?" Nora asked.

Hettie now trotted after another maid who had just appeared at a room farther down the corridor. "Della! Wait!"

"I have to fetch the laundry, miss." Della tried to go, but Hettie pulled her back.

"But what's happened? Someone screamed."

"Oh, the young master suddenly came down sick!" Della stared at the floor unhappily. "I wish I'd never come to this house." She hurried away.

Approaching them, Jane overheard their exchange. She kept walking until she reached the family wing, within listening distance of the children's room. Miss Molan's sharp voice as well as the doctor's voice filtered out from behind the door, and she heard Charlotte whimpering and sobbing miserably. The boy had seemed a picture of health when last Jane saw him. Had he had an accident?

When the door to the children's room opened and Miss Molan stepped out, Jane went to her. "Can I help at all?"

The governess was pale and seemed shaken. "The poor boy, the poor boy," she murmured, her voice barely audible.

"What's going on?"

Miss Molan raised her head and looked at Jane with a mixture of horror and sympathy. "The mother . . . oh, who could . . ." The young woman suddenly clutched Jane by the arms, wide-eyed. "When a mother is capable of something like that, God help her child."

"For heaven's sake, speak! Tell me what's happened!"

Miss Molan released her and wiped her eyes. "She tried to poison him. I'm not allowed to say that, but that's what it was, my lady. His own mother, oh, that is a tragic turn. Oh no, oh no . . ." Covering her face with her hands, she rushed away.

Hettie, who was standing behind Jane, said softly, "Ma'am, I can't believe that. Not Lady Charlotte. She loves her children!"

The door to Charlotte's room opened, and Dr. Cribb stepped out. "Doctor, please, Miss Molan has just given us a terrible fright."

The doctor cleared his throat. He seemed to be searching for the right words. "Lady Charlotte has suffered a nervous breakdown. I have sedated her with laudanum, but her son is of greater concern to me. He seems to have eaten or drunk something that has left him in a comatose state. It happens sometimes that children will chew on something and accidentally poison themselves, but it's highly unusual, really. This is not the time of year for belladonna or goldenrod."

"Cedric was poisoned? But he's alive?" Jane asked anxiously.

The doctor nodded thoughtfully. "He is delicate, but he has a hardy constitution, like his father. I wish I knew what he ate, then I could prescribe an appropriate remedy. For now all we can do is wait and pray." He gave Jane a sympathetic look. "Go to the young maid's funeral, my lady. There's nothing you can do here, but in church you can pray for Cedric."

St. Michael and All Angels lay before them, enshrouded in frosty morning mist above the River Coquet. The river flowed languidly through fields, its surface frozen where its waters spread and grew shallow. The small church was an architectural novelty consisting of three structures, nestled together and ascending in size like stairs, a place of refuge and consolation that had grown over the centuries. The village itself had fewer than sixty inhabitants, including the elderly and the very young. In winter especially, life in those rugged hills took its toll on the people who lived there. *No different here than in remote Cornwall,* thought Jane. But were the cities any easier for the poor?

The congregation that had gathered for Rachel's funeral was small, but at least Sir Frederick had provided for a decent burial. Jane was surprised to find that Rachel was to be buried in Allenton and not in Crookham.

"Look, ma'am, Zenada and Sally are up front," said Hettie quietly as they passed through the lower nave of the church.

The simple coffin had been set in front of stairs leading up to a raised altar. A protestant minister was standing beside a pulpit, and he came to meet them when they entered.

"My lady, it is an honor to welcome you to our house of worship." The minister was of average height, a stocky man with a friendly smile.

In a small village, new arrivals never went unnoticed, so it came as no surprise to Jane that he already knew who she was. What was disconcerting, however, was that no one else from Winton Park was in attendance. The thought had hardly occurred to her before the church door opened and O'Connor and Miss Molan entered. The gamekeeper and the governess, certainly an honor for a young maid.

After the service, members of the congregation each took a handful of earth and threw it onto the coffin in the open grave. It must have been a huge effort for the men to dig a hole like that in the frozen earth. Two young village lads stood off to one side, leaning on shovels, waiting to finish their sad work.

Alison had asked Jane to bring some flowers on her behalf, and Jane and Hettie each tossed two orchids onto the coffin. The cream-colored blooms drifted into the pit like giant snowflakes, landing gently atop the wooden cover. Overhead, the sky had grown cloudy, and a chill wind blew through the cemetery. The bare branches of the surrounding trees creaked and sighed as if proclaiming their sorrow at the miseries of human life.

Wrapped in a black shawl, Zenada seemed aloof and almost stony in her grief. She was supported by her daughter, Sally, who called Jane over. "My mother would like to say something to you."

The minister stood with O'Connor and Miss Molan a short distance away.

"My sincere sympathies, Mrs. Bertram, Sally." Jane wanted to take the grieving mother's hand, but when the woman made no sign of uncrossing her arms, she thought better of it.

"Have you been able to find out anything about my daughter's death, my lady?" Zenada's voice was a raw, dark whisper that mixed with the wind soughing through the old gravestones and Celtic crosses.

They were standing on historical ground. Romans had invaded these parts, subjugating the inhabitants, and Scots had fought here for their freedom. Today, a Roma woman was wondering why her daughter had met a violent death in the service of English nobility. *And apart from me,* thought Jane, *no one seems to have any serious interest in finding that out.*

"Not yet, but your daughter was an honorable young woman. I can assure you of that." At the very least, Jane wanted to give Rachel's mother that consolation.

"God preserve you, my lady."

The proud woman and her daughter left the graveyard slowly, and the two young men with the shovels began to fill the grave. The minister said good-bye to Jane and Hettie at the gate, and Jane spotted O'Connor and Miss Molan speaking together, then Miss Molan walking alone toward the village.

"My lady." O'Connor tapped his cap and stood in front of Jane with his hands in his pockets.

"Where is Miss Molan going? Shouldn't we take her back to the house with us?"

"I've no idea, but I shall be driving her back later. She wants to meet somebody. Thank you for coming here, my lady."

"I consider it my duty," Jane replied. "Lady Charlotte would certainly have come, too, if she were well enough."

O'Connor cleared his throat. "Terrible thing, with the boy."

"What did Miss Molan tell you?" Jane asked, flipping the fur-lined collar of her coat against the icy wind.

"That Cedric was apparently poisoned, and because Lady Charlotte doesn't want to send the boy to boarding school, one could easily imagine that—"

"That she deliberately poisoned her own child? A serious allegation, and one for which there is no proof."

Hettie, who had been uneasily looking up and down the street, said quietly, "I'm going to the alehouse, ma'am. I'm cold out here."

Both of them knew that Hettie wanted to keep an eye on Miss Molan, and Jane nodded her assent.

"And I must leave as well," said O'Connor. "Something in Winton Park is off, my lady, so off that it stinks to high heaven, if you know what I mean." O'Connor nodded. "I wish you a pleasant day."

What was he trying to say? That even women in the higher reaches of the nobility were capable of committing a crime? Gathering up her skirts, Jane set off after Hettie. The frozen ground crunched beneath her boots, and she caught up with Hettie within a couple of minutes.

"There you are, ma'am. Miss Molan's just gone into the Trout Inn." Hettie hesitated.

"We wanted to eat anyway, didn't we? Let's see if the trout they serve does justice to the name."

There was nothing in Allenton to justify a visit from travelers. The Trout Inn was the best of a disenchanting clutch of impoverished houses. Sir Frederick was the owner of the land they had been built on and therefore responsible for the houses of his lessees, but instead of enhancing the properties, his income was diverted buying expensive orchids or sent abroad to Colombia.

From the outside, the building looked skewed, its black wooden beams leaning considerably. It was not much better from the inside. Stinking of rancid grease and damp walls, the ceilings were so low that Jane was on constant lookout lest she bang her head. Squeaking shadows scurried along the walls, spoiling any appetite Jane might otherwise have had.

At one end of the room, which held six tables in all, was an open fireplace, welcoming enough for visitors to overlook the general lack of comfort and cleanliness.

"Oh!" Hettie cried happily as she flopped onto a chair in front of the fire and lifted her skirts.

"Careful, Hettie, or you'll catch your dress on fire!"

Two men with frozen faces were spooning down soup and drinking beer at a nearby table. There was no sign of Miss Molan.

"Excuse me, gentlemen, did a young woman in a black dress come in just now?" Jane asked the men, who looked like cattle herders.

The men looked at each other and grinned. "Another one?"

"I'm going!" called a woman's voice, then an older woman carrying a tray stumbled into the room.

Mugs and a pitcher swayed ominously, but the woman managed to set her tray down safely on a table. "Everyone in black today, and all of 'em oh-so-fine. Must've been someone big to bring such fine sorts out here. D'you want something to eat? We've still got soup, and we've always got trout."

Hettie looked angrily at their hostess. "Do you know who you're talking to, you old hoddy doddy?"

"If she ain't the Queen, then I don't care who she is." The hostess laughed hoarsely, and her considerable bosom quaked beneath her dirty apron.

"Our Gertrude don't give a fig for social classes!" The men joined the woman in her raucous laughter.

"Forget it, Hettie. We'd like something to drink, some wine and bread. And where might I find the lavatory?" Jane asked, removing two shillings from her purse.

The woman stopped laughing instantly and held out her hand for the coins. Her straggly gray hair was tied in an untidy knot, and her face was covered in small pimples.

"Down the hall, past the kitchen, in front of the steps on yer left."

Jane nodded. "I'll be back in a minute. Wait for me here. If Zenada and Sally come in, invite them to our table."

Avoiding looking into the kitchen, she walked to the rear of the house. A wooden stairway climbed to the first floor, and the corridor to the left, judging by the smell, led to the lavatory and out to the yard. She could hear pigs and chickens outside, along with the scrape of a shovel, accompanied by cursing. Jane glanced back up the corridor and saw a scruffy man's head disappear into the kitchen. There was no one else in sight, so Jane cautiously climbed the footworn wooden stairs, which creaked with every step she took. The frosty air found its way in through the fissured masonry and rickety windows, and Jane noted the thin layer of ice that had formed on the glass and wooden surfaces inside. Finally, she reached the second floor; standing at the banister, she listened for sounds coming from the dark corridor in front of her.

"Lissy, don't make things so hard for us. It doesn't have to be like this. We'll find a way, trust me." It was the voice of Mr. Hartman.

Miss Molan said something in reply that Jane did not catch, but then she heard, ". . . and what if the boy dies?"

The floorboards on the other side of the guest room door creaked, and Jane heard the bolt slide back. She tapped down the steps again as quietly as she could and stood at the bottom.

"The doctor was there, wasn't he? He will certainly take good care of the lord's heir." Hartman's voice was deep, with the kind of unplaceable accent that Jane had heard many times from well-traveled people. It was probably only natural for people to adapt themselves linguistically to their surroundings, she thought. Maybe Hartman was from the Continent, and his profession had brought him to England. Who knew what dreams Miss Molan might harbor? Jane heard the woman's skirts rustling on the stairs.

"I hope so. You have to get to know the boy before you can like him. He's a little devil, but I know how to handle him." Miss Molan descended the last steps on Mr. Hartman's arm and almost bumped into Jane, who acted as if she were on her way to the toilet.

"Oh, Miss Molan!" Jane stopped and looked expectantly from the dismayed face of the governess to her companion. "I was just on my way to the lavatory."

Seeing him this close, Jane realized that Hartman was an attractive man. His moustache was too bushy for Jane's taste and the lines of his face too soft, but she could understand the governess's interest in him.

"This is Mr. Hartman, an old friend and a teacher," said Miss Molan. "He applied for the position of tutor for Cedric."

Hartman gave Jane a small nod.

"May I ask how you know each other?"

Hartman began to explain. "From—"

"We were both employed in the house of Sir Robert Parks's sister, some years ago," Miss Molan interrupted. "We have stayed in touch since." The woman smiled mirthlessly.

"That would be Lady Darringham? In Surrey?"

Miss Molan nodded.

"It's very nice that at least you and Mr. O'Connor were able to come to Rachel's funeral. I thought there would be more people there, that she was popular in the house?"

"She wasn't there very long. My lady, please excuse me, but I have to be getting back soon and would still like to talk with Mr. Hartman for a moment."

"You can come with me in my coach. You'll find me in the dining room. Do you have plans, Mr. Hartman?" Jane asked politely.

"Uh, yes, actually. The staffing agency has offered me two other positions. I'll be leaving tomorrow."

"Then I wish you every success with those. Best of luck!" Jane turned back toward the dining room.

"My lady, the lavatory is that way!" said Miss Molan.

"Oh, well, I've changed my mind," said Jane, screwing up her nose.

20.

As the coach bounced over the frozen ground, Jane gazed out the window, watching the snowflakes drifting ever more heavily earthward. With the frost of recent days, an icy white blanket had formed quickly over the landscape, and when they climbed out of the coach at Winton Park, Hettie looked up at the sky then at her traveling companion. Miss Molan had ended up returning with O'Connor after all.

"The snow's even staying on the roof, ma'am. I hope we're not going to see much more of this. Oh, there's the butler," she whispered to Jane as they walked. "He might be good-looking, but I don't like him."

"I don't like him very much, either, but a butler carries a heavy burden of responsibility, and with the lords of this particular manor, he doesn't exactly have an easy time of it." Jane cleared her throat and climbed the front steps. "Good day, Mr. Draycroft."

"My lady. It was very nice of you to attend the funeral." He bowed a little deeper than usual and accompanied them inside.

"How is Cedric?" Jane allowed him to take her coat.

Draycroft turned away rather awkwardly. "Not very good, my lady. We are deeply concerned about the young Lord Halston."

"And Lady Charlotte?"

"There is nothing new I can say about her. Does my lady wish for something to eat?"

Jane saw Hettie's eyes light up. "Gladly. Have tea and scones brought to my room."

"Very good, my lady."

On the way to Jane's room, they passed maids running around nervously and heard Sir Frederick's imperious voice rumbling out of an open door.

"No, Charlotte! Enough is enough. You're not in your right mind. Doctor . . ." The door slammed shut, and Hettie stared at Jane in fright.

In the seclusion of Jane's room, Hettie said, "Poor Lady Charlotte. I can't believe she would do something so horrible to her own child, but that's what her husband seems to think, isn't it?"

"That's what it sounds like, but let's not jump to conclusions." But Jane, tossing her gloves on the bed and sitting in an armchair, felt exactly the same way as her maid.

Hettie helped her out of her boots. "Lady Charlotte isn't very happy, is she?"

Jane looked at the young woman, who was concentrating on loosening her bootlaces. "I'm afraid she isn't, Hettie. Really, any halfway normal person would go insane inside this gloomy box."

"Is that it? Has she gone mad?"

Sighing, Jane held on tightly to the arms of the chair as Hettie pulled off the tight-fitting boots. "No. On the other hand, there are certainly things that we don't understand. People are capable of the cruelest acts for seemingly incomprehensible reasons. Do you recall the case of the solicitor's jealous wife? She poisoned both her daughters because her husband loved them more than he loved her."

"Terrible! The woman was hanged, wasn't she?"

"Yes, it was a tragedy . . . but Charlotte loves her children! She would not seriously risk something happening to Cedric simply to keep him with her a little longer."

"What if she thinks her son is better off sick with her than healthy at boarding school?" Hettie brushed the boots and set them aside, then went to find a fresh dress for Jane.

Hettie's words gnawed at Jane. She could hardly eat any of the scones Draycroft sent up and flinched at every sound in the hallway.

"Didn't you think it odd that, of all people, Mr. O'Connor and Miss Molan came to the funeral?" said Hettie, stacking the used saucers and plates.

"Not really. Mr. O'Connor really did seem downcast. I'm sure that he liked Rachel, and she was a very pretty girl. And Miss Molan wanted to meet Mr. Hartman. For her, the funeral was simply a good excuse to do that. I'm going to visit Ally now. You could try to speak with Della or Gladys."

Out in the corridor, Jane paused and looked across to the Halstons' wing of the house. An oppressive sense of powerlessness crept over Jane when she saw Dr. Cribb, his face grim, come out of the children's room and go into Charlotte's.

"Jane!" Alison cried from her daybed when Jane entered the room. "You're finally paying me a visit! What is going on today? No one tells me anything!"

"For good reason, dear Ally. You are not supposed to be getting upset, but I simply have to ask you about Charlotte." Jane summarized what had happened as objectively as possible.

Alison's face filled with a mix of sympathy and horrified disbelief. "Whatever you and the others might think, I'll stand by Charlotte to the ends of the earth!"

"No one likes to think that a person they love could do something like that. That's only natural. But when you think about all your times together, were there ever any . . . odd moments with Charlotte? Did she ever strike you as especially jealous or possessive?"

"You must be joking! You know how close we were as children. It's normal for young girls to be spiteful when it comes to their first love," Alison replied forcefully, but something in her tone made Jane prick up her ears.

"Spiteful?"

Running her hands over her rounded belly, Alison closed her eyes. "It doesn't necessarily mean anything, but since you're asking, and considering the circumstances, it happened one summer out at my parents' country place in Kent. Charlotte was visiting along with two other friends. I'd been looking forward to the weeks with Isabelle and Georgina very much because it was their last summer in England before leaving for India with their parents. Two lovely girls. We did painting courses together at the Royal Academy, and they were both far more talented than me!

"Isa is similar to Charlotte: shy, rather pale, but pretty. Apart from painting, we also played music together. Isa has a wonderful voice! If she had wanted, she could have joined the opera. We four girls practiced a short program to perform at a garden party. I recited a poem, Georgina and Charlotte did a pantomime, and Isa sang. It was a beautiful song. Let me think . . . yes." She hummed softly for a moment, then sang, "Now sleeps the crimson petal, now the white . . ."

Alfred, Lord Tennyson had written the poem about the transience of beauty, and it was as melancholic as it was moving. Jane nodded. "And Charlotte was jealous of Isa's voice?"

"Wait, no, no, that too, but there was a young man, Claude, a guest from France at the party. We were so young—giggly, silly little girls. But Charlotte was a bit older and took everything awfully seriously. All of us had flirted with Claude, but he liked Isabelle the best. He had dreamy, dark eyes and soft, curly hair, and he wrote love poems to Isa and secretly read them to her in the rose garden. When Charlotte found out, she surprised them both there and pretended that she had caught them doing something indecent." Alison straightened one of her pillows. "It was horrible. Isa got in terrible trouble, and Claude had to leave. Her parents thought she had lost her virginity, and she was examined by a doctor. The poor girl . . . and all because Charlotte had made such a big fuss and spread mean lies about the two of them."

"She could have destroyed both their lives!" said Jane.

"She hadn't thought that far ahead. She was jealous. Later, she wrote Isabelle a letter apologizing for what she had done, but by then the girls were already in India and had taken that dreadful memory of their last summer in England with them."

"Charlotte's actions were self-serving and scheming. I would never have thought her capable of something like that."

Downcast, Alison said, "Neither would I, Jane, believe me. We didn't see each other much after that. Charlotte got married, and it was only at her wedding that we became close again. And then we both had children, and I no longer thought about that summer."

"And now she's unhappy and doesn't want to be separated from her son," mused Jane aloud.

"Oh, Jane, we might be doing her a terrible injustice!" Alison grasped Jane's hand.

"I hope so."

There was a knock at the door, and Hettie entered carrying two envelopes. "Excuse me, ma'am, this was just delivered for you. And this one is for you, my lady."

"Oh?" Alison tore open the envelope. "How sweet, Thomas misses me. The twins are well, and he'll come collect me soon." She pressed the notepaper to her lips. "Is that from David?"

"Hmm? Yes." Jane glanced up from the short, telegraphed message and turned abruptly to Hettie, who was waiting patiently. "He's been shot!"

Hettie clapped her hand to her mouth. "But the captain will get better again, won't he?"

With a grin, Alison said, "Another woman's heart broken by our captain."

"No, my lady, I mean, I like the captain very much, but not like . . . ," Hettie stammered, blushing.

"It's all right, I know what you mean." Jane refolded the telegram. "It's not a serious wound, but he can't come up here. That, and he's also chasing down a lead—in St. Giles," Jane added gloomily.

"Well, it's no wonder someone shot him!" Alison exclaimed. "What's he doing running around such a wretched part of London? At least he tells you what he's doing. Thomas doesn't share anything about his work with me."

"Maybe because Thomas's kind of parliamentary work is deadly dull." New conflicts constantly arose between the two biggest political parties, which led to continual delays of necessary reforms. One current battleground was about the workers' right to vote. Jane shared David's opinion that everybody should have the right to vote, that anyone who worked should also have a voice in how things were run; it was only fair. "Which minister is he working for now?"

"I think he might have moved into the trade ministry. Oh, Jane, you're right. Even if he had told me, I wouldn't have remembered, but right now, it's more important that we help Charlotte."

Jane slipped the telegram into her pocket. "Good. Where's Nora?"

"She went to find some lavender for me. The scent is calming." Alison took a deep breath. "I don't think I can get through another pregnancy like this one. After this child, I need a break."

Jane kissed her friend's forehead. "Be brave. We—"

A horrible scream resounded through the house.

"I'll come back later, Ally. Hettie, follow me!"

Trailed closely by her maid, Jane ran down the corridor and across the landing to the Halstons' rooms. The doors to both the children's room and Charlotte's bedroom stood wide open. Another scream, this time gurgling and hoarse, sent a shudder through Jane, and she felt Hettie's hand on her arm.

"Oh, ma'am, something horrible must have happened . . ."

There were muffled male voices, rustling, the sounds of furniture being pushed around, then a loud crash. Charlotte tore out of her room and fell into Jane's arms.

"Dear God Almighty, hold on to her!" Sir Frederick bellowed, and the doctor swore.

Jane held the quaking Charlotte tightly in her arms. Charlotte briefly stared at her, eyes wide; her pupils were dilated, and her gaze darted about frantically, but worst of all were the scratches on her face. Bloody trails streamed down her neck and chest, which a plain day dress barely covered. The lace neckline was torn and stained with blood. Strands of her dark hair had come loose and stuck to her neck and shoulders.

"Jane, help me," Charlotte whispered, her voice breaking, before Dr. Cribb and Sir Frederick rushed out of the room and pulled her from Jane's grasp.

Now Jane realized that the doctor had probably tried to give Charlotte an injection against her will. On her right arm, the sleeve was torn, dark bruises practically glowing against her pale skin, and blood flowed from a cut.

"What are you doing to her? Why are you doing that?" Jane demanded, following the men, who had dragged her friend back into her room, Charlotte screaming like a madwoman.

In front of the bed stood an armchair, and the two men forced Charlotte to sit, then bound her to the chair with leather straps. Jane would never forget the desperate woman's screams as she fought them with all her strength. Finally, Dr. Cribb poured a clear liquid onto a cloth and pressed it to Charlotte's face; a few seconds later the convulsive movements stopped, her body went slack, and she slumped in the chair. Gladys, looking composed, stood beside the bed.

Sir Frederick stumbled back against a chest of drawers. He held on to it as if in danger of falling. His face was dappled with red spots, and the skin around his mouth was deathly white. The muscles of his jaw were twitching and, like Charlotte, he had scratches on his cheeks and neck. Blood spotted his white shirt, and his breathing was rapid.

Miss Molan appeared in the doorway. "Has she been sedated?"

"Yes! Close the door and see to the children," Sir Frederick snapped. "And not a word to anyone."

The governess still wore her black mourning clothes, which seemed strangely appropriate. Glancing quickly at Jane, she hurried out. Jane was glad that Hettie had stayed outside, because the sight of Charlotte like this—injured and unconscious—was hard to bear. Her damaged body lay unnaturally in the chair, like a broken doll, her limbs held in place by the straps.

"We can untie her now." Jane tried to reach Charlotte but was immediately stopped by Sir Frederick's thundering voice.

"Don't touch my wife! She's caused enough trouble for today. And you will keep your nose out of this business." Sir Frederick pushed himself away from the chest of drawers and grasped Jane's shoulder in a painfully tight grip.

Though she cried out, it seemed not to bother Sir Frederick in the slightest. "And not a word about this, my lady, from you, either! This concerns me and my wife, no one else. Have I made myself clear?" He glared at her threateningly.

"Let go of me, Sir Frederick. I am your guest and you're hurting me!"

He released her, but his expression lost none of its threat. "This marriage has brought me nothing but misfortune." Suddenly, he turned away and buried his face in his hands. His shoulders heaved with stifled sobs.

Dr. Cribb checked Charlotte's breathing then came over to Jane. Gently taking her arm, he led her to the door. "Please go, my lady, there's nothing you can do here."

"But—"

"That woman is a danger to herself and to her children. Believe me, it's better if you leave now," the doctor insisted, trying to push her out the door.

"You want to lock Charlotte away, don't you? You're not going to take her to one of those disgusting asylums!" Jane braced herself against the door.

"She is ill and will be treated accordingly. Please don't make this any more difficult than it already is." Dr. Cribb's face brooked no protest.

When the door closed in Jane's face, tears of rage and concern brimmed in her eyes. She was never more painfully aware of her powerlessness than at that moment. Here in this stranger's house, she was no more than a guest to be tolerated, only a woman, someone who, when it came down to it, would not be believed, her words being ascribed instead to hysteria.

21.

London, December 1860

"Something's off, Captain." Blount was standing in the stairwell of a dilapidated tenement in Queen Street looking at an apartment door, which stood ajar. On impulse, David had decided they should visit Bill Pedley at home, despite his wounded arm. His instincts, it seemed, had not let him down.

David already had his army revolver in his hand. "Smells like death."

Blount growled his assent and nudged open the door with his foot. "Hello? Mr. Pedley? Bill?"

Inside, the narrow corridor was dark and stuffy. Behind the first door was a tiny, windowless room. David lit a match; in the flaring flame, they saw an unmade bed, a basin, and a clothes rack.

"Let's move on," David murmured.

The next room was the living room, or what remained of it. There must have been a tremendous struggle there, because the few pieces of shabby furniture were knocked over or sliced open. Glass panes on a cabinet were smashed in, and the contents strewn around. Shards of porcelain mixed with books and papers on the floorboards. A window was open, and the icy winter wind swept the city's stink into the room, but what made the men pull up short was not the stench of London but the sight of Bill Pedley's mutilated body.

The veteran lay on his back in a pool of blood. His head was strangely twisted, as if someone with near superhuman strength had broken his neck. Bill's wooden leg looked like it had been thrown aside, lying in one corner of the room, far out of Bill's possible reach. Bill was wearing trousers, a shirt, and leather slippers. Among the smashed crockery, David recognized shards of a teapot, and a piece of bread and butter lay beneath a chair.

"They tortured the poor bastard before they broke his neck." Blount was crouching by the body, examining Bill's hands. His fingernails had been torn out and his earlobes sliced off. Beside his head lay a crushed orchid.

Bill Pedley stared at nothing in wide-eyed sightlessness. The twisted expression on his face reflected the terrible fight that must have taken place. Blount closed the dead man's eyes.

"They didn't waste any time. This must have happened early this morning, right after our visit to St. Giles," said David, feeling a sharp pang in his injured arm.

"Big John?" Blount asked. His eyes scanned the room in search of clues as to the killer or to what they had been looking for.

"It's possible, but why? Because we asked about Korshaw? No one heard us talking."

"Clifford Cunningham?"

David shook his head. "Impossible. He was up to his ears in debt."

Blount picked up a couple of books. "If that isn't a good reason to kill . . ."

"Someone like Clifford Cunningham would know that Bill was just the middleman. Big John would make damn sure that he got his money. No, this looks like the work of several men. The door wasn't broken, so Bill must have opened it, which means he knew his killers. This was certainly not the first time they'd done something like this. I'd go so far as to say that they took pleasure in their work. Clifford might shoot someone in the heat of the moment, but he doesn't have the stomach for torture." David looked at the chaos around them.

"What if Bill had been taking bets on the side, and Big John found out about it?" Blount stared out the window. It was early afternoon, and street vendors were touting their wares.

"Maybe. That's always a possibility, and with a man like Bill, I think we can safely assume he was taking secret bets. Let's look for Korshaw's letter. If it isn't here, we'll know what they were after."

They set to work searching through the books that littered the floor. Although the furniture was old and worn, David noticed that Pedley had kept a number of art objects and weapons from his time in India: ivory figures of elephants, carvings inlaid with semiprecious stones, and two small paintings of Indian landscapes. One of them reminded David of the picture he had seen in Rosewood Hall, the one Jane loved so much.

"They left all of this behind? They must have been in a hurry." Blount went to a desk by the wall and pulled out all the drawers that weren't already lying on the floor.

David looked back at the dead man. "Someone must have disturbed them, but if that was the case, why did no one call the police? And why did they leave the valuables behind? It would have been easy to sell them."

Crouching, David rapped on the desk with his knuckles, searching for hidden spaces. He found a secret compartment and the mechanism to open it, but there was nothing inside.

A fire still smoldered in the fireplace, and the remains of letters and papers lay scattered among the dark embers. David poked through the burned scraps. "Looks like they did a thorough job."

"What about the pictures?" Blount turned the paintings around, but there was nothing hidden below the paper backings.

A letter could be anywhere—beneath the floor, behind a wall panel, or even under the wallpaper. David ran his hands over the walls, and Blount scoured the floorboards.

"The bedroom?"

David shrugged. "I'm afraid we've come too late, but let's not leave any stones unturned."

They found a candle and searched the narrow bedroom from top to bottom. It looked as if the murderers had done no more than lift the mattress, because everything else in the room was untouched.

"D'you hear that? In there!" cried an unfamiliar voice, and there was the loud clopping of boots on the stairs.

Smothering a curse, David threw open the front door. A surprised constable stood before him, his club raised.

"It's about time someone got here! We've been waiting half an eternity for you!" David snapped at the young bobby, who took a step back, perplexed.

An older man in a plain brown suit was standing behind him. "Impossible! My name's Kealton, I'm the building's caretaker, and neither of these men notified me that they was here! Arrest them! And where's Mr. Pedley? I heard strange noises up here this morning, and with these two here, I've been hearing them again. Something's going on in there!"

Still wearing his hat, David squared his shoulders. In his elegant suit and dark coat, he commanded respect. "Your name and district, sir."

The officer was a very young man who had clearly not been in the police force very long. "Uh, Gibson, Willie Gibson, Mayfair and Soho, sir."

"Who is your commanding officer?"

"Mr. Eastlake."

"Roscoe Eastlake, I see." David knew the man only by name, having heard Martin Rooke mention him. "This is a case for a special team, Gibson. Send a message to Mr. Rooke at once."

"Who are you to give orders?" said the caretaker.

"This is Captain Wescott, you cretin," Blount snarled at the caretaker, who stepped hesitantly aside. "A man to whom our country owes a great debt. This investigation is confidential, so clear off. Go make sure nobody sticks their curious nose in here and disturbs the scene of the crime."

"A man can claim anything. I never heard of no Wescott. Have you?" The skeptical caretaker, who clearly was not going to be put off easily, turned to the young officer.

The officer replied meekly, "Crimea. The Lucan case."

At that, the caretaker whistled through his teeth. "Of course! I apologize, Captain, and congratulations. I'll take care of everything. No one'll come up here who don't belong here, I promise you that."

A door across the way opened, and a woman peered out. "What's going *on* out here? D'you have to make such a racket?"

"Back in your room, Trudie, and don't put your head out here again. Count up your rent, instead. This here is a secret matter of the highest importance," the caretaker ordered her, adopting the imagined tone of an army sergeant.

Trudie screwed up her face indignantly, gray strands of hair hanging loosely beneath a puffy bonnet.

"Just a moment. Ma'am, perhaps you saw something this morning? In the stairwell, perhaps? Mr. Pedley had visitors, and we would very much like to know who they were," said David very politely.

The woman took a hesitant step forward, revealing her washed-out dress, patched many times, and her bare feet stuffed inside ragged slippers. "Because you asked so nicely, my good man, I'll tell you. I did see someone today, and three slippery-looking types they were, too, the kind you don't want nothing to do with, if you know what I mean.

There's lots of people who come to visit Bill, but normally it's scruffy gamblers or young gents whose fine old fathers have cut 'em off. No secret round here that Bill took side bets on the dogs." Trudie signaled to David to come closer. "My own husband placed his bets with Bill in Seven Bells. The old bugger won, too, then drank away his winnings!" she said, aggrieved.

"And what did today's men look like? This is very important. If you can help us, we would be grateful." David fished a shiny silver coin from his pocket.

The caretaker pushed his way forward. "I can tell you what they looked like." He wanted the coin for himself, but David closed his hand over it.

"And yet you didn't mention that right away, Mr. Kealton. Why not?"

"Give a man a chance to get the lay of the land. Where is Pedley, anyway?"

"Dead, back there in his living room. You didn't bother to check on him after the men left? I'm surprised, considering that you're the caretaker here." David narrowed his eyes and peered at the man, who turned and looked at the floor.

"Ha, Kealton, you were off with that whore of yours, weren't ye? Where you're always creeping off when Katie ain't home. You can't have seen those men at all," sniffed Trudie.

"You are bound to tell the truth, sir!" the bobby said importantly, and Kealton, abashed, gazed at his shoes and said nothing.

"Go, man, and make sure no one else comes in here!" Blount gave the man a push.

"And you, Gibson, go and fetch Rooke and his men," David ordered. "Ma'am?"

Trudie held out her hand, and David dropped the coin into her palm. The woman grinned at him with satisfaction, revealing gapped teeth. "There was three of 'em. One was bald and had a face full of scars. The other one, the one I reckon was the leader, he was a monster of a man. I didn't recognize his face, but one of 'is ears looked like a cauliflower."

"Big John," Blount murmured.

"And the third?" David asked.

"He was little, weedy, a foreigner of some sort, spoke a mishmash you couldn't understand, and he carried a knife. They were up to no good, I could see that clear enough. When the little man spotted me in the doorway here, I locked it up quick smart, else they might well have sliced me up, too." Trudie's swollen eyes looked fearfully at them. "They ain't coming back, are they?"

"I think they got what they came for. You didn't go into Pedley's rooms after that?" Wescott watched her carefully.

Trudie vehemently shook her head. "No, Captain, cross my heart. I did my washing and cooking and kept my eye on my daughter's littl'uns. I only just came out when you was talking to Kealton out here."

David believed the woman; her fear of the killers was not feigned.

"Thank you. Oh, and can you let us borrow a lamp?"

David and Blount spent the time until Rooke and his people arrived combing every chink and corner of Pedley's apartment, but all they found was a small tin box hidden behind the bed that contained bills and a number of letters from India. None, however, were from Korshaw.

Later, sitting with Rooke in his office at the police station, the detective pushed the small box across his desk to David. "Take it with you if you want. You're deeper into this than I am. What do you think?"

It was beyond question that Big John was involved in the murder, but they could not prove that because Trudie had sensibly refused to testify. No one could blame her, because no one would be there to protect her from the criminals' revenge if she spoke out against them.

The handwriting on the letters was a woman's script. "Love letters?" David asked.

"Come off it. Not the items in the box. I mean Bill. The orchid. Coincidence?"

David slowly shook his head. "Those damned flowers turn up everywhere we look. The first murder happened at Veitch and Sons. The victim was an orchid-keeper. No, let's go back further, to the maid at Winton Park. She lived in the house of an orchid breeder. And now there's Bill, who was acquainted with Korshaw. He was left with a crushed orchid lying beside his head. I don't believe in coincidences."

"So what do you believe in, David?" Rooke laced his fingers behind his head and leaned back.

"Nothing, not since the war. Humans are evil, grasping creatures. Worse than any animal, because a human will kill not to sate his appetite or protect his family. Humans kill for material gain or to take revenge, or simply because they feel like it." It had been a long and difficult day. His arm hurt, and he longed to feel the warmth of his wife beside him.

"Evil wears many faces, and I have a sinking feeling that Bill's death is the start of something that will keep us busy for a very long time." Rooke rocked forward and rapped on the table. "Go home, David. Have someone examine that wound. You don't look good."

David stood up and took the dented box with him. "See you tomorrow."

Colombia, October 1860

Dear Sir Frederick,

I could not in good conscience even tell you what today's date is. I am hardly in any condition to write and can only hope that these lines do indeed reach you. Our ascent into the cordilleras was steep and arduous, but everyone made it back down the other side in one piece. Maracaibo Lake seemed to be waiting for us in all its botanical plenitude.

Our route to the mysterious flowers so sacred to the Motilones proved more difficult than anticipated. Not only did it turn out that Rudbeck was still there, but the Indians were preparing for one of their most important religious rituals. Disturbing such a ceremony would have been indefensible. Death would have been the least we could have expected.

So we descended the steep path and were happy that we had gotten our mules across the mountains healthy and unhurt. Farther below, we saw a long procession of Indians dressed in colorful garments, moving silently along narrow mountain trails toward a dense forest. It was a sight at once uplifting and frightening, for the men were armed with bows and spears. The cool mountain regions lay above us, and it was fascinating to watch the way the rainforest rose from the plains and swallowed up the colorful figures, one by one.

"Señor, we must not disturb them. The Motilones perform their ritual at a secret place, a holy place. It is a great event. It is rumored they have a store of gold hidden in the jungle. Look there, señor, it is the zipa—the high priest. He will lead the rites," José whispered reverently beside me.

"They can't hear us," I said, wanting to ease his mind. "You can speak normally."

"Oh, no, señor. You don't know what they can hear. No one does. If we speak badly of them, they will take their revenge. They have ears everywhere. A cousin of mine found that out for himself, and it was terrible to see!" José's dark-skinned face had turned pale, and his jaw trembled. The man was truly afraid.

Dennis joined us. "What was it, José? What did you hear?"

"Shh, señor, not so loud!" José glanced nervously around, especially in the direction of the bearers, who were crouching with their usual inscrutability beside their trunks and sacks, rolling leaves to smoke.

"Oh, José is just talking more cock and bull . . . Come on, let's go. We can't stand around here all day!" I said. The path on which we had stopped was only a few feet across, and I am not one of those nimble goats that likes to stand around on mountainsides.

The bearers seemed unaffected by all this, but a sense of foreboding overcame me when I saw them talking among themselves right afterward, gazing upon the colorful procession disappearing into the rainforest.

I nodded to José. "Tell them they have to come as far as the Motilone camp if they want to get paid. That was the deal."

"Derek, look! There's a white man with the priest!" Dennis exclaimed.

I saw a man in light, tropical attire walking behind the zipa. He turned his head in our direction. "It's Rudbeck."

"Who else?" Dennis laughed. "It would be strange to find another white man here, wouldn't it? Though I guess you can never know. You and I are both here, after all."

"But why would a white man be allowed to attend their sacred ceremony?" I asked José, who knew the customs of the Motilones better than we did.

José finished shaking hands with one of the bearers. "They will come down to the edge of the village but no farther. Then they will turn back. They won't cross the plain to the sea."

"Good enough, but now tell me, how is it possible that Rudbeck is with them?" We had started moving again, descending carefully. We were still several hundred meters above the edge of the forest, along the perimeter of which we would find the village. The Motilones had long been aware of our presence, but there was no sign of them approaching us, preoccupied as they were with their sacred ceremony.

"They will not take Rudbeck all the way. The ritual happens at a crater, at a lake in the forest. I cannot say

exactly how it involves the gold. No outsider has ever seen the ceremony itself. No one who has lived to tell, at least."

Would Rudbeck really be stupid enough to believe he could uncover the secret of the Motilones' gold? Assuming they actually had any gold, of course. It was certainly possible, and we knew that precious stones are indeed mined in these mountains, but until today, I had only ever heard of the Motilones in relation to the Sobralia mystica.

"The Sobralia, *perhaps?" I said, struck by a sudden thought. "Is that the gold of the Motilones? Is it to be found there, at the lake?"*

José balanced himself against a boulder as he slid down a patch of scree. "As far as I know, the ritual has nothing to do with the orchid. Señor, would it not be a good idea to go to the village immediately? There will only be women, children, and a few old men there. Maybe one of them will be able to tell us where the zipa goes to get their miraculous flower."

I agreed. Let Rudbeck look for gold. We were on the right path, I could feel it. My esteemed Sir Frederick, if I am good for anything, it is for tracking down orchids, and I give you my word, that morning, there in the cordilleras, I could feel my scalp tingling with anticipation. The flower was practically in my grasp. I could feel it!

Nothing and no one would be able to keep me away from the Sobralia mystica *today. We might have let the old man's black orchid slip through our fingers, but that just made me all the more determined to be successful with this venture. I won't bore you further with all the details. Suffice to say, the village women were busy preparing the feast for after the ceremony. Although they met us not with hostility but with indifference, it was clear that we were not welcome. From what I understood of the ritual, it involved an initiation for the young men of the tribe, and for that reason only the old, toothless men remained in the village. But those old, toothless men could still wield a blowpipe, which did not appeal to me, nor did I want a horde of crazed Motilone women snapping at my heels.*

Thus, for a time, we stood in front of the village, which stretched for quite a distance along the edge of the rainforest. The Motilones do not like to live close together, and they are known for fighting one another. We were out of sight of where the women were cooking. A boy approached us, a curious adolescent. "José, ask the boy about the flower and show him this." I took from my pocket a string with a little silver pipe on it, with which I could imitate bird calls.

The pipe was dear to me, and expensive, but the preferred prize had to be appealing enough for the boy to overcome his fear of the zipa. I blew into it for a few moments, demonstrating how one could create different sounds. The boy's eyes grew wider and wider, and he reached out his hand for the rare toy.

Jose explained what we were looking for. The boy, who wore no more than a cloth around his loins and shoulders and carried a bow and a quiver of arrows, had eyes only for the pipe. He nodded.

Our bearers were grumbling, but I exhorted them to stay with us as we had not actually entered the village. Secretly, I hoped that we would be able to find the flower and leave again immediately. The Motilones' ceremony was a gift from the gods, a perfect opportunity. How else would we have found an opportunity to seek out the holy site without being drilled through with poison arrows?

I hung the pipe around the boy's neck, and we followed him. It is strange how naïve and trusting these savages become when they want something. They then seem to me like small dogs or children promised sugar if they are obedient. Perhaps it was pure luck that this young lad had no fear of the priest and wanted the pipe more than he wanted salvation.

Turning to Dennis, I asked him whether we still had petroleum along with the ointment we used to keep gnats at bay. "We should slather ourselves in the stuff. The Sobralia *is protected by aggressive insects." We pushed our way into the forest. Looking ahead, we could see that the path first led downhill before climbing again. With every step, the vegetation grew denser, and the green canopy quickly formed an impenetrable roof overhead. The jungle is all-consuming.*

I promised our bearers double their pay if they stayed with us. They quickly discussed this and decided in my favor. We had not entered the village, after all, and we wanted to move on that same day. For an hour, we marched through that hilly terrain. The rainforest was interrupted time and again by enormous rocky outcrops that formed clearings or fell away into canyons.

The Indian boy grew uneasy. In a patchwork of Spanish and local dialect, he told José that we needed to go to a specific rock in the next canyon. José looked at me.

"He should show us exactly where the flowers are, or at least exactly which rock we're looking for." In that dense undergrowth, and without precise directions, we would have been lost in minutes.

Somewhere in the jungle we heard the roar of a big cat, maybe a jaguar. Those elegant hunters stalk these forests and can spell doom for a solo wanderer.

"The boy says we should have the bearers wait here with the mules and the baggage. The way from here is very difficult," José translated for the boy, who was gesticulating wildly.

Indeed, the way was all but impassable, blocked by numerous fallen trees, boulders, and pools of water, but eventually, bathed in sweat, we reached a gap in the rock walls. Only a slim man could fit through it. But through the gap I saw one isolated, overgrown pinnacle, thrusting upward like a druidic stone, pressing its tip against the canopy of leaves above. And as forewarned, I also saw those aggressive, buzzing insects, swarming around the rock like a horde of watchmen. Taking the pipe and its string from around my neck, I handed it to our adolescent guide, who held it wide-eyed and reverently in his hands. One final look back, then he disappeared into the jungle.

With a huge grin on his face, José handed me our crucible of foul-smelling ointment to ward off the insects. Dennis and I smeared it on every inch of exposed skin, and even José, confronted by those uncommonly large insects, slathered himself with the stuff. Then, each of us carrying a basket, we squeezed through the slot in the rock wall. I turned my eyes upward. Immediately, I saw fine roots, and above them shimmered the magnificent blooms of white and yellow; even from there, I could make out a delicate sprinkling of red!

My heart beat faster. I was so close to the flowers I had coveted for so long! Such a wealth of glory and achievement awaited us on that pinnacle of rock, beneath the canopy. We found a tree that was easy enough to climb, and I was certain the zipas used exactly that tree to reach their holy flowers. And then, my God, there we were, within reach of the most priceless treasures of the orchid kingdom, so long yearned for. The dream of every orchid collector was about to be fulfilled—by me. I would be the first to take the holy flower of the Motilones and show it to the rest of the world!

Was it the right thing to do? Was it, perhaps, a sin? In that moment, I did not think about it. I simply closed my eyes as the furious insects descended on me. They resembled enormous hornets, but the oily, stinking substance kept them at bay, at least initially. In all my joy and euphoria, I briefly forgot how sensitive those plants are. If I harbored any ambition to get them back to England, I would have to act with caution.

Gently, I pushed my fingers into the thin layer of humus in which the orchids grew. Slowly, carefully, I extracted a dozen of the small plants, placing them in the basket I carried on my back. With the stinging or biting insects now coming perilously close, I was just about to take another plant when I heard a cry.

"Derek!" The fearful voice was that of our young botanist.

As fast as possible, I half-slid and half-fell back down the tree, tearing my skin on the rock but ignoring the pain because I heard José cursing and Dennis crying out. With one hand, I drew my revolver from my belt, and with the other I broke my fall on a large branch, tumbling to the ground and stumbling over Dennis's body. My hand landed in a pool of blood. "Dennis?"

But the young man did not move. I heard a suppressed cry, a groan, and in the weak, shimmering light that penetrated the canopy, I saw two human bodies entangled in a deadly battle. José and Mungo Rudbeck!

José seemed to have suffered a head wound, for he had blood running over one eye. If I did not want to lose a second friend that day, I had to act immediately. When the two men briefly separated and Mungo glared at me with bared teeth, I did not hesitate. I fired. Mungo's eyes opened wide, and his hand flew to his breast. He stumbled backward against the rock and slid to the ground.

José groaned. "Gracias, señor. You saved my life!"

"Dennis?" I went back to the traveling companion who had become such a dear friend, but I was unable to do more than confirm his death.

Furiously, I turned on Mungo, slumped against the rock. "Why did you have to kill him? He was not a competitor, only a young man, an idealist."

Mungo, a muscular young man with dark skin and slightly almond-shaped eyes—I believe his mother was mixed-race—spat at me. "You always were too soft, Derek. There's no place for that in our line of business. Only the strongest survive. As it turns out, you had the better nose, at least this time."

He coughed, and blood trickled from the corner of his mouth. I handed him a handkerchief, but he waved it aside. "When you leave, give me my revolver. I don't want the Motilones to catch me."

"Why not? I thought you were friendly with them. Weren't you walking with the zipa just now?"

"He didn't want to leave me alone with the women. That's the only reason he took me along with them. Besides, I promised him a barrel of rum. That good old zipa loves the stuff." Mungo let out an abrupt laugh. "But then I saw that you had moved on, and the wheels in my brain started to turn. I told the zipa that I would follow

you and keep my eye on you. He's not stupid. He realized long ago that orchid hunters like us would rather slit each other's throats than hold hands."

Crouching beside him, I waved José over. "Do you have any cachaça left?"

José had wound a scrap of cloth around his head injury. He withdrew a small flask from the bag he carried over his shoulder. "Guarro!" he spat. "Pig!" But he still handed me the bottle.

Mungo greedily drank a mouthful, staring at me with burning eyes. "Now show me those goddamned miracle orchids! That's why you're here. I saw the roots. White . . . are they white or yellow?"

Close to death, the fanatical flower hunter had eyes only for his quarry. To be honest, I would hardly have acted any differently had I been in his position. I took the basket from my back and carefully took out one of the plants. I held it out to him almost tenderly. "They are radiant, as if lit from inside. See the tiny red spots?"

His eyes locked on the ornate flowers. For men like us, they were worth more than a mountain of gold bars. Lifting his blood-smeared hand, he reached for the flower, but I pulled it back.

His mouth twisted mockingly. "You won't live to enjoy it." He coughed, then laughed.

I quickly returned the orchid alongside the others in the basket. "José, come, we should leave this place."

"The shot, Derek. Have you forgotten the sound of the gunshot? The Motilones are sure to be on their way, a swarm of angry wasps wielding poison arrows with which to impale you. But you won't die. You'll only be paralyzed, and then the bloodthirsty monsters will take you back to

their village. They'll torture you and torment you for what you've done . . . how you've defiled their holiest of holies!"

Mungo could hardly get the words out. He coughed and spat blood, and his face was a twisted mask of hate and pain. The surrounding rainforest felt like a living thing, and those dreadful insects buzzed louder and closed in around us. Our ointment seemed to be becoming less efficacious. One of the filthy beasts landed on Mungo's cheek, and the man bellowed in pain.

José hurled a volley of curses at him in Spanish. He had little sympathy for Mungo's plight.

"Leave him, but we should take Dennis out of here." We picked up our dead friend, but before we departed from that fateful place, I picked up Mungo's revolver from the ground. Emptying the cylinder and removing all but one bullet, I threw him the gun. He managed to pick it up then pointed it at me, trembling.

"One bullet, Mungo. That's all you have. Adieu!"

His curses and the shot that followed still reverberate in my ears, like the rustling and hissing of the jungle that deepened all around us.

I very much hope that these valuable flowers reach you undamaged.

Your faithful servant,
Derek Tomkins

22.

Winton Park, Northumberland, December 1860

"I can't say a word to Alison! Promise me she won't hear a breath of it, Hettie. She would get too worked up, and then I'm afraid she might lose the baby," Jane implored her maid, who was busy pinning up Jane's hair before dinner.

"I'll have a word with Nora soon, ma'am. She should make sure the other maids don't go spreading silly rumors." Hettie clipped the last comb in place. "Lady Alison is going to have her baby soon, isn't she?"

With a sigh, Jane stood. She had chosen a plain, chestnut-colored dress for dinner. She could have eaten with Alison in her room, but her friend's curiosity was too great. Jane knew that if she wanted to help Charlotte, then she would have to find out what was going on in the house. "I'm afraid so. The only consolation in all of this is the presence of Dr. Cribb."

Hettie fetched a scarf from the cupboard. "It's chilly in here. This house is like a sieve. Please take this along, ma'am." She wrapped the scarf around Jane's shoulders, then gazed at Jane, a worried look on her face. “I really don’t know if the doctor’s to be trusted. Poor Lady Charlotte.”

“We don’t know what truly happened. I hope I can find out more during dinner.” The house had grown very still; even from the children’s room, there was not the faintest voice or laugh to be heard.

On her way downstairs, Jane listened for any sound at all from the family’s wing, but everything remained silent. With a heavy heart, she went down to dinner. The long table was set for three, and the dark room seemed even more oppressive than usual. Jane found Dr. Cribb and the master of the house deep in conversation by the fireplace.

“Ah, our houseguest. Please, my dear, what can I offer you to drink?” Sir Frederick greeted her, his expression serious.

“A sherry, if I may.” Jane waited until the maid handed her the glass before asking, “How is Charlotte?”

Dr. Cribb’s eyebrows twisted in a frown. “You should not have had to witness this tragic development, my lady. Please don’t draw any quick conclusions. I had to sedate Lady Charlotte for her own protection. She was hysterical, completely beside herself.”

Hysterical, thought Jane. That was the word, so popular, so frequently used to describe any woman who defied social conventions or her husband’s commands. “I know Charlotte as a loving mother, not as hysterical.”

Sir Frederick stared grimly into the flames. “You hardly know her, and please excuse the observation, but your interest in our family affairs seems remarkably pronounced.”

“I mean no disrespect, Sir Frederick. Please believe me when I say that my reason for asking stems purely from my concern for your wife, and because Alison is so attached to her. That is perhaps a weakness of women, that we care too much.” Jane smiled apologetically.

“I beg to differ, my dear,” said Dr. Cribb. “That is what makes your sex so attractive, but there are situations where a woman’s natural concern can take on an abnormally possessive aspect and become pathological."

"Are you suggesting that Charlotte is insane? That there's reason enough to have her locked away in an institution—"

"Nobody wants that," Sir Frederick angrily interrupted her. "Me least of all, but if it comes down to sparing my wife from prison or even from the rope, then I would rather see her committed. How else am I supposed to explain to a court that my wife was found beside her son's bed with a bottle of laudanum in her hand?"

Jane paled instantly. "Oh, no! That doesn't mean that she was going to give any of it to Cedric, does it?"

"*Did* give it to him, my lady. I'm sorry to say. Miss Molan entered the room just in time to prevent anything worse." The doctor sighed regretfully.

Jane wished that David were there. She wanted to talk with him about how the situation was unfolding here. He was not the kind of man to act in haste, but instead he was able to cast circumstances in a fresh light and find the gaps in a chain of evidence. On the other hand, without her intuition and her often rash decisions, they would never have stumbled on to Mary's trail or Rachel's secret.

"My lady? Would you come to the table?" Sir Frederick interrupted her thoughts, and dinner was served.

During the meal, Jane avoided referring again to either Charlotte or the children, and instead she praised the cook: "The roast grouse with glazed carrots is excellent."

But the master of the house merely nodded absently. "I received a package today. From London. I may now declare that I am the first Englishman to possess a *Sobralia mystica*!"

"Congratulations! How extraordinary!" Dr. Cribb raised his wine-glass. "Now here's to successfully cultivating it!"

Sir Frederick's face, which had until then been serious and rather strained, suddenly brightened. "Thank you, my friend."

Jane also raised her glass. "Is that the black orchid you were telling me about?"

"Oh, no. If I ever actually got my hands on that specimen, I'd hire a dozen of the best guards. A man with a black orchid has to fear for his safety, maybe even for his life!" Sir Frederick's cheeks were flushed, and it had nothing to do with the red wine.

"My man in Colombia found the holy flower of the Motilone Indians for me and managed to spirit a number of the plants out of the country. Every time such plants survive their journey undamaged, it is a miracle. If you like, I'll show you the orchids after dinner," he offered.

"It would be an honor," Jane replied.

Before the meal was over, however, the doctor was called to attend to his patient upstairs, which did nothing to improve Sir Frederick's mood. He downed a glass of port. "Allow me to check on the health of my wife and son. Mr. Draycroft will bring you to the greenhouse later."

"Of course. I'll write a letter in the drawing room."

A short while later, as Jane found herself standing in front of the porcelain figurines that Charlotte loved so much, a crippling sadness overcame her. She felt not only useless but naïve and helpless, caught in a tangled web of a family drama and a mysterious plot that was impossible to view with any clarity. It was this blindness that infuriated her most of all, because she trusted her innate belief that a crime had been committed regarding Rachel's death. A terrible suspicion crept over her. What if Charlotte was truly mad and also responsible for Rachel's death?

Taking pen and paper from Charlotte's desk, she started to write to David, knowing that it would help her put her churning thoughts in order. She had been scratching the quill across the paper for several minutes when a soft voice behind her asked, "My lady, may I disturb you?"

Jane jerked around. "Heavens, you gave me such a fright!"

One of the young maids was standing behind her with downcast eyes and hands clasped in front of her. "I'm sorry, my lady. I'll leave."

"No, no. Stay, please!" Jane put the pen aside and wiped her fingers with a handkerchief. "You're Della, aren't you?" She recognized the dark-haired laundry maid whom she had only ever seen darting shyly through the corridors.

"Yes, my lady." The girl's bonnet and apron were immaculately white, and her dress was neatly ironed. Mrs. Gubbins allowed no errors with the servants' attire. Voices came suddenly from outside the door leading to the hall, and Della jumped a little.

"Della, what can I do for you?" Jane encouraged the skittish young woman.

Jane could see clearly that Della was having great difficulty saying what was on her mind. "You went to Rachel's funeral."

"I was glad to be able to."

"And you went to visit Rachel's parents. No one from the house ever did that." Della took a deep breath. "Not even Sir Frederick."

"I would not hold that against him. He has a lot of things to worry about."

"He should have visited them, but all he has in his head are his flowers. People don't matter a jot to him." Della looked around fearfully and stepped closer to Jane. "My lady, I know that Rachel was going out to meet someone on the night she died."

"I think so, too, Della. Do you know with whom?"

Della nodded. "You can't tell anyone that you heard it from me."

"I promise."

The young woman lowered her voice to the merest whisper. "She went to meet Mr. Draycroft."

Jane looked at the anxious girl in surprise. "Really? Why are you only telling me this now?"

"Because no one's going to investigate Rachel's death. She wasn't a loose woman. She was a good person." Tears came to Della's eyes. "She was so pretty, my lady, and always so sad."

There was a knock at the door, and Mr. Draycroft entered. "My lady, may I show you to the greenhouse? I've brought your coat."

"Thank you, Della. Please take the towels to my room, then look in on Lady Alison, would you? She would no doubt appreciate some extras, too."

Della nodded, then turned and scurried past Mr. Draycroft, keeping her eyes on the floor.

Jane folded the letter she had begun, then tucked it in her pocket and stood. As they walked, she asked Draycroft, "Have you ever considered a position in London? I'm certain that an attractive man such as yourself could earn much more there than you do here."

If her forthrightness took the butler by surprise, he did not show it. "Thank you, my lady. I am happy enough here."

He held the front door open for her, and the frosty night air rose to meet them. Jane turned up the fur collar on her coat. The snow had stopped, and a blanket of white crackled beneath her shoes.

"I know a house where they would welcome you with open arms, so to speak. The woman of the house is lonely, if you know what I mean." Jane wanted to lure him out of his professional reserve, and it seemed she had achieved that when Draycroft softly laughed.

"Ah, I see, my lady. I'm afraid I would be a disappointment." He stopped walking, and when Jane turned to look at him, his smile spoke volumes.

Jane thought of the exceptionally correct dealings she had witnessed between Draycroft and the female staff, all of whom seemed to adore him. "You . . . are not attracted to women?"

"My lady, I admit nothing and I deny nothing. I have no desire to go to prison."

Homosexuality, Jane knew, was punishable with a prison term, depending on which judge tried the case. There were certain liberal circles where they laughed at such moral prudishness, but in public such "abnormal tendencies" were vilified.

"You have my word that nothing we say to each other will go any further, Mr. Draycroft."

"Thank you, my lady."

"But I do have a question. On the night of her death, Rachel had arranged to meet someone. Where were you that night?"

Raising his chin, Draycroft said, "In the stables. There is a stablehand . . ."

He was speaking the truth, Jane realized from his tone of voice. "Then why would you send a message to Rachel asking her to go to the hunter's hut on the moor?"

Draycroft opened his eyes wide in sudden shock. "Do you think that I . . . ? No! I swear I did no harm to Rachel. If such a message exists, then I would like to see it. I wrote no such thing."

"Would you give me a sample of your handwriting?"

"Of course. Wait a moment." He reached into a pocket of his suit. "This is a list of tasks that I assign to the male members of staff. Would that do, my lady?"

"Thank you," said Jane, pocketing the note. "Please forgive me for asking, Mr. Draycroft."

The butler indicated where the illuminated greenhouse shimmered beyond some tree trunks, and they continued walking on the frozen gravel path. "Rachel should never have taken her position here. She was not happy. If you ask me, she was on the run from something. But she did her work, and I am not in charge of the female staff. Have you already talked with Mrs. Gubbins?"

"She doesn't seem to be the kind of housekeeper in whom one can confide."

"Nor is her husband. The stable master carries out his duties with a strict hand."

Jane could well imagine what would happen if Mr. Gubbins caught Draycroft and his young friend in one of their secret trysts.

"Here we are, my lady." The butler held the greenhouse door open for her.

"Thank you for everything, Mr. Draycroft."

The greenhouse was comfortably warm after the chill night air, but was not as hot as Jane had expected; it was more like the spring climate in the hills near her home, and she realized that the temperature had been lowered a little since her last visit. Even at this late hour, gardeners were busy with the plants and with keeping the ventilation system clean. A gentle breeze seemed to waft from below, causing Jane's dress to flutter a little.

"Ah, my lady, come in, come in!" Sir Frederick's tall figure appeared from behind the large tree that filled the center of the greenhouse.

Several open wooden boxes stood on the floor. Some contained linen sacks that had been sliced open, and Jane glimpsed earth and straw inside. Sir Frederick had rolled up his sleeves and was cutting thin hemp rope into pieces. Empty plant pots stood on a workbench beside a small trowel and other tools. Sir Frederick's eyes were practically aglow as he lifted a small pot containing a rather unspectacular orchid from a shelf. "This is the one!"

Jane reached for the pot, but Sir Frederick set the white-yellow orchid down on the bench.

"It is exhausted from its long journey. We want to let it sleep again soon. Look at this delicate grain, the red dots. It is perfect! A beauty!" he said rapturously, his eyes trained on the object of his affection. "It is a marvel that this flower has survived. But look here, at these buds. In a few weeks, they will be a show of magnificent blooms. Then I will present it in London. Oh, you won't believe the expressions on the faces of Cunningham, Parks, and even Day. They'll see that I'm the best grower in the country. Not one of them has yet managed to find a *Sobralia mystica*, and each one of them has sent more men out into the world than I have. My instincts about Tomkins were correct. When it comes to people, they always are. Spies in my house be damned! I knew from the start that Derek Tomkins was the best in his profession."

"Spies?" The small flowers seemed to be staring at Jane and laughing at her. *What a lot of fuss you're making about me,* they seemed to be saying, even as they were probably pining for the warm climes of their home country.

Sir Frederick gazed at his orchid like a man besotted. "What? Oh, I had a number of applications from gardeners whom I knew immediately were Cunningham's men."

Gardeners, thought Jane. *Are they the only ones he means? Not a servant girl, perhaps, previously employed by Cunningham?* "Where do these miracle flowers grow? It feels cooler in here compared with my last visit."

"You noticed that?" Once again, Sir Frederick seemed surprised at her perceptiveness. "Well, the temperature will be further reduced as December progresses to cause as little distress as possible to the plants. It is the resting phase in the orchids' growth cycle, although the various species need to be handled differently. Cattleya orchids, for example, prefer temperatures between 54 and 66 degrees, and in the East India section we maintain the temperature between 60 and 72 degrees."

Peering into the open boxes, Sir Frederick crouched and took out a small sack that was still closed. Involuntarily, he let out a cry. "That is not possible. Adam!"

One of the gardeners hurried over and threw his hand over his mouth when he saw what Sir Frederick was holding. "Sir, I'm sorry. I must have overlooked that one!"

The middle-aged man reached for the little sack but Sir Frederick roughly pushed him away. "You stupid, useless fool! How could you have overlooked this? Do you have the slightest idea what this plant is worth? You won't earn as much in your entire miserable life! Your Sunday off is canceled—for the next two months!"

The man attempted to defend himself. “Sir, please, my mother is lying in—”

“Go! One more word, and I’ll take the whip to you!” The man excused himself and backed away, head hanging. Sir Frederick, his face still red with wrath, set about freeing the orchid from its container.

From inside the sack appeared a disappointingly small plant with dried leaves and withered roots. By that point, Jane thought it best if she took her leave.

As Jane reentered the main house, Hettie came running excitedly. “Ma’am, you should come at once. Lady Alison is bleeding!”

23.

Seymour Street, London, December 1860

David read Jane's telegram a second time before letting out a groan. "I don't believe it!"

He ran his fingers through his hair. Certainly, Jane was smart and confident enough to face whatever challenges she confronted in the chilly north, but her improvident approach was constantly getting her into hair-raising situations—and driving David mad with anxiety. He had to admit, however, that in this particular case she was blameless.

Blount sat across the table, on which lay Bill Pedley's letters. "I hope nothing has befallen Lady Jane?"

Apart from Jane, Blount was the only person David trusted unreservedly. Since his and Jane's wedding, he appreciated the man even more knowing that Blount was utterly devoted to Jane. "No, although I am starting to fear that she might run into some danger up there. Someone went to the trouble of luring Rachel onto the moor with a counterfeit message. The butler has assured Jane that he was not responsible for the note, and if I understand her correctly, his interests lie less in pretty girls than in stableboys."

"Hmm. If that's truly the case, he's out of the running for suspects. He could be lying, of course," Blount considered.

"Let's assume for the moment that he's telling the truth. Then there would have to be at least one person in the house who would know Draycroft's handwriting and who could also forge it. A kitchen maid would be able to write no more than her name, at best."

"The housekeeper, perhaps? What was her name again? And her husband, that uncouth chap who runs the stables?"

"There's more. It seems Lady Charlotte tried to poison her son and has now been locked up in her own house. And there's a tutor the governess has been meeting in secret." David glanced up from Jane's unusually thorough telegram.

"That could mean everything or nothing at all. Love affairs and petty intrigues among servants are common enough. Look here, Captain, this could be something." Blount tapped on a letter he had separated from the others.

"Another love letter from that Cynthia and I'll shoot myself." David grinned, reaching for the pages. Cynthia had apparently been in India at the same time as Pedley and Korshaw and had fallen in love with Bill, but Pedley had not returned her affections as much as she would have wished, and no marriage proposal had eventuated.

"'Madras, July 1853. My dearest Bill,'" David read aloud, "'I will miss you very much and cannot support your decision to leave India permanently. What do you expect to find in England? Like me, you have no family there anymore. Why can't we start a new life together here? I would dearly love to look after you. Your wound does not deter me in the slightest, as I've told you a thousand times!

"'A man without a leg is far more appealing to me than a man without a heart! And there is so much goodness and decency in you

that it brings me to tears to think that I will never again see your face.'"
The letter continued in that vein for several lines. David skipped the rest of the paragraph and then, suddenly, the enamored woman had his attention again.

"'Do you remember that exciting English couple who wanted to go off to Burma with Korshaw? I almost joined them. We planned to board a boat in Calcutta that was bound for Bassein. Some new scenery and a bit of adventure would have done me good, but things took a strange turn. Maybe it has already made the papers in England?

"'Well, if not, then I will be the first to report it. Korshaw was behaving more intolerably than ever, which was probably because someone had caught on to him. Did he really believe he could get away with his crooked business deals forever?

"'If I had been his client, I would have stuffed the miserable fraud into a sack of snakes. But it would probably hurt Korshaw more to lose his money. Still, I had already bought my ticket for the crossing and arranged for my baggage to be taken aboard when I received a letter from a dear friend who intends to marry in Madras a month from now. I am supposed to be her maid of honor. Well, to cut the story short, I canceled my trip and stayed behind in dusty India.

"'And now I think I made a wise decision! The Satterleys did in fact travel to Burma with Korshaw. I had grown particularly fond of the young woman; she was very clever, although rather solitary. Well, life in foreign climes demands a lot, doesn't it? One can't spend every day singing and dancing. Incidentally, the natives here drive me round the bend with their lethargy and indifference. They have absolutely no sense of time! But back to the Satterleys.

"'Peter and Velma, as I knew them, were such a nice couple. He had been promoted to lieutenant and was supposed to take up a new post in Burma. I have not been able to find out exactly what happened, but there was a frightful scandal when Peter died under mysterious circumstances shortly after they arrived. Everyone was talking about it, because British officers are not found dead in their bedrooms every day. He had not laid a hand on himself, nor was a snakebite involved. God, there are so many poisonous creatures in that country, and when everything's said and done, I don't think anyone will ever find out how the poor man died. There are some very persistent rumors going around that his wife poisoned him!

"'Isn't that terrible? Velma, who was always so nice and with whom I so enjoyed a hand of bridge. No, I can't believe she would do such a thing. Either way, it seems she is not completely blameless in the matter, because people say that she was having an affair with an adventurer. Korshaw, perhaps? I'm starting to think that anything is possible, and that I am seemingly incapable of reading my fellow man or woman. Oh, my dearest, am I too credulous, too trusting? Since that scandal came to light, I have heard no more from her. She simply disappeared, just like Korshaw. But perhaps you might hear something of one or both of them?

"'I would be obliged if you would write by return post and tell me how you are. I am foolhardy enough to hope that we might meet again. Forever yours, Cynthia.'"

David put the letter on the desk. "So Peter and Velma Satterley were with Korshaw in Burma. Peter Satterley? I've never heard the name in connection with any scandal, but I'm sure I can find out more. I'm going to the club, Blount."

"Cynthia who, Captain?" Blount turned the envelope over.

"One of the gentlemen who spent time in India will know. Our expatriate British community is well-informed." David looked at his pocket watch, a piece he had inherited from his mother. "What's going on with Levi? Has he been back to see that Gundorov in Holborn?"

"Not as far as I know. He's been spending a lot of time studying with Josiah. The boy would like to become a pharmacist."

"Interesting. If he works hard, I'll certainly help him along."

The club offered a number of benefits that David appreciated, not least of which was its wonderfully predictable routine. Mr. Bale greeted him on arrival, and upon entering the venerable old rooms, David was met by soft music, the scent of cigars, and the absolute certainty that should the rest of the world perish, Brooks's would survive.

Among all the familiar faces, David sought out those he knew had served or lived in India. In particular, he sought the second sons of noblemen, those for whom no great inheritance waited and who, as a result, entered military service in search of their own fortune. Others were only killing time until they received their portion of their father's estate, however small it may be. Yet others were running away from gambling debts or an arranged marriage.

"David! Wonderful to bump into you here. Otherwise I would have come knocking on your door tomorrow." Thomas was striding toward him from an adjoining drawing room.

"Thomas!" The men clapped each other on the back, and Thomas invited David to have drinks in the library.

"So what are our wives up to?" Thomas asked. He seemed thinner, as if he'd been working hard and not sleeping enough. The previous weeks and the crisis surrounding Russell and Josephine Simpson had obviously taken a toll on him.

David kept the details of the tragic events surrounding Charlotte to himself, instead mentioning Sir Frederick's orchid mania and Jane's investigation of Rachel's death. "While we're talking about orchids—and the damn things seem to be following me everywhere this winter—does the name Satterley mean anything to you?" He briefly reported on the man's death.

Thomas listened in amazement. "My goodness, how is it that you always manage to stir up the worst hornets' nests? Or should I be blaming Jane?"

The warm whisky went down easily. David swirled the golden liquid in the glow of the fire and grinned. "Or rather Alison, wouldn't you say?"

Thomas rubbed his forehead. "You're right. Satterley? Was he an army man? Or was he in the Indian Civil Service? We're always having trouble with that lot."

The Indian Civil Service, better known simply as the ICS, comprised the so-called elite of British Civil Service officers in India. These men displayed their superiority over the Indian population openly and with such self-evident arrogance that subsequent conflicts in the colonies were almost inevitable. The Sepoy Rebellion in May three years earlier had brought things to a head and had showed the British occupying forces that their ignorant suppression would no longer be tolerated without protest.

"A low-ranking officer, married to an Englishwoman named Velma. They were friends with Korshaw . . . the gardener murdered at Veitch and Sons. It seems they traveled together to Burma." David summarized the story for Thomas. "And our one-legged Bill was in Madras at the same time as Korshaw. Something was going on there, something that Bill thought important."

"But his premature death prevented him from telling you what it was. Hmm, orchid hunters? Korshaw was certainly an adventurous man. Burma . . . wait, it's coming back to me. Yes, that was a very pretty scandal indeed and a popular topic in the salons that season! The Englishwoman who poisoned her husband ran off with an intrepid explorer. That must have been the Velma in the letter."

"Was there anything in the papers? Pictures of the woman?"

"Now you're asking too much. Mr. Bale will know, though." Thomas sent for the butler, who suggested looking through past newspapers for the months in question, then went off to collect them.

As they waited for the newspapers to be brought out—Brooks's, of course, maintained its own archive—David spotted young Everett Ralston across the room and nodded to him. "Does Ralston still have much of a future after being tangled up in that affair with Josephine Simpson?"

"What do you think? His father is a High Court judge who got him a position in the ICS." Thomas sneered. "If you're looking for the embodiment of an elite civil servant, look no further than Everett Ralston. He's off to Madras in the New Year. And once again, we've managed to keep Lord Russell's reputation spotless. He's supposed to succeed Palmerston, who's a good man. We need better social-welfare laws not only here but in India as well, and that will only happen over there with more self-determination for the Indians."

"Men as corrupt as Korshaw can do a lot of damage. Perhaps that was it, that Bill thought Korshaw had somehow harmed the British crown?"

"There are many like Korshaw overseas, in it for themselves and to hell with the British and the Indians and everybody else. Strangely enough in this case, it keeps coming back to orchids," Thomas mused. "So was Korshaw the adventurer Velma absconded with?"

"I doubt it. It seems that everyone who knew Korshaw painted him as a shrewd businessman, but also as a fraud and a playboy. Not the kind to go off by himself, traipsing through the jungle for months on end with every snake, bug, and native trying to kill him."

A shudder went through Thomas at the thought. "What a horrid idea! Who in their right mind would do something like that voluntarily? Not long ago, Sir Charles Wood, our secretary of state for India, was looking for an undersecretary. I told him thank you and turned it down. You never know when someone's going to take it into their head to pack you off to the subcontinent."

The butler returned, setting a pile of newspapers on the table. "Would the gentlemen like anything else?"

"No, thank you," said Thomas, reaching for the *Times*. David reached for the *Morning Post*.

Various articles briefly relayed Satterley's mysterious death and the disappearance of his wife, who was invariably described as blond and petite, although there were no pictures of her to be found. David thought of Etta Ramsey, the young woman from Ilford who had been cheated by Korshaw, but immediately cast the thought aside again.

"A good evening, gentlemen," said a deep voice in front of them, and David looked up at no less a personage than Lord Cunningham himself.

In his perfectly tailored suit and with a gold watch chained to his vest, the gray-haired man personified everything that the British nobility represented. Cunningham held a seat in the upper house and acted as an advisor to the same Sir Charles Wood, the secretary of state for India, whom Thomas had just mentioned. He pulled a number of other strings, too, David knew. In contrast to his son, however, the father was able to maintain control over the passions he so zealously pursued. His face testified to a dissolute life, but David also knew that the man's ruddy nose and heavily veined cheeks could easily belie a keen intellect and strength of will.

The two younger men stood to greet Lord Cunningham. "Would you join us, sir?" Through his parliamentary work, Thomas was better acquainted than David with Lord Cunningham. The older man nodded and sat down. Mr. Bale appeared instantly, setting down an ashtray, a whisky glass, and a bottle of the best scotch without being asked. Cunningham was not part of their immediate circle of friends, and David assumed that a very specific reason lay behind his decision to honor them with his presence.

After a few general remarks about foreign policy and the weather, Cunningham asked after their families.

"My wife is expecting our third child, though I'm afraid she is confined to bed at her cousin's house up north. Doctor's orders, though

I hope to bring her home soon. Luckily, Lady Jane is with her," said Thomas.

"She is a guest at Sir Frederick's, isn't she?" Cunningham asked.

"Correct, sir." Thomas, momentarily distracted, waved to another guest.

"Lady Jane, yes . . . we heard a great deal about your unconventional wife last season, Wescott." Cunningham was peering at David through watery blue eyes.

"We owe it to her that we were able to expose Devereaux and his trafficking in human lives. I am very proud of her," said David emphatically.

"The world changes, and the people change with it. In my day, a woman would never have been able to take such liberties." Cunningham cut the tip off a cigar, held it between his lips, then spat before one of the butlers offered him a light.

"I see no disadvantage in having an intelligent, independent woman by my side. On the contrary, she enriches my life," David replied. He noticed Thomas's forehead rumple nervously.

"Well, I am not one to gainsay you, though I am happy to say that I, for one, have no more surprises to expect in that regard," Cunningham said, puffing on his cigar. "These days, I dedicate myself solely to collecting orchids. Flowers are beautiful, silent, and pleasing." He let out a droning laugh, coughed, and continued, "Having said that, they are not cheap. Still, one likes to have something to flaunt, am I right?"

"Orchids are certainly an expensive pastime. Deadly sometimes, too, I've come to realize." David saw one side of Cunningham's sideburns twitch.

"You mean that poor gardener, the man from Veitch? Terrible affair, that. A good man. He recommended a number of outstanding plants to me. A real loss for Veitch," said the lord, taking a swig of whisky.

A young butler brought a message for Thomas, who promptly stood and left. When he was gone, Cunningham said, "Wescott, I rate you highly as an experienced officer and a man of honor. Few have the guts and backbone to stand up to a man like Lord Lucan in court."

"Thank you, sir." *And a compliment usually leads to a request,* David thought.

Cunningham cleared his throat. "I know that you are investigating some delicate matters and that you're working with Martin Rooke."

"Sir?"

"Well now, I've heard that you met my son, Clifford, at Seven Bells. I take it that you were not there to bet."

"No, sir."

"My son, unfortunately, was. He has a weakness for games of chance, no matter the kind. It is not always easy to protect one's children." Waiting for a response, Cunningham gazed at David with half-closed eyes through the haze of cigar smoke.

"Who would you need to protect Clifford from? From himself, or has he made some enemies?"

"Come on, Wescott. We both know that Bill was blackmailing young men with their IOUs, and now he's got his just deserts." Cunningham leaned back in his armchair. His pose radiated superiority, but there was also something hesitant about the man. "In which directions are you investigating?"

"I can't tell you anything about that, sir."

"Then let me put my cards on the table. My son visited Pedley and wanted his IOUs back, but he did not kill that louse."

"Were you there, too?" asked David matter-of-factly.

"Most certainly not! That's got nothing to do with it. I know my son, and I know that he is not capable of murder. You have no reason to pester him with questions."

"Don't we? Thank you for explaining my job to me, but I will decide for myself who is a suspect and who is not." David had, in fact, long since crossed Clifford off his list, but he would not be intimidated by anyone.

"I have tried to settle this amicably, Wescott." Cunningham banged his glass onto the table. "You don't seem to know with whom you are dealing." He rose to his feet, the ash from his cigar tumbling onto David's armchair.

David made a point of seeming unimpressed, but inside he was seething. "I think I do, but all men are equal before the law, aren't they, Lord Cunningham?"

The nobleman sniffed contemptuously and turned away.

24.

Winton Park, Northumberland, December 1860

Jane sat by Ally's bed and stroked her friend's hand. Ally's face was pale as she lay nestled on pillows, and Jane wiped the sweat from her forehead with a moist cloth.

"Oh, Jane, I'm so sorry to cause so much trouble for all of you! As if there weren't problems enough without mine," said Ally, who was trying very hard to keep her fluttering eyelids open.

"What nonsense! I'm simply happy that your bleeding has stopped. Are you in any pain?"

Dr. Cribb had discovered that Alison's cervix had opened early, which meant they could expect an early birth. Still, because Ally was strong, and because she had survived the birth of twins and was already well into her eighth month of this pregnancy, the doctor remained confident that all would be well, and he had sent for the village midwife.

"No," Ally said bravely, and she squeezed Jane's hand. "It's just that I would have much preferred to bring my child into the world at home in London. With Thomas nearby, although—" A contraction seized her, and she pressed her lips together.

Feeling rather panicky, Jane hoped the midwife would arrive soon. "What should I do?" Jane murmured aloud, more to herself than to Ally.

"This is normal, Jane." Ally looked at her with warm, blue eyes. "The contractions come and go. All things considered, I'm glad Thomas is in London. He's far more nervous than me about these things. Have you been to see Charlotte?"

"They won't let anyone into her room." She had neither seen nor heard Charlotte since the previous day.

"She needs you more than I do. Go. Nora is here, and Dr. Cribb will be back soon."

Jane kissed her friend's flushed cheeks.

"Thank you, Jane," Ally called after her as Jane left the room.

Ever since her talk with Draycroft, Jane had observed everyone in the house with suspicion, continually wondering who could have had an interest in Rachel's death. As much as she replayed events in her mind, though, she could find no real connection between the pretty Roma girl and the Halstons' other staff. A secret liaison with a servant, a stablehand, or O'Connor was out of the question; if that had been the case, it would not have been necessary to lure Rachel to the hut using Draycroft as bait.

Opening the door to her room, Jane called out for Hettie, who was repairing small tears in the hems of Jane's skirts.

"Hettie, you have to help me. I want to see Charlotte."

"But she's been locked in," said Hettie, though Jane could clearly hear the enthusiasm for an illicit adventure in her voice.

"Bring your sewing things." Jane gathered up her skirts, and they made their way down the corridor to the opposite wing. When she drew close to Charlotte's bedroom, she heard voices coming from the children's room. Miss Molan was apparently playing with Eleanor, and little Pebbles was barking. O'Connor, on orders from Sir Frederick, had brought the dog back to the house that morning.

"Who has the key?" Jane murmured as she examined the lock on Charlotte's door.

Hettie was scanning the corridor. "Sir Frederick. Mrs. Gubbins also has one on her large key ring."

"And Gladys?"

"No, Gladys has to ask Mrs. Gubbins to let her in whenever she wants to visit Lady Charlotte. In the meantime, she's downstairs helping with the laundry."

Jane poked around in the lock with a hairpin, but to no avail. "Hmm, give me the knitting hook." The tool had a wire hook on the end.

Hettie handed it over and watched in fascination as Jane deftly picked the lock. "Well done, ma'am."

"Shh. Stay here and keep a lookout. If someone comes, knock twice." Jane slipped into Charlotte's room and was immediately enveloped in a nauseating stench. It was normal for bedrooms to get stuffy if they were closed up because the mattresses were usually stuffed with horsehair then covered with four or five sheets. Though it varied dependent on the housekeeper, a household's sheets were usually rotated every two weeks. This meant that sleeping on a freshly made bed was rare, and bedbugs were a constant problem.

Living in her uncle's house, however, Jane had grown used to meticulous cleanliness and had since kept her own home scrubbed and spotless. This included a weekly changing of the sheets. Mrs. Gubbins, however, took a thriftier approach, as Jane had discovered to her chagrin. And there, in Charlotte's room, the stink of old sheets mixed with the reek of vomit.

Charlotte lay on her bed in a nightdress and dressing gown, clearly under the influence of powerful sedatives. The heavy curtains had been closed, and the room lay in a permanent twilight. Pressing her hand to her mouth, Jane hurried to the window and threw it open. On a sideboard she found a number of bottles containing scented oils.

Rose? Too weak. Lavender? Good. Smelling salts? Just the thing. Jane trickled a drop of lavender oil onto a handkerchief and held it under her nose. Then she went over to the bed and wafted the smelling salts around Charlotte's face. The poor woman looked more dead than alive, hardly a surprise considering how much laudanum and ether she'd probably been given. Indeed, it seemed almost a miracle that the frail woman was still alive.

"Charlotte, dear Charlotte! It's me, Jane. Don't worry, I want to help you." She patted Charlotte's cheek and lifted her head from the pillow.

A bowl of water stood on the bedside table. Jane moistened a cloth and wiped Charlotte's mouth and nose clean. Then, using all her strength, she pulled Charlotte's limp body away from the vomit and to the other side of the bed, until she finally had Charlotte lying clear of the mess. Charlotte's hair fell wildly over her forehead, and some life slowly returned to her weak body. She coughed, gasped for air, and began to choke. A bucket stood beside the bed. Jane picked it up hastily and held it in front of Charlotte, but all the poor woman could spit out was phlegm before sinking back onto her pillow in exhaustion.

"Here. Breathe this in again." She waved the smelling salts under Charlotte's nose, and Charlotte finally opened her eyes.

Her pupils were dilated and black, but they began to focus, coming to rest on Jane's face. In a hoarse, barely audible whisper, she said, "Why is he doing this to me? I didn't do anything."

"Charlotte, tell me exactly what had happened in Cedric's room before Miss Molan got there."

Charlotte's lips were dry and cracked, her skin mottled, and the dark shadows under her eyes made her look like a ghost. "Nothing! Ceddie was lying on the bed. He was asleep."

Speaking was clearly a strain for her, but Jane did not let up. "What then? Something must have happened."

She held a glass of water to Charlotte's lips, and the sick woman sipped a little before continuing, "There was a bottle beside his bed. I don't know any more . . . I was trying to read the label when he woke up and saw me and began to scream. I tried to calm him down, just calm him down, but he kept on screaming. I held him tightly. It was horrible . . ."

"And then?"

Charlotte closed her eyes again and nodded. "She pulled me away from my son and said I wouldn't be able to do anything more to him. That I had already done enough damage." A strangling sob racked her emaciated body. "I love my children. They are *my* children! They belong to me . . . don't take them . . ." She mumbled some confused, unintelligible words.

"It will be all right. It was all a misunderstanding. Frederick wants only the best for your children." But Jane was uncertain what to make of Charlotte's words. Her reaction was excessive, obsessive. What if the doctor was right? What if she would rather drug or injure her children than be separated from them?

"Charlotte, listen to me." She stroked Charlotte's cheek and waited until the woman had opened her eyes and was looking at her. "You can't scream and thrash anymore. Do you hear me? You have to be calm and reasonable, or they will lock you up."

Groaning, Charlotte's lips quivered. "Don't lock me up, no—"

"If you act normally, then you won't have to take this stuff anymore. Then you will be able to think clearly again. Do you understand?" Jane held her chin firmly and looked her in the eyes.

Charlotte nodded gently and tears filled her eyes. With a sigh, Jane picked up the moist cloth and pressed it into Charlotte's hand. "Here. And . . ."

She heard two knocks at the door and jumped to her feet. "I'm not supposed to be here!"

Terrified, Charlotte frantically shook her head. "Don't go, please," she begged. "They hate me! They never wanted me here!"

Jane heard a woman's voice at the door and saw the doorknob slowly turn. Where could she hide? Behind the screen? Her feet would be visible. There was only the small space behind Charlotte's four-poster bed, the curtains of which were draped around the headboard. Jane pushed herself into the space and quickly arranged the drapes to cover herself.

Moments after she had pulled in her hand, she heard Mrs. Gubbins's domineering voice. "What's all these stories, my lady? You're causing us nothing but grief. Poor Sir Frederick, the things he has to put up with. He doesn't deserve any of this. What a misery. You should be ashamed of yourself, doing something like that to him and his children."

Jane heard Charlotte whimper.

"Oh, whine all you like. That's all you ever do. The first Lady Halston would never have done that. She would never have let herself go like you have. Look at yourself. It's disgusting. I'll send Gladys up to change the sheets. It's a waste is what it is. We changed the sheets just last week, and now look what you've done."

Jane stayed as still and calm as she could, breathing softly, trying not to move the bed-curtains. Mrs. Gubbins was so busy with Charlotte that she took no notice of the heavy material.

It sounded as if Mrs. Gubbins was fluffing the pillows. Water splashed, and the metal bucket rattled. "Well, haven't you done a fine job here, messing your bed while the bucket's on the floor. Not like we've got much else to do. We're only here for the likes of you, after all."

"Get out of here!" Charlotte croaked.

"I'll go once I've got things squared away here, and then I'll see to it that everything else in this house is shipshape. Oh, go ahead and close your eyes. Drink your medicine, and you'll be right as rain." Jane heard a cork pop out of a bottle, then a spoon being picked up.

The bed shook. It sounded as if Charlotte was refusing to take the laudanum. "You ungrateful woman! You've spat on me!"

Had Charlotte meant Mrs. Gubbins when she'd said they never wanted her here? Was it Mrs. Gubbins who hated Charlotte so much? So much that she would devise a plot to get Charlotte committed to an asylum?

"And just when Sir Frederick is about to see his biggest triumph. You don't appreciate them wonderful flowers at all. It means nothing to you that your husband's one of the best experts there is when it comes to orchids. At least *I* read *The Gardeners' Chronicle.*"

The bottle was put down, and the spoon clanked as it fell onto the tray where the medicines stood. Jane heard the little dog bark from across the corridor.

"I'm off now. I'm sending Gladys up to make the bed, then I'm going to tell Sir Frederick about your obstinate, churlish behavior. If you ask me, the doctor ought to give you another injection."

The rattling of keys accompanied Mrs. Gubbins to the door, which then closed behind her, the key turning in the lock. Jane cursed silently. Hettie would never be able to pick the lock! She was sitting in a trap, but at least the overbearing Mrs. Gubbins had not noticed that the door had been unlocked and the window opened.

Cautiously, Jane extricated herself from her hiding place, then pinched her nose to stifle a sneeze. She quickly leaned over Charlotte, who had curled up like a child and was crying softly into her pillow. "Charlotte, I'm going to go speak to Sir Frederick, and I'm going to swap the laudanum for water. Then you can drink some when they tell you to, all right?"

Jane plucked the cork out of the small bottle, poured the laudanum into the orchid pot that was standing on the dressing table, and refilled the bottle with water. "Look, just water." She shook the bottle to mix the few remaining drops of opium solution with the water, giving it a brown color similar to the original potion.

"All right," Charlotte murmured, her teeth chattering.

From the other side of the door, Jane heard Hettie call out quietly. "Ma'am!"

Jane thought fast. She could not climb out through the window, and the house had no balconies. The door that joined Charlotte's room to her husband's was a possibility. "Hettie, go into Sir Frederick's bedroom and open the connecting door."

"What if someone catches me?"

"Then run!"

Jane went to the center of the long wall, where the door to the adjoining room was. As expected, it was locked, but after a few seconds the key turned on the other side, and then Hettie was standing there, beaming at her.

"Quickly, ma'am. It sounds like there's a whole crowd coming up the stairs!"

They ran through Sir Frederick's bedroom, which was only slightly larger than his wife's and furnished with similarly plain furnishings. Jane put her hand on the doorknob at the exact moment that voices passed by in the hallway.

"That's Sir Frederick with Mrs. Gubbins and Gladys," Jane whispered, silently praying that the master of the house would not enter his bedroom.

The trio outside seemed to be in a hurry. They heard Charlotte's door being unlocked, then closed again. Jane opened the door and looked up and down the corridor carefully—apart from an occasional potted plant, it was empty—then dragged Hettie out behind her. After she had silently closed the door, she exhaled loudly.

"Good. I have to speak to Sir Frederick alone. But how am I going to manage that without making him angry?" Jane tapped her foot, then noticed Della hurrying excitedly up the stairs toward her.

"Oh, my lady, have you seen Mrs. Gubbins? Her daughter is here. Imagine! She's been away in India!" Della was trying to catch her breath.

"Such a lovely woman." She giggled. "I would never have guessed she and Mrs. Gubbins were related."

Jane smiled. "Wait here, Della. I know where to find her."

She knocked at Charlotte's door, which Gladys opened. As far as Jane could see, Sir Frederick was sitting on the side of his wife's bed, and Mrs. Gubbins was talking to him intently.

"Tell Mrs. Gubbins that she is needed downstairs urgently. She has a visitor." Before Gladys could close the door again, Jane wedged her foot in and pushed past Gladys. "Sir Frederick, could I have a minute of your time?"

Staring at her darkly, Mrs. Gubbins addressed Gladys. "Whoever it is can wait."

"Mrs. Gubbins, surely you don't want to keep your daughter waiting? Especially after she came all the way from India?" Jane warbled.

"Go," Sir Frederick growled. "I detest nervous biddies hopping around like chickens."

Her expression stony, Mrs. Gubbins left, and Gladys closed the window and drew the curtains. It had certainly grown cold in the room, but the stench, at least for now, was bearable.

"Gladys, go and get two new pillows and fresh bedcovers," said Jane before the maid could begin peeling off the sheets.

Reluctantly, Gladys looked at her. "But—"

"Immediately," Jane insisted.

Sir Frederick was still sitting on the edge of the bed, holding his wife's hand. Charlotte lay with her eyes closed. "I don't understand this. I would not have thought it possible."

"Sir Frederick, if you will allow me to speak about this, I don't believe that Charlotte did anything to hurt your son. It could have been someone else in the house," Jane began tentatively.

Sir Frederick abruptly released Charlotte's hand and stood. "What are you talking about? Who would have grounds to do anything to my son? Keep your nose out of my business!" he thundered.

"And what about Mrs. Gubbins? She makes your wife's life hard because she can't get over Charlotte's predecessor!" Jane shouted back, louder than intended.

Sir Frederick paused, taken by surprise. "Really? I did not know that, but Charlotte is the woman of the house, and she has to command the necessary respect herself. I can't be responsible for everything. The big orchid exhibition will take place in London this January. The Queen herself has announced that she will attend and present the prize for the rarest and most beautiful orchid. I have other things to worry about than my servants' squabbling!"

"Look at Charlotte. Please don't let the doctor inject her again. She is utterly exhausted. I—"

At that, Charlotte opened her eyes. Upon seeing Jane and Sir Frederick together, she sat up sharply. "You traitor!" she screamed, glaring at Jane. "You've made a pact with the devil, you—" Charlotte choked and gasped for air, her eyes staring wildly.

Sir Frederick angrily ground his teeth. "Enough! Go and see to Lady Alison. This is my job."

Reluctantly, Jane stepped out into the corridor. Passing the staircase, she glanced down to see Mrs. Gubbins talking with a young blond woman who could only have been her daughter.

Before returning to Alison, Jane wrote a telegram to David; she was beginning to doubt if she could help Charlotte at all anymore.

25.

London, December 1860

Together, David Wescott and Martin Rooke made their way along the street toward Veitch and Sons Royal Exotic Nursery. The recent snow had frozen the streets into a filthy mass. Coaches had a hard time driving over the sharp-edged ruts, and injured horses were commonplace. It was a difficult time for those who lived on the streets, too. Without a warm place to sleep, simply surviving became difficult.

"So what's become of that urchin you took in, David? Robbed you blind and fled on his heels, I'll wager?" Martin joked. His closely cropped hair was hidden beneath a woolen cap. David had never seen him in a top hat.

"Actually, no. Myron is a clever young lad, and he hasn't disappointed me. Levi has taken him under his wing and is teaching him to read and write."

Martin Rooke laughed. "Watch out, or word will get around." Then, more seriously, he said, "This cold weather will take its pound of flesh."

Chestnut sellers had set up their small stoves on street corners and could not fend off the needy swarms who merely wanted someplace to warm their frozen limbs.

"I don't think Myron is about to let anyone take his place." They had reached the steps leading up to the elegant entrance of Veitch and Sons. "Why is Veitch only now coming to you with this information?"

Rooke whacked his snow-smeared boots with his walking stick. "That's what we're about to find out."

They were greeted by a young man wearing a black suit and green apron emblazoned with the company crest. He took one look at Rooke's calling card and led them straight to Mr. Veitch's private office.

The old man greeted them with an anxious smile. A tray with tea and shortbread stood on his desk. "Gentlemen. Please take a seat and help yourselves."

David doffed his hat and set it on the table, and Rooke rolled up his woolen cap and tucked it into his coat pocket.

Veitch, a white-haired gentleman with a pince-nez on his pale nose, waited until both men had served themselves tea. "The cold has come too early. It is so damaging to my plants. I'd be lost without my greenhouses, but heating them in the winter is expensive. Without my exclusive clientele and their willingness to pay, I would have to close up shop."

Rooke cleared his throat. "Mr. Veitch, you called us here to tell us about Korshaw's concealed activities."

The businessman sighed. "The impatience of youth. I do not chatter idly, dear sir. My only aim is to make clear to you what this is all about. We are not some corner nursery, but a company with international associations. I supply orchids to the Continent, and I have customers in France and Prussia."

"I met Lord Cunningham at my club. He is a major orchid collector and another of your customers, if I understood him correctly?" David inquired politely.

"One of many notable gentlemen. That brings me to the reason for your visit: Korshaw was involved in independent dealings with my customers. Such an impertinence . . . and I trusted the man! I took him into my company with no good references and offered him a fresh start. Sheer ingratitude, that's what it was. Sheer ingratitude!" Veitch was shaking.

Rooke and David exchanged a glance, then David asked, "I take it Korshaw was dealing in orchids? Where was he obtaining them?"

Veitch slid forward to the edge of his chair. "Yes, of course! Orchids are the only way to get rich in this business these days."

"You do realize, Mr. Veitch, that you have just given us a motive for Korshaw's murder?" David watched the grower's reaction curiously; he did not believe the man capable of murder.

"What? Oh, balderdash, I'm not about to kill my best gardener. That is what he was—an exceptional gardener. He did tell me that he had been a businessman in India, but his true talent was with flowers, and especially orchids. The plants seemed to thrive in his presence; it was as simple as that."

"So he wasn't selling your orchids on the sly?" Rooke asked, nibbling on a piece of shortbread.

"No, no, which is why I never noticed his side dealings. Then Sir Robert Parks paid us a visit and requested another violet *Pleione praecox*! Do you see where this is going? I haven't offered such a flower in over a year. *Pleione praecox* is a long-petaled orchid, very large and rare, and correspondingly expensive. Other customers started coming in to ask about different rare orchids I have never sold. It finally dawned on me that Korshaw had been using my customers to sell his own orchids. I immediately went through the paperwork in his desk and came across a list of names. Most of them I know—as orchid hunters." Veitch reached into a file, withdrew a crumpled sheet of paper covered with cramped handwriting, and handed it to Rooke.

Both men scanned the list. Most of the names were accompanied by a month and a country. "Mungo Rudbeck, September, Mexico. Walter Mitscherlich, August, Burma. Derek Tomkins, September, Colombia, and so on. Can you tell us who else these men were working for?" Rooke asked.

Veitch made a face. "Crooks, the lot of them, if you ask me. Playing their backers against each other. Rudbeck works for Parks, Mitscherlich for Sander, and Tomkins exclusively for Halston, as far as I know."

David inhaled sharply. "Well, what do you know . . ."

"Halston," Rooke said thoughtfully. "Any news from there?"

After leaving Veitch's office, they walked for a while through the wintery, gray London streets, each man deep in thought. Eventually, David said, "I'll send a telegram to Halston. He needs to tell us the exact nature of his business relationship with Tomkins, but if I remember correctly, he said that Tomkins worked exclusively for him. He seemed proud of that."

"Is that a reason to kill Korshaw? Or to have him killed?" Rooke nodded to a policeman walking his beat.

They passed a stand offering soup and battered fish that catered primarily to the poor, who had no cooking facilities in their homes and therefore had to rely on street vendors for meals. Wherever he looked, David saw hungry people standing in front of shop windows, eating whatever they could buy for a few pennies. The smells of fish, peas, kidney pie, and pastries mixed with the stink of horse dung and human excrement.

"Hardly. Halston certainly has a temper, but he'd be more likely to go after his own man, Tomkins, than Korshaw. But Korshaw had other customers. Perhaps one of them felt cheated or defrauded. Cunningham, perhaps?"

David thought of Rachel, who had worked for Cunningham before entering the Halston household. "What if Rachel, the maid at—"

"I know who you mean," said Rooke.

"What if Cunningham used Rachel to infiltrate Halston's collection, and the whole story about the importunate son was simply made up?"

"And so Halston got rid of her?" Rooke stopped and turned away from a barefooted youngster shoveling dog feces into a bag with his bare hands. The boy would no doubt attempt to sell it to a tannery or a maker of leather gaiters.

"But how does his sick wife figure into all this . . . no, it doesn't fit together." Wescott pulled on his top hat a little tighter as a gust of icy wind swept between the buildings. Too many things did not fit together. "Have you made any headway with the Pedley affair?"

"Not really. We paid a visit to Seven Bells, but either they got wind of us coming in advance or they shined themselves up right after the murder. They were as clean as new pins. Nothing we could do. Big John laughed at us."

"As expected. What about Satterley and the black widow?" David had told Rooke all he knew about that case.

"She must have changed her name. I wasn't able to turn up any recent documents for a Velma Satterley. Are you still coming for a drink?" Across the street, a hanging pub sign squeaked in the wind, but David had the stink of the street in his nose, which robbed him of both his appetite and his thirst for beer.

"Thank you, but I think I'll just take a coach home. Jane might have sent a telegram."

The moment David stepped through his front door on Seymour Street, he found Levi and Blount waiting for him. "What's the matter?" he asked in alarm.

"A message from Lady Jane." Blount handed him the envelope. "She sent it express."

Levi, who had waited his turn to talk, then said, "Myron would like to tell you something, Captain."

David hurriedly read Jane's message. God, poor Charlotte was actually in danger of being locked away forever, Alison could give birth at any moment, and the housekeeper had a blond daughter who happened to be visiting from India. "I have to go to Northumberland! Blount, we leave as soon as possible."

After helping him out of his coat, Blount took his hat and walking stick. "But listen to what Myron has to say first. The boy has traversed half of London."

"I'll be in the library." David went straight to his desk and poured himself a glass of whisky, then reread Jane's telegram. "That scheming old witch!" As he knew from Jane, Mrs. Gubbins hated Charlotte, and now it turned out that her daughter had been in India. Maybe Rachel had uncovered something, or perhaps she'd overheard something she shouldn't have.

There was a tentative knock on the door, and Myron entered. The boy was barely recognizable from his former self. A few days of decent food, a warm bath, and new clothes had worked wonders. In front of David now stood an alert young lad whose eyes glowed with self-confidence. "Myron, I hear you're learning to read and write?"

"Yes, Cap'n. I can already write me name and a few words. The grub's smashing, and the kitchen's warm, and Mr. Levi's nice and so's Mr. Blount and—"

David tousled the effusive boy's hair. "It's all right, I know . . . but you wanted to tell me something?"

The boy's face turned radiantly proud. "I heard you talking about orchid hunters and that gardener who died. I've got lots of friends. The boys on the streets, we stick together . . . most of us, anyways. We've got eyes and ears everywhere. One of me friends, his name's Tom. He's got an uncle who was a soldier in India. Now he drinks and earns his keep working down on the docks if he isn't . . . well, that don't matter."

David tried to imagine what kind of business an army veteran and dockworker could get himself involved in and decided not to pry. "Yes?"

"Well, Tom's uncle went into a pub in St. Giles and saw Korshaw. He called out and waved, but all Korshaw did was turn his back and disappear into the crowd."

"Which pub?" asked David, already suspecting the answer.

"The Seven Bells it was. But that ain't all. Tom's uncle figured Korshaw had something to hide if he didn't want to see an old pal from the colonies, so he went after him and followed him all the way to the docks. This was in the middle of the night. Korshaw went right up to a sailboat from overseas that had just tied up. The ship was being unloaded, lots of crates of spices and ivory, that kind of thing. Then Tom's uncle got a shock because he saw Korshaw talking to a man that he himself was afraid of."

Myron looked at the floor.

David had been listening and watching the boy intently. "Are you keeping something from me, Myron?"

The boy fiddled with the sleeve of his jacket, a warm, tweed item that Josiah had outgrown. "I'm sorry, Cap'n. No one does nothing for free. Tom's uncle will only tell you the name face-to-face, and only if you pay 'im for it. He'll be working at the West India Docks all today."

Whether or not work was to be had at the docks depended on the arriving ships. Some weeks, two hundred trading ships or more tied up. Other weeks they were lucky to see thirty. Early mornings, the dockworkers gathered at the gates, hoping to be chosen for the day. More often than not, three hours of work was all they got, and what they earned was barely enough to live on.

"What's his uncle's name?"

"Dan."

"I hope you didn't promise him anything?"

Myron's eyes widened. "No, cross my heart! It's true enough, Cap'n, that we poor folk have to do what we can with whatever comes our way. A second chance don't come often."

David stifled a grin. "Then let's see if what Dan has to say is worth a penny."

"Yes, Cap'n!" Myron all but jumped along beside David, who strode back into the hall. "It's bound to be!"

"Blount! We're going to the docks!"

The West India Docks consisted of two docks, with a third under construction, on the Isle of Dogs, a tongue of land inside a bend of the Thames in London's East End. In the early afternoon, the coachman drove his three passengers along West Ferry Road. The sight of an undulating sea of masts, rigging, and a wide variety of ships made David's heart beat faster.

A railway line had been added since the construction of the harbor facilities proper sixty years earlier, making the loading and unloading of the big ships considerably more efficient. Even Blount looked out of the coach window with interest.

"They can sail from the import dock directly into the export dock, and the goods are hauled straight off to the farms," David explained to Myron. "There's a four-master being unloaded as we speak."

Myron pushed up the window and poked his head out into the cold. "The dockworkers are coming with sacks. Can I climb out?"

David banged on the wall of the coach with his stick, and the coachman drew his vehicle to a halt. After climbing out, David went over to the coachman. "Here's the first half." David gave the coachman what they had agreed on. "You'll have the rest once you've driven us home again. Where will we find you?"

"Corner of Emmet, in the Peacock's stables."

The Peacock was the kind of guesthouse typical of the docks, offering cheap bunks for seamen, along with prostitutes and reasonably good food. The sheds and depots stood a little farther north, along with the police station, customs offices, and the harbormaster's office. Past that came more warehouses and the workshops of carpenters, wagon makers, painters, blacksmiths, mechanics, and, set a little back from the fray, a workhouse and tiny cottages for the harbormaster's employees.

The docks were correspondingly chaotic. Seamen, tradesmen, dockworkers, street vendors, horse-drawn carriages, pack mules, and all manner of doubtful characters—who would even gather scraps of old rope if they could trade them for money—were milling about in a cacophony of noises and hollering. Myron seemed in his element as he nimbly dodged a cart that had slid out of the slippery traces, then pointed ahead at the porters.

"He'll be there! Come on!" Chest puffed out, his new boots polished, and his cap pulled low on his forehead, he strutted through the throng.

Blount, who wore a long coat and cape over his suit and who had taken to wearing a new bowler hat, stamped dourly through the ankle-deep, frozen sludge. Close to the river, snow never lasted long, unless the year was particularly cold and the frost bit hard for weeks. Like David, Blount kept one eye on dubious figures moving around the dock or standing in small groups, his revolver within easy reach beneath his coat.

"Not sure this was such a good idea, Captain," he murmured after they were jostled by two tough-looking dockhands. "What if it's a trap?"

Five men in rough coats with knives tucked into their belts suddenly emerged from behind a stack of crates, blocking their path. The one in front fixed them with a derisive squint and said something in

Russian to the others. Blount returned the insult in fluent Russian, making sure they saw his revolver, and the men let them pass.

Myron looked up admiringly at Blount. "I want to be just like you, sir. That was respect!"

"So where's our informant? We don't have all day," Blount grumbled.

The men on the docks, coarse characters to whom life had given nothing for free, hauled their sacks to waiting carts. One of them snatched his cap from his bald head and wiped the sweat from his face with a rag. The heavy work had left its mark on his body. His cheeks and nose were covered in a dense web of blue veins. The last two fingers on his right hand were missing, and he walked with a limp. Heaving his sack onto the cart, he stretched with a pained grimace and was about to shuffle back to a ship when he noticed Myron.

"Eh, Myron!"

"Eh, Dan. I kept me word!" Myron replied and proudly stepped aside.

Blount and David stepped forward, all too aware of the curious glances of the other dockworkers.

"Don't you 'ave some fine friends, Dan? Or are they lambs to slaughter?" A dark-skinned man let out an ugly laugh and dropped his sack close behind Dan as if by accident. "Oops."

David signaled to Dan to come closer. "Can you meet us at the Peacock? I'll pay for the time lost."

"And two dark ales and a beef soup!" Dan demanded, putting his cap back on. "Eh, Myron, looks like ye've landed on yer feet. If only Tom had yer kind of luck . . ."

Dan turned to a young man who was crouched on top of a crate. "Can y' take over for me, Bob?"

The young man didn't need to be asked twice. He jumped down immediately and ran to the enormous East Indiaman ship bobbing in the icy Thames water.

Suddenly, a soft, whirring noise sliced the air, and Myron, who had been standing in front of Dan, opened his mouth in a silent scream.

Dan immediately grabbed the boy under his arms, staring in disbelief at the handle of the knife protruding from the boy's skinny body. "Myron . . . come on, lad, say something!"

Turning instantly, Blount was already in pursuit of the assassin, one of the Russians from moments before. All five were running, scattering. David looked around, but all he saw were impassive faces, with only a few showing honest emotion. Violence and crime were the norm there. You closed your eyes and kept on, hoping to survive.

Myron's eyes stared lifelessly at the gray winter canopy. "Let me take him," said David, lifting the dead boy in his arms. The handle of the knife jutted skyward accusingly.

David had prepared himself for many things, including an attempt on his own life or Blount's, but he was not prepared for the death of this small and innocent boy. Gently, he closed Myron's eyes and swallowed back his own rising tears. "Whoever did this will pay. We'll find him."

"Sir, I think it was me they was after," said Dan beside him, stroking Myron's limp hand.

David cleared his throat. "No doubt. You need to tell me what you know."

Anxiously scanning the docks, Dan suddenly seemed as tense as a deer that has scented its hunter. "Not here."

In the meantime, someone had alerted two police officers who had been patrolling the other side of the dock. They ran over.

"Do you know who did this?" asked the elder officer.

"My assistant is pursuing the presumed killer. Russian, I'd say," David said.

"And you are . . . ? Were you in business with the Russians?" The officer took out a notebook.

David identified himself and demanded that Rooke be called, which defused the officer's suspicions. Together, they carried David's sad cargo into the harbor office.

They laid Myron on a bench, removed the knife, and covered the boy with a blanket, then someone handed David and Dan tea and rum. David blamed himself for Myron's death, and he was angry with himself for not seeing that something like this might happen. "I should've forbidden Myron to come along!" he muttered angrily to himself.

"Captain," said Dan quietly, sitting beside him on a stool. "I get what yer feeling, but the boy knew what he was doing. He was a clever rascal. And you made him feel worth something. I ain't never seen him so happy as in these last few days."

David looked up sadly. "A brief happiness . . ."

"Better a moment of happiness than a long and miserable life, eh? Listen, I'll tell ye who I saw Korshaw with, then I'll be dropping out of sight."

"I'll give you some money, enough to let you disappear for a while. It's the least I can do," David promised.

"Korshaw was about the rottenest piece of filth I ever ran across in India, a treacherous, two-timing rat ye wouldn't believe if he told ye the sun rose in the morning. I'd been stationed in Burma for three months and met him at the casino in Bassein. He was with an adventurer, a man he wanted to do some big deal with. Korshaw always had some kind of crooked business going, but the other fellow was on to him, I'd a sense of it. I knew he'd be in hot water if he ever cheated this fellow. Korshaw was murdered, wasn't he?"

Dan had spoken in a low voice, scanning the room as he spoke, but the only man in sight was a constable at a desk, busy with paperwork.

"It was supposed to look like suicide, but it was murder," David confirmed.

"When I saw the two of 'em together back then, I had a feeling it wouldn't end well. Know what I mean? How sometimes ye just sense that somebody's going to come to harm? I've read occasional bits and pieces about that adventurer in the papers since India. He's an orchid hunter, a real specialist."

"What's his name?" David could not stand the sight of the dead boy any longer.

"Tomkins. Derek Tomkins."

26.

For a raven ever croaks, at my side,

Keep watch and ward, keep watch and ward,

Or thou wilt prove their tool.

Yea, too, myself from myself I guard,

For often a man's own angry pride

Is cap and bells for a fool.

Alfred Lord Tennyson

Winton Park, Northumberland, December 1860

Jane woke with a stabbing pain in her side. Her corset had twisted and was poking painfully into her soft skin. Only a man could have conceived of such an instrument of torture as suitable clothing for a woman! Sitting up, she straightened the detested undergarment. The winter sun shone weakly through the window, the curtains only half-drawn.

The first thing she saw was her friend's bed. After an arduous night marked by fear of more bleeding, Alison had fallen into an exhausted sleep.

Nora lay on the carpet beside Alison's bed, and Hettie had curled up in an armchair. Jane smiled. The two young women had been a great help and could not have been more attentive to Alison. Jane rose from the worn chaise longue, stretched her arms, and rolled her stiff neck to and fro.

Still wearing her evening dress from the night before, and with her hair bedraggled, Jane knew she must look like one of the fallen girls that frequented St. Giles. She swept the curtains open, and Nora was instantly wide-awake.

"Oh, good gracious! Pardon me, my lady. I'll put water on and get breakfast started right away." She looked over at Alison.

"Get changed first, Nora. Lady Alison is still sleeping."

Nora seemed relieved and gave Hettie a shove as she left the room. Hettie grumbled indignantly, then fell out of her armchair in surprise when she realized where she was.

Dr. Cribb had stayed with his patient until well past midnight. He had done what he could to stop the contractions from getting any stronger. He wanted to be sure that Alison's bleeding had caused no harm, and his efforts seemed to have been successful.

After Jane had bathed, dressed, and eaten some breakfast, she remembered Mrs. Gubbins's visitor and went out into the hall, where she met Mr. Draycroft.

"Good morning, my lady," he greeted her, inscrutable as ever.

"Good morning, Draycroft. Yesterday evening, a visitor arrived for Mrs. Gubbins and her husband. From India, I heard? How thrilling!"

"You mean Mabel, Mrs. Gubbins's daughter?"

"Yes, of course. I would love the opportunity to talk with her. I spent my childhood in India, you know," said Jane.

"If you would like to wait in the green drawing room, my lady, I will have Mabel brought to you."

"That's very kind, thank you."

Jane walked through the chilly entrance hall and was happy to discover that a fire had already been lit in the drawing room. When

Charlotte's porcelain figures caught her eye, however, she was overcome by a desperate sadness. What could she do to help the poor woman? Jane would gladly have talked with Cedric himself, but she was not allowed in his room, and Miss Molan watched over the boy like a mother hen.

A young messenger entered the drawing room with a telegram for her. Jane tore open the envelope, and her hand instantly rose to her lips. "New development. Black widow is blond. Myron dead. Korshaw friends with Tomkins in London. I arrive tomorrow. Be careful. David."

What could that mean? Tomkins was in England? But hadn't Frederick just received a letter from Colombia? And the black widow was actually blond? That could only refer to the woman who had poisoned her husband in India, which David had mentioned in his last report to her. The key to everything seemed to be Korshaw. Oh, it was all so exasperating!

Jane gazed through the window. Ice crystals had formed around the edges of the glass. Outside, thick icicles hung from tree branches, and the artfully carved hedges seemed covered in a layer of frosting. The snow had only been cleared from the entrances, and rounded white caps crowned the stair posts. From where she stood, Jane saw Miss Molan carrying a jug and walking on the path that led around the outside of the house to the kitchen.

The soft sound of someone clearing her throat brought Jane out of her thoughts, and she turned to see Mrs. Gubbins standing behind her. Her graying hair was pulled back tightly, and a string with two keys on it hung from her belt.

"I asked to see your daughter, not you," said Jane.

"Draycroft said the same to me. Unfortunately, my daughter is not well. Her long journey has left her ill, and I hope that my lady will forgive her for not attending."

"What's wrong with her? I hope she hasn't come down with some kind of tropical disease? Or a fever? Something like that can be extremely annoying and can come and go for years."

"No, it's nothing like that. She is simply exhausted and needs rest," Mrs. Gubbins quickly reassured her.

Jane raised her eyebrows. "That's a relief. Then I'm sure she'll be strong enough to join me for tea this afternoon."

Mrs. Gubbins hesitated, then nodded. "Very good, my lady."

"Oh, and where is your daughter lodging? Does she have a comfortable room?" Jane inquired.

"My husband and I live in the stable master's quarters. We have a guest room there."

"I'm glad to hear it. It must be wonderful for you to finally see your daughter again after . . . how long has it been?"

"Mabel's been away for eight years, my lady." Mrs. Gubbins's hands trembled as she spoke, and Jane read the trembling as a sign of emotion in the normally composed woman.

"Thank you." Jane watched the housekeeper leave. Mrs. Gubbins clearly not only expected perfect behavior from her staff, but she had also built an iron cage of discipline around herself.

What if Rachel had seen a photograph of Mabel then read a newspaper article about the black widow and put two and two together? *No time to lose,* Jane thought, hurrying up to her room.

"Hettie, take out my coat. We're going for a walk."

She told Hettie about David's telegram but did not mention Myron's death. David had mentioned the boy to her, a boy he had wanted to give a second chance. And this was the same man accusing her of being too softhearted? Jane smiled to herself.

"Ma'am, how far are we going? Should I be putting on my heavy boots?"

"Just as far as the stables." Jane pocketed the small pistol David had given her to defend herself. It fired only a single shot, but sometimes one shot was enough.

Over a sturdy day dress, Jane wore a short velvet coat with long tails and a fur collar. Since her gloves were unlined, she kept her hands tucked inside her muff instead. Hettie loved the new tweed coat that

Jane had custom-ordered for her. The girl had never had any new clothes made just for her, and it was a pleasure for Jane to see Hettie so happy.

"It's actually lovely up here." Jane and Hettie were standing on the terrace in front of the park, looking out over the snow-covered fields toward the treetops, beyond which lay the river and the moor. The skies were once again hung with gray clouds.

"Humph. I'll be happy when we're back in London. Or even better—in Cornwall! Ma'am, will we be at Mulberry Park for Christmas?" There was yearning in Hettie's voice, a longing for the stretch of land she called home. She began to hum, "O, come all ye faithful—"

"I'm afraid not. Christmas is only two weeks away. Even if Ally brings her child into the world today or tomorrow, she can't drive home again immediately. And Charlotte . . . oh, Hettie, whatever are we going to do?"

Jane saw a man striding through the trees, a gun over his shoulder and a hound at his side: O'Connor. He had seen her as well and headed toward them.

"That Mr. O'Connor, ma'am." Hettie pulled her shoulders back. "Strange that he isn't yet married . . ."

"Maybe he has a dark secret," Jane joked, and her thoughts turned to Miss Molan. Perhaps something was going on there, and they had skillfully managed to keep it under wraps?

"Good morning, my lady. Miss Hettie," O'Connor greeted them pleasantly. "Guests don't normally put up with Winton Park this long. It gets particularly lonely up here in the winter, unless you like to hunt. After Christmas, we always expect a big hunting party, though I'm not at all sure Sir Frederick will follow tradition this year."

"You mean because of Lady Charlotte?" O'Connor's dog had positioned itself beside Jane. Thinking of Rufus, she scratched its head as they walked. She was also beginning to feel the need to return home.

"That too," said O'Connor, offhand as usual.

Jane's instinct told her that O'Connor was a good man, so she decided to talk with him more frankly. "Rachel was lured onto the moor by someone in the house. We know that with certainty."

The gamekeeper's expression darkened. "You're sure? That's not good. If Rachel was having an affair with the butler, I could take him to task—"

"No! Take my word for it, Mr. Draycroft had nothing to do with it," Jane assured him hurriedly.

O'Connor glanced at her in surprise. "You seem very certain of that."

"I am. Without explanation, you will simply have to believe me. Did you know that the Gubbinses have a daughter who's been away in India?" Jane turned them onto the path that led to the stables.

O'Connor stopped and looked at her dourly. "Where's this going, my lady? Are you implying something?"

"What? No! What makes you think that?"

His expression relaxed. "Then you didn't know. Mabel and me, we were quite close, once."

"Oh!"

Hettie inhaled loudly.

"It's long over. She wanted something different, and she got it. Now, if there's nothing else, my lady, I've other things I have to be doing." He tipped his cap and went off with his dog in the other direction.

When he was out of earshot, Hettie said, "He has some nerve! Though he doesn't seem to have much good to say about Mabel Gubbins. And if she takes after her mother even a bit, he can count himself lucky to be rid of her."

Jane's thoughts, however, were leaning in a different direction. Mabel had got what she wanted. What had O'Connor meant by that? "Come on, Hettie. Mabel has a few questions to answer."

As they stepped into the courtyard in front of the stables, they saw Mr. O'Connor talking with Miles. The stable master's quarters were attached to the end of the stable building. "Hettie, I want you to go over there and ask the men something about horses, anything to distract them. I want to get to the Gubbinses' rooms without being seen."

"What should I ask?" Hettie said unhappily.

Jane simply gave her a small push toward the men then ran along the hedge, briefly pausing behind a parked carriage. She saw Hettie gesticulating wildly and steering the two men into the stable, and she grinned.

As quickly as her dress and the frozen cobblestones would allow, Jane hurried to the single-story stable master's quarters. She saw a shadow move behind one of the windows. She had to knock twice before the door opened a few inches.

"Yes?" The female voice inside sounded anxious and young.

"Miss Mabel Gubbins? I'm Lady Jane Allen, here as a guest of the Halstons. May I speak with you for a minute?"

The door opened further, and Jane entered a narrow vestibule leading directly into a small kitchen and a living room that was hardly any larger. The rooms were very warm, which Jane assumed had to do with the daughter's return from India and her need to readjust to English climes.

"Please, my lady, have a seat in the living room. Tea? I've just brewed some."

Mabel Gubbins spoke very softly and with a slight accent. She may have been thirty, but her features were girlish, and she looked younger. Her flaxen hair was parted carefully in the middle and tied back into a knot, and large, blue eyes gazed out from a round face. Her demeanor was courteous, her expression eager and friendly. Was this the face of a woman who had poisoned her husband then run off with an adventurer?

"Tea would be lovely." Jane took a seat and set her muff aside. "Miss Gubbins," she began.

"Mabel, please," said the young woman, handing Jane a cup of aromatic tea.

"Excuse my barging in like this, Mabel, but I am so happy to finally talk to someone who has just returned from India, as I grew up there."

Mabel had wrapped a tartan shawl around her shoulders and perched on the edge of a chair. It was the posture of someone used to being subordinate, not the posture of a self-assured officer's widow. That, or Mabel was an exceptionally good actress.

"Really? I was there for eight years, but now I'm very happy to be home. The climate was not good for my health, and with all the humidity there, the pianos were always out of tune. Horrible!" A smile flashed over Mabel's face.

"Are you a musician?"

"I teach music. I don't have the courage or the confidence to perform onstage, which you need as a professional musician. That was my dream once, but now I teach gifted girls and am happy if they can learn to love the music for itself." Mabel paused. "Pardon me. When it comes to my music, I get carried away."

"Oh, no, quite the opposite, I find it extremely refreshing. Women have a hard enough time finding a useful occupation that is also socially acceptable."

Mabel's eyes lit up. "I know! There are so many female talents that can never come to the fore. I try to make my students realize that they are capable of more than just a marriage of convenience." So, Mabel Gubbins was a secret supporter of women's rights. Where did she get that from?

"Then may I assume you are not married?"

Mabel lowered her eyes. "No. I . . . well, some years ago I had to make a choice, and I have not regretted it."

"Tell me about India! I miss the smells of the spice markets, the forests, the heat, all the wonderful colors!"

The exotic climate might well have caused her grief, but Mabel apparently felt some connection to India, and she was more than happy to tell Jane about it, describing her travels through the various British administrative regions. "The only place I would not like to return to so quickly is Burma," she concluded. "The people there are not my sort, and the heat is even more unbearable."

"But you were there?"

"My last employers moved from Calcutta to Bassein to try to deepen some business relationships."

"And are you going to continue teaching now that you're back in England?"

"I've accepted a new position in Kent. Lady Teynham was looking for a woman to teach music to her daughter."

Jane nodded. "I wish you every success there, Mabel. It was a pleasure speaking with you. I'm sure your parents are proud of you."

A shadow crossed Mabel's face. "Yes. Thank you, my lady."

A bowl containing a small heap of powder caught Jane's eye. "Spices from India?"

Mabel shook her head. "Oh, no. No, Miss Molan was good enough to let me have a few crushed henna leaves. I have some cloth that I wish to dye."

Jane froze inside. The leaves of the henna plant were traditionally used in India for making a dye to decorate hands. The color was an intense brown, and the dye could also be used for fabric or hair. Trying to keep her tone light, Jane asked, "Where would a henna plant grow here?"

Mabel laughed and said, "You're right, henna won't grow in this cold, but Sir Frederick allowed Miss Molan to grow a henna plant in his hothouse. I think it is very nice of him, considering that he needs all the space he can get for his orchids. My mother is actually very worried about him and says that ever since the death of his first wife he's been quite obsessed with these flowers. Sad, isn't it? When you lose your great love, then live with someone who doesn't understand you? You know . . ."

Jane was already on her feet. "Mabel, you have no idea how much you have helped me! I'm sorry, but I have to go!"

Out in the yard, Jane searched quickly for Hettie, finding her at the stable entrance with Miles, Mr. Gubbins, and a black horse. "Hettie!" Jane called to her.

The maid said something to the men, who laughed, then Hettie hurried over to Jane. "Yes, my lady? Have you found something out?"

"My lord, yes! How could I have been so blind? Tell me, Hettie, what did you say to the men?"

"Oh, ma'am, it was so childish. I asked about the horses' teeth, why they put up with having a bit in their mouths. You know, that sort of silly girlish twaddle, but they liked it." Hettie was grinning broadly.

"You're an absolute wizard, Hettie!" Jane said and patted her cheek. "But listen closely—Miss Molan is our suspect. She came out of the house this very morning carrying a pitcher."

They were hurrying through the park, and Jane only slowed her steps when they were close to the servants' wing. "She would have poured it out somewhere around here. And fool that I am, I didn't give a second thought as to why she would have bothered going outside at all."

"I can't say I follow you completely, ma'am." Hettie stumbled along behind Jane. "Oh, look, ma'am. Someone tipped out a dark liquid here."

They were standing above the small yard in front of the kitchen. A hedge shielded them, keeping them out of sight from the staff down below. It was a good place to get rid of something secretly, and if it hadn't snowed, the liquid would have seeped away unnoticed into the earth. As it was, a dark fringe had settled into the snow.

Jane crouched. "Clever Miss Molan. She poured it into the hedge, but she forgot that the ground was frozen and that not everything would drain right away. Once the earth was saturated, the rest of it spread into the snow." She scratched up a chunk of snow and raised it to her nose. It smelled distinctly of wet hay. She held it out to Hettie to see. "Do you know what this is?"

"Blood?"

"No. Henna."

"What?"

"It's a dyestuff from India. You can use it to color cloth or skin. Or hair." She looked meaningfully at Hettie.

The import of Jane's words struck home instantly. "My goodness, no! Then she's . . . We have to get to Lady Charlotte!"

27.

London, December 1860

The man had spent the entire night sitting on the cell floor. He had touched neither the porridge nor the water, and he had not said a word. The other inmates kept a respectful distance from him, which only confirmed David and Blount's suspicion that they were dealing with a professional assassin.

Now, the next morning, David and Blount were in Martin Rooke's office. "Martin, I'm running out of time," David said, his anxiety showing. "I have to drive north! Jane is in danger, I can feel it, but—"

"We can't let Myron's murderer go free, and we have to find out why he killed the boy and not the uncle." Rooke was standing at the window, arms crossed.

"We don't know if I caught the right one," growled Blount. "I'm starting to think it was one of the others, the one with the big mouth."

He rubbed his knuckles, which were chafed from the fight he'd had with the man when he'd finally caught up with him at the docks.

Blount had a split lip, and one of his ribs was probably broken. If he were given the opportunity to interrogate the prisoner, Blount might have returned the favor.

Outside, a church clock struck ten, and street vendors began offering the day's first meal. "Martin?" David drummed his fingers impatiently on the desktop.

Martin Rooke rubbed his chin and went to the door, which stood ajar. "Berwin!" he bellowed down the corridor.

A sergeant was at the door moments later. "Sir?"

"Bring last night's prisoner into my office."

"The Russian? The silent one?"

"Did we arrest anyone else?" Martin snapped.

"No, sir." The young sergeant left hurriedly.

"You both speak Russian, don't you?" Rooke placed a low stool in the center of the room and pushed the chairs and the table out of the way.

"Blount speaks several dialects. Also Hungarian," David replied, taking off his coat.

Blount and Rooke did the same, Blount cursing as he withdrew his left arm from his sleeve. Levi had helped with his bandages, but every movement hurt and would do for some time yet.

"Blount, don't touch him! You've done enough. This is my job." David grimly rolled up his sleeves.

Rooke grinned. "You sound like you're the only one who's going to enjoy himself."

"They could prosecute you. You're a regular officer."

"Extraordinary situations call for unconventional means." Rooke lifted a booted foot onto the stool. "If he doesn't open his mouth, then I'm in the wrong profession."

It took a few minutes, but Berwin finally dragged the prisoner in. "He was resisting, sir."

The broad-shouldered Russian had a bleeding nose, and a new lump had appeared on his shaved head. He held his hands, balled into fists, in front of his body. The handcuffs used by the Metropolitan Police were made of heavy iron and could not be removed without a key or tools.

"Put him on the stool, Berwin, and tie up his ankles," Rooke ordered.

The Russian looked around, weighing up his surroundings and his enemies, searching for any opportunity to escape. His muscles were tense, and a vein in his neck pulsed; he grinned contemptuously as Berwin tied his feet together with a leather belt. When the young sergeant straightened up again, the prisoner spat in his face and uttered an obscenity.

Rooke said, "Berwin, go make some tea. Preferably in another station, if you know what I mean."

The sergeant paled. "Yes, sir."

When the door had closed behind him, Blount said in Russian, "Don't try anything, you rat, and your profanity won't get you anywhere."

The man gaped at him, astonished.

"What's your name?" David asked.

The brute simply spat and swore again. David and Rooke exchanged a glance. Rooke, standing behind the Russian, grasped him by the shoulders, and David hit him on both ears. He had not cupped his hands, nor did he strike him hard enough to burst his eardrums, but the blow was painful enough to let the prisoner know that they were serious.

The man shook his head and let out a stream of invectives in Russian until Blount shouted in his face, "Shut up!"

Once again, David asked in Russian, "What's your name?"

The man stared obstinately toward the door. The muscles in his neck bulged.

"All right." David took a position in front of the man, and Rooke grabbed him roughly by the chin.

The prisoner's eyes widened in sudden fear. It looked as if he had already experienced what he knew would follow, or had done it himself to others. "No, please! Taras!"

Rooke released the man's head.

"Taras. Taras what?"

"Komarow. I didn't kill the boy."

"Who did?"

Taras shook his head. "He'll kill me."

"We could kill you, too," David said.

"Yes, but then you would have nothing," Taras answered.

"What do we have now? A Russian who told us a name, which could be real or false." David turned away.

"Ask him if the boy was the target," Rooke growled.

David translated, but the prisoner said nothing. In Russian, Blount said, "I could smash his knees." Picking up a policeman's baton that was standing in a basket in a corner of the room, he tapped it on the man's kneecap. Slowly, he raised the club.

"No!" Taras cried. Sweat formed on his forehead. "The boy was the target."

"Why?" David took out a handkerchief and filled it with coins from his pocket. When Taras again fell silent, he hefted the handkerchief in his hand, feeling its weight, then held it out to Blount. With a grin, Blount added more coins. David knotted the handkerchief and whacked the tight little sack against the edge of the desk. He did not like torture at all.

"If you force me to hurt you, it will hurt me more. But make me angry and I can't guarantee anything," he said softly.

"If you think your miserable life is worth two cents, then talk!" Blount added. "The captain is pressed for time, and that makes him . . . unpleasant."

Still standing behind the man, Rooke watched the captain and Blount intently.

"What will you do with me if I talk?" Taras looked at them dubiously, eyes narrowed to slits.

David conferred briefly with Rooke, then said, "We'll set you free."

"And if I say nothing?"

"Then you'll be hanged as a Russian revolutionary who planned an attack on the House of Lords," David said, admiring Rooke's creative suggestion.

"You can't do that! There's no proof!" Taras shouted.

"We even have witnesses." David hoped urgently that the man would finally talk. He wanted to take the afternoon train.

Taras snorted and cursed then finally said, "I don't know why the boy had to die, but we were paid to find you and kill him. Just him, no one else. If we'd wanted otherwise, you'd all be dead."

"Oh, you think so?" Blount said with a snarl.

"You're quick, and you think like one of us. That's the only reason you caught me, but sooner or later, we would have gotten you." Taras looked from Blount to David. There was nothing in his eyes but the unsettling certainty that he meant what he said.

"Who hired you?"

"Ask Big John. Now beat me to death. That's all I have to say." Taras closed his mouth and gazed at the door, his dull eyes those of a man awaiting his fate.

David translated their exchange for Rooke, who shouted down the corridor for Berwin. The sergeant was back in the room so fast that he could not have been far away.

"Take him back to his cell," Rooke ordered.

"Are you really going to let him go?" Blount asked.

"Yes, but the first solid ground he'll feel under his feet will be in Australia," said Rooke. They all knew that what might happen on the convict ship to Australia was another story.

"Big John?" Rooke had straightened his shirt and put his jacket on again.

"Are you coming along?" David was already putting on his coat and hat.

"Of course. I'm not going to let you go to St. Giles alone."

St. Giles was no less dangerous in daylight than it was at night, but it was certainly uglier, revealing the hateful face of poverty at its worst. The Bank of England and London's magnificent boulevards and parks were just a few streets away, but there in Old Nichol, a labyrinth of stinking alleys hemmed in by dilapidated tenements, a visitor moved in another world. Different rules applied there, and anyone from outside who entered that haven of destitution, violence, and crime would be sniffed out immediately and either sucked into the vortex or spat out again.

The corpses of dogs and cats lay in and around pools of dirty water. Makeshift repairs to buildings' broken windowpanes had been made with newspaper and scraps of wood. Rooke wore a bowler hat and carried a revolver and baton beneath his coat, as did Berwin, who followed at his heels.

"The death rate here is five times higher than in the rest of London," said Rooke, dodging a pig that was trotting down the lane.

"That's the effluent. The people here drink the fouled Thames water and dump their rubbish on the roadside, and as long as that continues, nothing here will change," David said. His eyes were everywhere at once, scrutinizing all movement, peering into every entrance, but no one seemed to be following them today.

They reached the entrance to the Seven Bells unmolested. The door opened immediately, as if someone was expecting them, and they were led wordlessly into the large barroom where Big John sat behind a heavy wooden table. It looked as if he had just eaten, for he tossed his knife onto a meat platter and wiped his mouth on his sleeve.

A few thin rays of light entered the room through the grimy windows, and it was only when they stepped closer that they saw the two armed bruisers on either side of Big John's chair. Rooke glanced warningly at David.

"Captain, you honor me! Oh, and our very special friend, Mr. Rooke, is with you. Didn't we meet for the first time recently?" Big John, holding the better cards, savored the situation.

"So you rely on foreign murderers these days?" said David, referring to Taras.

"One can never have enough good people, wouldn't you agree? But joking aside, I have no idea what you're talking about," said Big John calmly. "May I offer you something to drink?"

"Why the boy? Why did you have the boy killed? He did nothing to you," said David accusingly.

Big John's small, piercing eyes looked at David almost with sympathy. "As I said, I had nothing to do with it. I wash my hands of it." He dipped the tips of his fingers in a bowl of water that was standing on the table, then dried them on the tablecloth.

Leaning forward, Rooke spoke in a low voice. "Taras Komarow has told us a very different story."

For a moment, the former boxer seemed to be weighing various courses of action. Then he drank a mouthful of beer and gave his men a signal, at which they moved to the opposite corner of the room. There were no guests in the bar yet; officially, the Seven Bells was only open in the evening.

"Did he?" Big John murmured. "He can't have told you much, because he knows nothing. That's what keeps an organization healthy, you know. Every little cog only gets the bit of information it needs. Naturally, I planned it that way. I won't stand for my people playing me for a fool." He was referring to Pedley's murder, but as he well knew, they could not prosecute him without witnesses. "On my mother's grave, the boy's death does not rest on my conscience. Sometimes even I am just following orders."

"Then you know who was behind it?"

Big John reached below his seat and produced an envelope. "You have a mortal enemy, Captain, and you probably don't even know it. Revenge can wear many faces. I like you, though you may not believe it. Here."

He handed David the envelope. "And now, please excuse me. I have some urgent business that needs my attention. Or was there something else, Mr. Rooke?"

Rooke clenched his jaw. All of them knew that, legally speaking, he could prove nothing against Big John. "We're not done with you yet, Big John. Everyone makes mistakes."

"Then take care you don't slip up first," Big John replied.

In silence, the men left the grim establishment, watching every shadow until they were well outside St. Giles. David took the letter out of his pocket and tore it open only when they had reached a coach station.

Isn't it true that the loss of someone you care about hurts more than a knife in your own back? This is just the beginning. D.

David turned the piece of paper over in the light. It was heavy and expensive but bore no watermark.

"My God," he muttered. He knew that Charles Devereaux was hiding behind that signature. Who else could it be?

Rooke had been watching David and only glanced at the words when David handed him the letter. "Is that . . . ?"

"Devereaux, yes. I took Jane from him, and I destroyed his trade in young girls and his business here in England." A shudder went through David, because if Devereaux had truly returned, then David really did have an enemy capable of anything. He looked earnestly at his friends. "Not a word about this to Jane!"

"We need to hurry, Captain," said Blount. "The train leaves in an hour."

28.

Winton Park, Northumberland, December 1860

The wintry air and their tight dresses did not make it any easier for Jane and Hettie to return quickly to the house. But when they arrived, the next piece of bad news was already awaiting them.

Gladys came from the kitchen, and she had clearly been crying. "This is all so terrible! I want to leave this place. I can't stand by and watch this—"

"Watch what?" Jane asked, taking the maid's trembling hands in hers and rubbing them soothingly.

"Lady Charlotte has had a terrible attack. She looked like a she-devil. She was raving and scratching, and Mr. Draycroft and Sir Frederick had to hold her down so that the doctor could give her morphine. A person can't live like that!" Gladys sobbed.

"Where is Miss Molan?" Jane looked around, just as Della came running down the stairs.

"The baby is coming!" Della cried. "Gladys, help me. We need more water and clean towels!"

At that moment, Alison needed her more than poor, sedated Charlotte did. With great haste, Jane and Hettie doffed their coats and hats, washed their hands, and ran to Alison's room. Dr. Cribb was standing over the bed with the midwife, telling Alison how to breathe.

"I know how I'm supposed to breathe. This is not my first child!" Alison puffed. Her cheeks were bright red. Nora had untied her mistress's hair, and sweaty strands clung to Alison's face.

They had spread fresh linens out for Alison to lie on, and several basins of water stood at the ready. On the table lay clean cloths and the doctor's medical instruments. Jane knew enough about childbirth to know that it was better, if at all possible, not to use the tongs and other instruments.

"Jane!" Alison nearly cried with relief. "Come here!"

Jane raised her eyebrows at Dr. Cribb, but he merely nodded. "Sit with her. It will be a few hours yet. Lady Alison is in pain and refusing to take chloroform, although it really does provide some relief during the birth."

"Can it hurt her or the baby?" Jane asked. She sat on the edge of the bed and held Alison's hand.

Almost imperceptibly, the doctor hesitated. "No, not really. Not when it is given in the correct dosage. My colleague, Dr. John Snow, invented an effective chloroform inhaler that even the Queen has come to appreciate. During the birth of her eighth child, Prince Leopold, she was greatly helped by the application of chloroform." Cribb went to the table and picked up a cloth handkerchief and a syringe. "We will lay this cloth over the mother's mouth and nose, and I will then determine precisely how much chloroform is needed to ease the pain. I would go so far as to claim that giving birth under chloroform is pain-free."

Alison looked exhausted, but said, "As long as I can bear it, I will take no chloroform. Oh, yes, I've read about it, and I know there have been some deaths, too!"

"Keep going, Ally, you can do it." Jane shared her friend's opinion. She did not believe that doctors had enough experience with this relatively new anesthetic.

The contractions came and went, and Jane read to Alison, entertaining her with funny stories and ensuring the room was aired regularly. The latter of these tasks proved harder than suspected because the midwife, Mrs. Potts, a churlish woman from Allenton, thought that cold air and too much light would harm the mother.

"I've brought a lot of children into this world, and I have *never* allowed windows to be opened! The room must be kept dark and warm. It has always been that way, and it has stood the test of time," Mrs. Potts complained, screwing up her round nose in annoyance.

"Fresh air is important. The mother has to get oxygen into her lungs, not the same stale air that we've already exhaled a hundred times!" Jane replied unflinchingly. Dr. Cribb had gone to check on Charlotte, and she was left to prevail against the stubborn midwife alone.

"I'm so hot, Jane," Alison murmured. She groaned as the next contraction came.

"Nora, open the window for a minute. I'll close the curtains around Ally's bed so no drafts can get through. Any objections, Mrs. Potts?"

The woman sorted her equipment loudly, grumbling about silly, ignorant girls who thought they knew everything. "Do you want to be there when I give her the enema?"

"Thank you, Mrs. Potts, but I don't want to interfere in that area of expertise. Besides, I must go speak with Dr. Cribb. Stay strong, Ally, I'll be back in a minute."

Even in her exhausted state, her friend was still pretty. *No, the right word was* radiant, thought Jane, smiling at Alison, who grimaced back at her.

As soon as Jane stepped out into the hallway, she heard Dr. Cribb's voice. He was standing on the landing of the stairs, talking to Sir

Frederick. When the two men saw her, Sir Frederick turned away and went downstairs. Cribb was waiting for her.

"My lady, how is Lady Alison?"

"Keeping her chin up, and my God, I admire her for that!" said Jane.

The doctor smiled. "That is a gift that women have. They bear the most extreme pain and are rewarded with the greatest happiness."

"Which brings me to Charlotte. She is a good mother, and she has suffered a terrible injustice. Doctor, I am certain that someone in this house is treating her very badly."

"Those are strong words, my lady. Who do you suspect?" The doctor glanced around, checking for eavesdroppers, but they were alone on the landing. The grandfather clock in the hall struck five, and it was already dark outside.

"Where is Miss Molan?"

"Sir Frederick just told me that Miss Molan had to excuse herself because of a pressing family matter. Something about her sister. She had to go to Allenton but will be back later." Cribb looked at her curiously.

"Miss Molan left? Just like that? What about the children?"

"Gladys is with them right now. It's only for a few hours, and I can also help look after Cedric . . . who is coming along nicely, by the way."

Was the governess trying to fly the coop? "Did Miss Molan take any bags with her?"

"Why would she? It is only a short trip to Allenton. What is this, my lady? Do you suspect Miss Molan? She is Sir Frederick's mainstay right now," Cribb declared with some indignation.

So that's how it was, thought Jane. "I'm simply a bit surprised, to be honest. She is usually so self-sacrificing, but I guess it's understandable when it comes to her own family. How is Charlotte?"

"She's asleep. The last attack was devastating. I can only hope that she comes through it unharmed."

"Unharmed?"

"That is to say, I have seen patients who have suffered such hysterical attacks frequently. At some point, the brain suffers irreparable damage."

Horror-struck, Jane stared at him. She had to do something. One more attack and Charlotte would certainly be lost. "Thank you, Doctor, for being so open with me about this."

Dr. Cribb nodded. "I do everything in my power, my lady, but even I have my limits."

The door to the guest wing flew open. Mrs. Potts called, "Doctor, it's almost time!"

Jane let the doctor go ahead and wondered what she ought to do. Alison would understand if she wasn't there. She had asked Jane to come north in the first place because she was worried about her cousin. Jane ran downstairs and spotted Draycroft leaving the library.

"Mr. Draycroft," she said, as softly as she could.

The butler strode over to her immediately. "My lady?"

"I need your discreet assistance. It is a matter of life and death: Lady Charlotte's, to be more precise." Jane knew it was no lie. "I need a coach, and I need Mr. O'Connor to go with me, as quickly as possible."

"Yes, my lady. But Sir Frederick let Miss Molan take the closed carriage. All we have is the open carriage."

"That will do. If Miss Molan returns in my absence and wants to see Lady Charlotte, you have to stop her from doing so. Do whatever it takes!"

Draycroft inhaled sharply. "You can count on me, my lady."

"Where is Sir Frederick?" Jane asked cautiously.

"In the library, but he will go out to the greenhouse soon. He is expecting an important guest."

"Tonight?"

"Possibly."

"Then I have to hurry!" Jane lifted her skirts and ran back upstairs.

First, she hurried to Alison's room, but there was not yet the level of excitement in the room that an imminent birth would spark. Dr. Cribb was discussing something with the midwife, and Jane crouched by her friend.

"Oh Jane, you're back!"

"Ally, listen to me. I have to leave you alone for a while. I can't explain why, but if I'm to save Charlotte, this is my only chance. You're in good hands here, and I'll hurry, I promise." She kissed her friend on the cheek.

Alison squeezed her hand. "Go, go! When you come back, I'll show you my beautiful child."

Jane stood and pulled Hettie with her out of the room. "Dress warm, we're going for a drive."

In her room, Jane rummaged inside her muff.

"What should I take?" Hettie gathered coats and boots for both of them.

"Bring your knife along. And where the devil is my pistol?"

A short time later, they snuck down to the entrance hall undetected. Draycroft awaited them there. "O'Connor will meet you along the way. Good luck, my lady."

Seated in the open carriage with Miles driving the horses, Jane sighed and said, "I hope we're doing the right thing!"

"You don't really think that Miss Molan is visiting her sister in Allenton, do you? Today of all days."

"No. It is simply too improbable. She's meeting her lover or her accomplice or whomever else, and she's using her plot against Charlotte to gain something for herself. Oh, I've been so stupid! If Miss Molan can handle henna so well, then she probably knows exactly what plants can spark a seizure or cause hallucinations."

"But no one would suspect that, ma'am," said Hettie as the coach rumbled along the frozen drive.

O'Connor was waiting for them on his horse at the edge of the forest. The coach pulled up, and Jane spoke briefly to the gamekeeper.

"My lady. Where do you want to go?"

"To the Trout Inn in Allenton, unless there's another place around there for a rendezvous?"

"There's the hunter's hut on the moor, but that would be rather uncomfortable at this time of year."

"And hardly possible to get there with a coach, unless I'm mistaken."

"No. The path is narrow, and no coachman in his right mind would even think about driving there now."

"Then we go to Allenton!"

The icy wind and the darkness made the drive to Allenton seem endless, and Jane's worries made the drive feel even longer. If her suspicions were wrong, she would look ridiculous, and if she was right, then she had no idea what awaited her when she confronted the probable poisoner. She knew for certain, however, that if she wasn't able to stop Miss Molan that night, then one way or another it would mean the end for Charlotte.

"God help us," she murmured, and she reached for Hettie's hand.

Miles finally drew the horses up, then turned to the two women. "Here we are, my lady. I'll stay with the horses, though if you need help, I will gladly come along."

O'Connor had already dismounted and now helped Jane out of the carriage. Two lamps hanging on the carriage offered meager light. The village lay mostly in darkness, with only the outline of the church still visible, although a fire burned yet in the local smithy, casting its glow over the village street. The blacksmith's hammer beat a rhythm on his anvil; somewhere a dog howled; and distant laughter sounded from one of the houses. Inside the Trout Inn, a celebration seemed to be taking place. Jane heard the sound of a fiddle from inside the tavern, and a woman's clear voice sang:

As I was a-walking one morning in May, I spied a young couple a-making of hay. Oh, one was a fair maid and her beauty shone clear. The other was a soldier, a bold grenadier.

"Do you have a plan, my lady?" asked O'Connor, unbuttoning his jacket and peeling off his gloves, which he tucked under his belt.

"If Miss Molan is here, I hope we have the element of surprise on our side," said Jane, and she glanced up at where she knew the guest rooms to be. "I suspect she's meeting someone there."

"Who would that be?" O'Connor peered up at the windows doubtfully. Two were lit, but the curtains were drawn.

"I suspect that she is acquainted with the orchid hunter, Tomkins, and that they have been hatching some kind of plot that involves the Halstons."

"If Tomkins is really up there, then he's dangerous. Let me go ahead, my lady." O'Connor placed a hand on the fence surrounding the inn. "I can't believe it. Miss Molan seems like such a proper person. So eager." He paused, thinking. "Probably too perfect, and more concerned with Sir Frederick than is proper. Some women are like that. All right. Shall we?"

A moment later, Jane and Hettie followed O'Connor into the barroom. The few tables inside were full. In a back corner stood a woman and a dark-haired man with a fiddle. The woman's almond-shaped eyes were lined with black, and golden armbands clinked with every movement she made. It was none other than Zenada, who stood there swaying and singing the ballad.

Was it a coincidence that she would encounter the murdered girl's mother there that very evening? Zenada sang on, paying no mind to the newcomers, although her eyes flashed when she recognized Jane.

"What is it with all you people today?" The proprietress entered with a tray full of beer glasses, and she set it loudly on one of the tables.

"Lady, you were here once before, weren't you? We ain't got a table free, 'less you want to sit with these nice gents here." Gertrude clapped one of the seated men on the shoulder.

"Behave yourself, Gertrude. We're looking for a young woman, the Halstons' governess," said O'Connor.

Gertrude let out a laugh. "Did she get away from you again, gamekeeper? She was here after the funeral. She likes to live it up, don't she? Miss Hoity Toity."

"Is she here?" asked Jane, offering the woman a coin that she promptly pressed into her cleavage.

"Upstairs. Second door on the right."

Jane walked past Zenada to the stairs, feeling the Roma woman's eyes on her back.

"Hettie, you wait down here. If we need help, go get Miles, understood?"

Hettie pouted. "But I could—"

O'Connor, who was already at the top of the stairs, sharply raised a hand, and Hettie fell silent. Now Jane also heard the sound of agitated voices coming from a room.

"No, Derek!" Melissa Molan cried. "Listen to me! It isn't the right time, not yet. She'll be out of the way soon enough."

The man's voice was clearer. "I've waited long enough, and you promised me. I can't stay in England. Someone will find out the truth about Mungo's death, and then I'll have to pay. And so will you! Or do you think you can hide forever behind fake brown hair?"

Jane climbed the stairs carefully, trying not to make them creak. O'Connor looked at her as if to ask, *Now?*

"Not yet," she whispered.

They were both standing outside the door. Apart from some rustling and the scraping of a piece of furniture, there were no other sounds from inside. Then something thumped onto the floor, and the man moaned. Jane wanted to move away, but O'Connor stopped her. "My lady, that is not the sound of lovemaking . . ."

He raised his pistol, cocked the hammer, and kicked open the door of the room. Miss Molan let out a shrill cry, and something crashed and broke, but no shot was fired. Jane pushed her way through the half-open door and saw Miss Molan facing O'Connor, a knife in her hands and her face cold and expressionless.

"What are you waiting for? Shoot me and you'll hang. I haven't done anything!" She lifted her arm high and tried to stab O'Connor, but he grabbed her by the wrist and twisted her arm until she screamed and dropped the knife. Then he forced her onto a chair.

"See to the man, my lady!" the gamekeeper ordered.

On the floor were the remains of a shattered wineglass, and the adventurer's head lay in a pool of red wine. Derek Tomkins's eyes were wide open, his pupils dilated and wandering, unfocused. The man seemed to be in extreme pain and groaned while his body convulsed uncontrollably. Jane kneeled beside him and tried to cradle his head, but he reached for his throat, gasping for air, then his body suddenly went limp.

"What did you give him?" Jane shouted at Miss Molan. Looking around, Jane spotted an empty wine bottle and a pitcher of water on top of a low cupboard. Flames flickered in the fireplace, a small sack at its center.

But rather than answer Jane, Melissa Molan only stared in fascination at the dying man. O'Connor twisted her arm again until she cried out.

"He's beyond help. It was belladonna," she said, exultant. As Jane knew, in high concentrations, deadly nightshade was lethal.

"In the wine?" Jane reached for the bottle.

"He would have tasted it in the water."

Jane took a blanket from the narrow bed, rolled it up, and pushed it under Tomkins's head. The man's breathing was barely perceptible, and his skin was red and felt hot to the touch. "Hold on!"

Hettie rushed into the room. "Ma'am, are you all right?"

"Get Miles and another strong man. We have to get Tomkins to Winton Park."

Hettie looked at the orchid hunter curiously. Despite his deep tan, his face had taken on an unhealthy color. "What's wrong with him?"

"She poisoned him. Go, run, every minute counts!"

"My lady, pass me that scarf there, please," said O'Connor.

Taking the thin scarf from the bed, Jane passed it to the gamekeeper, who used it to tie Miss Molan's hands behind her back. The governess sat stiffly on the chair and did not struggle. "There is no antidote. He'll die, just like Lady Charlotte will."

Jane crossed the room and slapped Miss Molan's face hard. "You monster!"

Hettie finally returned with the men, who laid the unconscious Tomkins on a sheet and carried him down to the carriage. They went out through a back door to avoid causing an uproar, and Jane paid Gertrude off for her silence. When Tomkins was safely in the carriage, O'Connor came downstairs with Miss Molan.

"Get your hands off me!" she snarled, trying to bite O'Connor, but he gripped her even tighter.

Zenada was waiting for them at the foot of the stairs. The grieving mother had wrapped a dark cloth around her head. When her gold armband flashed, Jane at first thought the glinting metal was a knife. But Zenada merely raised her hand to Miss Molan's forehead and briefly murmured a few Roma words. To Jane, she said, "That is my daughter's murderer. She will die a slow, agonizing death and burn in hell until the end of days."

"What rubbish is that you speak, woman? They'll hang me, and I am laughing about it already!" Miss Molan mocked, but her voice was trembling.

"Zenada, we have to return to Winton Park. Come with us," said Jane, but the Roma woman simply turned and walked away.

Jane sat in the closed coach with Hettie while Miles drove Miss Molan—her hands still bound—in the open carriage, followed closely by O'Connor. The coachman drove the horses as best he could, but the darkness and a driving snowstorm slowed their progress.

Lightly patting the cheeks of the unconscious Tomkins, Jane lifted his arms in an effort to pump air into his chest, but the man lay sprawled across the upholstery, completely still. "I fear the worst, Hettie."

"Ma'am, this isn't your fault."

"I should have seen the truth earlier. I should have seen how corrupt and false she was."

"Evil wears many faces, ma'am," said Hettie. Moments later the coach pulled up in front of Winton Park.

29.

The open carriage stopped in the snow-covered courtyard just behind them. O'Connor jumped from his horse and called for Draycroft, who was already waiting for them.

The gamekeeper yanked open the door of the closed carriage and turned Tomkins's head to check his condition. Tomkins was still unconscious. "Get someone to help you carry this man, and send for Dr. Cribb, fast!" he ordered Draycroft. "If it isn't already too late," he murmured, training his angry gaze on Miss Molan, who was resisting Miles's help in getting down from the open coach.

Jane and Hettie climbed out of their carriage and into the frigid night air. "How is Lady Alison?"

The butler smiled. "She has a healthy little boy, my lady." He then waved to a servant, who came running down the steps of the house followed by Dr. Cribb and Sir Frederick.

"What the deuce is going on here? Lady Allen! Are you responsible for this commotion?" Sir Frederick thundered, pushing his way through to the carriage. "Tomkins! My God, say something, man! Cribb, don't just stand there, help get him into the house."

While the men attended to Tomkins, Sir Frederick looked around. Enough light came from the windows of Winton Park to illuminate the area around the front entrance. The sweating horses steamed in the cold air, stamping their feet restlessly in the snow. Flurries of servants came to see what all the excitement was about, but Mrs. Gubbins soon put a stop to the ogling and shooed them back inside.

"Why is Miss Molan bound? What do you think you're doing getting mixed up in the affairs of my house?" Sir Frederick bellowed at Jane. "Untie her at once!"

Miles looked uncertainly at Jane. In a fury, Sir Frederick snatched the whip from the driver's box on the coach and advanced on Miles, but Jane pushed between them.

"No! Listen to me! This woman tried to kill Charlotte. She is the one behind Rachel's death and is responsible for Tomkins's condition," she said, loudly and without flinching.

Sir Frederick turned pale, and the hand holding the whip dropped to his side. He stared at Miss Molan in incomprehension.

"She is a murderer," Jane continued. "She poisoned her husband in India years ago and found her way into your house under a false name."

"That can't be true! Miss Molan, I entrusted my children to your care. Defend yourself!" In shock, he stared at the governess, but she simply raised her chin defiantly and turned away.

"Take her into the house," Sir Frederick ordered.

Jane reached for his arm. "Charlotte is in danger."

"O'Connor, deal with Miss Molan. Lock her up somewhere. Mrs. Gubbins, see to the rest and . . ." He looked around helplessly, then finally stumbled up the stairs beside Jane.

Dr. Cribb came out of the servants' wing, where they had carried Tomkins. His expression was somber. "There was nothing I could do."

"Then help Charlotte!" Jane called as she hurried upstairs.

She heard Mrs. Gubbins bringing the unnerved servants to order, and she followed Dr. Cribb into the bedroom that had become Charlotte's prison cell. Sir Frederick followed them.

"Charlotte! We're here to help you," Jane said as she entered, then pressed her hand to her mouth to keep herself from crying.

Since she had last seen her, Charlotte seemed to have grown thinner and was now only a shadow of herself. Her gaunt body appeared lifeless beneath the too-heavy blankets, but her eyelids fluttered slightly, and her cracked lips moved.

After examining her medicine bottles, Dr. Cribb leaned over Charlotte and lifted her eyelids. "Her pupils are dilated and just as wide as Tomkins's."

"Miss Molan poisoned Tomkins with belladonna, but Charlotte is still alive. Maybe the governess gave her something else," said Jane.

Sir Frederick was holding on to a bedpost tightly. He shook his head. "Belladonna? She poisoned Tomkins with deadly nightshade? My God, we were sharing our home with a murderer."

"There isn't much I can do except make Lady Charlotte vomit, to clear out whatever poison might still be in her stomach. I am not aware of any antidote," said the doctor. "I only know that belladonna kills by causing paralysis of the lungs."

"Not necessarily," said Sir Frederick, who seemed to have pulled himself together. "Deadly nightshade has been in use for centuries. I read a treatise by Friedlieb Runge in which he describes the modus by which the poison acts. He spoke of a remedy. Let me find it!" He hurried from the room.

"Send me Gladys—and Mrs. Potts. She's still here somewhere. And then you should get something to eat, my lady," said Dr. Cribb. "Lady Charlotte will pull through."

The doctor was right about the food. Jane felt weak and chilled to the bone, and in that state she would soon be of no use to anyone. In the kitchen, she resolutely sent Gladys and Mrs. Potts upstairs, though they were loath to leave their own dinner, then she quickly ate some rabbit stew and a chunk of sweet bread before heading back upstairs herself. But before going back to Charlotte and the situation at hand, she first had to pay her friend a visit. Everything else would have to wait. She tapped at Alison's door and cautiously entered.

Nora, with a happy smile on her face, came to meet her. Quietly, she said, "My lady, everything went well. She was so brave, and what a wonderful little fellow she now has! Take a look."

Jane moved across to the cradle that Charlotte's own children had used and peered down into the crinkled face of a newborn boy, smacking his lips softly in his sleep. "He's beautiful!"

"Jane," she heard a weak voice say from the bed, and she turned and hurried across to Alison.

Throwing her arms around her friend, Jane joyfully kissed her on both cheeks. Despite the trial of the birth, Alison's complexion was rosy and she looked content.

"I'm delighted you came through it so well!" Jane said.

"Me too, believe me. Isn't he marvelous? Thomas will burst with delight. A son!" Ally squeezed Jane's hand. "But what's happened, Jane? You don't have to protect me any longer."

Jane briefly reported the situation, then finished by saying, "And now Miss Molan has some questions to answer."

"It all sounds so horrible. Do you think she'll tell you anything?" Just then, Ally looked past Jane and grinned. "But I'm sure David will know how to get someone to talk, won't he?"

"If he were here," Jane began, frowning in confusion as Alison nodded theatrically. Slowly, she turned around.

Snow still festooned his hair and coat, and the smells of leather and horse surrounded him. "Please excuse my entering unannounced."

Reaching his hand toward Jane, he took her in his arms. He briefly pressed her to him and kissed her forehead before letting her go again. "Alison, my compliments. I hear you now have a son!" He looked into the cradle, then kissed Alison's hand. "Thomas will come tomorrow morning. He would gladly have accompanied me here tonight, but Lord Russell can't get by without him just yet, it seems."

"Who cares about a tea crisis in China? We have a son!" Alison complained jokingly. "Now go deal with that murderous woman."

David looked at Jane in alarm, and she grimaced apologetically. "I had to do *something*, David, or she would have killed Charlotte." She took him by the arm. "Come on, you have to question her."

"What? But . . . ," he protested feebly.

When they were outside the room, Jane explained all that had happened, and David glowered ever more darkly as she spoke. "At least you took O'Connor with you. Jane, things could have taken a very different turn! Just imagine if Tomkins—"

But Jane cut him off with a vehement shake of her head. "David, we have to talk to her now, before she gets over the shock of being found out. How did you even get here? The streets are terrible, and now they're under snow, to boot."

"The coachman took us as far as Belsay. From there, we rented horses. My telegram was supposed to warn you about the murderer, Jane, not encourage you to apprehend her! I had something I had to take care of myself, or I would have been here earlier." He swept a loose strand of hair out of her eyes.

"I'm so sorry about Myron," said Jane. "Why him?"

David's mouth hardened, and his eyes narrowed. "Life on the streets is dangerous, and as soon as you have a bit of luck, you make enemies."

"Captain!" called Dr. Cribb from the end of the hallway. "We're so happy you are here. Sir Frederick is down in the library."

They found the master of the house poring over the scientist Friedlieb Runge's essay. After a brief greeting, Sir Frederick said, "I know what can help her: the seeds of the Calabar bean. It's a legume from West Africa."

"West Africa?" Jane repeated in despair.

"I know where such plants are being grown. Lord Alfred Sinclair has some. He lives just outside Ashkirk. Cribb, if I get the seeds by tomorrow evening, does Charlotte stand a chance?"

"We should leave no stone unturned, of course," the doctor replied. "But I would put more faith in the patient's will to live."

"Where is Miss Molan now?" Jane asked.

"In the cellars. Lady Jane, Captain, my behavior toward Charlotte has been inexcusable." Sir Frederick took a deep breath. "I have done her an injustice, but she also gave me every reason to. And on top of everything, my best supplier is dead. This is a horrible turn of events."

Jane listened to Sir Frederick's specious apologies with growing revulsion. Not a word of sympathy came out of his mouth. All he thought of was himself and his reputation, and even his attempt to obtain the antidote, she knew, was simply another way of indulging his passion for plants.

David interrupted Sir Frederick. "Sir, if you will allow me to, I would like to question the prisoner. As soon as we hand her over to the authorities, the opportunity will be lost."

"Go ahead. I will pen a message to Lord Sinclair." Sir Frederick had already turned back to his book. "Perhaps we could write a joint paper on the effects of the antidote, or . . ."

Cribb followed them out into the hall, where Blount was waiting. Jane was pleased to see her husband's loyal companion again.

"My lady, we are extremely happy to see you safe and sound," he said.

"Thank you, Blount." Jane looked at the men around her. "I would like to be there when you interrogate her. I know some things that might be helpful."

"Cribb?" David turned to the doctor.

The gray-haired physician nodded, his face stony. "Let us go."

30.

As the small group led by Draycroft made their way past the kitchen, silence fell, and the kitchen maids and other servants paused in their duties and whispered among themselves. The butler opened the door leading down to the cellars, where it was noticeably colder than upstairs. In front of the first heavy wooden door, Draycroft said, "Mr. Tomkins is here. Miss Molan is up ahead."

Jane swallowed. Miss Molan was in the same room where they had laid out Rachel. Watching her with concern, David held her trembling hand. "You don't have to be there, Jane."

"Yes, I do." She took a deep breath then followed her husband into the chilly room.

Miss Molan stood bolt upright in front of a pile of boxes, a blanket slung around her shoulders. The table on which Rachel had lain had been pushed back against a wall. A chair stood beneath a slit window, and a lantern had been suspended on the wall.

"I'm freezing," Miss Molan snapped. She lifted up her hands, which were now tied in front of her. "And what's this?"

"For your own safety. So you don't harm yourself." David pointed to the chair. "Please sit down, Miss Molan."

In a low voice, Draycroft said, "I searched her pockets, just in case. If you need me, I will be in the kitchen."

The butler departed, leaving the door open.

David turned to the prisoner. "Miss Molan, I represent the criminal investigation office in London, and if you cooperate and tell us your motives and the sequence of events as you see them, I will be able to present your testimony as mitigation before a court."

Miss Molan seemed to consider this, and after some seconds, she sighed and sat on the chair. "If I tell you everything, may I say good-bye to the children?"

"If Sir Frederick allows it, yes."

The young woman lifted her chin. She knew that she had lost, but she was not broken. She eyed Jane coolly. "The day you came to Winton Park was the day my misfortune began. I might have carried out my plan perfectly, but you stuck your meddling nose into everything."

"It was Lady Alison who suspected that something strange was going on," Jane replied.

"Oh yes, of course, our little blond princess. You fools have no idea what it means to be born without a silver spoon in your mouth." Melissa Molan's face twisted in loathing as she spoke.

"What did your husband do to deserve being poisoned? Your real name is Velma Satterley, isn't it?" David asked.

Miss Molan exhaled sharply. "Peter was a failure, and a boring one at that. I would have expected more spunk, more courage when it came to taking a risk. Then I met Derek Tomkins. He was a real man. He knew the world, and he showed me what it meant to truly live!"

"You could have gotten a divorce from Peter."

"That would have taken too long, and he wouldn't have wanted one, in any case. He was too traditional. I know my way around plants, at least that was one thing I learned in India. There are so many wonderful plants. You can do the most surprising things with them." She laughed hoarsely. "Belladonna is just one of many poisons I've made. But what matters is the dosage, isn't it? A little here, a little there, and suddenly you start to hallucinate, act irrationally, become aggressive, seem confused . . ."

"Poor Charlotte," Jane whispered.

"Oh, that woman is hysterical without drugs, and she's utterly incapable of standing up to her own son. Cedric needs a firm but loving hand. We understood each other from the very start. If I were his mother, he would be his father's pride and joy! I even found the perfect tutor for him, an old admirer of mine, but Sir Frederick didn't want him." At the reference to Sir Frederick, her voice softened.

"Sir Frederick is an intelligent man, but what he lacks is a strong woman beside him. I would have supported him, helped him with his flowers. He often talked to me in his greenhouse, he even let me plant my henna bush there." Miss Molan looked up. "That was it, wasn't it? That was my mistake. But I had to dye my hair. Somewhere, someone would have recognized me with blond hair—a chance meeting at a party, in a park . . . With brown hair, I turn into unassuming Miss Molan. Plus, Sir Frederick likes dark-haired women. His first wife had brown hair, too, like mine."

"What about Rachel?" Jane asked.

"Such a pretty thing. Sir Frederick had his eye on her the day she arrived, and she would not have turned him down. Oh, not her! I know women like her. And then, stupidly, she saw me come out of Sir Frederick's office after we'd . . . well, you know." She smiled smugly.

"I don't believe that's true!" said Jane.

"Why not? He's a man, after all, and I could give him what his wife wouldn't. You don't believe it because we kept it a secret. Otherwise, where would that have left him? With a mad wife and an affair with the governess?"

"So you forged a letter and lured Rachel out onto the moor," said David.

"It was so easy. Rachel had been making eyes at our handsome butler, and it was child's play to tempt her into a rendezvous with a few encouraging lines. Out in the dark, all it took was a good push, and the moor swallowed its victim."

"Getting rid of a rival is one thing, but how does Tomkins fit into the picture?" David handed Blount his notebook and pencil.

"Derek and I were bound by a complicated story. One ought never to mix business with affairs of the heart. I traveled with him through Burma for several months, then to Madagascar, but the life he led would have killed me. Then there was Korshaw. A canny trader, that one. He met Peter and me in India, then followed what happened afterward in the newspapers. Well, like I said, he was not stupid, and he could put two and two together. That was yet another reason for me to assume a new identity and sail to England, that and the tropical climate, which was making me sick.

"Derek and I had a plan. He was a brilliant plant hunter. He had a particularly keen sense for orchids and could find the rarest kinds, which he sold at a premium. He promised me a life in America as soon as he got enough money together. Then I took the position with the Halstons, and Sir Frederick practically fell in love with Derek, who supplied him with the best orchids he could find.

"Sir Frederick, naturally, thought that Derek was working exclusively for him, but—my God!—why would he do that? Sir Frederick is miserly and does not understand that Derek was standing with one foot in the grave every time he went on his expeditions. What does he think, that the wildmen there come out singing songs and simply hand over their sacred flowers, just like that?" Miss Molan looked at the gathering around her. "Of course, Sir Frederick had no idea that Derek and I knew each other. But it wouldn't have mattered anyway, because Derek was simply among the very best at what he did. He even managed to steal the sacred orchid of the Motilone Indians! Oh, that was good. He was able to spirit it out of the country for Sir Frederick, managing to shoot his closest rival, a man named Rudbeck, dead at the same time. Rudbeck was working for Sir Robert Parks. Derek did so much for Sir Frederick, and Sir Frederick barely thanked him for it."

David raised his hand. "What about Korshaw? I heard that Korshaw and Derek were seen together on the docks in London."

"Korshaw was greedy. Derek supplied him with the best-quality plants he could find, and that was fair! But when Korshaw saw me at an orchid auction in London with the Halstons, he recognized me. Well, Derek took care of that particular problem as soon as he returned to England. And since nobody knew he was here, he said he could plan our passage to New England in peace and quiet. The liar!"

Stunned, Jane could only listen as the woman—whose proper façade no one had seen through—calmly explained her murderous scheme. "What went wrong? Why did Derek Tomkins have to die? He wanted to take you with him."

"Ha!" Miss Molan sniffed. "I thought the same. No, he came here to buy time, to stall me! Derek lived a life filled with adventure and women. Oh, yes, I knew he had other women. He was a good-looking man, funny and charming, too. At the Trout Inn, he said he'd give up his other women for me, but then he chuckled, as if he was laughing at me, and I knew he wouldn't change his ways!"

Jane leaned closer to David. The cold was creeping into her limbs.

"At that moment, I realized which man I would choose. Sir Frederick trusted me, and he would turn to me once his wife was out of the way. He can't stand hysterical women, and I know exactly how to handle him. I'm the right woman for him!" she declared, her hands balling into fists. "If *I* had been born the daughter of an aristocrat . . ." She stared at Jane, her eyes filled with hate.

"So that belladonna you used on Tomkins and Charlotte—did you give some of it to Cedric, too?" asked Dr. Cribb.

"Oh, Doctor, if only you'd spent a little more time getting to know plants. No, I would never have poisoned Cedric. I just gave him some lobelia, that's all; a good remedy for hay fever or hives, but in bigger doses it causes nausea. I also gave him a little laudanum to make him sleep." Miss Molan smiled knowingly.

"You let a child suffer for your madness!" the doctor said in horror.

"Madness?" Miss Molan laughed. "A woman who takes her life into her own hands and clears away obstacles in her path isn't mad. Farsighted is what I would call it."

Sir Frederick's voice was heard in the passage. "In here?"

"Yes, sir, just ahead," said Draycroft. The two men stepped inside the makeshift prison cell.

"You two-faced, murderous witch! What have you done to my family?" Sir Frederick roared. He tried to attack Miss Molan but was held back by David and Blount.

"Frederick! How can you say that? I did it all for you! We loved each other!" As if on command, tears flowed down Miss Molan's cheeks.

"What is this madwoman raving about?" Sir Frederick's cheeks flushed red with fury. "She's lying! Every word is a lie! Why did you kill Tomkins? I know that he had something extraordinary for me, so where the deuce is it?"

"Go scour the fireplace in that lovely room at the pub. Maybe you'll find a few charred scraps of the last black orchid Derek managed to save from the shipment." Every word she said dripped with the triumphant pride of the loser.

"No . . . no!" Sir Frederick bawled. Turning on his heel, he stalked out of the room.

The following morning, David and Jane were standing in the green drawing room waiting for Thomas to arrive. Velma Satterley, alias Melissa Molan, was still locked up in the cellars while she awaited transfer to the authorities. For the murders she had committed, death by hanging was certain.

"I am so happy that Charlotte is recovering," Jane exclaimed. "Dr. Cribb is confident that she will be well again even without the antidote. But what will become of her and Sir Frederick? I mean, he still . . ."

David had picked up one of the colorful porcelain figurines. "That's none of our business, Jane. Let's leave it to Charlotte and Sir Frederick to pick up the pieces the best they can."

"But—"

"No!" David placed the figurine back on the table. "And please, never collect anything like this." Taking Jane's hand, he drew her closer to kiss her, but a noise at the door caused them to pull apart.

Sir Frederick came in holding a dish that held a small pile of ashes.

"Look at this." His voice shook a little.

David and Jane stepped closer and discovered the remains of a small plant sack, a few charred leaves, and the barely recognizable stalk of a plant.

"This was a black orchid. A black orchid!" Sir Frederick sobbed. He touched a blackened leaf tenderly. "Tomkins, that dog in a doublet, he actually did it! The letters, you remember?"

Jane nodded, but Sir Frederick continued, heedless of her response. "I had my doubts, of course. I thought his depictions were perhaps exaggerated, that he dramatized, you know, to keep me paying his way and drive up the price of his work. But he wasn't lying. God, I would have paid him anything!"

Ever pragmatic, David said, "The man was probably counting on that."

The orchid grower gazed dismally at the remains of the little plant that had cost an orchid hunter his life. "And what if he did? I'd have given him any sum he requested. That stupid woman, that insane, vile creature! If I'd been at the Trout Inn, I'd have throttled her with my own hands. The terrible part is that Tomkins told no one where he found the orchid. These men are individualists, lone hunters who would rather take their secrets to the grave than pass them on to a rival. If I were a younger man, I'd go out into the wilds myself."

He seemed to come to his senses then, raising his eyes from the orchid's remains. In a calmer tone, he said, "What you must think of me. Only a lover of orchids could understand what I'm going through. Poor Tomkins is dead . . . but the loss of such a singular flower is beyond common comprehension."

"It seems passion and blood are inseparable from this flower," Jane observed quietly.

Frederick Halston poked around in the remnants of the exotic plant. "Maybe there's still something I can save." He looked to Jane. "I don't want to hold you up. You have had to suffer enough in your stay here. We owe you a debt of gratitude."

Before David or Jane could say anything more, he walked into his office, murmuring to himself, "You would have to cross this plant with a Calanthe. If that worked, then . . ."

When the door closed, Jane said, "Unbelievable! Even now, he has more time for his orchids than for his wife."

David stepped over to the window, just as a carriage rolled across the heavy carpet of snow in the courtyard. "Thomas is here!"

He was relieved to see that Thomas had arrived and could look after Alison. He wanted nothing more than to leave Winton Park. At the same time, he knew that a dark shadow still hung over them, but he would say nothing to Jane of the threatening letter he had been given at the Seven Bells. Not until absolutely necessary.

"David, there's just one thing, before we join the others," Jane began.

He looked at her, puzzled.

"Never grow orchids."

31.

Mulberry Park, Cornwall, New Year's Day 1861

Heavy snow was falling on the front lawn. The enormous, ancient mulberry trees looked as if they had been coated with powdered sugar. Rufus ran madly through the snow, snapping at the falling flakes, rolling on his back and barking joyfully when Jane threw a snowball for him. It was good to be back. She had wanted so much to be home again, and for Jane, home meant this unprepossessing place in Cornwall.

It was here that Jane felt her uncle's presence the strongest. She missed Henry dearly, and not only because this was her first Christmas without him. Mary, who now called Mulberry Park home when she wasn't at the boarding school, was staying with them, and Mrs. Roche had recovered from a bad cough. Floyd was back to his old self again, and Dr. Woodfall had come to visit a few days earlier and stayed on, though not entirely of his own free will. Richard Woodfall would have preferred to spend New Year's Day with his own family, but the snow had made the roads and lanes impassable. Jane had come to appreciate his presence because living with David had become more and more of a strain.

Ever since their return from Winton Park, he had been more taciturn and bad-tempered than usual. Nothing seemed to please him, and he evaded all questions. He spent hours alone in his office and was constantly sending Blount off to the post office. When he did take her in his arms and kiss her, there was often a sadness in his eyes that tore at Jane, deep inside. How could she help him if he would not share what was on his mind?

"Jane! You'll catch your death if you're not careful!" Richard Woodfall called, stamping through the snow.

She turned around and threw a handful of snow at Rufus, who leaped up at her. "Rufus! No jumping!"

Trying to dodge, Jane stumbled, falling backward into the snow. Laughing, she clambered to her feet, fending off Rufus's cold nose, which was sniffing and snorting at her face in canine concern. She grasped Woodfall's outstretched hand gratefully.

"You great ox!" she scolded Rufus playfully as she beat the snow from her coat and skirts. Rufus barked and ran away.

"Everything all right?" asked Richard Woodfall. His pale eyes were as roguish as ever.

"Nothing broken, Doctor. Apart from Rufus, there's not much that can knock me down," she said, straightening the fur-lined hood of her coat.

"Have you read this morning's paper? Cunningham won first prize for his Cattleya la-something-or-other. Shall we walk a little? I have to stretch my legs after that breakfast. Mrs. Roche seems to be trying to fatten me up."

Jane clapped her hands to free her gloves of snow. "I'd love to take a walk. And yes, I did read that about Cunningham. I could imagine Sir Frederick turning scarlet with anger. Then, of course, I thought of Charlotte. I'm glad she and the children have gone to Italy. She can recuperate fully there and get some distance from everything."

"Won't she have to give her testimony at the trial at the end of the month?"

"No. Sir Frederick will do that. One can't really put the poor woman through that. I've written everything down in a statement to the court, but I may still have to appear as a witness. If I see Miss Molan again, it would be my pleasure to testify against her."

"You're a fearless one, Jane. I know no other woman ready to so selflessly put herself out for others." Richard spoke with an undertone that made Jane prick up her ears.

They had reached the end of the lawn, and Jane stopped walking. "But?"

"Well . . . you often put yourself in danger," said Richard.

"Has David been talking to you? Are you supposed to warn me to be more cautious?" she said, more rudely than she had intended.

"Jane, your husband is deeply concerned."

"So I've heard. Unfortunately, he never shares those concerns with me."

Richard gently grasped her arm. "He has his reasons. I've known him longer than you have, and right now I have the impression that something is weighing heavily on his soul."

"Why can't he tell me that, Richard?" Jane faced him and tried to read what was behind his friendly expression.

"Let's go back. This snow is never going to stop."

Briefly, Jane looked up at the gray sky. The snow was settling like a heavy curtain all around them. "If this keeps up, you might have to harness a sleigh behind your horse."

"Just like when I was in Russia." Woodfall went on to describe icy Russian winters, which were far from romantic. Instead they were times of deprivation that claimed many lives. "Still," he concluded, "some part of me misses those days."

They had reached the steps leading up to the main entrance, where they found David waiting for them.

"What are you rattling on about, Richard?" he said by way of a greeting. "Jane, is he boring you again with his old war stories?"

"Not at all. Thank you, Richard." Jane swept past David into the house. She was disappointed and angry that her own husband would tell her less about his past than a near stranger would.

She let Floyd help her out of her coat and was about to go up to her room when David's voice held her back. "Jane, come into the library. Please."

Turning, she saw him already striding ahead then waiting in the doorway for her, his expression flinty. As soon as she entered before him, he swung the door closed.

"What is the matter with you? Have I done something? You ignore me and go out walking with Richard instead." His voice grew louder, and the scar on his cheek turned a deeper shade of red. His dark hair, which he wore a little shorter now, fell over his forehead.

"I ignore you? Oh, David, please, that's silly. You've buried yourself in your papers for weeks, barely saying a word to me, and with hardly a glance my way." She lifted her chin. "Except in our bedroom. At least there I seem to fulfill a need."

David's nostrils flared, and his voice was hoarse as he shot back, "You are intentionally provoking me, Jane, and my patience has its limits."

"Really? How, pray tell, am I straining the limits of your patience? Help me understand, please, because I don't know what else to do!" She stepped toward him, holding out a hand. When he didn't move, she moved closer and looked him directly in the eye. "I am lonely, David. I miss my uncle. He was my family. Now all I have is you. And what are we, David? Is our marriage really only a formal arrangement? I know nothing about your family. You haven't even introduced me to your father."

His eyes flashed. "My father? You think my father is family? I would spare you that particular encounter. Should you ever get to know him, you would soon realize that the last thing you want from him is to be a father!"

"David." Although they were standing just a few inches apart, Jane felt so far away that she thought she might lose him forever. Tears filled her eyes.

"Don't." His voice was raw as he pulled her into his arms. "I'm so sorry, Jane. I very much want to be a better husband to you."

Sniffing, she tilted her head back. "You're not so terrible. Now, for example."

When she saw a spark of humor flicker in his eyes, she knew that all was not yet lost.

"Jane," he began. His voice was so serious that she felt her stomach clench anxiously. "Myron, the boy from the streets, the one who was killed on the docks."

"That poor little man. You really liked him, didn't you?"

"He deserved a chance, but someone begrudged him that because they wanted to hurt me." David closed his eyes briefly and took a deep breath. "Someone from whom I once took something is now out for revenge."

Slowly, a grim suspicion formed in Jane's mind, and her hands burrowed into his jacket.

"I've been making inquiries. Rooke has been helping me in London, and Thomas, too, with his connections in India. The Seven Bells in St. Giles doesn't belong to Big John, but to an English businessman in India."

"Devereaux," she whispered.

David nodded and stroked her back. "Do you now understand why I'm so worried about you? Why I don't want to let you out of my sight for even a minute, because I don't know if there is some hired killer somewhere just waiting for the right moment to strike?"

"Why didn't you say anything?" How could she have doubted him so deeply? she wondered.

"Because I needed to be sure. What was I supposed to do? Lock you in the house?"

She raised her eyebrows. "What do we do now?"

"I'll find him. There is no other way."

"When do we leave for India?"

"We?"

"How do you expect to keep an eye on me if I stay here?"

"Let's discuss that later."

Afterword

Why a black orchid? I am a great admirer of parks and greenhouses, which is ideal when undertaking my research because I get to spend time among ancient ruins and relics, and in parks steeped in history. Plants have been collected for centuries. They were used as food, for religious ceremonies, and for medicinal purposes.

One fascinating figure is the doctor Paul Hermann, who in the seventeenth century was commissioned by the Dutch East India Company and who became one of the first to go in search of rare plants. Botany soon developed into an area of study quite distinct from medicine, and suddenly, in the Age of Enlightenment, numerous scientific expeditions carried thousands of new kinds of plants back to Europe. Alexander von Humboldt, for example, brought back over six thousand different plants, barely half of which were already known to Europeans. In the pre-Victorian era, William John Swainson collected plants in Rio de Janeiro. He used orchids as packing material for the plants he sent to London, believing the orchids to be a kind of parasitic weed. However, one orchid bloomed during the crossing, triggering an orchid frenzy in England that soon spread throughout Europe.

A few years ago, I visited Kew, as the Royal Botanic Gardens in London are more generally known. Among other attractions, an herbarium and the Palm House—today one of the oldest existing Victorian hothouses—were built in the 1840s. Construction began on the Temperate House, which housed plants from the temperate regions of the world, in 1860. Indeed, in England and Europe in the mid-1800s, numerous botanical gardens and huge trade nurseries were established, a development assisted by the advent of faster ships, which made it possible to transport tropical plants back to Europe more expediently and in relatively undamaged condition.

It was in Kew that I first heard about the nineteenth-century obsession with orchids, for it is in Kew that the sketchbooks of probably the most famous orchid grower, John Day, are housed. Orchids are among the strangest, most fascinating, and most intimidating flowers. They practically laugh at observers, returning their stares, and there is something uniquely erotic about them. It is no coincidence that they take their name from the Greek *órkhis*, meaning "testicle." The flowers themselves are described as having lips and mouths.

Even Confucius called the orchid the queen of aromatic plants. From 1840 onward, more and more wealthy collectors, obsessed with orchids, sent notorious orchid hunters out into the world to bring back the rarest and most beautiful specimens from the jungles of South and Central America and from Asia. At auctions, individual specimens could attract prices of up to 12000 Goldmarks (approximately US $100,000). These adventurers forged paths into unexploited rainforests and through swamps, defying poisonous snakes, hostile indigenous peoples, diseases, and natural disasters. These reprobate soldiers of fortune were responsible for wiping out entire orchid populations by simply cutting down the trees on which the sought-after plants lived.

Insights into the orchid hunters' adventurous lives can be found in letters between the orchid grower Frederick Sander (1847–1920) and his hired plant hunters, and in Victor Ottmann's account of his experiences in tropical America, published in 1922.

The notorious black orchid soon became synonymous with an unattainably rare treasure, not least because of the tales spread by the orchid hunters themselves. Specimens were found that approached the black ideal—dark-violet orchids. In South America in particular, very dark specimens were found, several on the slopes of the Pichincha volcano. Only in recent years have growers like Fred Clarke in Florida managed to create a hybrid sold as a truly black orchid—the Fredclarkeara After Dark.

Please excuse the fact that some of the dates and information in this novel may not agree precisely with actual history or geography, but this story is intended more to entertain than to instruct. Sometimes, the historical circumstances were bent to fit with the story arc or the wills of my characters. I hope very much that any such bending has been for the reader's pleasure!

Find out more about the Lady Jane series at www.annisbell.com.

Acknowledgments

As with any of my novels, my readers deserve my biggest thanks! I receive a tremendous amount of support in my work in so many marvelous and different ways, and I am humbled and grateful for all of it.

I would like to thank the amazing team at AmazonCrossing for their competent, creative, and ever-enthusiastic help!

My heartfelt thanks also go to everyone who assisted in the creation of Lady Jane's adventures, and to my family most of all—for everything, always—you are simply wonderful!

About the Author

Annis Bell is a writer and scholar. She has lived for many years in the United States and England, and currently splits her time between England and Germany. The first book in her Lady Jane Mystery series was *The Girl at Rosewood Hall.*

About the Translator

Born in Australia, Edwin Miles has been active as a translator in the literary, film, and television fields for many years, and has worked, among other things, as a draftsman, teacher, white-water rafting guide, and seismic navigator.

After undergraduate studies in his hometown of Perth, he completed his MFA in fiction writing at the University of Oregon in 1995. While there, he spent a year as a fiction editor on the literary magazine *Northwest Review*. In 1996, he was short-listed for the prestigious Australian/Vogel's Literary Award for young writers for a collection of short stories.

After many years living and working in Australia, Japan, and the United States, he currently resides in his "second home" in Cologne, Germany, with his wife and two very clever children.

Printed in Poland
by Amazon Fulfillment
Poland Sp. z o.o., Wrocław